Bloodlust
&
Bonnets

Andrews McMeel Publishing
a division of Andrews McMeel Universal
1130 Walnut Street, Kansas City, Missouri 64106

www.andrewsmcmeel.com

19 20 21 22 23 SDB 10 9 8 7 6 5 4 3 2 1

ISBN: 978-1-4494-9747-7

Library of Congress Control Number: 2019937381

Editor: Melissa R. Zahorsky
Art Director: Spencer Williams
Designer: Sierra S. Stanton
Production Editor: Elizabeth A. Garcia
Production Manager: Chuck Harper
Colorist: Rebekah Rarely

ATTENTION: SCHOOLS AND BUSINESSES
Andrews McMeel books are available at quantity discounts with bulk purchase for educational, business, or sales promotional use. For information, please e-mail the Andrews McMeel Publishing Special Sales Department: specialsales@amuniversal.com.

Bloodlust
&
Bonnets

by Emily McGovern

Andrews McMeel
PUBLISHING®

PROLOGUE

Somewhere in Great Britain at the tail end of the Regency...

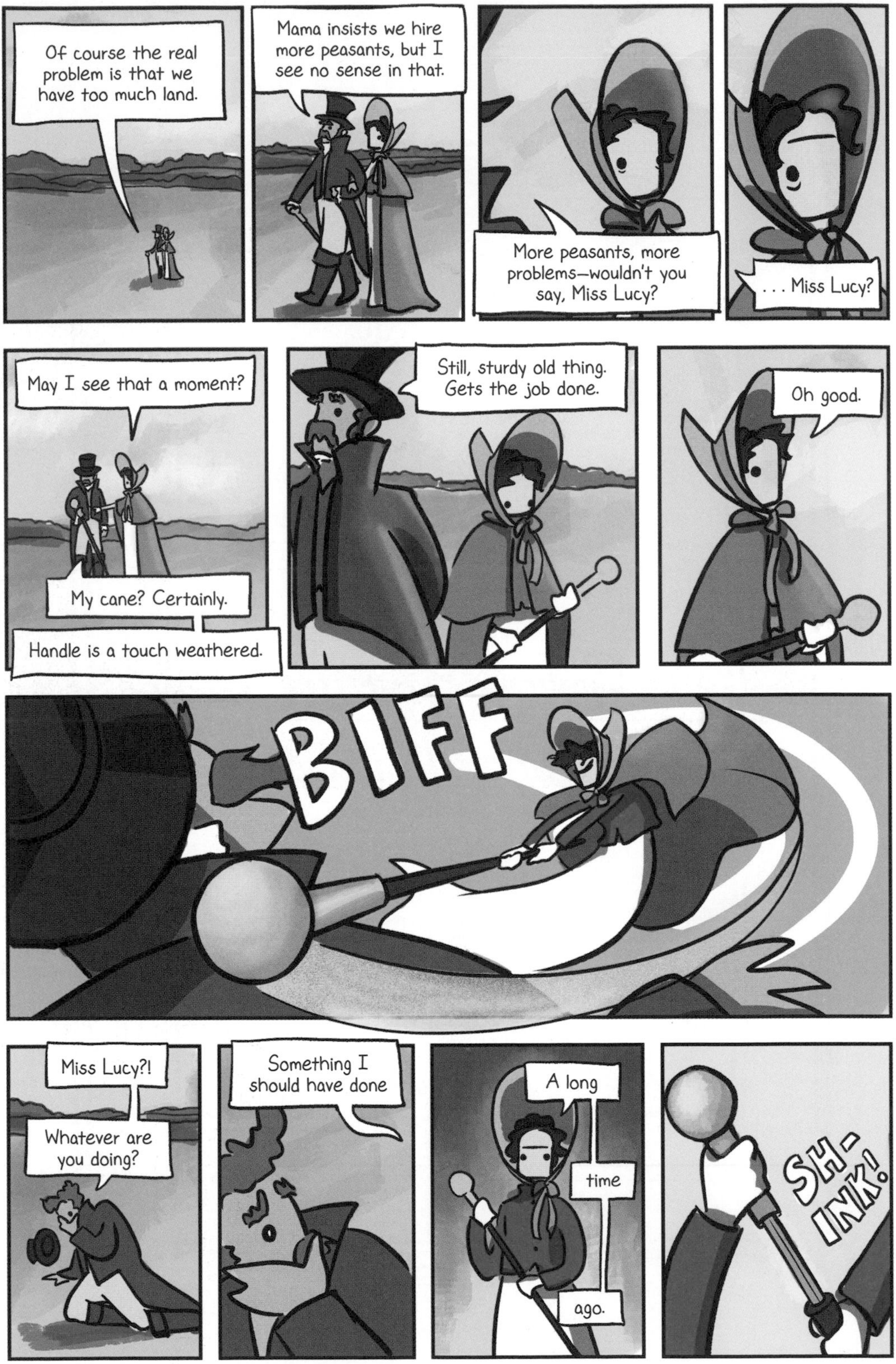
Of course the real problem is that we have too much land.
Mama insists we hire more peasants, but I see no sense in that.
More peasants, more problems—wouldn't you say, Miss Lucy?
. . . Miss Lucy?
May I see that a moment?
My cane? Certainly.
Handle is a touch weathered.
Still, sturdy old thing. Gets the job done.
Oh good.
BIFF
Miss Lucy?!
Whatever are you doing?
Something I should have done
A long
time
ago.
SH-INK!

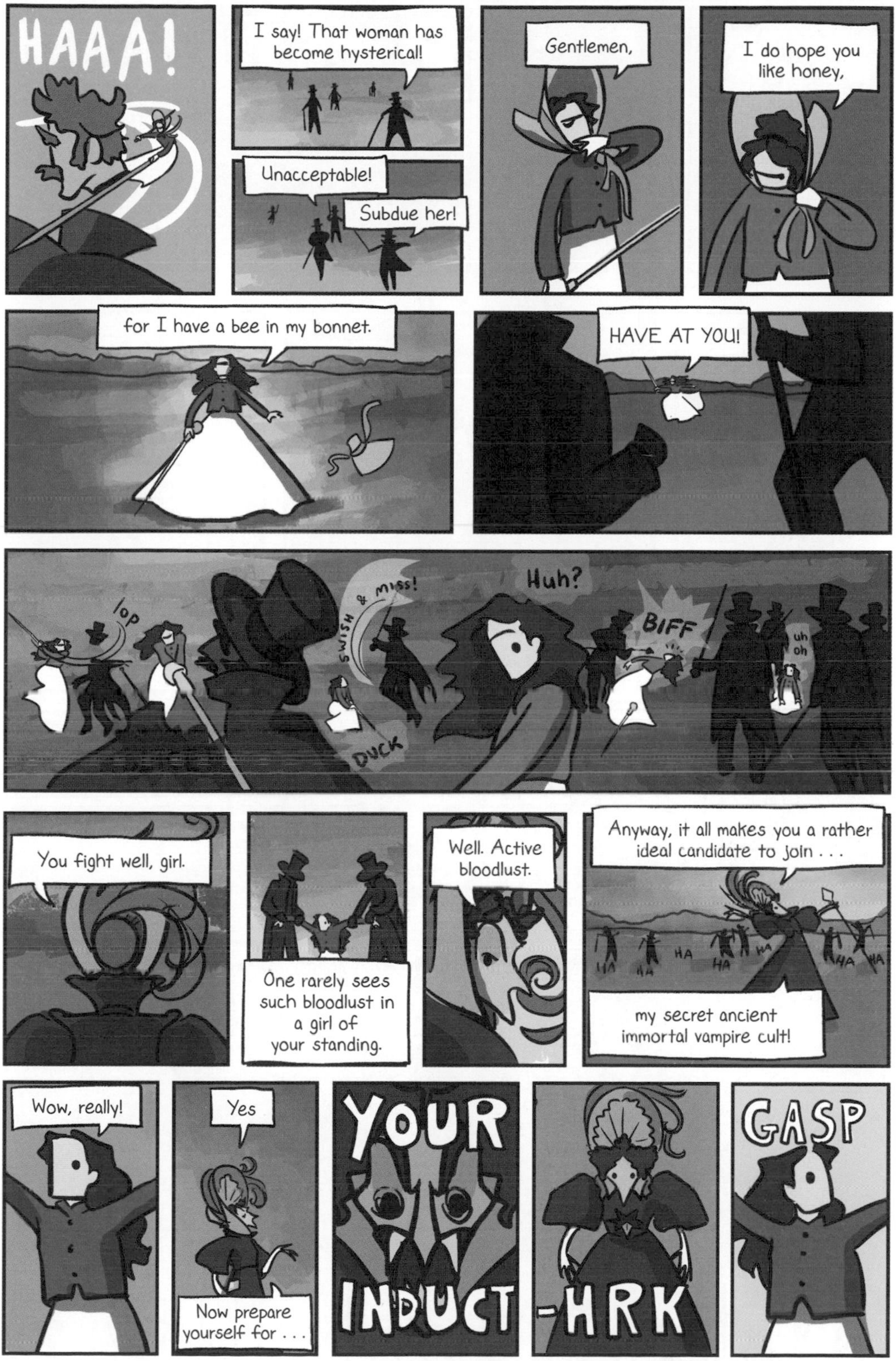

HAAA!
I say! That woman has become hysterical!
Unacceptable!
Subdue her!
Gentlemen,
I do hope you like honey,
for I have a bee in my bonnet.
HAVE AT YOU!
lop
SWISH & MISS!
DUCK
Huh?
BIFF
uh oh
You fight well, girl.
One rarely sees such bloodlust in a girl of your standing.
Well. Active bloodlust.
Anyway, it all makes you a rather ideal candidate to join . . .
HA HA HA HA HA HA HA
my secret ancient immortal vampire cult!
Wow, really!
Yes
Now prepare yourself for . . .
YOUR INDUCT
-HRK
GASP

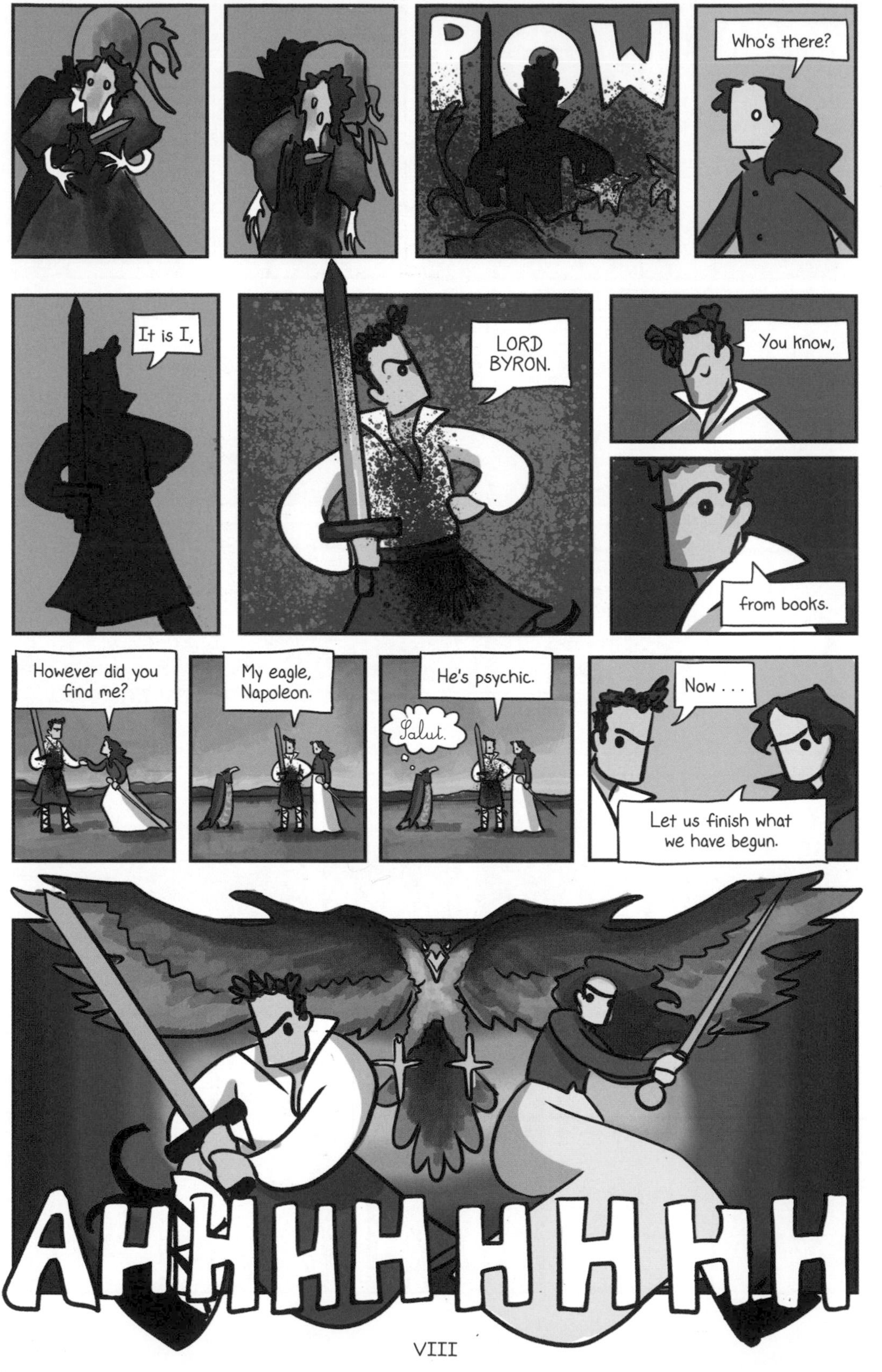
POW
Who's there?
It is I,
LORD BYRON.
You know,
from books.
However did you find me?
My eagle, Napoleon.
He's psychic.
Salut.
Now . . .
Let us finish what we have begun.
AHHHHHHHH

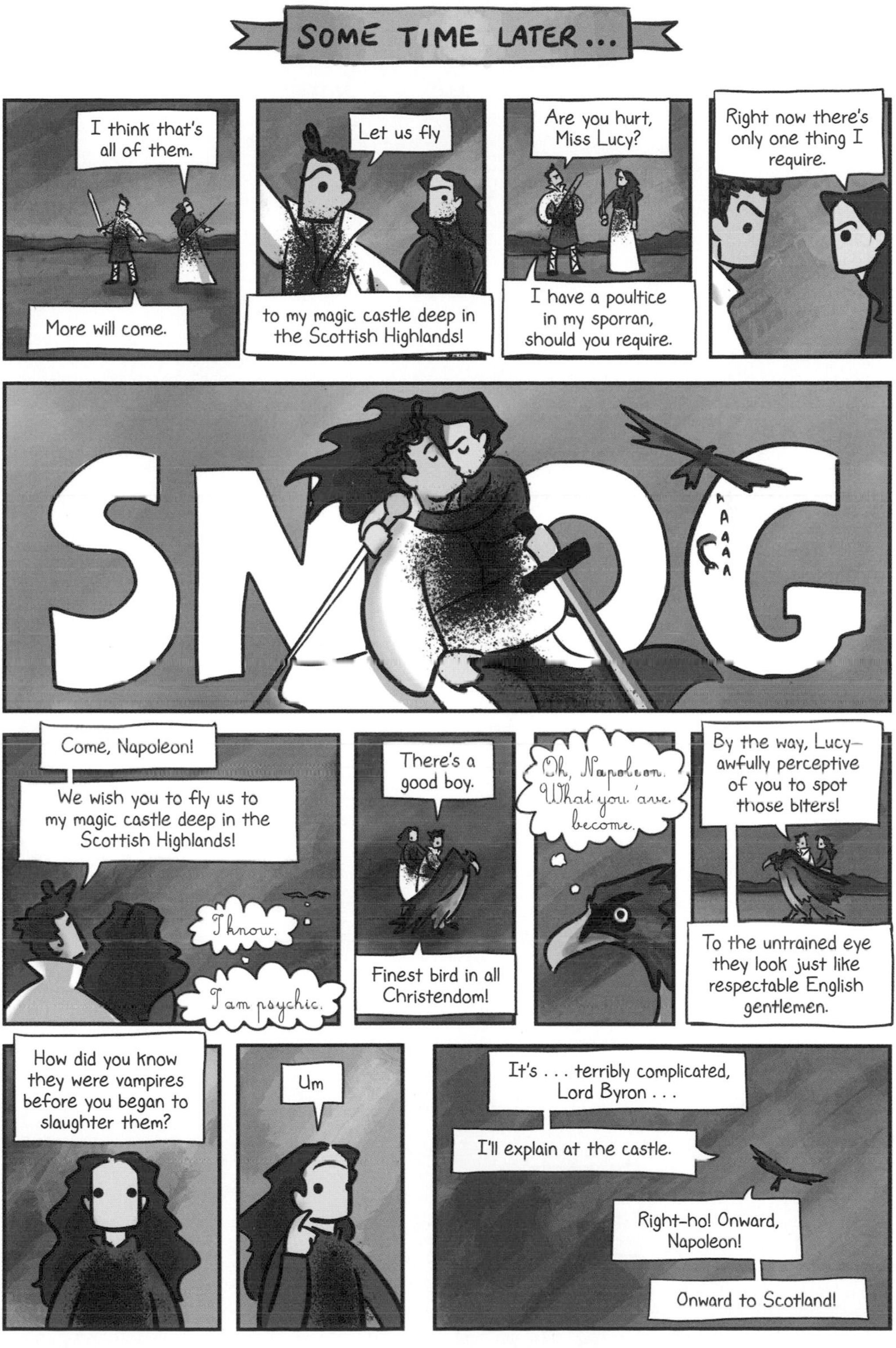
SOME TIME LATER . . .
I think that's all of them.
More will come.
Let us fly
to my magic castle deep in the Scottish Highlands!
Are you hurt, Miss Lucy?
I have a poultice in my sporran, should you require.
Right now there's only one thing I require.
SMOOG
AAAAAA
Come, Napoleon!
We wish you to fly us to my magic castle deep in the Scottish Highlands!
I know.
I am psychic.
There's a good boy.
Finest bird in all Christendom!
Oh, Napoleon. What you 'ave become.
By the way, Lucy— awfully perceptive of you to spot those biters!
To the untrained eye they look just like respectable English gentlemen.
How did you know they were vampires before you began to slaughter them?
Um
It's . . . terribly complicated, Lord Byron . . .
I'll explain at the castle.
Right-ho! Onward, Napoleon!
Onward to Scotland!

CHAPTER I – THE CASTLE

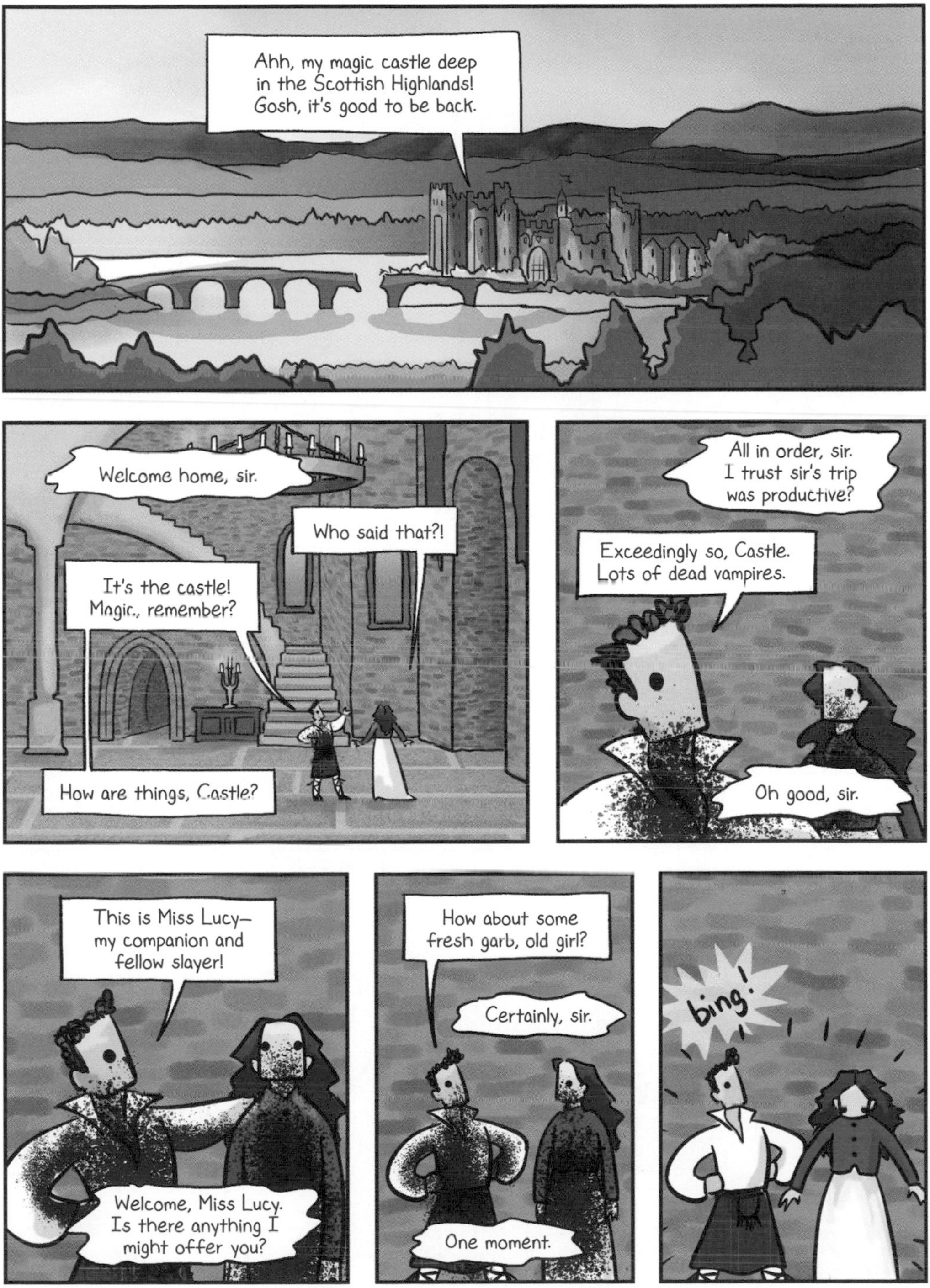
Ahh, my magic castle deep in the Scottish Highlands! Gosh, it's good to be back.
Welcome home, sir.
Who said that?!
It's the castle! Magic, remember?
How are things, Castle?
All in order, sir. I trust sir's trip was productive?
Exceedingly so, Castle. Lots of dead vampires.
Oh good, sir.
This is Miss Lucy— my companion and fellow slayer!
Welcome, Miss Lucy. Is there anything I might offer you?
How about some fresh garb, old girl?
Certainly, sir.
One moment.
bing!

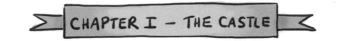

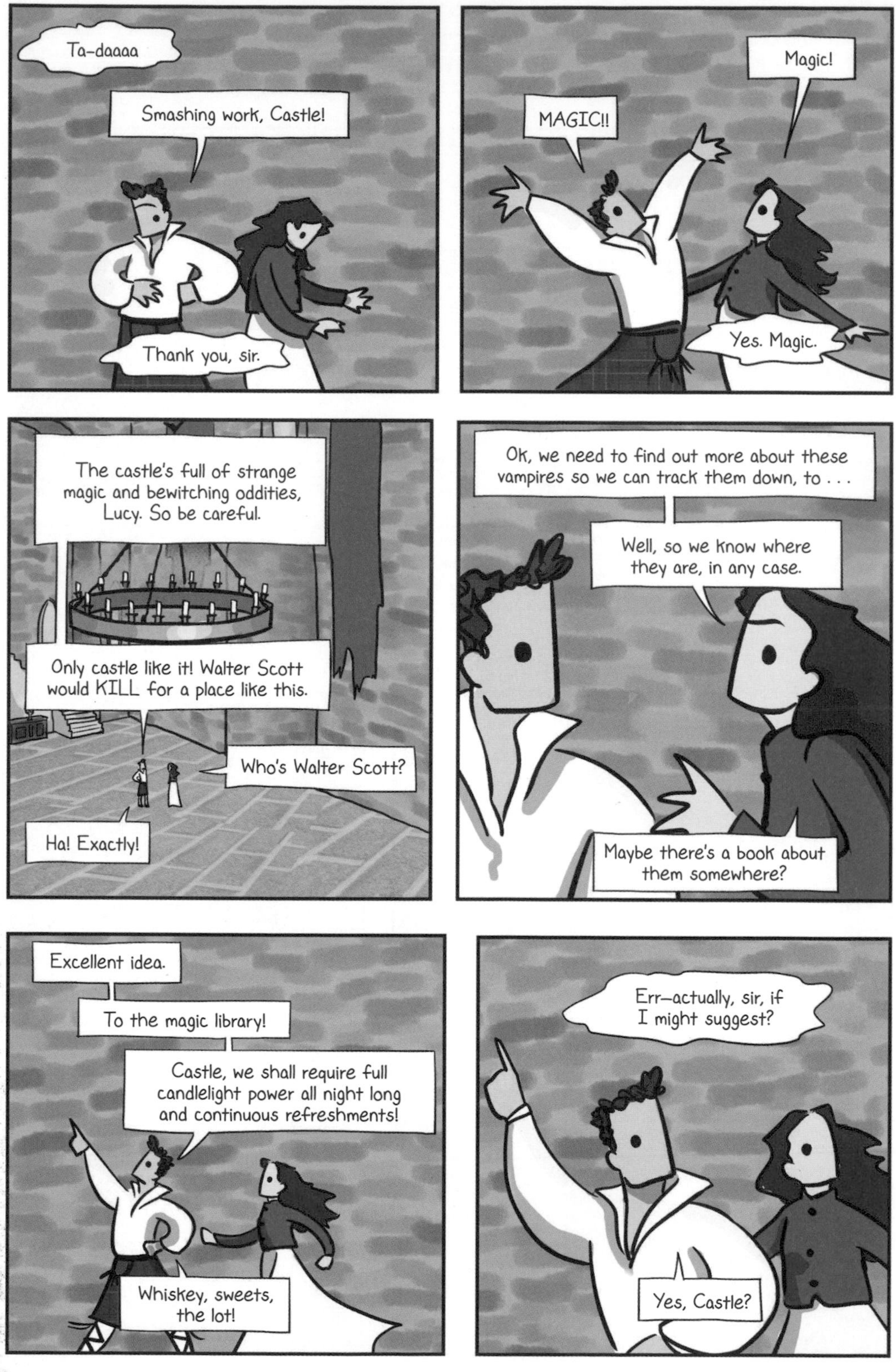
Ta-daaaa
Smashing work, Castle!
Thank you, sir.
MAGIC!!
Magic!
Yes. Magic.
The castle's full of strange magic and bewitching oddities, Lucy. So be careful.
Only castle like it! Walter Scott would KILL for a place like this.
Who's Walter Scott?
Ha! Exactly!
Ok, we need to find out more about these vampires so we can track them down, to . . .
Well, so we know where they are, in any case.
Maybe there's a book about them somewhere?
Excellent idea.
To the magic library!
Castle, we shall require full candlelight power all night long and continuous refreshments!
Whiskey, sweets, the lot!
Err—actually, sir, if I might suggest?
Yes, Castle?

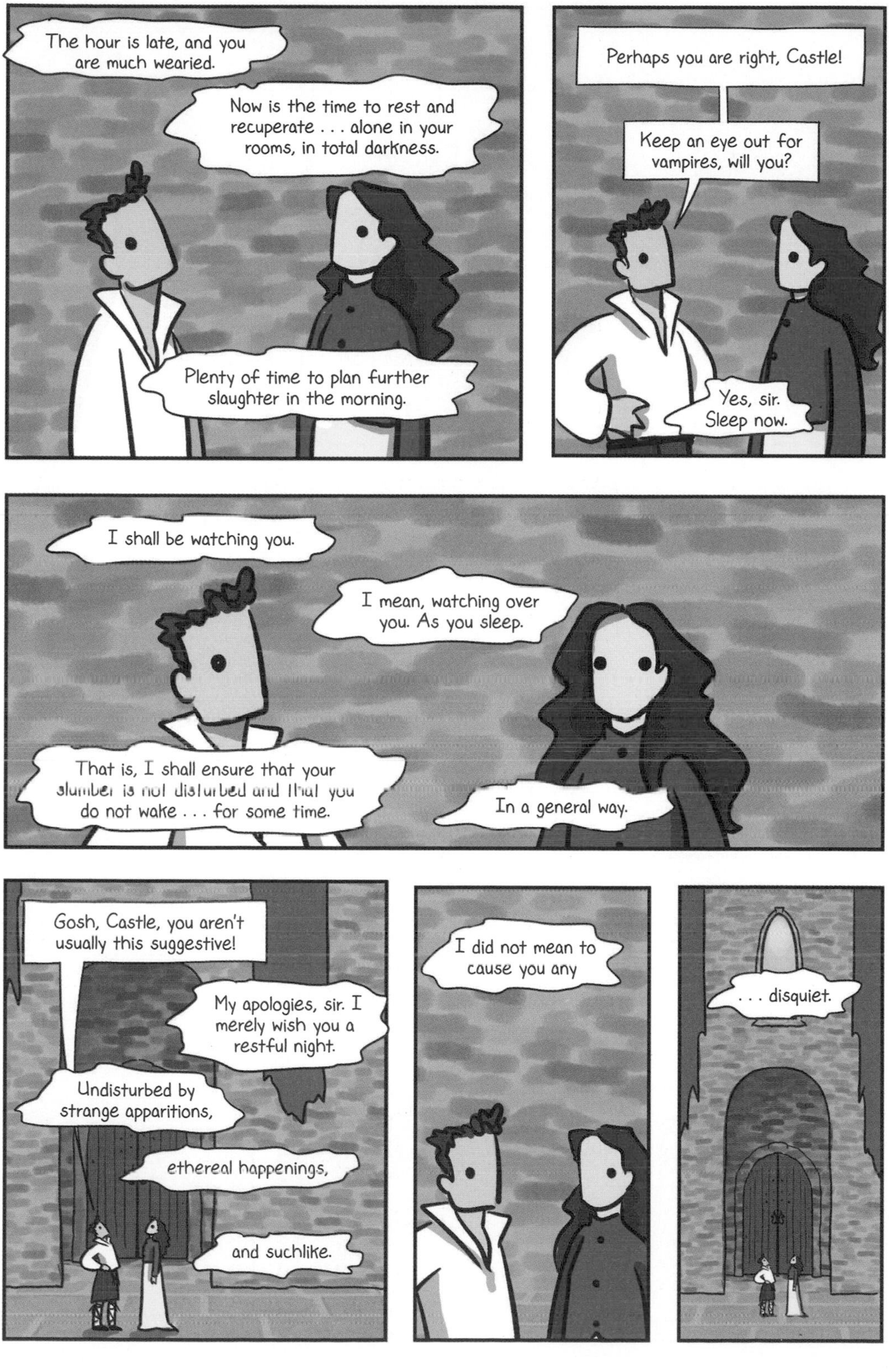
The hour is late, and you are much wearied.
Now is the time to rest and recuperate . . . alone in your rooms, in total darkness.
Plenty of time to plan further slaughter in the morning.
Perhaps you are right, Castle!
Keep an eye out for vampires, will you?
Yes, sir. Sleep now.
I shall be watching you.
I mean, watching over you. As you sleep.
That is, I shall ensure that your slumber is not disturbed and that you do not wake . . . for some time.
In a general way.
Gosh, Castle, you aren't usually this suggestive!
My apologies, sir. I merely wish you a restful night.
Undisturbed by strange apparitions,
ethereal happenings,
and suchlike.
I did not mean to cause you any
. . . disquiet.

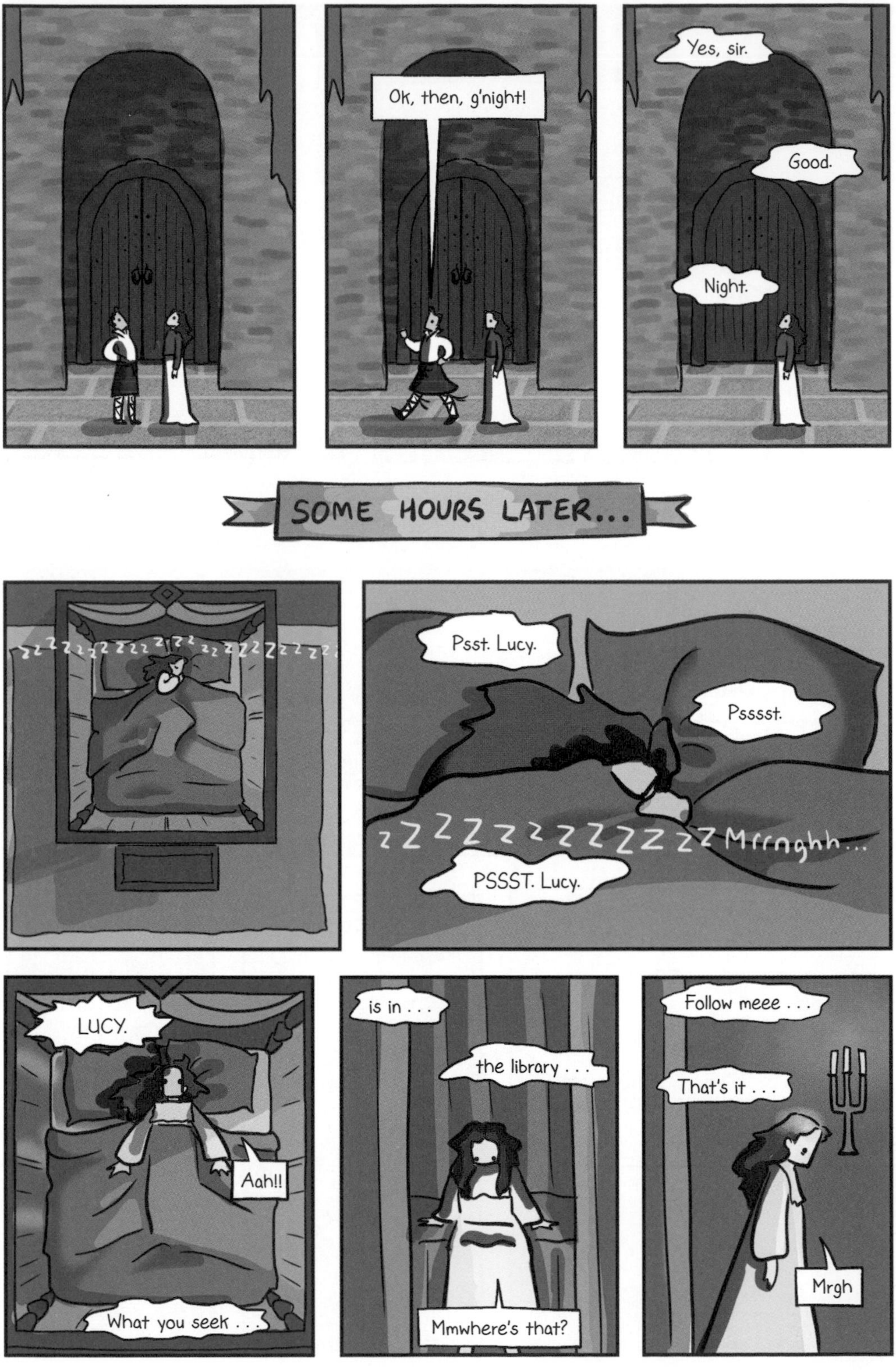
Ok, then, g'night!
Yes, sir.
Good.
Night.
SOME HOURS LATER...
zzzzzzzzzzzzzzzzzzzzzz
Psst. Lucy.
Psssst.
zZZZzzzZZZZzzZ Mrrnghh...
PSSST. Lucy.
LUCY.
Aah!!
What you seek . . .
is in . . .
the library . . .
Mmwhere's that?
Follow meee . . .
That's it . . .
Mrgh

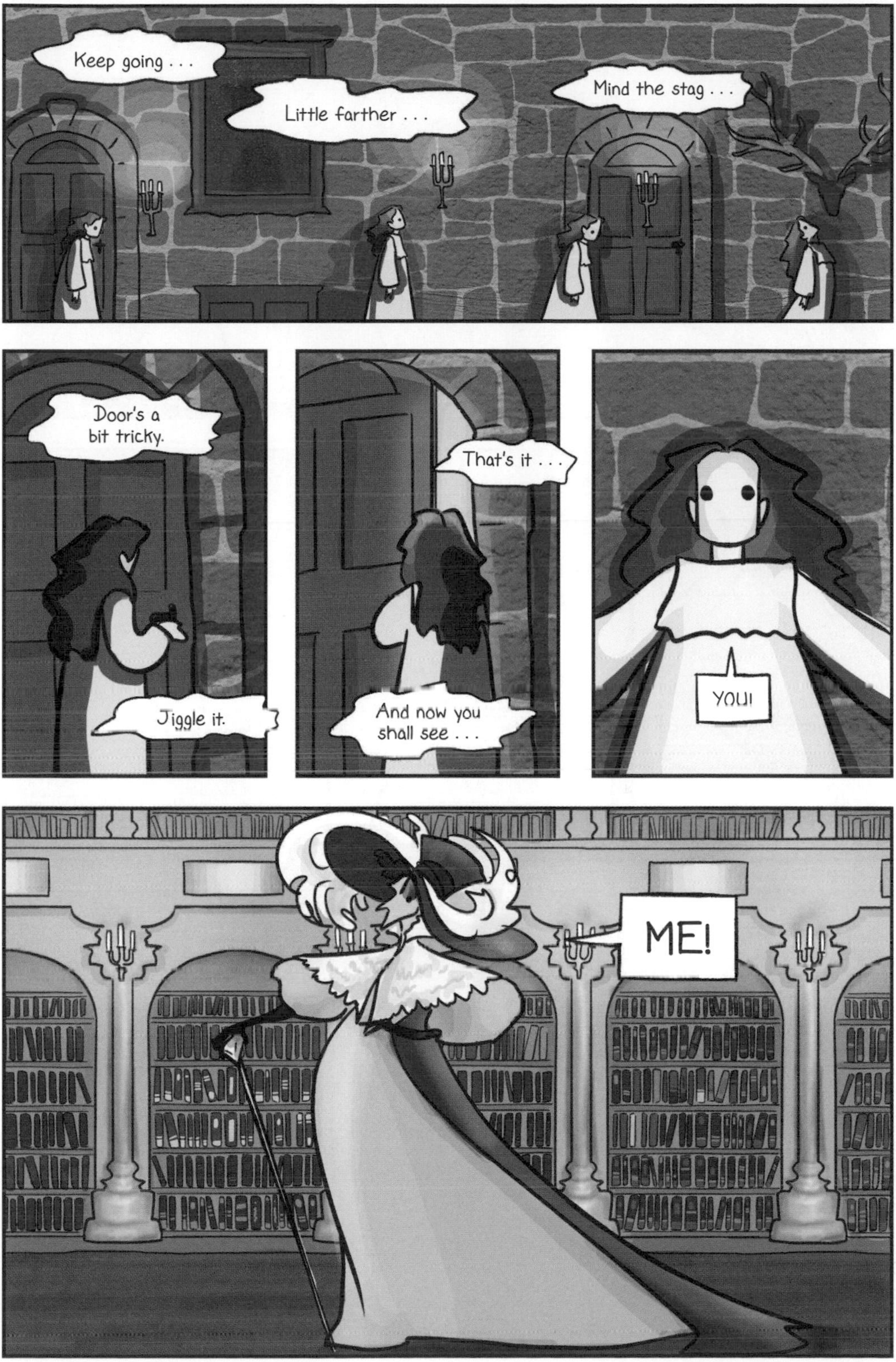
Keep going . . .
Little farther . . .
Mind the stag . . .
Door's a bit tricky.
Jiggle it.
That's it . . .
And now you shall see . . .
YOU!
ME!

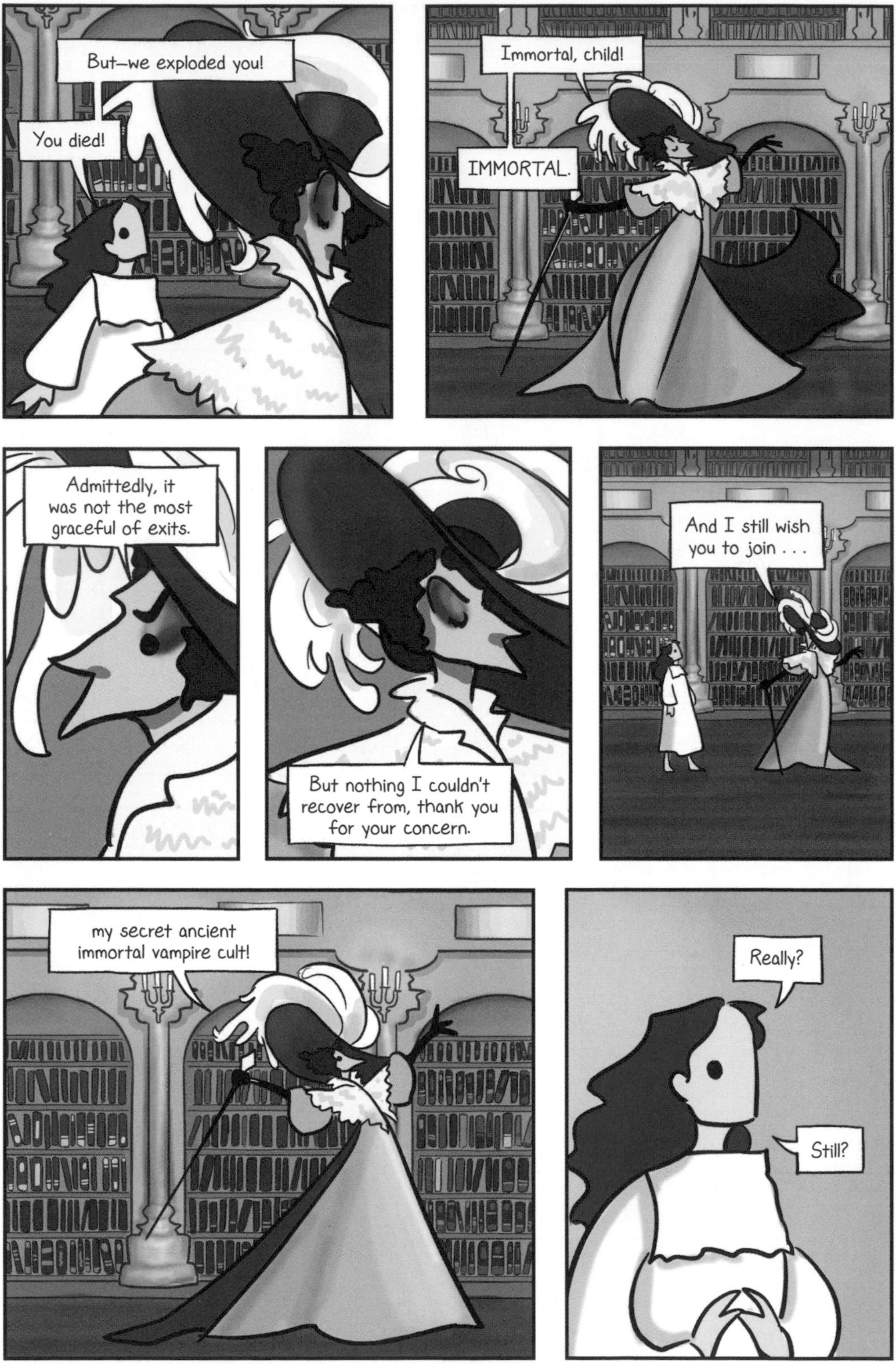
But—we exploded you!
You died!
Immortal, child!
IMMORTAL.
Admittedly, it was not the most graceful of exits.
But nothing I couldn't recover from, thank you for your concern.
And I still wish you to join . . .
my secret ancient immortal vampire cult!
Really?
Still?

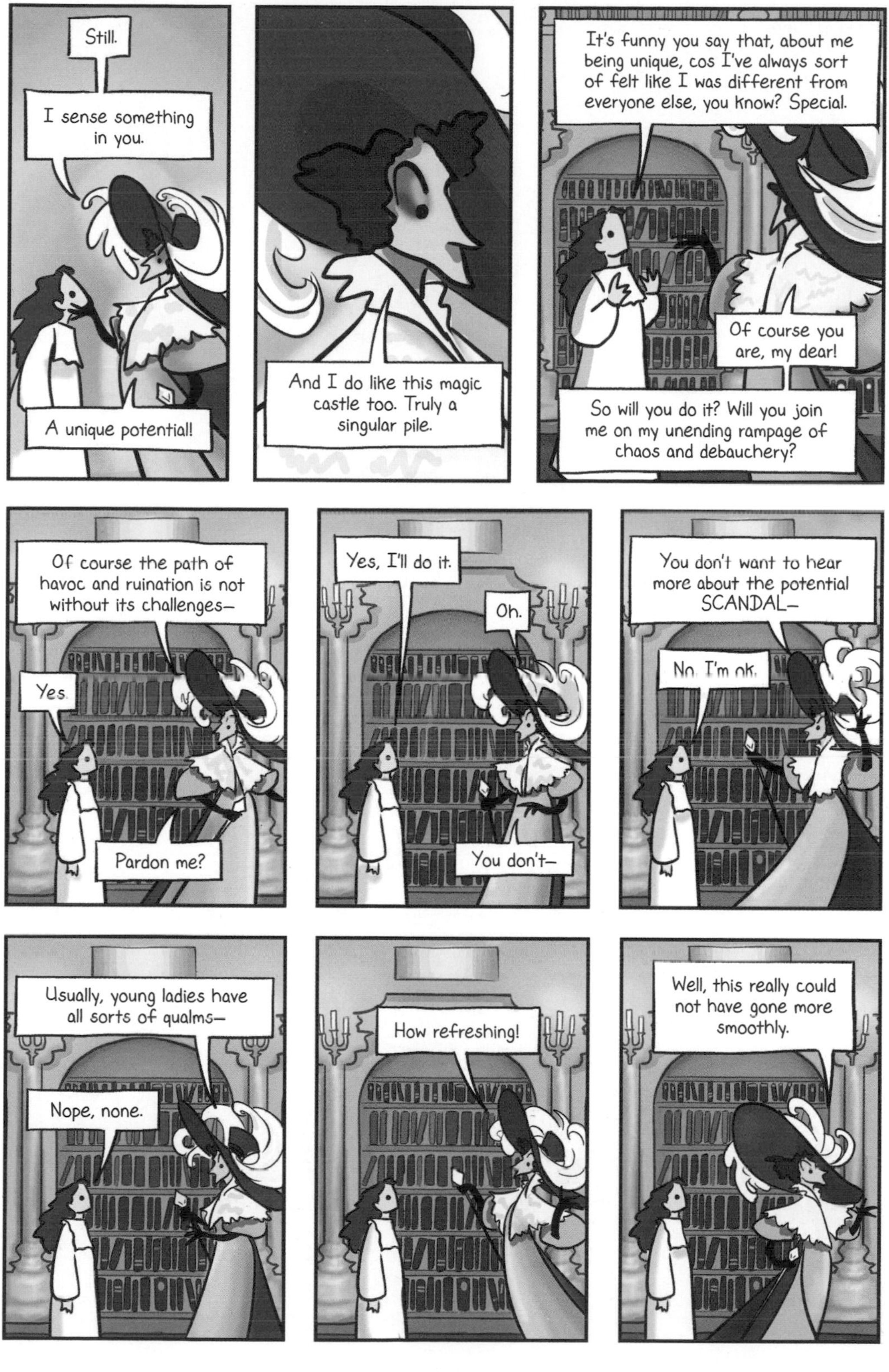
Still.
I sense something in you.
A unique potential!
And I do like this magic castle too. Truly a singular pile.
It's funny you say that, about me being unique, cos I've always sort of felt like I was different from everyone else, you know? Special.
Of course you are, my dear!
So will you do it? Will you join me on my unending rampage of chaos and debauchery?
Of course the path of havoc and ruination is not without its challenges–
Yes.
Pardon me?
Yes, I'll do it.
Oh.
You don't–
You don't want to hear more about the potential SCANDAL–
No. I'm ok.
Usually, young ladies have all sorts of qualms–
Nope, none.
How refreshing!
Well, this really could not have gone more smoothly.

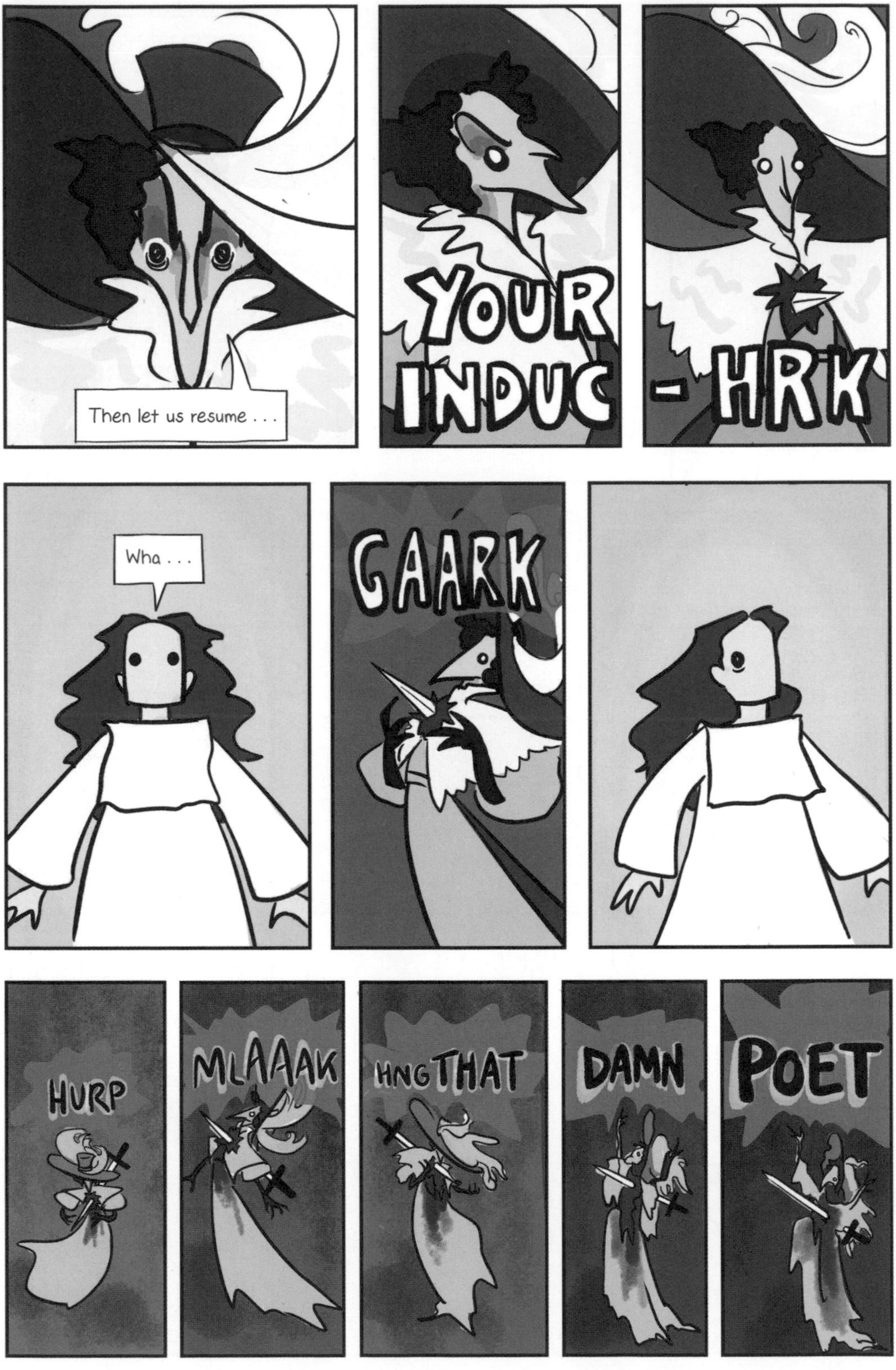
Then let us resume . . .
YOUR
INDUC
- HRK
Wha . . .
GAARK
HURP
MLAAAK
HNG THAT
DAMN
POET

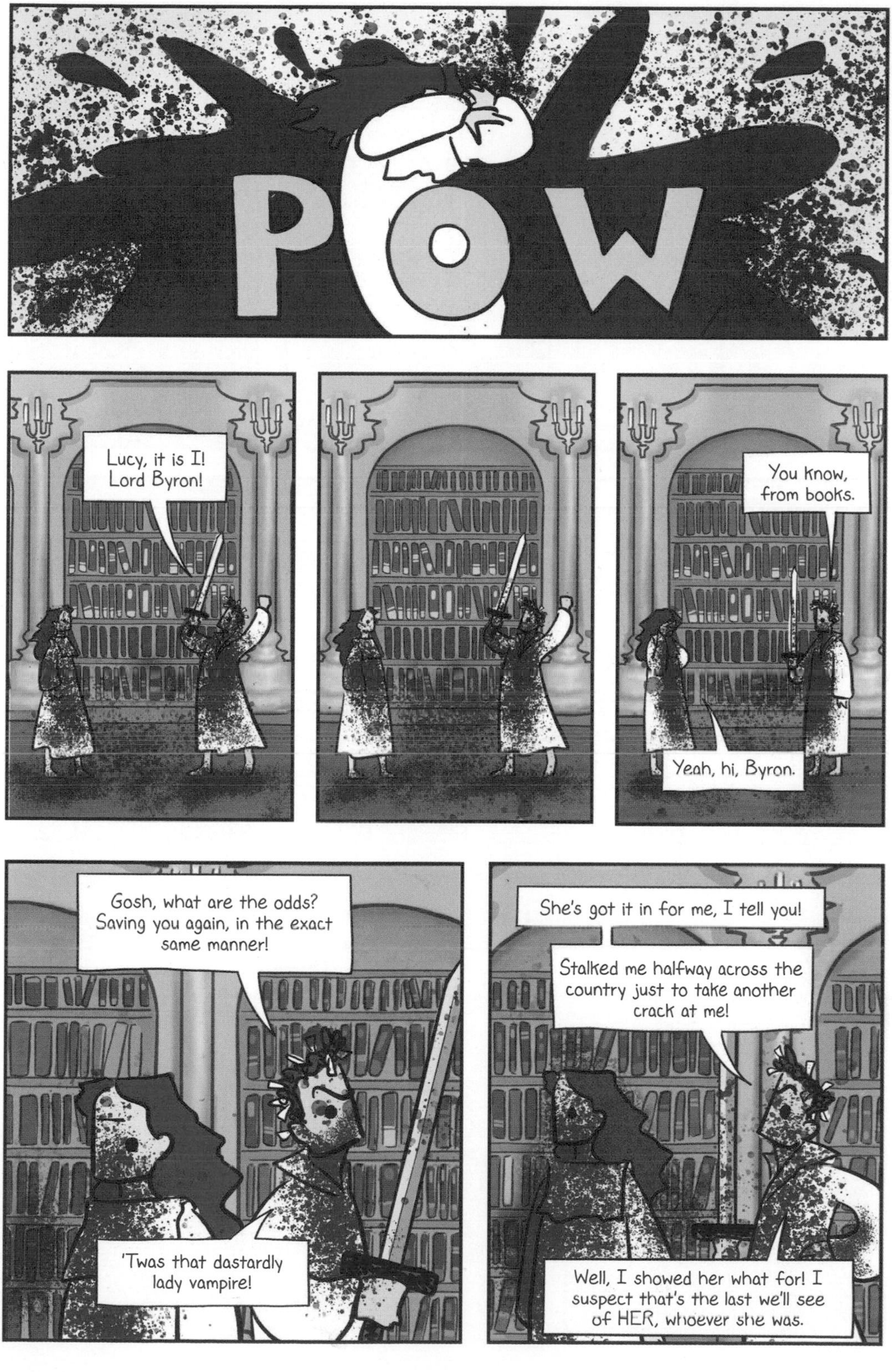
POW
Lucy, it is I! Lord Byron!
You know, from books.
Yeah, hi, Byron.
Gosh, what are the odds? Saving you again, in the exact same manner!
'Twas that dastardly lady vampire!
She's got it in for me, I tell you!
Stalked me halfway across the country just to take another crack at me!
Well, I showed her what for! I suspect that's the last we'll see of HER, whoever she was.

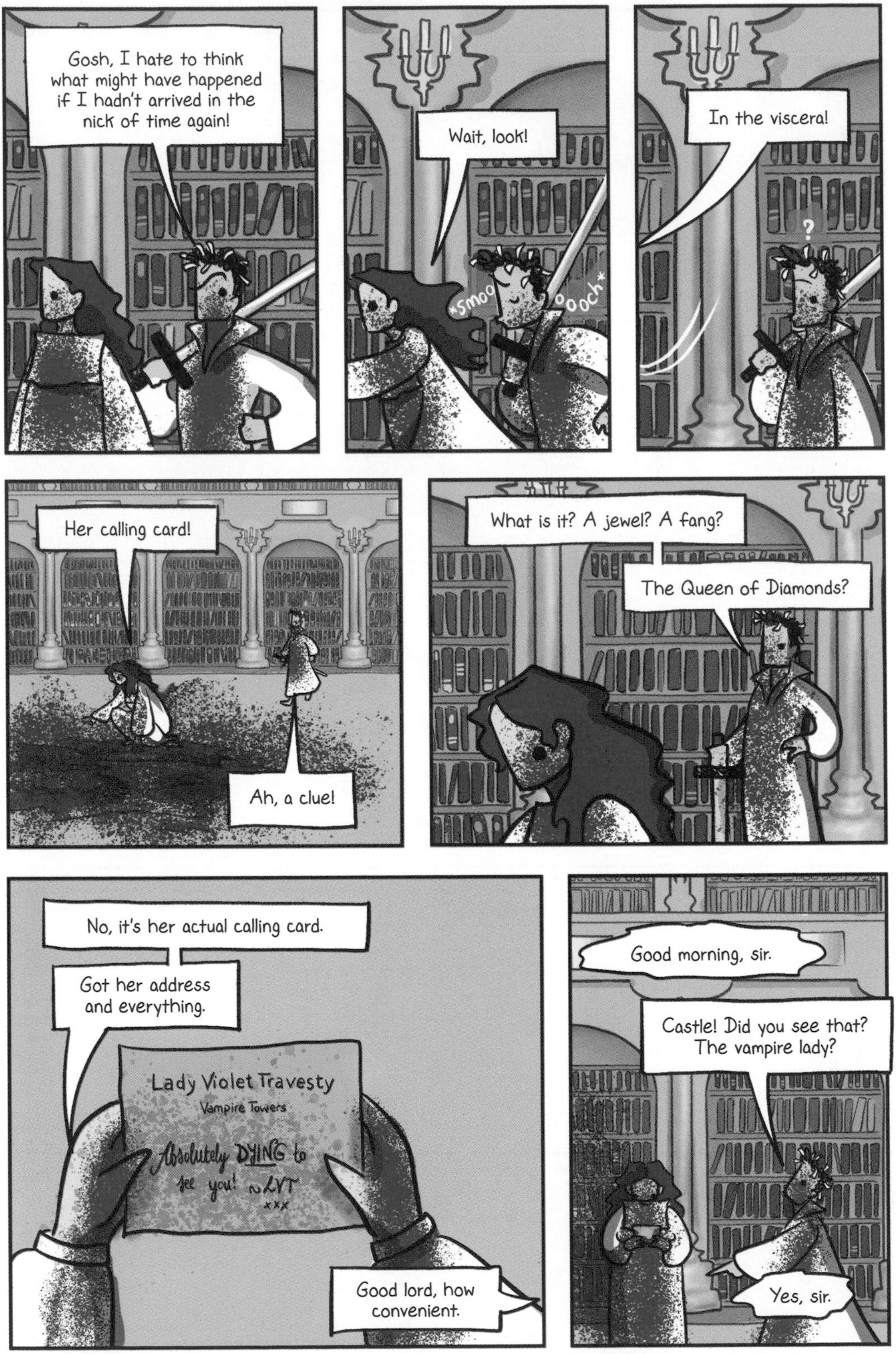
Gosh, I hate to think what might have happened if I hadn't arrived in the nick of time again!
Wait, look!
smooooch
In the viscera!
?
Her calling card!
Ah, a clue!
What is it? A jewel? A fang?
The Queen of Diamonds?
No, it's her actual calling card.
Got her address and everything.
Lady Violet Travesty
Vampire Towers
Absolutely DYING to see you! ~LVT
xxx
Good lord, how convenient.
Good morning, sir.
Castle! Did you see that? The vampire lady?
Yes, sir.

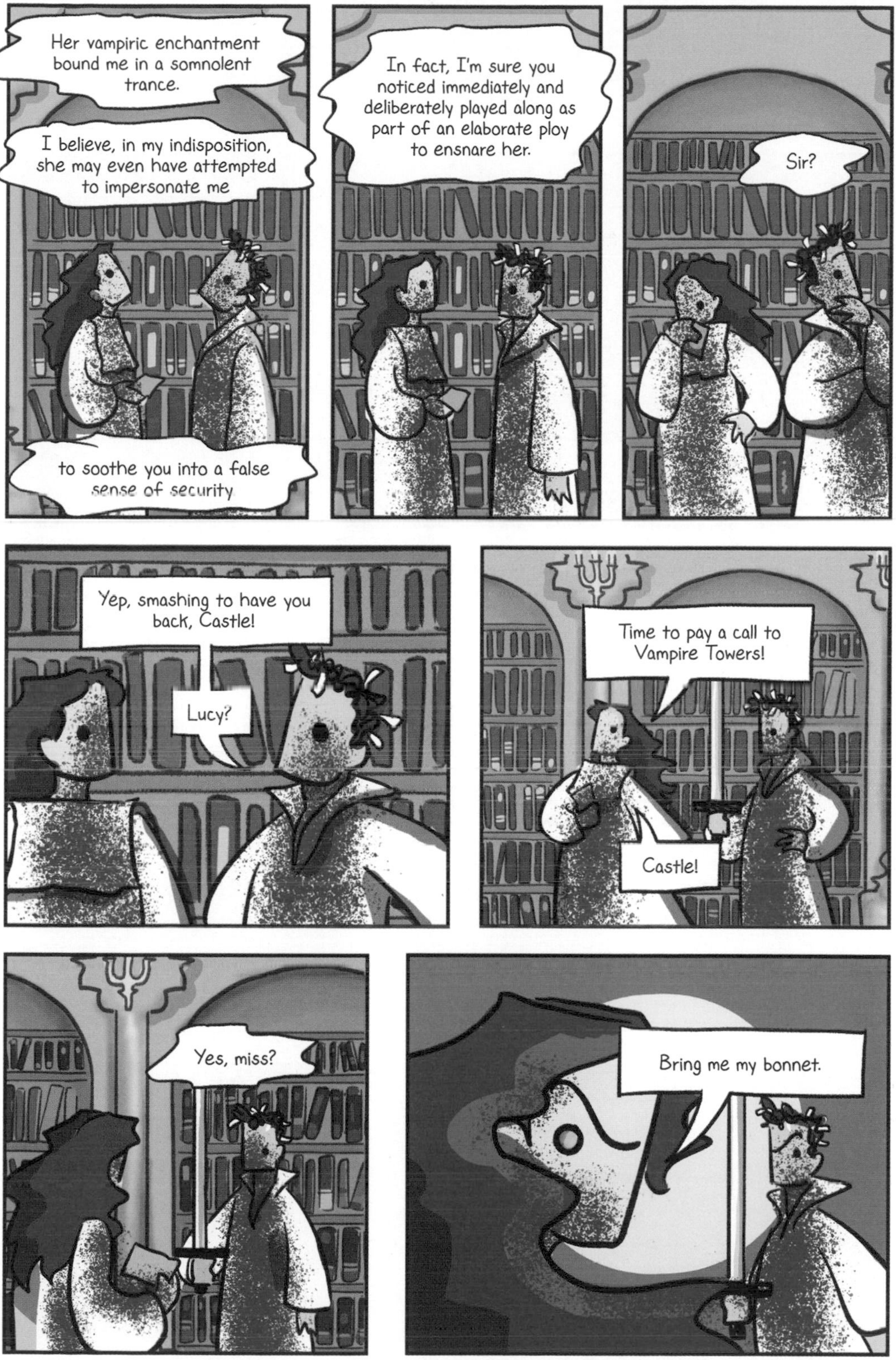
Her vampiric enchantment bound me in a somnolent trance.
I believe, in my indisposition, she may even have attempted to impersonate me
to soothe you into a false sense of security
In fact, I'm sure you noticed immediately and deliberately played along as part of an elaborate ploy to ensnare her.
Sir?
Yep, smashing to have you back, Castle!
Lucy?
Time to pay a call to Vampire Towers!
Castle!
Yes, miss?
Bring me my bonnet.

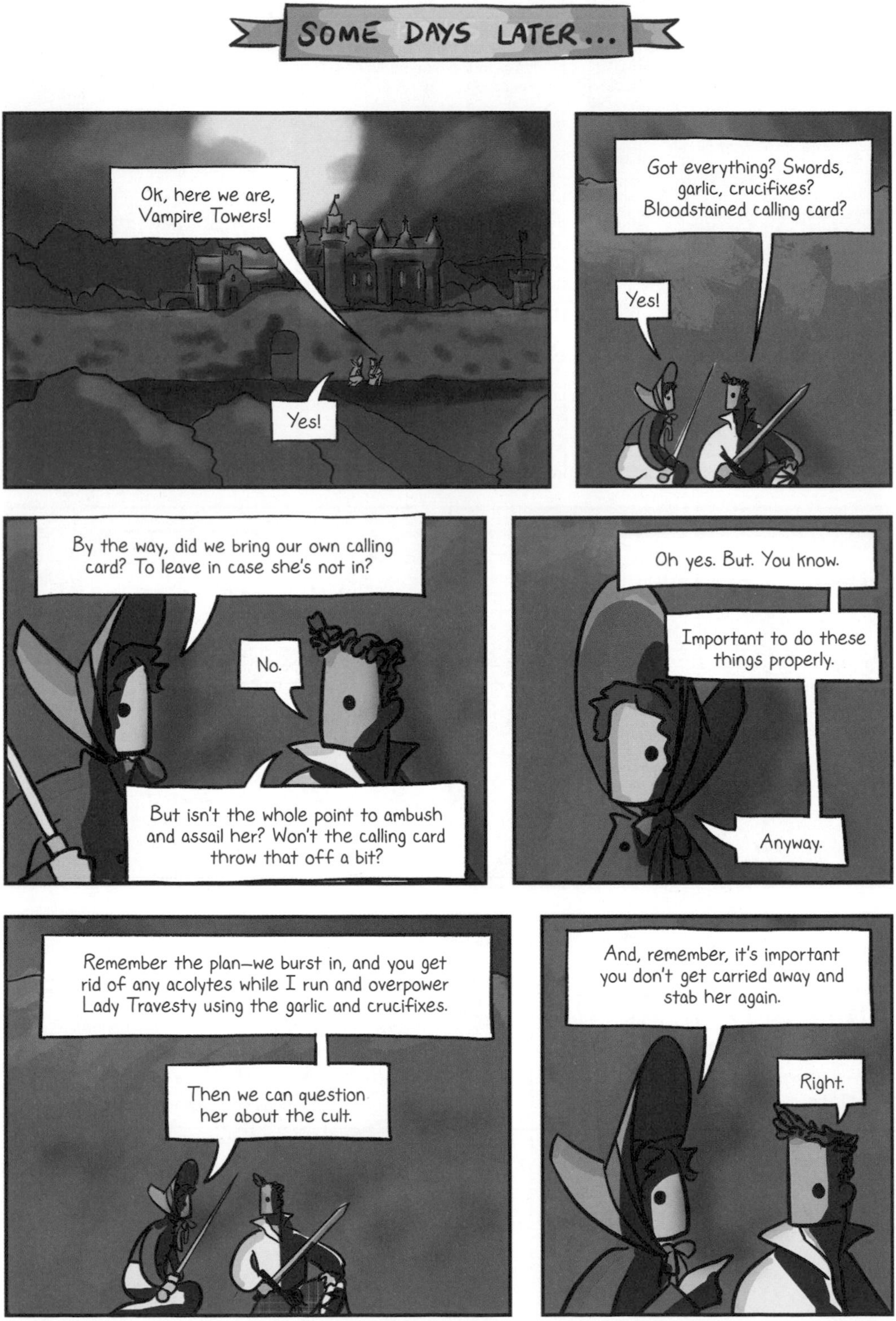
SOME DAYS LATER...
Ok, here we are, Vampire Towers!
Yes!
Got everything? Swords, garlic, crucifixes? Bloodstained calling card?
Yes!
By the way, did we bring our own calling card? To leave in case she's not in?
No.
But isn't the whole point to ambush and assail her? Won't the calling card throw that off a bit?
Oh yes. But. You know.
Important to do these things properly.
Anyway.
Remember the plan—we burst in, and you get rid of any acolytes while I run and overpower Lady Travesty using the garlic and crucifixes.
Then we can question her about the cult.
And, remember, it's important you don't get carried away and stab her again.
Right.

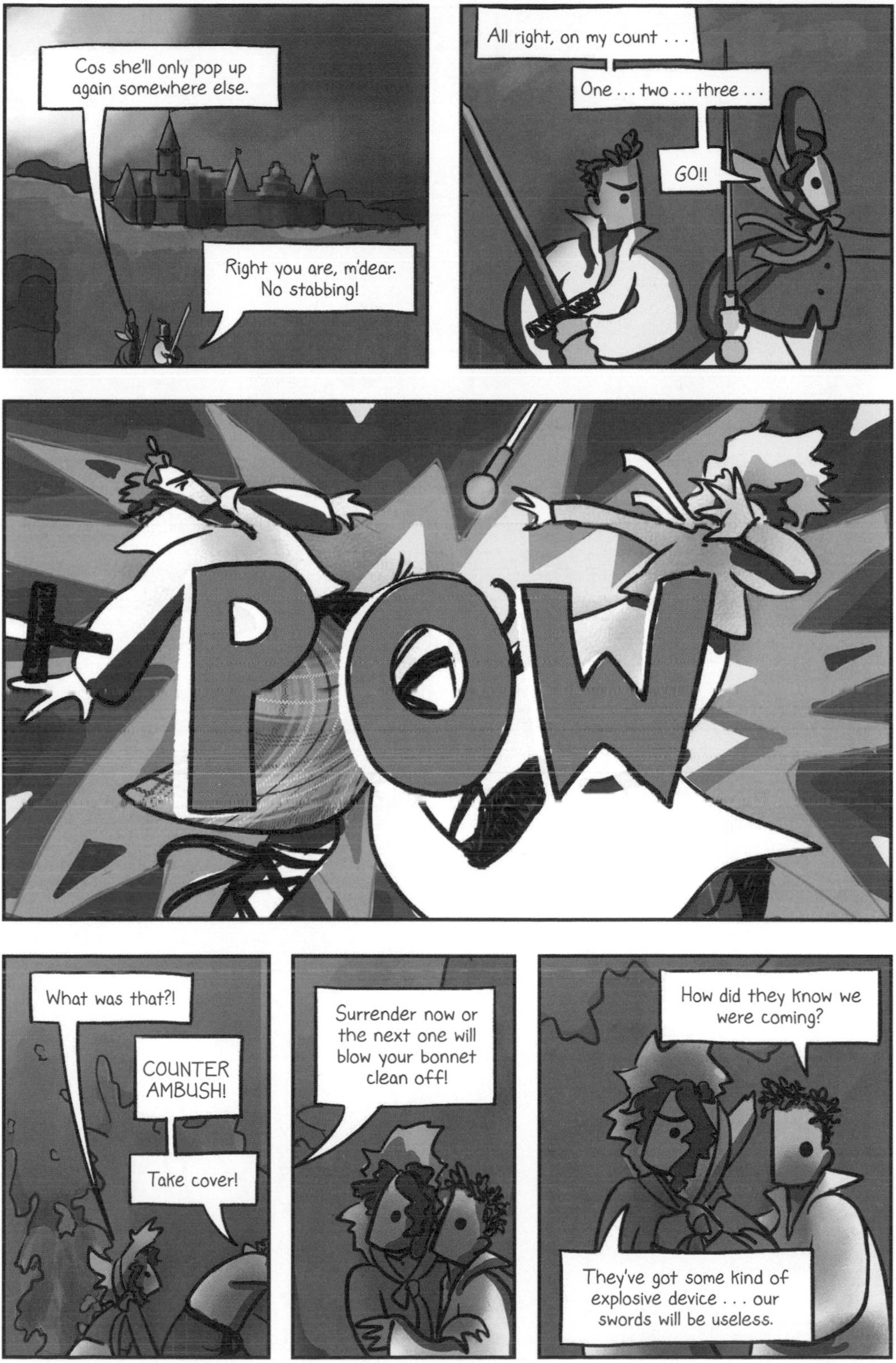
Cos she'll only pop up again somewhere else.
Right you are, m'dear. No stabbing!
All right, on my count . . .
One . . . two . . . three . . .
GO!!
POW
What was that?!
COUNTER AMBUSH!
Take cover!
Surrender now or the next one will blow your bonnet clean off!
How did they know we were coming?
They've got some kind of explosive device . . . our swords will be useless.

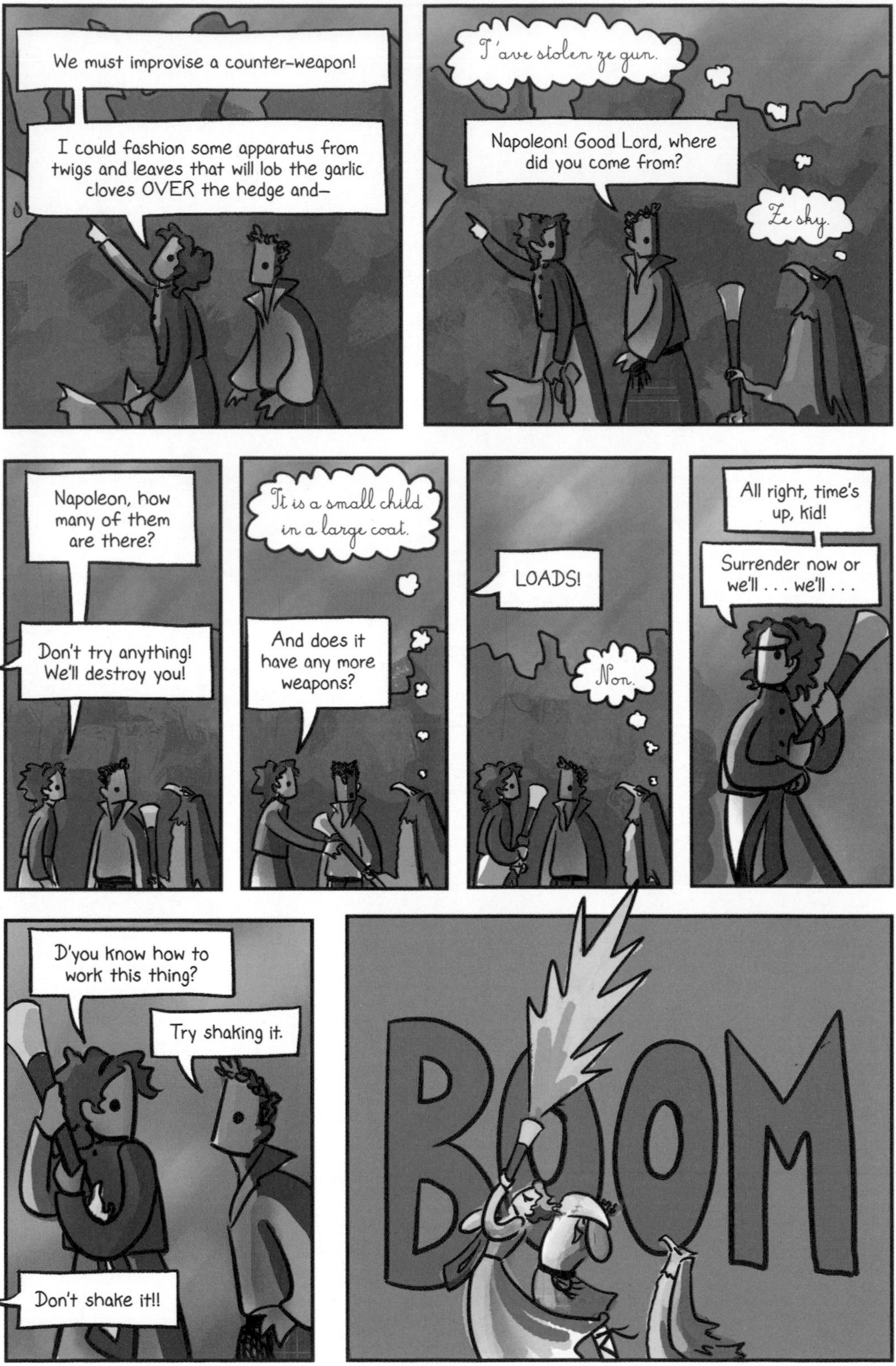

We must improvise a counter-weapon!
I could fashion some apparatus from twigs and leaves that will lob the garlic cloves OVER the hedge and–
J'ave stolen ze gun.
Napoleon! Good Lord, where did you come from?
Ze sky.
Napoleon, how many of them are there?
Don't try anything! We'll destroy you!
It is a small child in a large coat.
And does it have any more weapons?
LOADS!
Non.
All right, time's up, kid!
Surrender now or we'll . . . we'll . . .
D'you know how to work this thing?
Try shaking it.
Don't shake it!!
BOOM

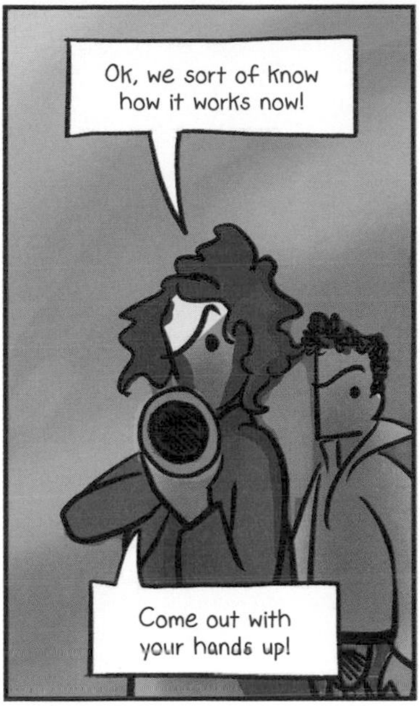
Ok, we sort of know how it works now!
Come out with your hands up!
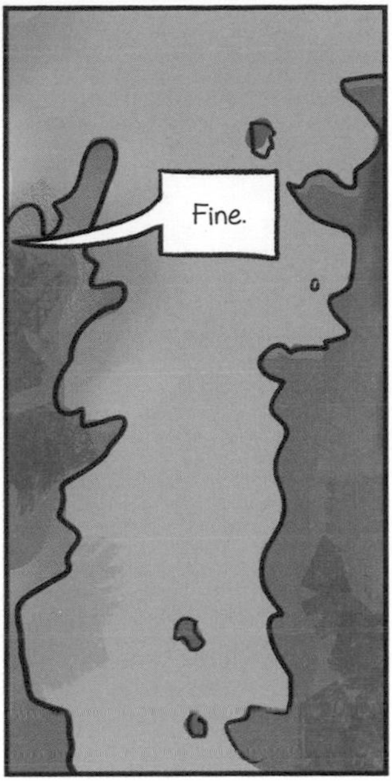
Fine.
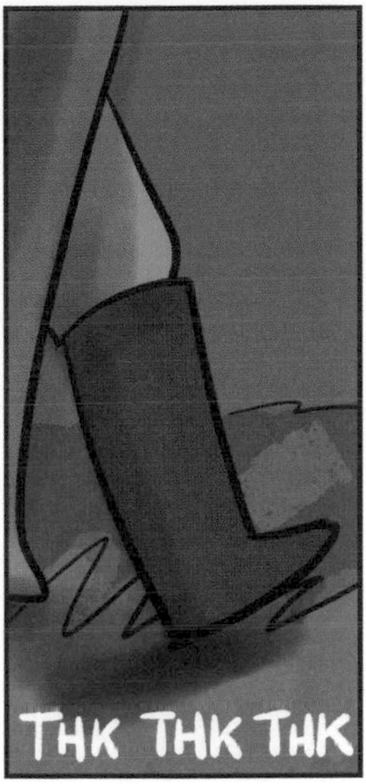
THK THK THK
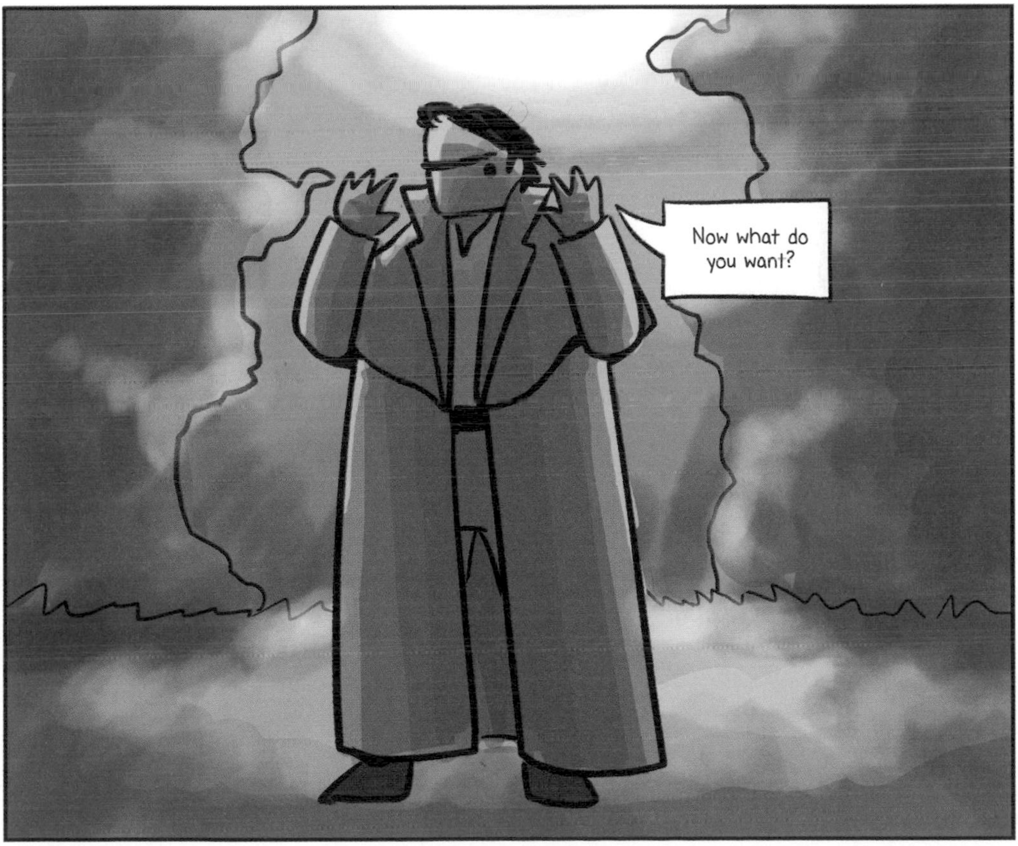
Now what do you want?

CHAPTER II – THE QUEST

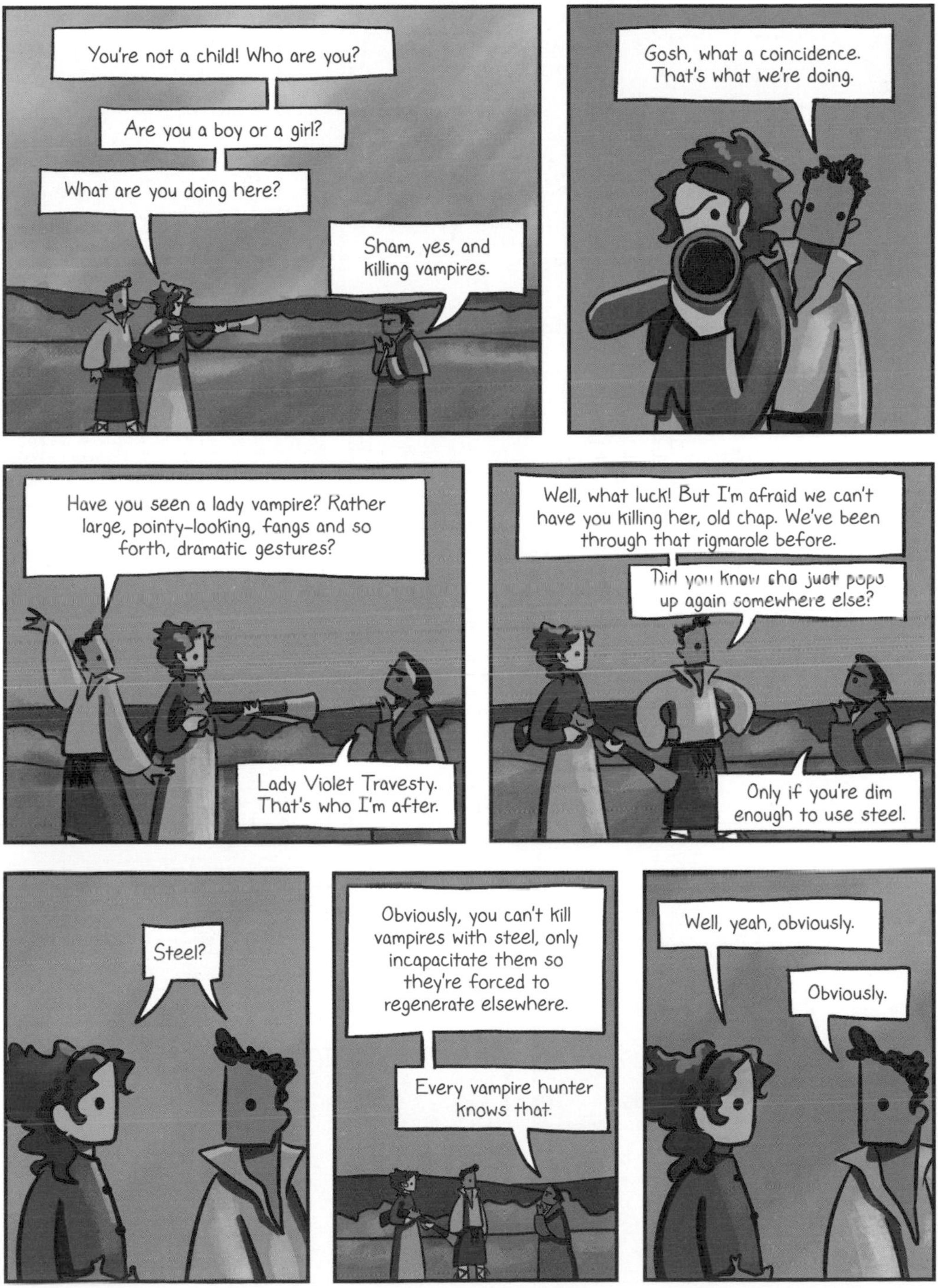
You're not a child! Who are you?
Are you a boy or a girl?
What are you doing here?
Sham, yes, and killing vampires.
Gosh, what a coincidence. That's what we're doing.
Have you seen a lady vampire? Rather large, pointy-looking, fangs and so forth, dramatic gestures?
Lady Violet Travesty. That's who I'm after.
Well, what luck! But I'm afraid we can't have you killing her, old chap. We've been through that rigmarole before.
Did you know she just pops up again somewhere else?
Only if you're dim enough to use steel.
Steel?
Obviously, you can't kill vampires with steel, only incapacitate them so they're forced to regenerate elsewhere.
Every vampire hunter knows that.
Well, yeah, obviously.
Obviously.

Anyway, we don't want to kill her or make her pop up somewhere else. We want to capture and question her.

Can't have you using this thing and killing her stone dead.

It won't kill her.

Hah! So you don't know how to get her either!

It's a modified blunderbuss loaded with a special mix of gunpowder and crushed garlic.

Enough to stun her but not kill her or allow her to escape.

Well, you . . . certainly have thought this through . . .

Too bad, now we've got it.

And sort of know how to use it.

Yeah

Look, I've got a suggestion I think will suit everyone.

SOME MINUTES LATER...

Ok, ready?

Ready!

Lady Travesty will be in one of the castle's inner rooms. I'll blast through the first wave of henchmen, then you two take on the rest while I run through and stun Travesty.

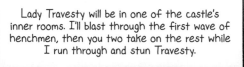

18

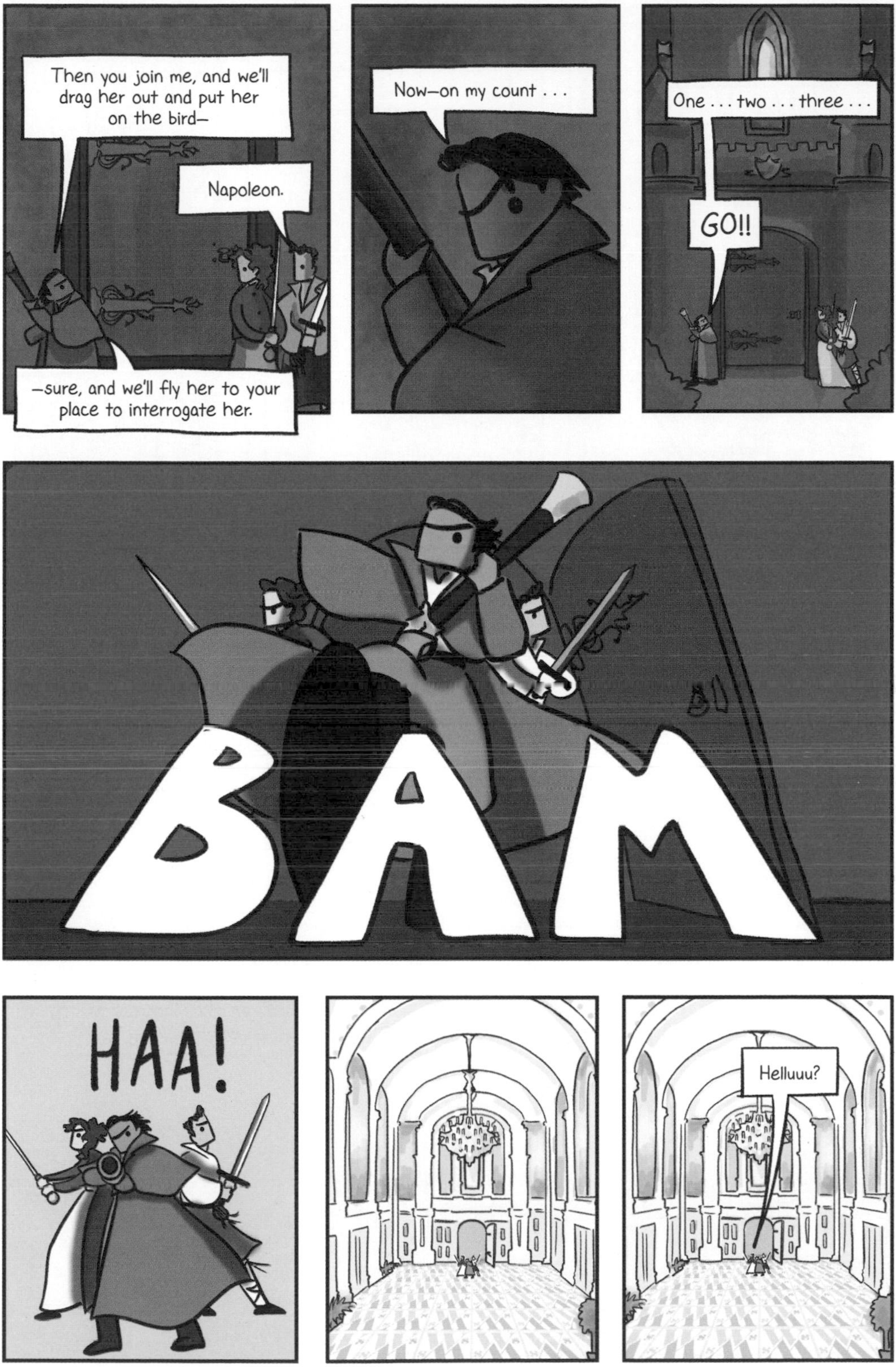

Then you join me, and we'll drag her out and put her on the bird—
Napoleon.
—sure, and we'll fly her to your place to interrogate her.
Now—on my count . . .
One . . . two . . . three . . .
GO!!
BAM
HAA!
Helluuu?

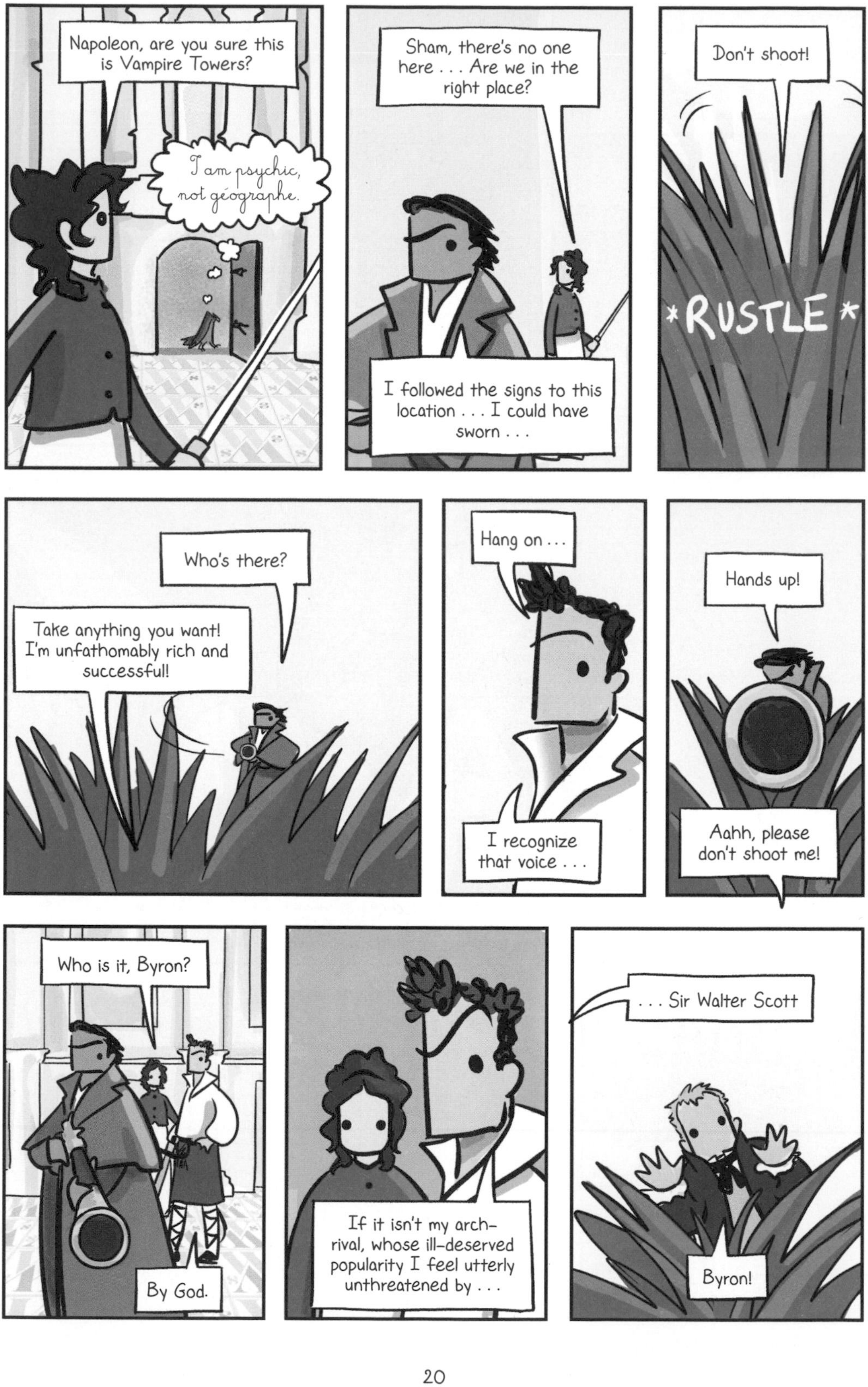
Napoleon, are you sure this is Vampire Towers?
I am psychic, not géographe.
Sham, there's no one here . . . Are we in the right place?
I followed the signs to this location . . . I could have sworn . . .
Don't shoot!
RUSTLE
Who's there?
Take anything you want! I'm unfathomably rich and successful!
Hang on . . .
I recognize that voice . . .
Hands up!
Aahh, please don't shoot me!
Who is it, Byron?
By God.
If it isn't my arch-rival, whose ill-deserved popularity I feel utterly unthreatened by . . .
. . . Sir Walter Scott
Byron!

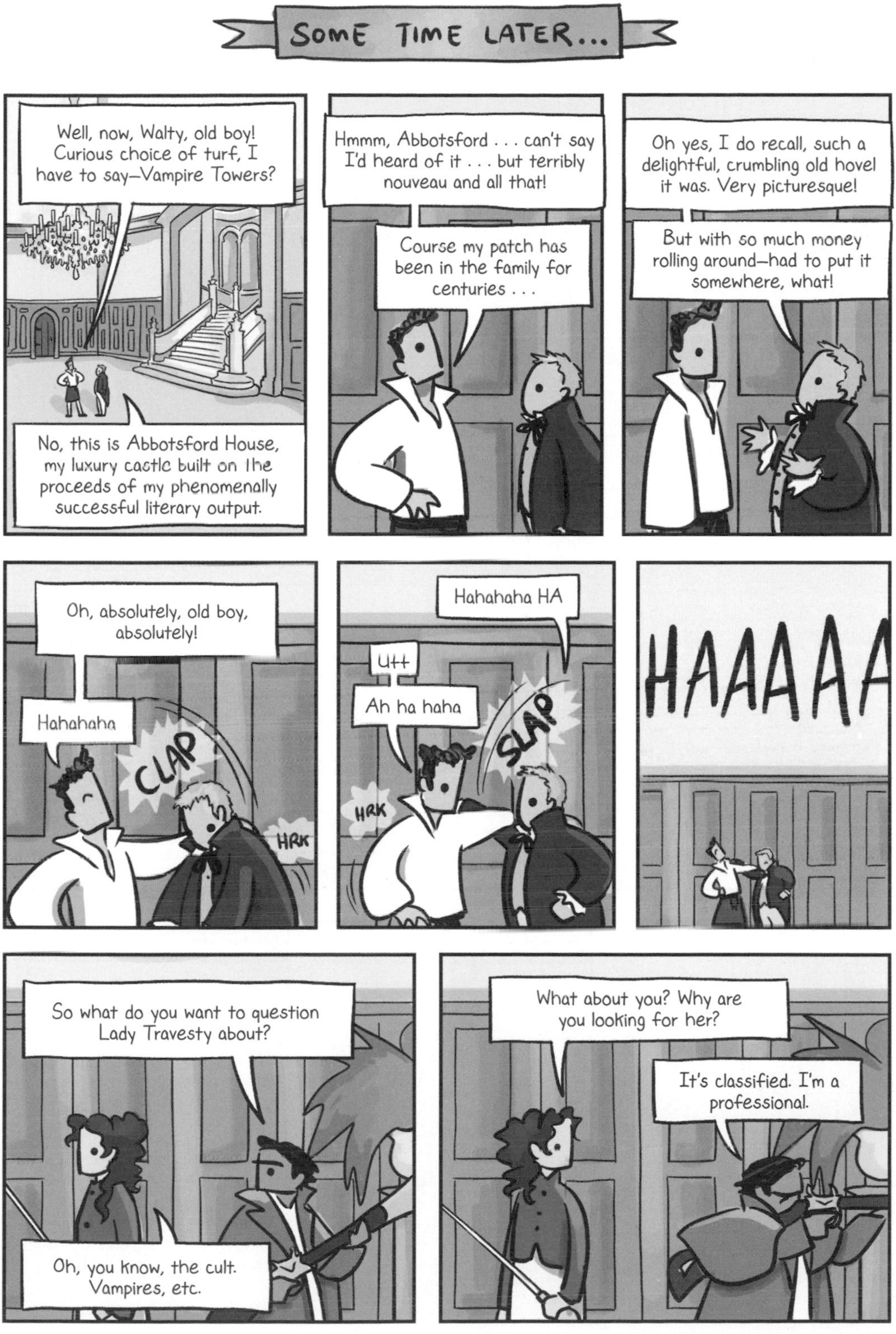
SOME TIME LATER...
Well, now, Walty, old boy! Curious choice of turf, I have to say—Vampire Towers?
No, this is Abbotsford House, my luxury castle built on the proceeds of my phenomenally successful literary output.
Hmmm, Abbotsford . . . can't say I'd heard of it . . . but terribly nouveau and all that!
Course my patch has been in the family for centuries . . .
Oh yes, I do recall, such a delightful, crumbling old hovel it was. Very picturesque!
But with so much money rolling around—had to put it somewhere, what!
Oh, absolutely, old boy, absolutely!
Hahahaha
CLAP
HRK
Hahahaha HA
Utt
Ah ha haha
SLAP
HRK
HAAAAA
So what do you want to question Lady Travesty about?
Oh, you know, the cult. Vampires, etc.
What about you? Why are you looking for her?
It's classified. I'm a professional.

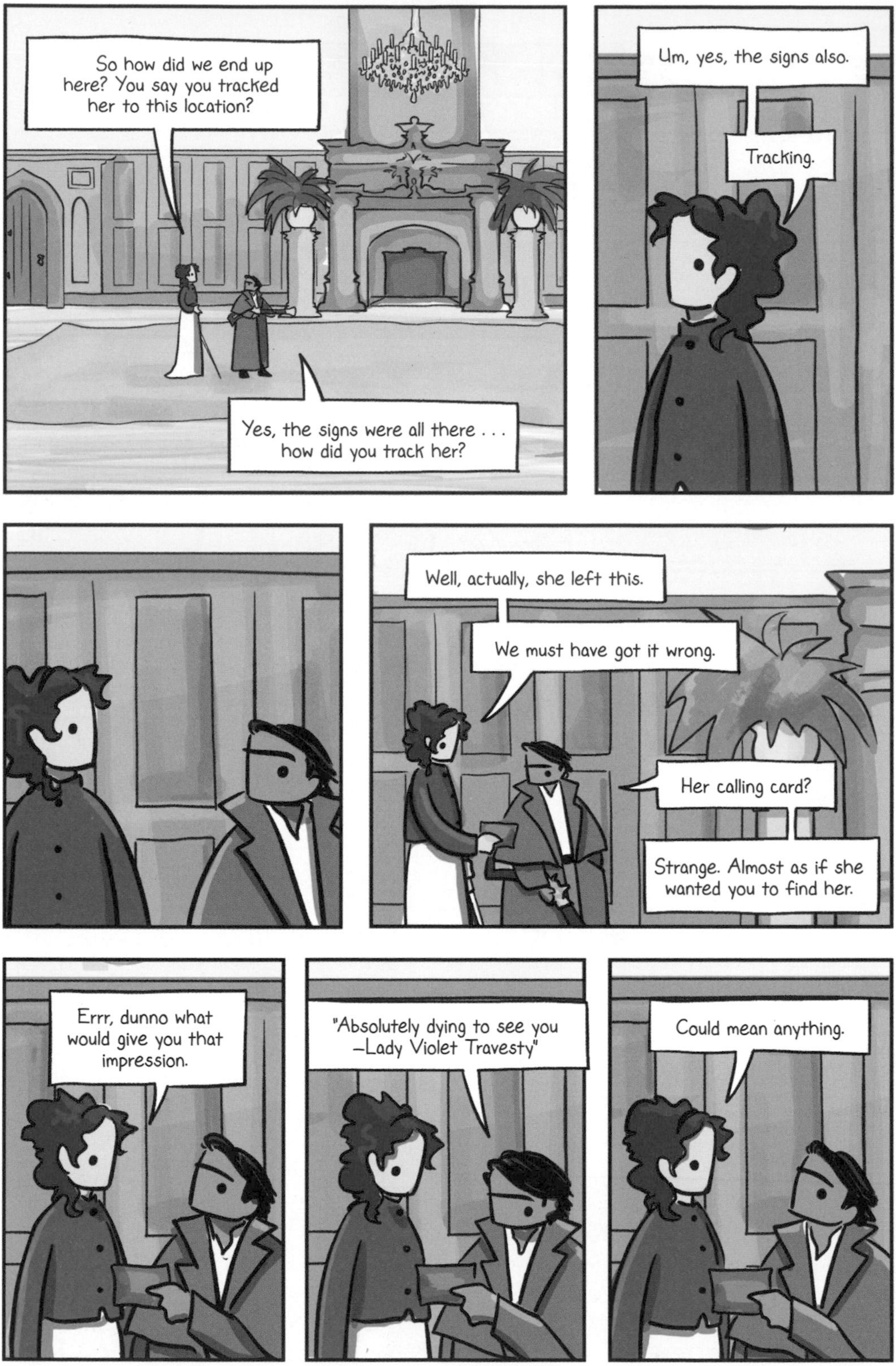
So how did we end up here? You say you tracked her to this location?
Yes, the signs were all there . . . how did you track her?
Um, yes, the signs also.
Tracking.
Well, actually, she left this.
We must have got it wrong.
Her calling card?
Strange. Almost as if she wanted you to find her.
Errr, dunno what would give you that impression.
"Absolutely dying to see you –Lady Violet Travesty"
Could mean anything.

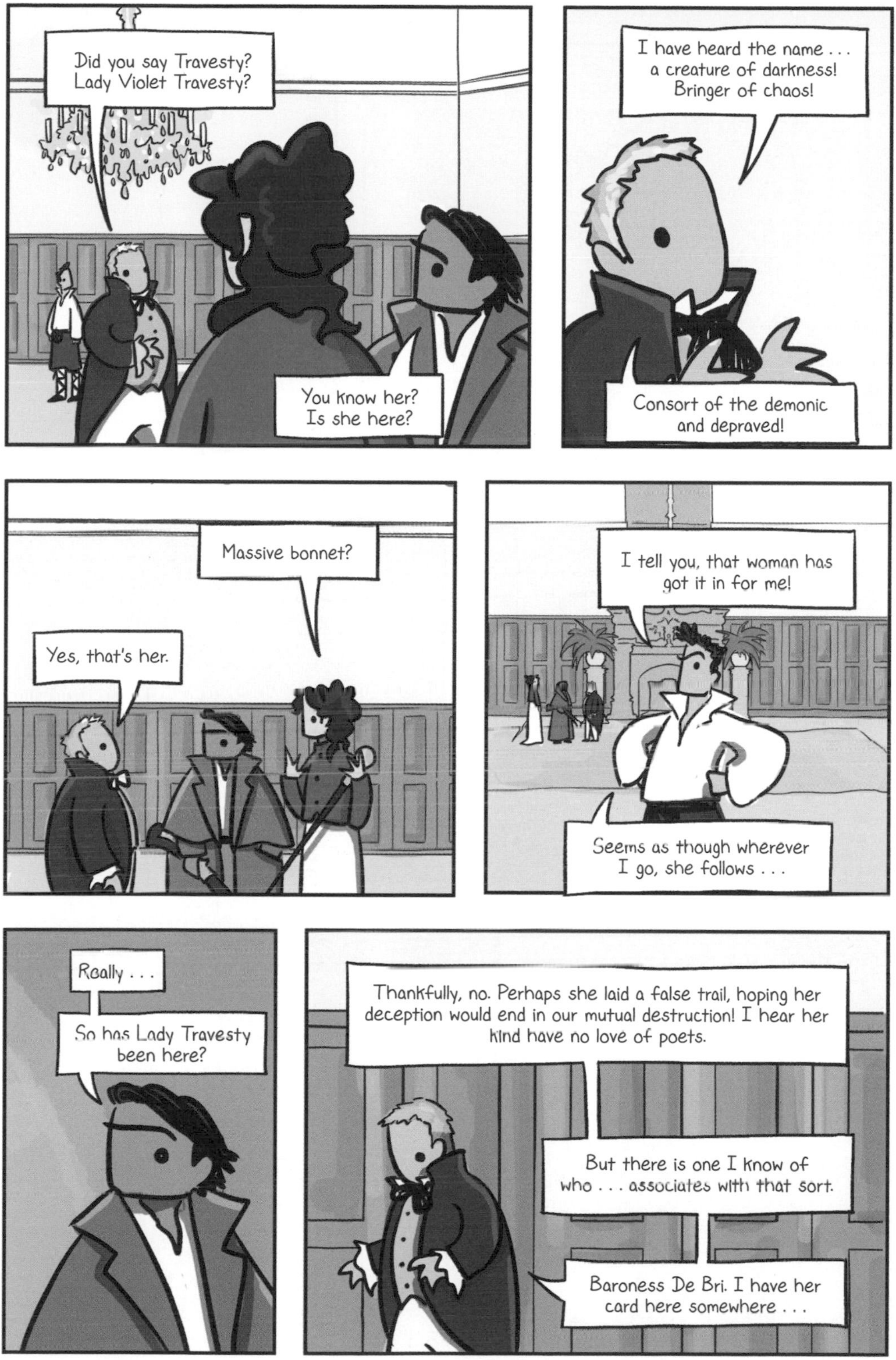
Did you say Travesty? Lady Violet Travesty?
You know her? Is she here?
I have heard the name . . . a creature of darkness! Bringer of chaos!
Consort of the demonic and depraved!
Massive bonnet?
Yes, that's her.
I tell you, that woman has got it in for me!
Seems as though wherever I go, she follows . . .
Really . . .
So has Lady Travesty been here?
Thankfully, no. Perhaps she laid a false trail, hoping her deception would end in our mutual destruction! I hear her kind have no love of poets.
But there is one I know of who . . . associates with that sort.
Baroness De Bri. I have her card here somewhere . . .

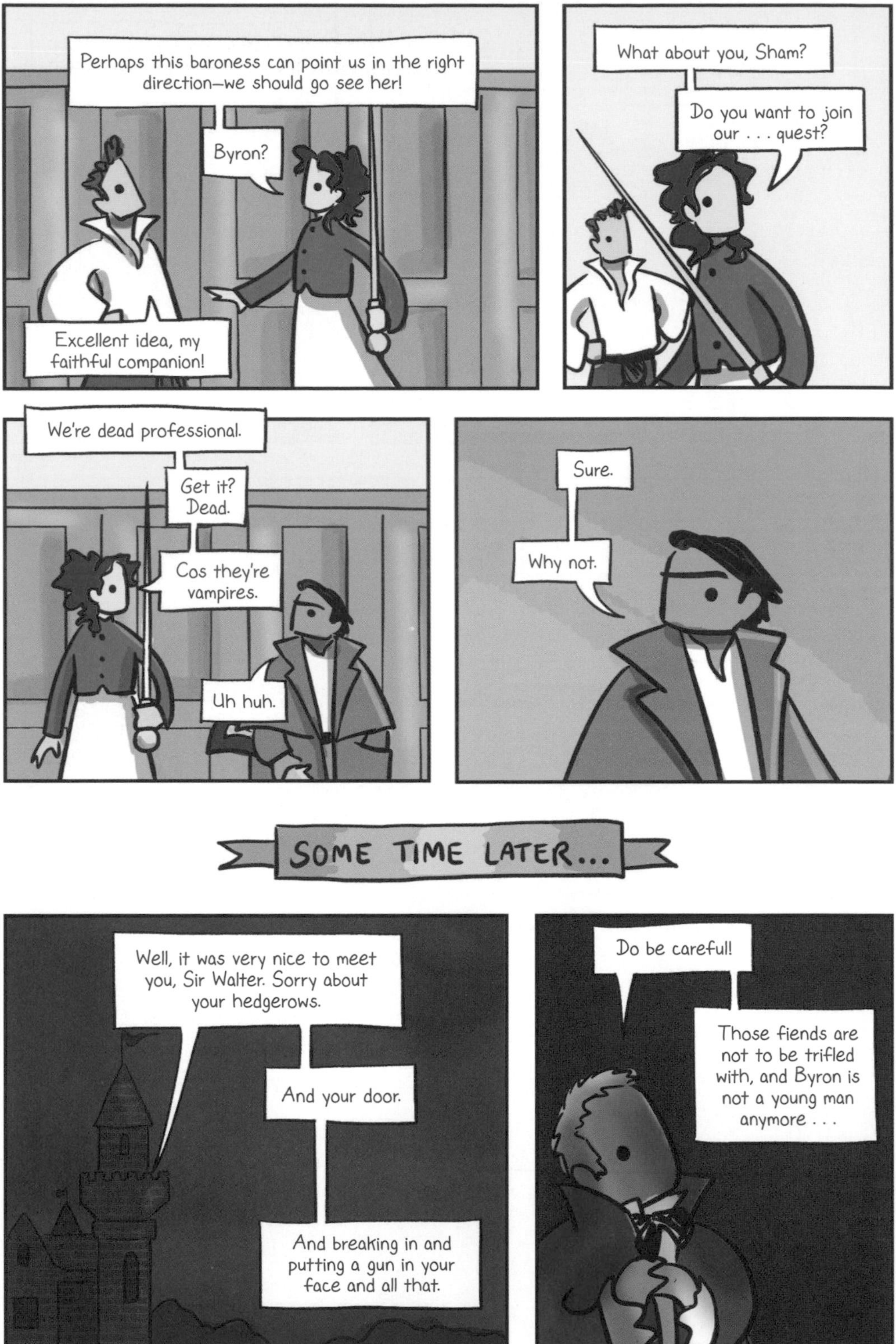

Perhaps this baroness can point us in the right direction—we should go see her!
Byron?
Excellent idea, my faithful companion!
What about you, Sham?
Do you want to join our . . . quest?
We're dead professional.
Get it? Dead.
Cos they're vampires.
Uh huh.
Sure.
Why not.
SOME TIME LATER...
Well, it was very nice to meet you, Sir Walter. Sorry about your hedgerows.
And your door.
And breaking in and putting a gun in your face and all that.
Do be careful!
Those fiends are not to be trifled with, and Byron is not a young man anymore . . .

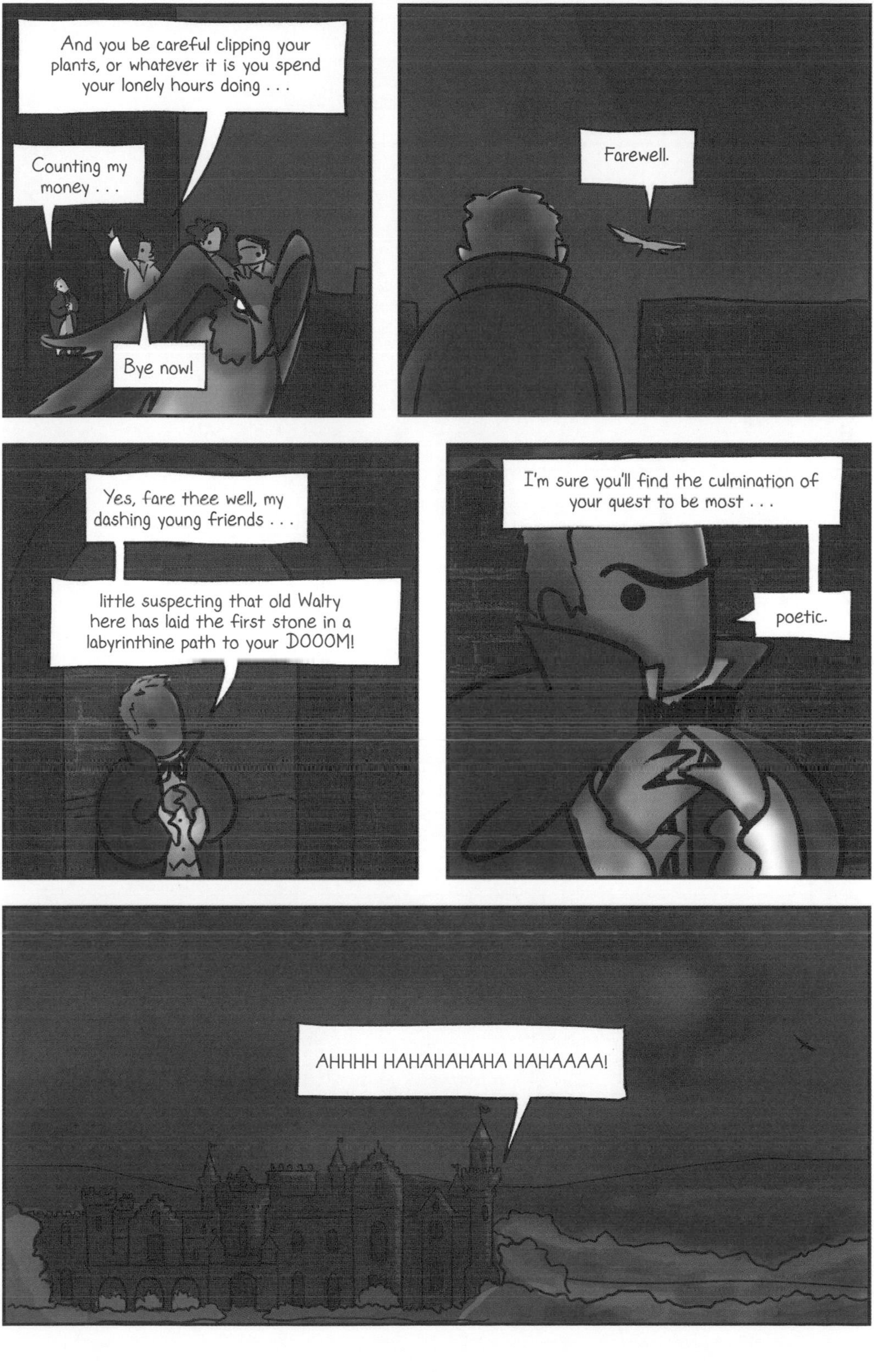
And you be careful clipping your plants, or whatever it is you spend your lonely hours doing . . .
Counting my money . . .
Bye now!
Farewell.
Yes, fare thee well, my dashing young friends . . .
little suspecting that old Walty here has laid the first stone in a labyrinthine path to your DOOOM!
I'm sure you'll find the culmination of your quest to be most . . .
poetic.
AHHHH HAHAHAHAHA HAHAAAA!

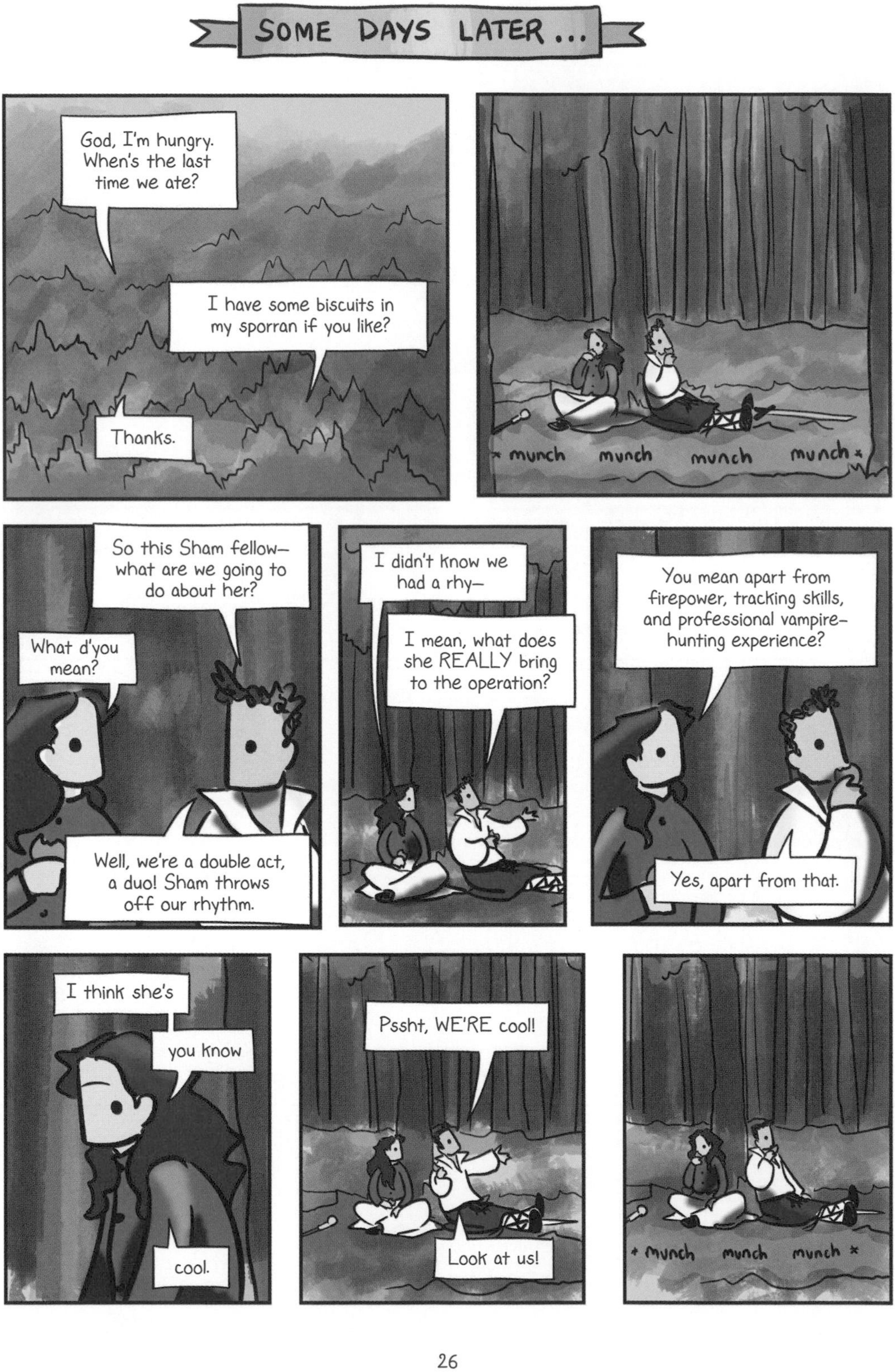
SOME DAYS LATER ...
God, I'm hungry. When's the last time we ate?
I have some biscuits in my sporran if you like?
Thanks.
munch munch munch munch
So this Sham fellow— what are we going to do about her?
What d'you mean?
Well, we're a double act, a duo! Sham throws off our rhythm.
I didn't know we had a rhy—
I mean, what does she REALLY bring to the operation?
You mean apart from firepower, tracking skills, and professional vampire-hunting experience?
Yes, apart from that.
I think she's
you know
cool.
Pssht, WE'RE cool!
Look at us!
munch munch munch

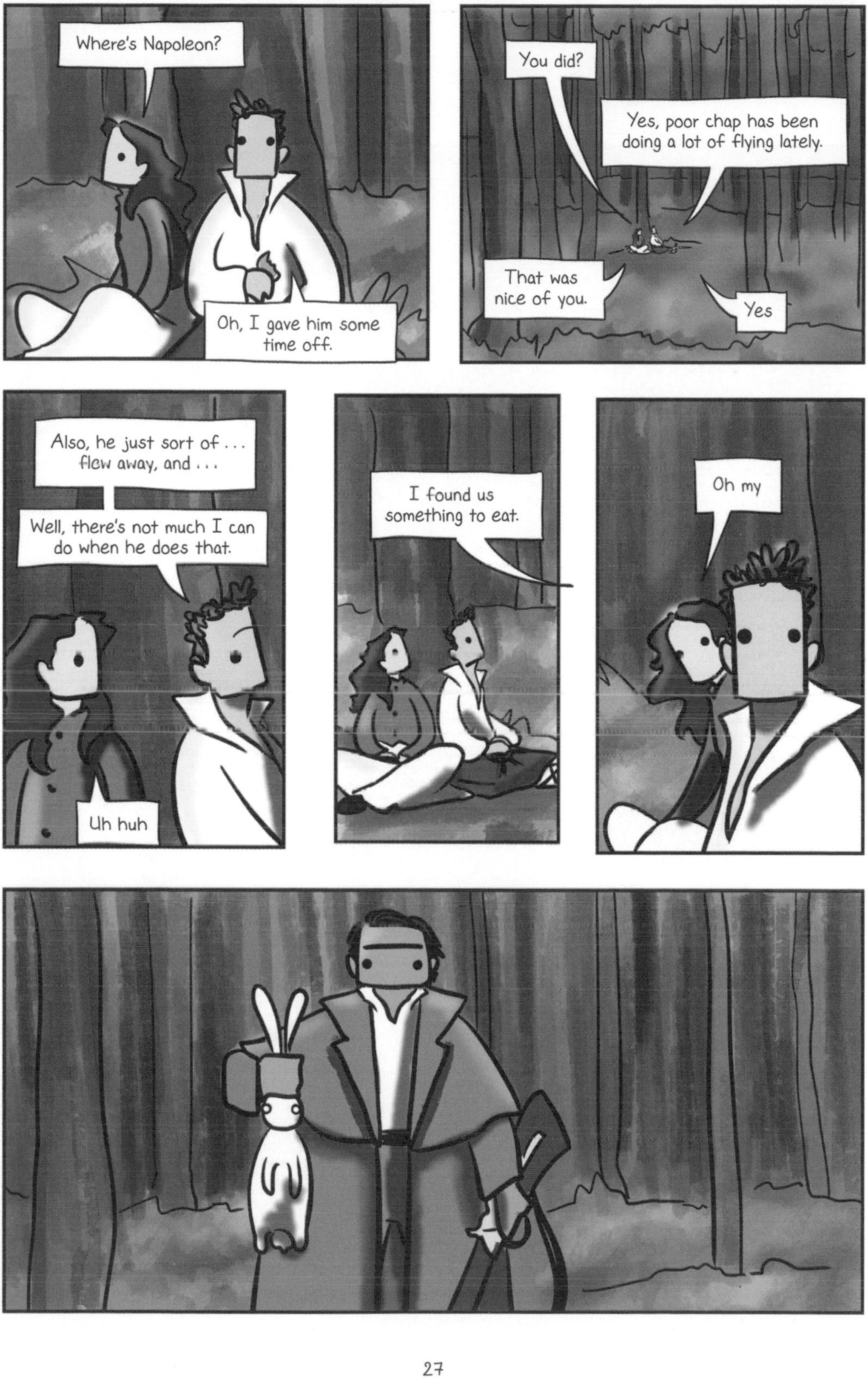
Where's Napoleon?
Oh, I gave him some time off.
You did?
Yes, poor chap has been doing a lot of flying lately.
That was nice of you.
Yes
Also, he just sort of . . . flew away, and . . .
Well, there's not much I can do when he does that.
Uh huh
I found us something to eat.
Oh my

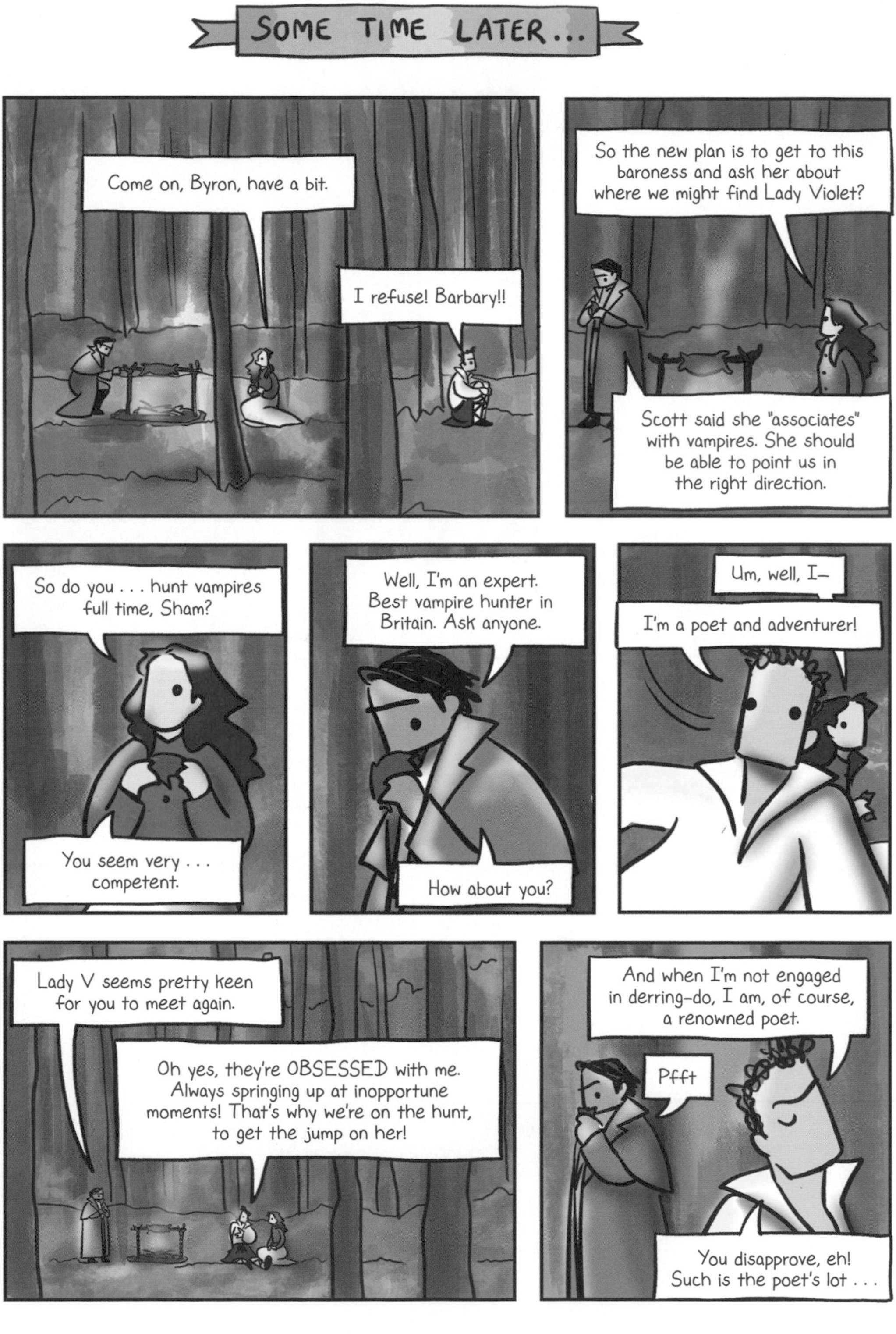
SOME TIME LATER...
Come on, Byron, have a bit.
I refuse! Barbary!!
So the new plan is to get to this baroness and ask her about where we might find Lady Violet?
Scott said she "associates" with vampires. She should be able to point us in the right direction.
So do you . . . hunt vampires full time, Sham?
You seem very . . . competent.
Well, I'm an expert. Best vampire hunter in Britain. Ask anyone.
How about you?
Um, well, I–
I'm a poet and adventurer!
Lady V seems pretty keen for you to meet again.
Oh yes, they're OBSESSED with me. Always springing up at inopportune moments! That's why we're on the hunt, to get the jump on her!
And when I'm not engaged in derring-do, I am, of course, a renowned poet.
Pfft
You disapprove, eh! Such is the poet's lot . . .

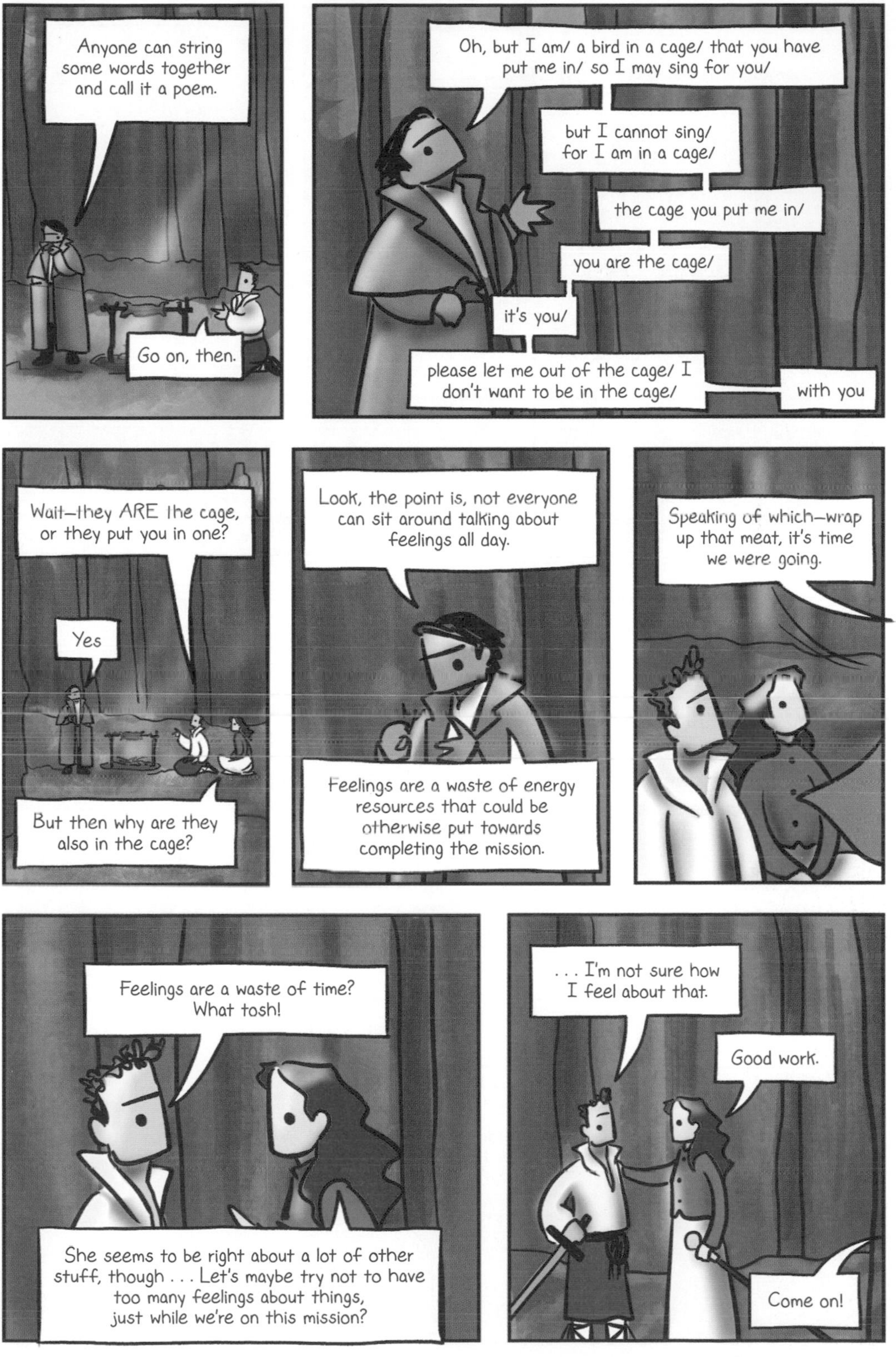

Anyone can string some words together and call it a poem.
Go on, then.
Oh, but I am/ a bird in a cage/ that you have put me in/ so I may sing for you/
but I cannot sing/ for I am in a cage/
the cage you put me in/
you are the cage/
it's you/
please let me out of the cage/ I don't want to be in the cage/
with you
Wait—they ARE the cage, or they put you in one?
Yes
But then why are they also in the cage?
Look, the point is, not everyone can sit around talking about feelings all day.
Feelings are a waste of energy resources that could be otherwise put towards completing the mission.
Speaking of which—wrap up that meat, it's time we were going.
Feelings are a waste of time? What tosh!
She seems to be right about a lot of other stuff, though . . . Let's maybe try not to have too many feelings about things, just while we're on this mission?
. . . I'm not sure how I feel about that.
Good work.
Come on!

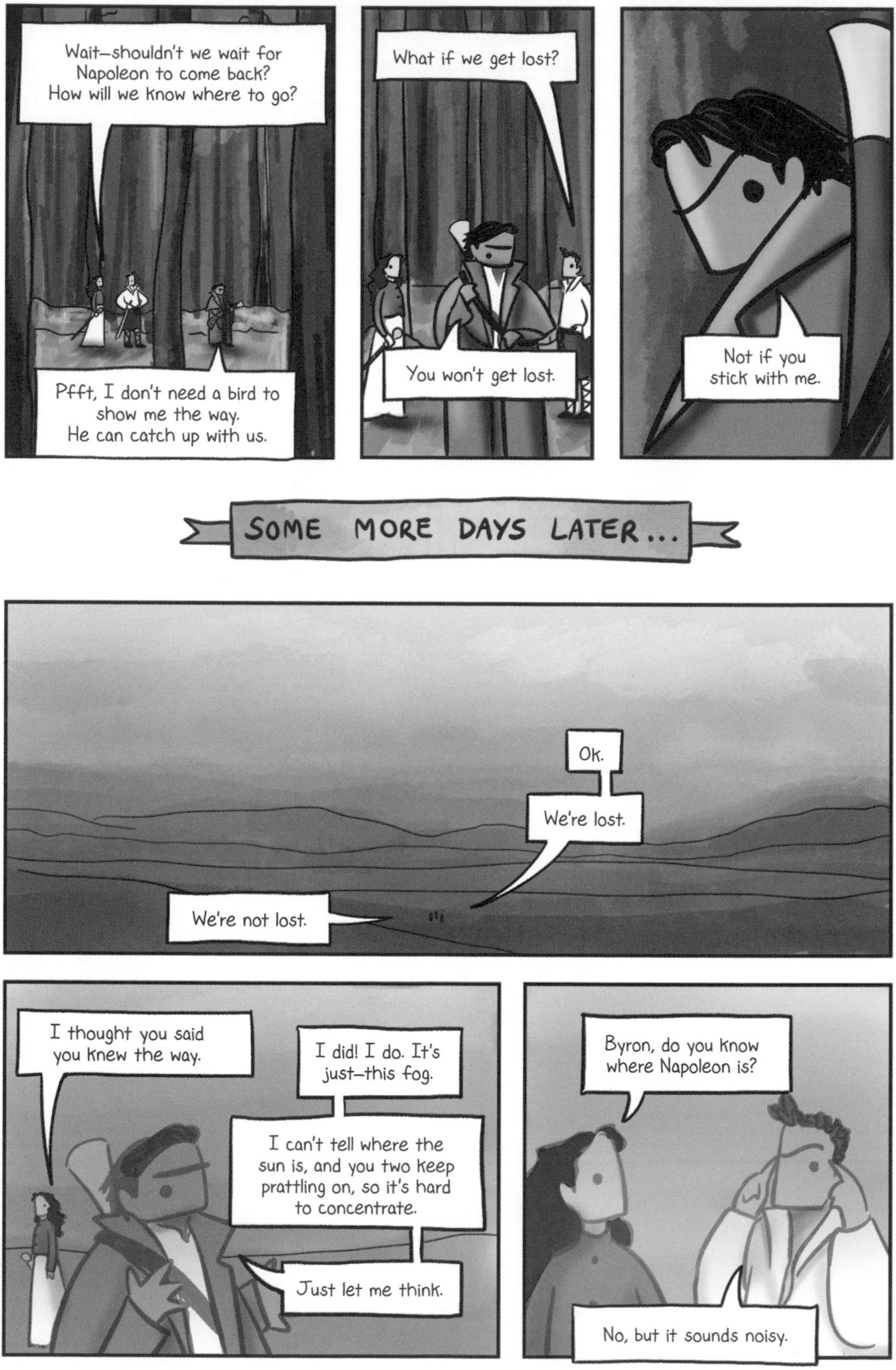
Wait—shouldn't we wait for Napoleon to come back? How will we know where to go?
Pfft, I don't need a bird to show me the way. He can catch up with us.
What if we get lost?
You won't get lost.
Not if you stick with me.
SOME MORE DAYS LATER...
Ok.
We're lost.
We're not lost.
I thought you said you knew the way.
I did! I do. It's just—this fog.
I can't tell where the sun is, and you two keep prattling on, so it's hard to concentrate.
Just let me think.
Byron, do you know where Napoleon is?
No, but it sounds noisy.

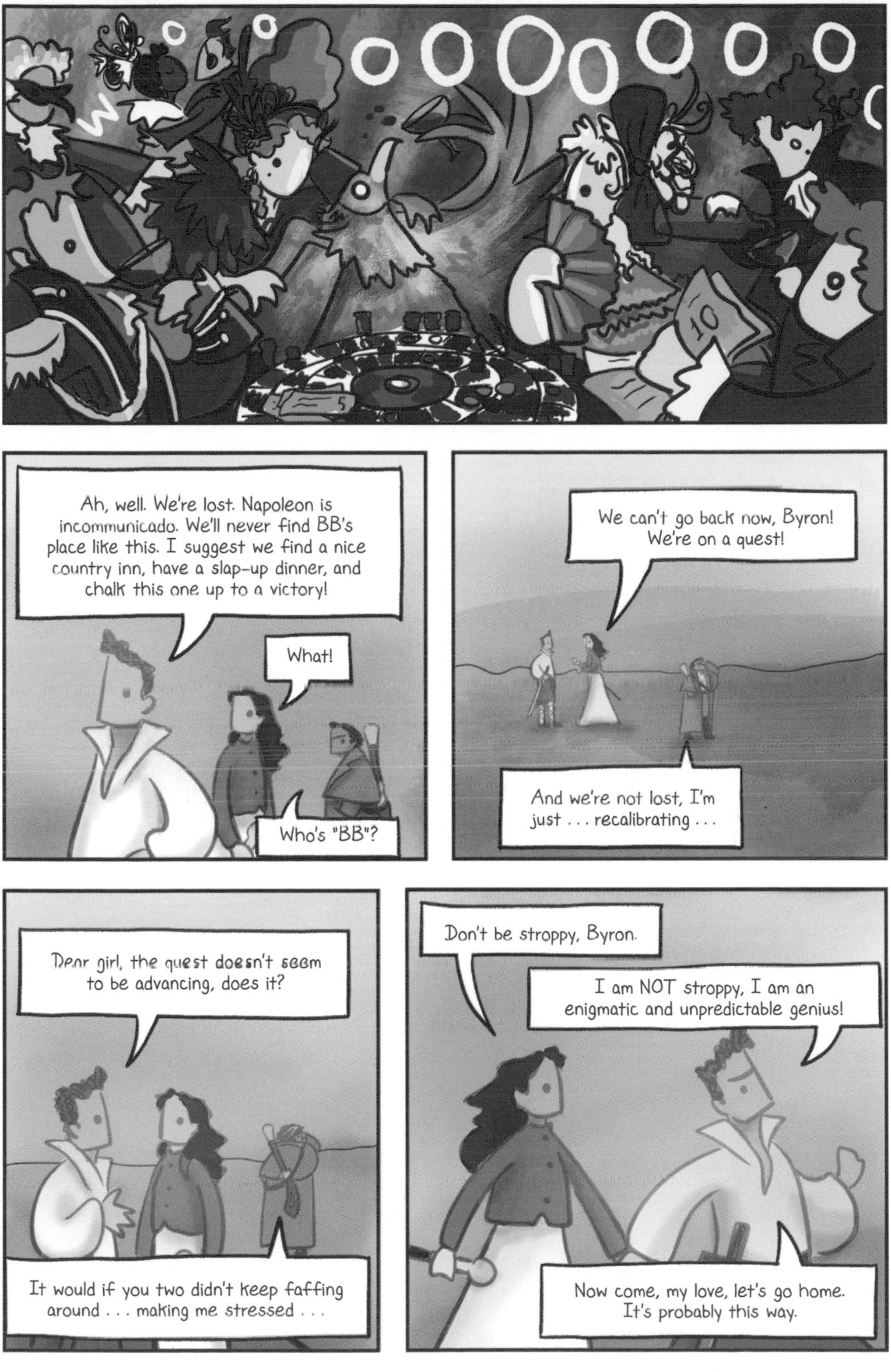
10
9
5
Ah, well. We're lost. Napoleon is incommunicado. We'll never find BB's place like this. I suggest we find a nice country inn, have a slap-up dinner, and chalk this one up to a victory!
What!
Who's "BB"?
We can't go back now, Byron! We're on a quest!
And we're not lost, I'm just . . . recalibrating . . .
Dear girl, the quest doesn't seem to be advancing, does it?
It would if you two didn't keep faffing around . . . making me stressed . . .
Don't be stroppy, Byron.
I am NOT stroppy, I am an enigmatic and unpredictable genius!
Now come, my love, let's go home. It's probably this way.

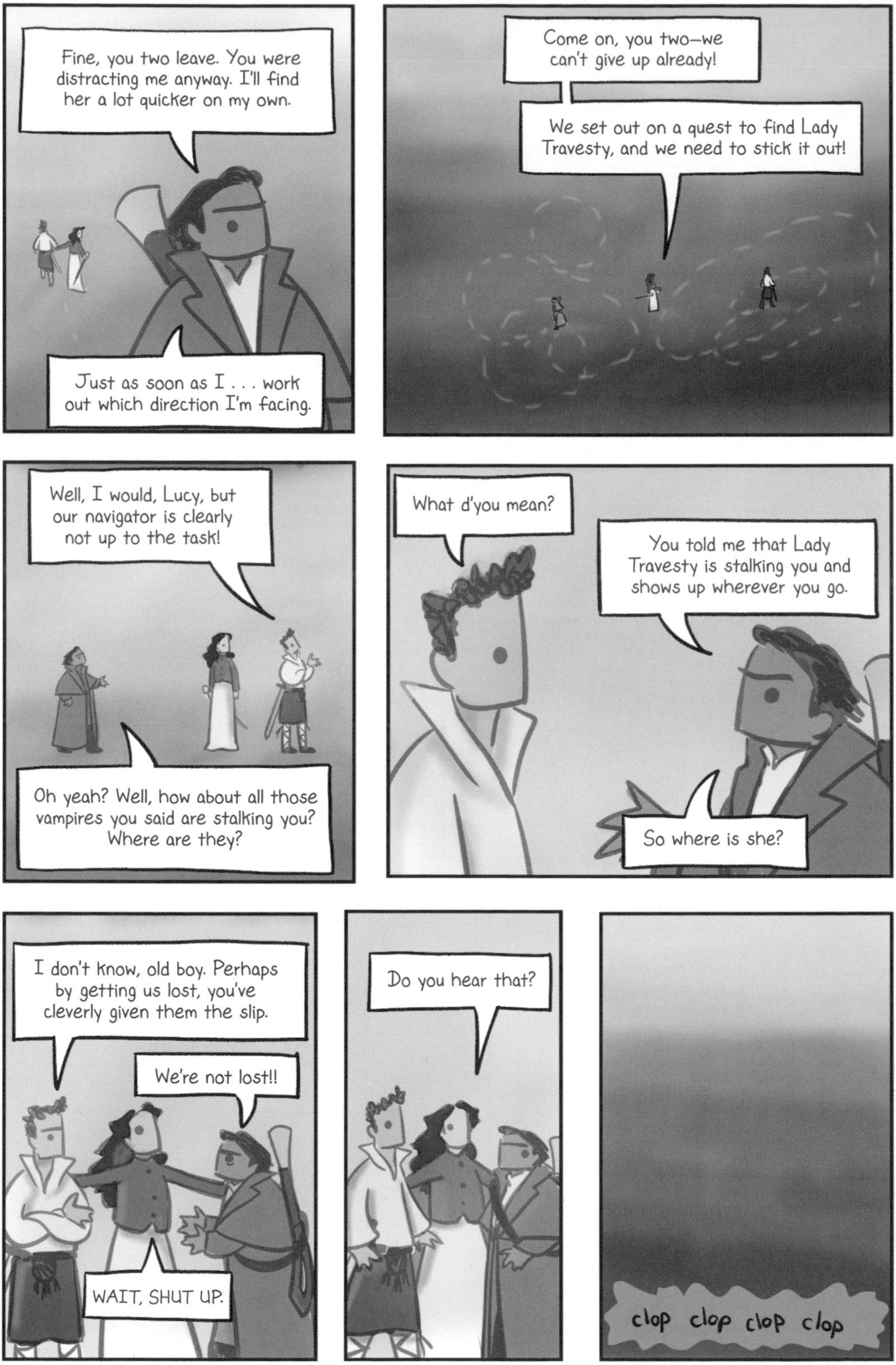

Fine, you two leave. You were distracting me anyway. I'll find her a lot quicker on my own.
Just as soon as I . . . work out which direction I'm facing.
Come on, you two—we can't give up already!
We set out on a quest to find Lady Travesty, and we need to stick it out!
Well, I would, Lucy, but our navigator is clearly not up to the task!
Oh yeah? Well, how about all those vampires you said are stalking you? Where are they?
What d'you mean?
You told me that Lady Travesty is stalking you and shows up wherever you go.
So where is she?
I don't know, old boy. Perhaps by getting us lost, you've cleverly given them the slip.
We're not lost!!
WAIT, SHUT UP.
Do you hear that?
clop clop clop clop

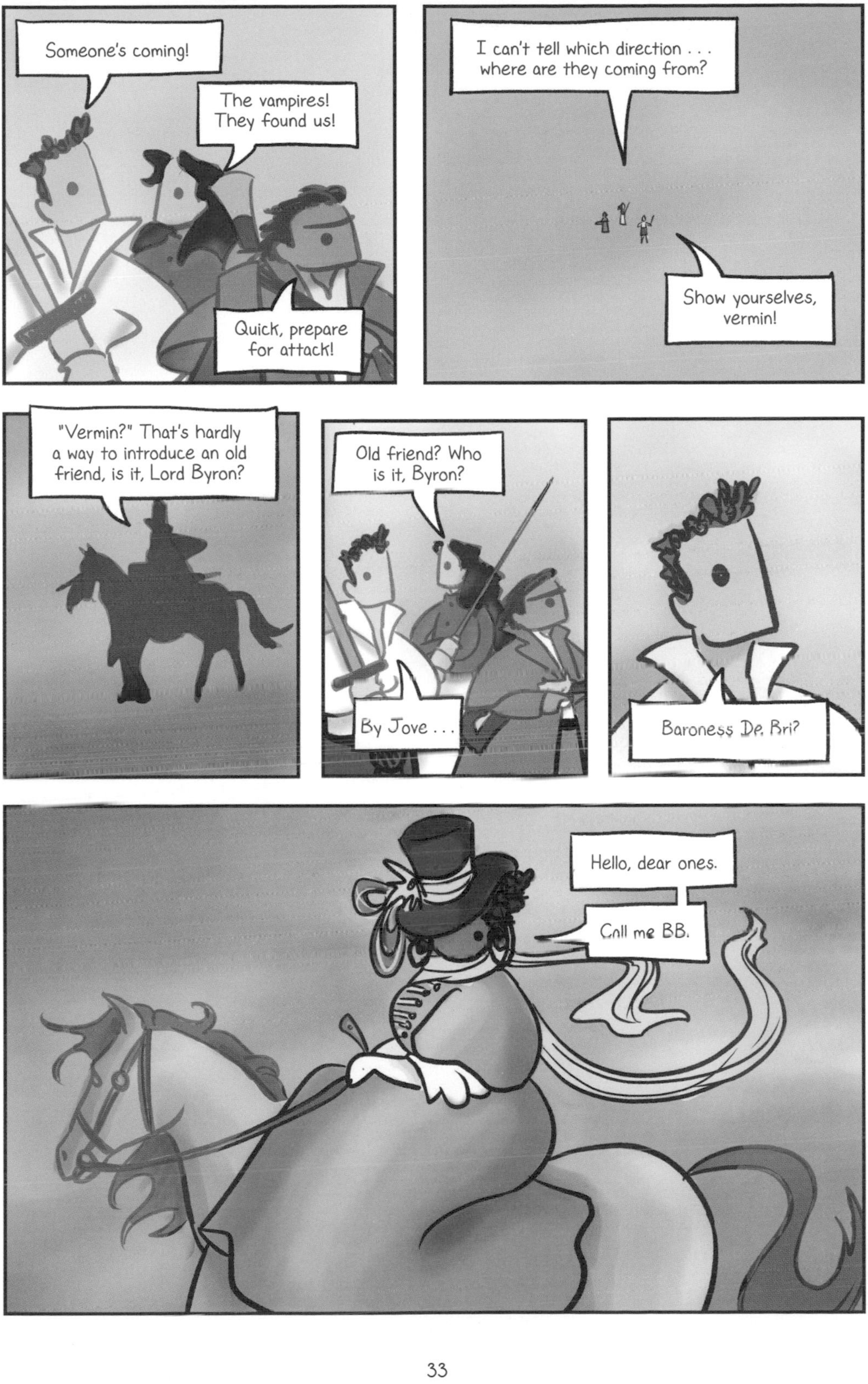
Someone's coming!
The vampires! They found us!
Quick, prepare for attack!
I can't tell which direction . . . where are they coming from?
Show yourselves, vermin!
"Vermin?" That's hardly a way to introduce an old friend, is it, Lord Byron?
Old friend? Who is it, Byron?
By Jove . . .
Baroness De Bri?
Hello, dear ones.
Call me BB.

CHAPTER III – THE BALL

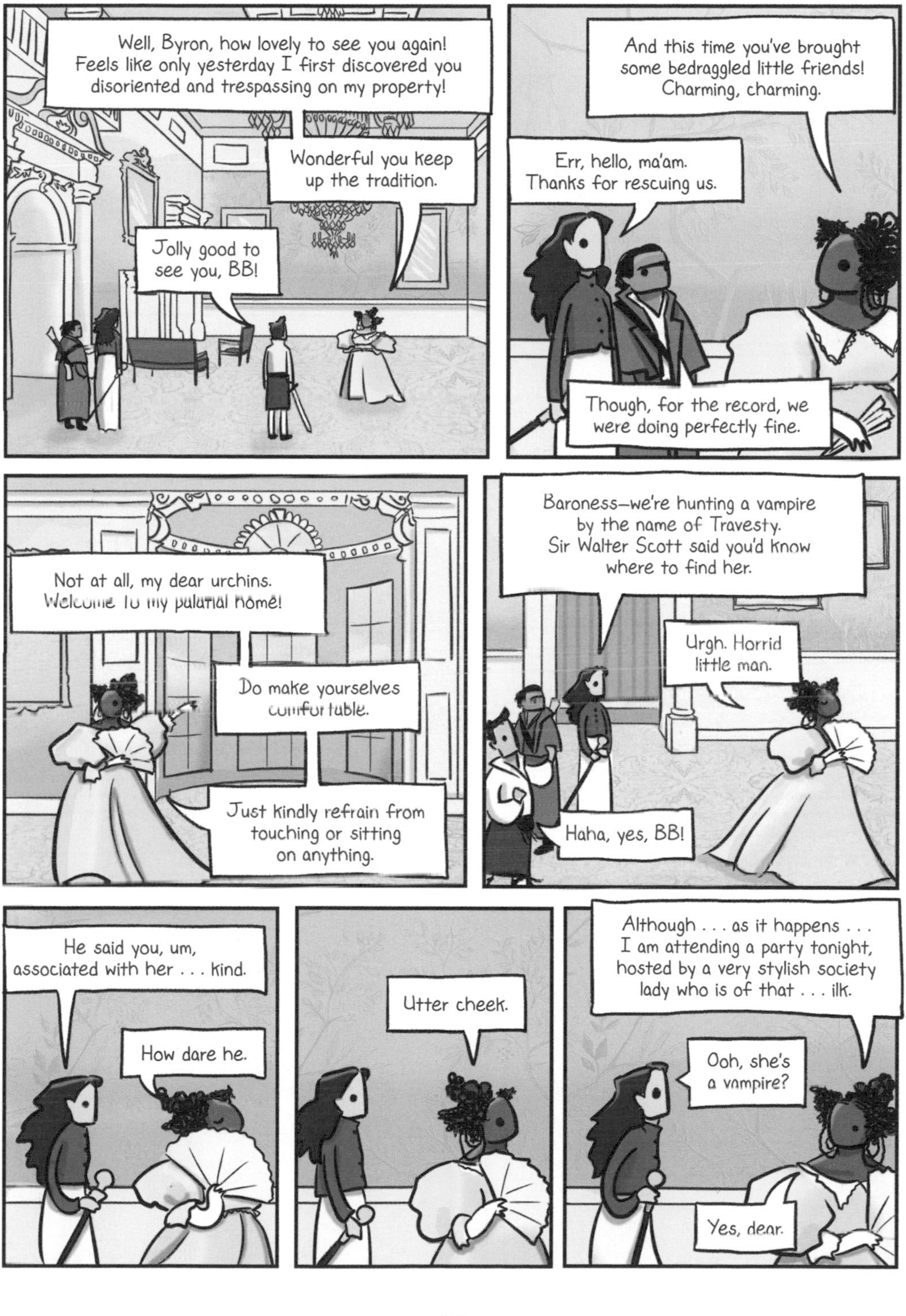

Well, Byron, how lovely to see you again! Feels like only yesterday I first discovered you disoriented and trespassing on my property!
Wonderful you keep up the tradition.
Jolly good to see you, BB!
And this time you've brought some bedraggled little friends! Charming, charming.
Err, hello, ma'am. Thanks for rescuing us.
Though, for the record, we were doing perfectly fine.
Not at all, my dear urchins. Welcome to my palatial home!
Do make yourselves comfortable.
Just kindly refrain from touching or sitting on anything.
Baroness—we're hunting a vampire by the name of Travesty. Sir Walter Scott said you'd know where to find her.
Urgh. Horrid little man.
Haha, yes, BB!
He said you, um, associated with her . . . kind.
How dare he.
Utter cheek.
Although . . . as it happens . . . I am attending a party tonight, hosted by a very stylish society lady who is of that . . . ilk.
Ooh, she's a vampire?
Yes, dear.

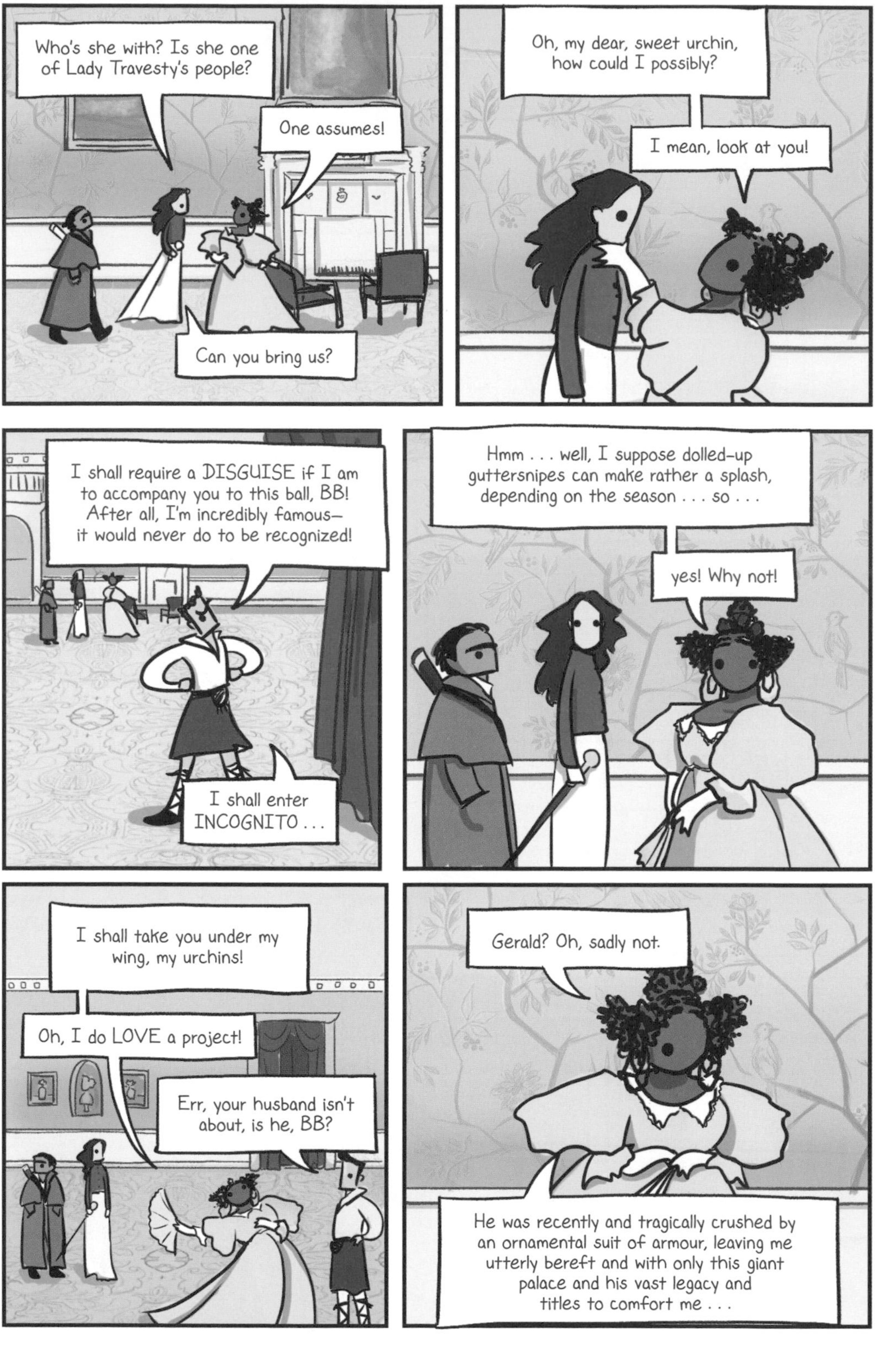
Who's she with? Is she one of Lady Travesty's people?
One assumes!
Can you bring us?
Oh, my dear, sweet urchin, how could I possibly?
I mean, look at you!
I shall require a DISGUISE if I am to accompany you to this ball, BB! After all, I'm incredibly famous– it would never do to be recognized!
I shall enter INCOGNITO . . .
Hmm . . . well, I suppose dolled-up guttersnipes can make rather a splash, depending on the season . . . so . . .
yes! Why not!
I shall take you under my wing, my urchins!
Oh, I do LOVE a project!
Err, your husband isn't about, is he, BB?
Gerald? Oh, sadly not.
He was recently and tragically crushed by an ornamental suit of armour, leaving me utterly bereft and with only this giant palace and his vast legacy and titles to comfort me . . .

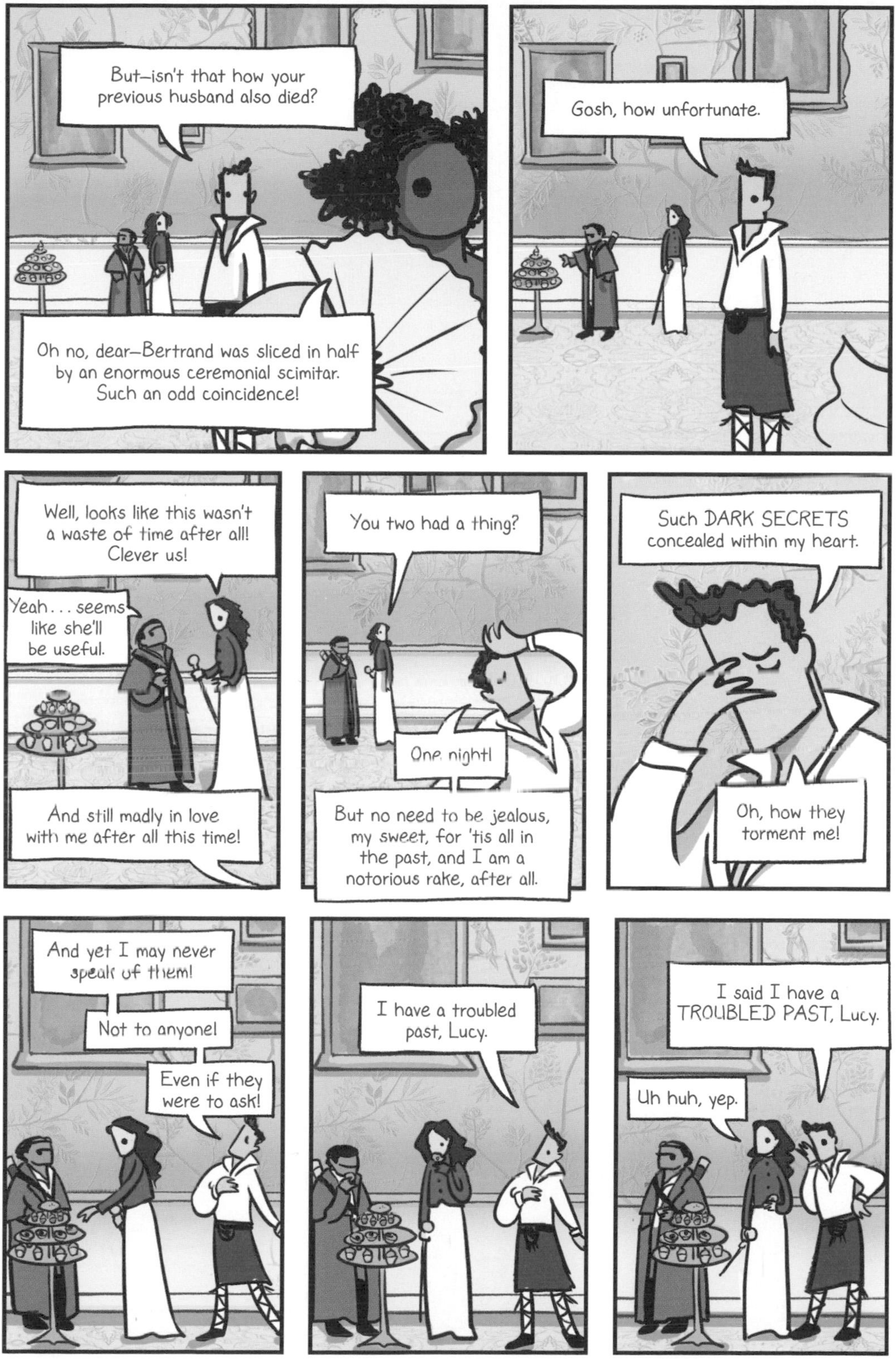
But—isn't that how your previous husband also died?
Oh no, dear—Bertrand was sliced in half by an enormous ceremonial scimitar. Such an odd coincidence!
Gosh, how unfortunate.
Well, looks like this wasn't a waste of time after all! Clever us!
Yeah . . . seems like she'll be useful.
And still madly in love with me after all this time!
You two had a thing?
One night!
But no need to be jealous, my sweet, for 'tis all in the past, and I am a notorious rake, after all.
Such DARK SECRETS concealed within my heart.
Oh, how they torment me!
And yet I may never speak of them!
Not to anyone!
Even if they were to ask!
I have a troubled past, Lucy.
I said I have a TROUBLED PAST, Lucy.
Uh huh, yep.

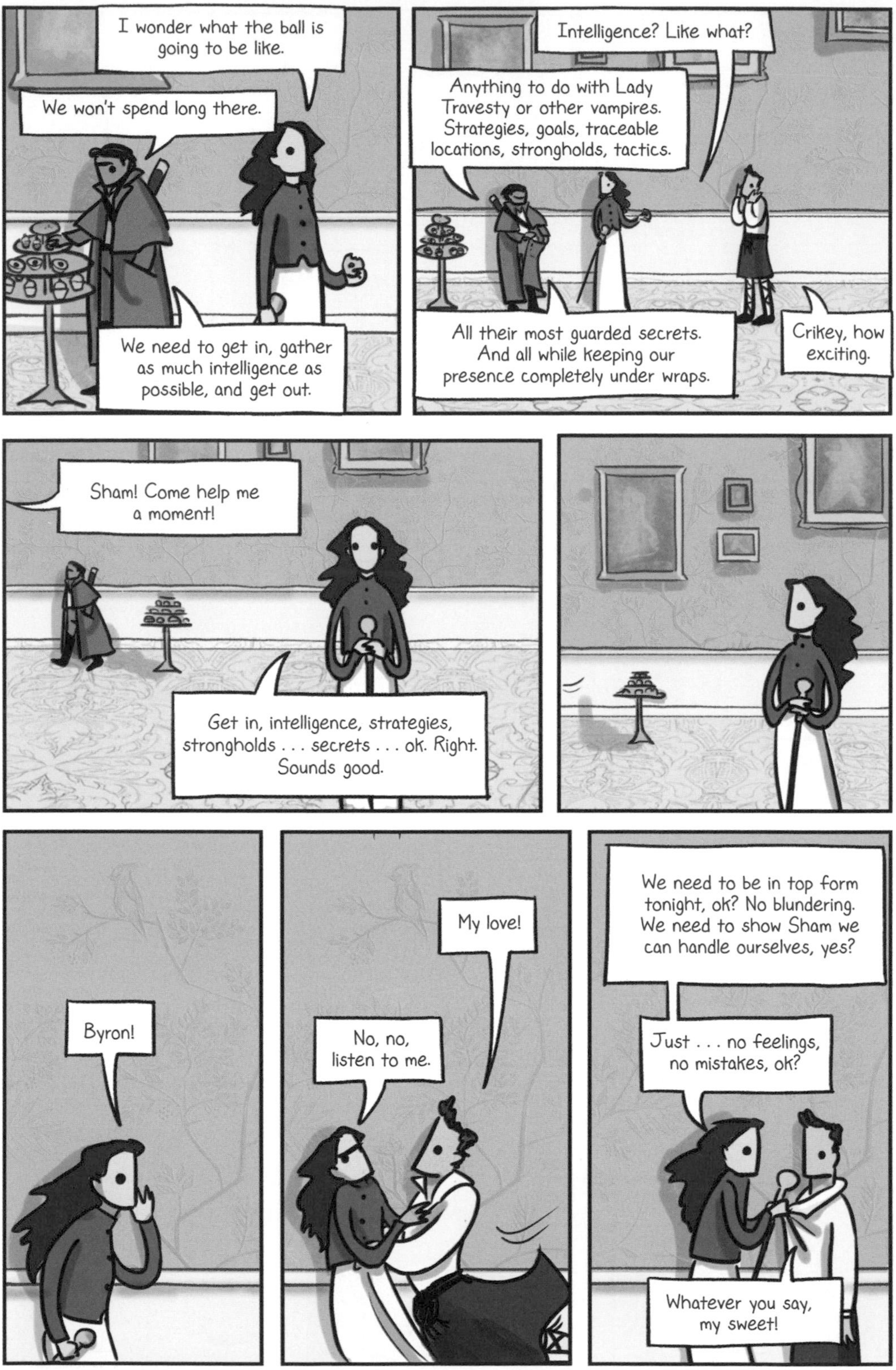

I wonder what the ball is going to be like.
We won't spend long there.
We need to get in, gather as much intelligence as possible, and get out.
Intelligence? Like what?
Anything to do with Lady Travesty or other vampires. Strategies, goals, traceable locations, strongholds, tactics.
All their most guarded secrets. And all while keeping our presence completely under wraps.
Crikey, how exciting.
Sham! Come help me a moment!
Get in, intelligence, strategies, strongholds . . . secrets . . . ok. Right. Sounds good.
Byron!
My love!
No, no, listen to me.
We need to be in top form tonight, ok? No blundering. We need to show Sham we can handle ourselves, yes?
Just . . . no feelings, no mistakes, ok?
Whatever you say, my sweet!

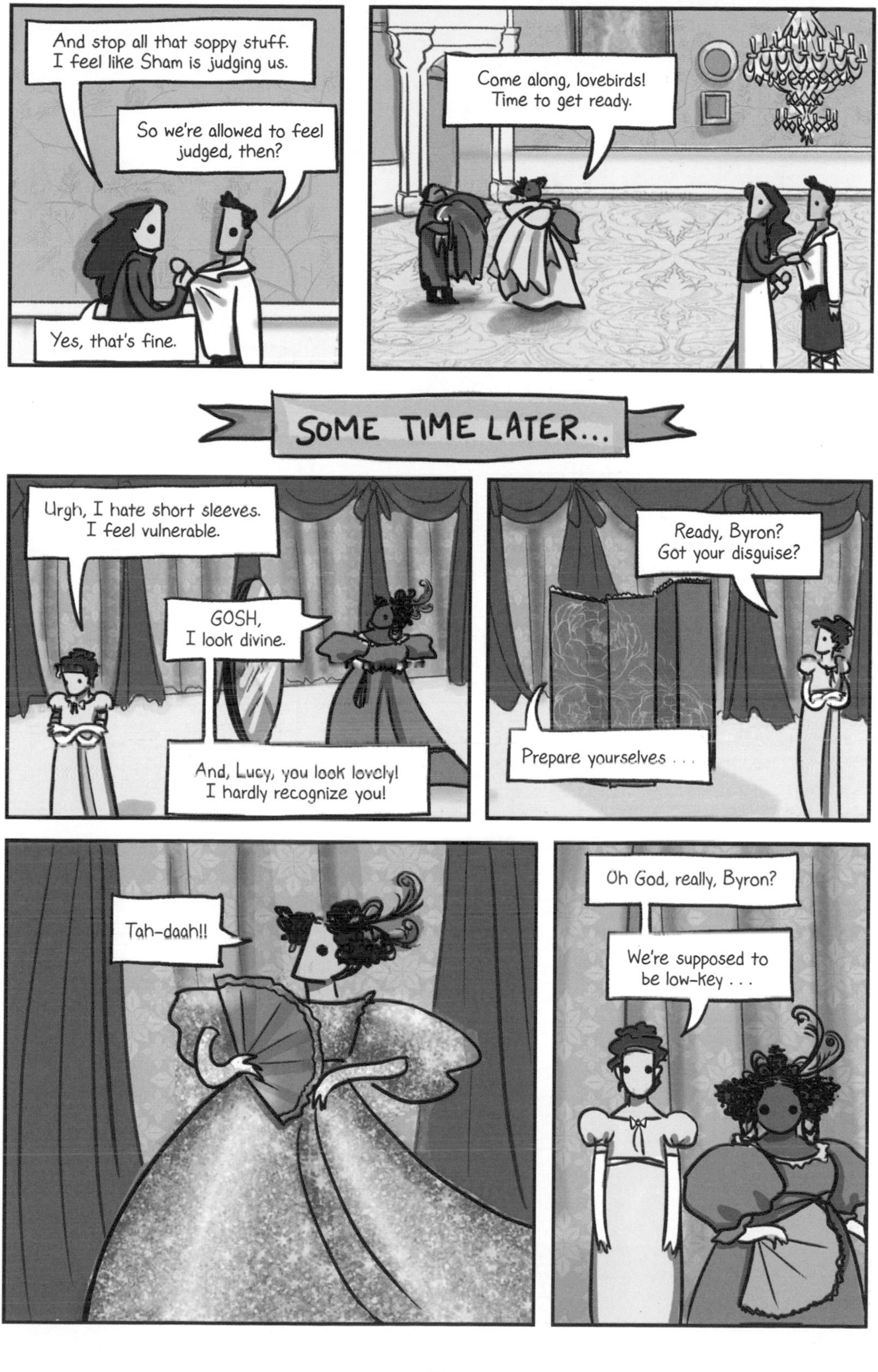

And stop all that soppy stuff. I feel like Sham is judging us.
So we're allowed to feel judged, then?
Yes, that's fine.
Come along, lovebirds! Time to get ready.
SOME TIME LATER...
Urgh, I hate short sleeves. I feel vulnerable.
GOSH, I look divine.
And, Lucy, you look lovely! I hardly recognize you!
Ready, Byron? Got your disguise?
Prepare yourselves . . .
Tah-daah!!
Oh God, really, Byron?
We're supposed to be low-key . . .

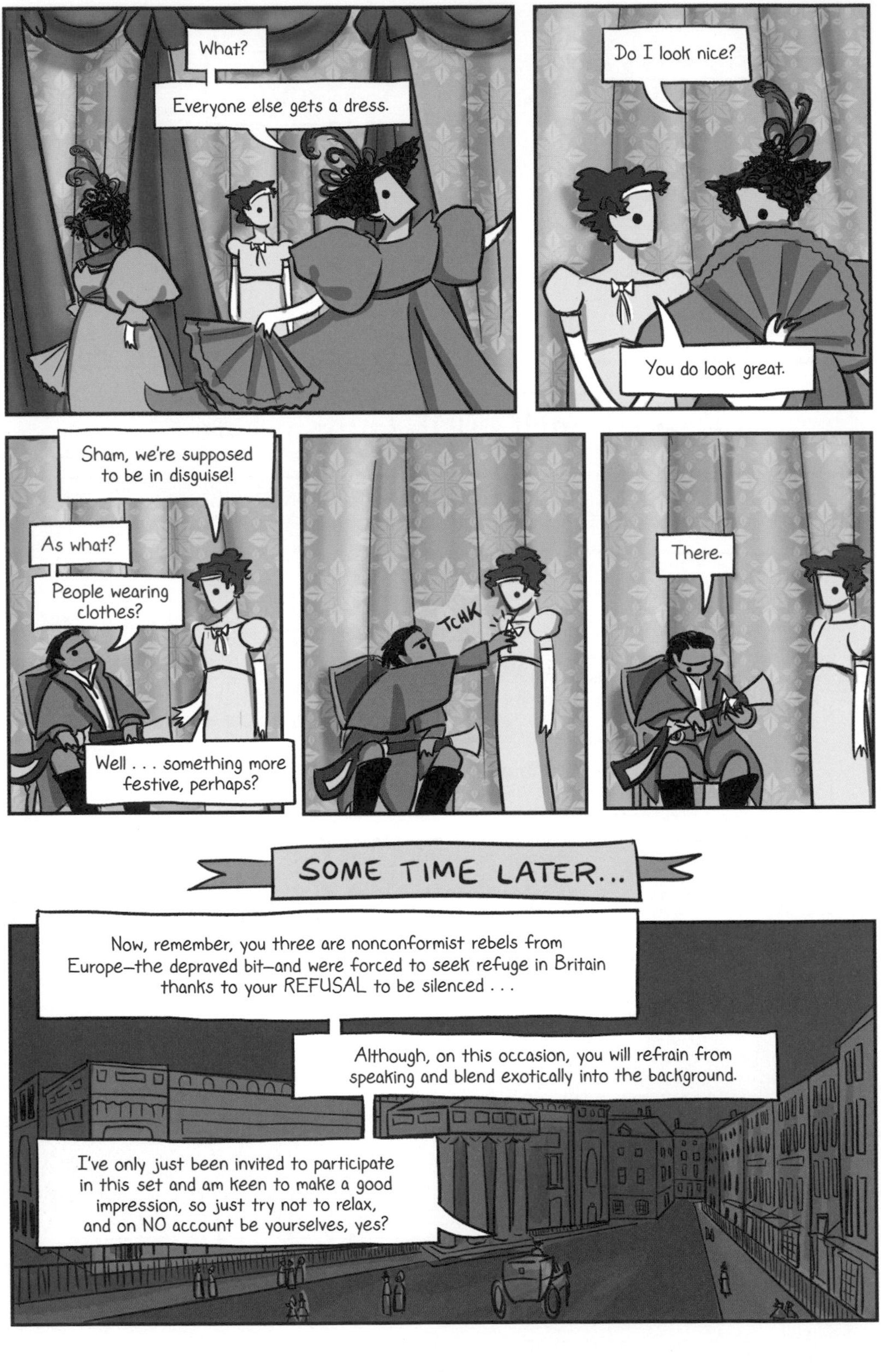
What?
Everyone else gets a dress.
Do I look nice?
You do look great.
Sham, we're supposed to be in disguise!
As what?
People wearing clothes?
Well . . . something more festive, perhaps?
TCHK
There.
SOME TIME LATER...
Now, remember, you three are nonconformist rebels from Europe–the depraved bit–and were forced to seek refuge in Britain thanks to your REFUSAL to be silenced . . .
Although, on this occasion, you will refrain from speaking and blend exotically into the background.
I've only just been invited to participate in this set and am keen to make a good impression, so just try not to relax, and on NO account be yourselves, yes?

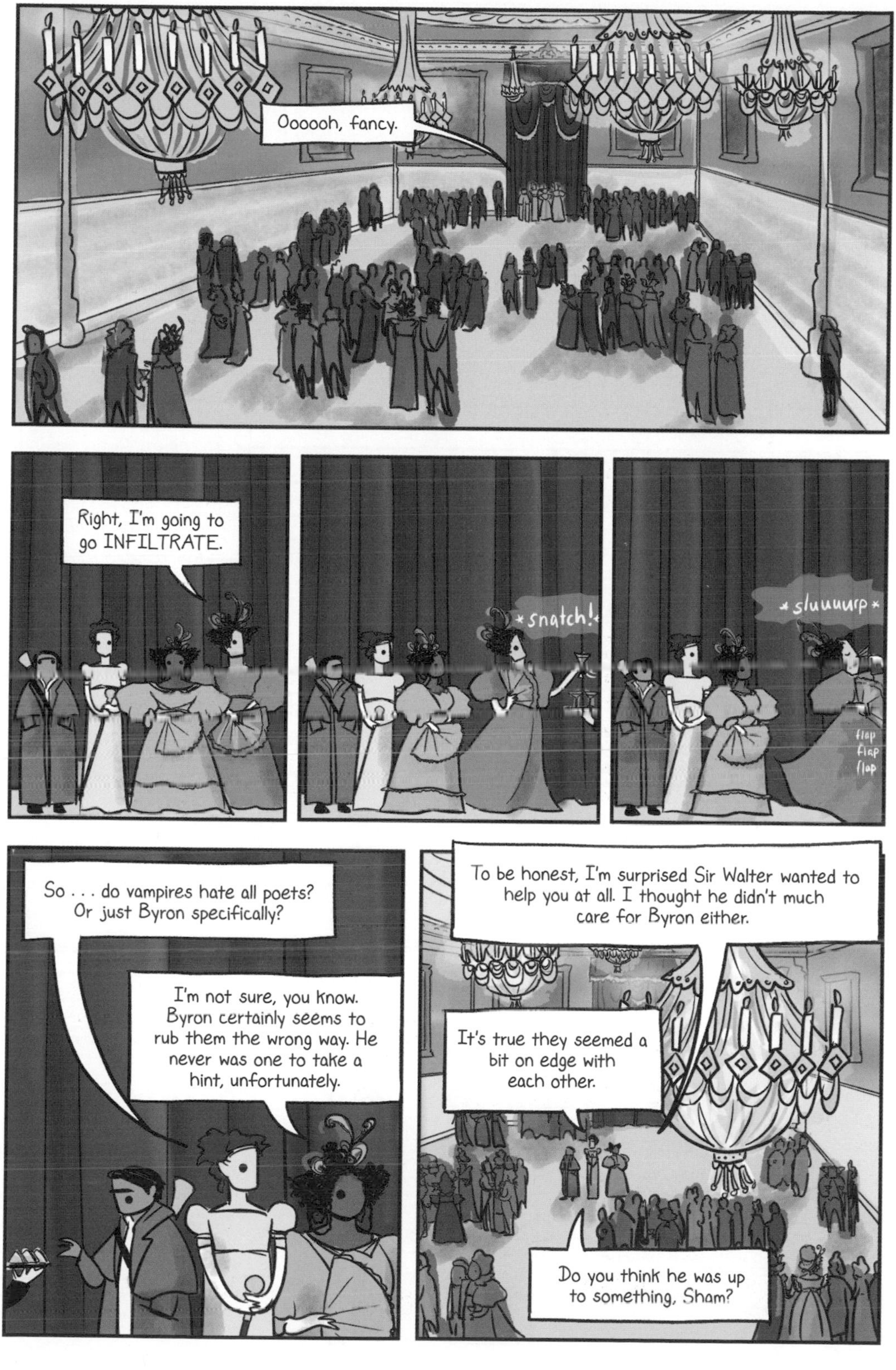

Oooooh, fancy.
Right, I'm going to go INFILTRATE.
snatch!
sluuuurp
flap
flap
flap
So . . . do vampires hate all poets? Or just Byron specifically?
I'm not sure, you know. Byron certainly seems to rub them the wrong way. He never was one to take a hint, unfortunately.
To be honest, I'm surprised Sir Walter wanted to help you at all. I thought he didn't much care for Byron either.
It's true they seemed a bit on edge with each other.
Do you think he was up to something, Sham?

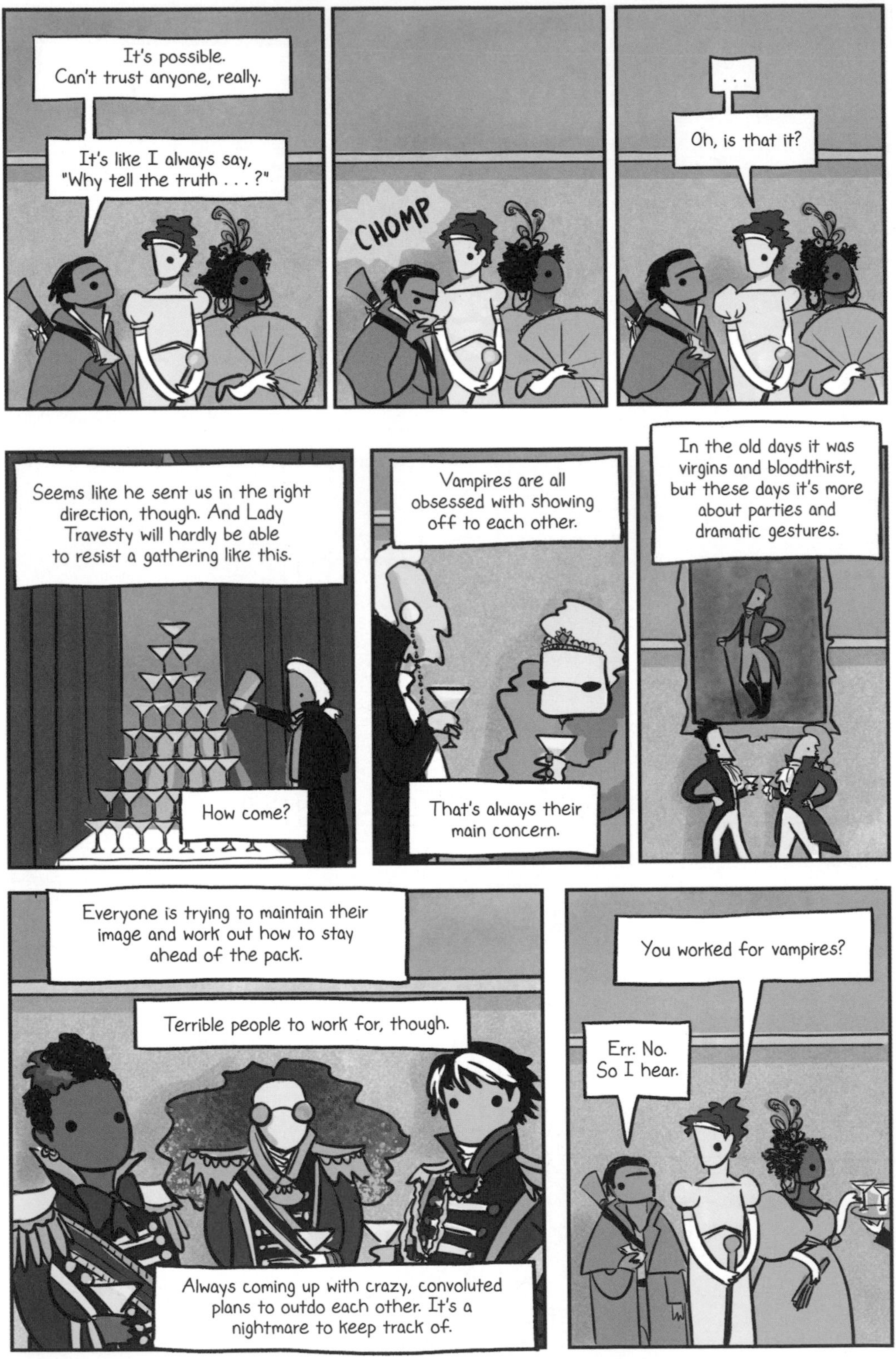
It's possible.
Can't trust anyone, really.
It's like I always say, "Why tell the truth . . . ?"
CHOMP
. . .
Oh, is that it?
Seems like he sent us in the right direction, though. And Lady Travesty will hardly be able to resist a gathering like this.
How come?
Vampires are all obsessed with showing off to each other.
That's always their main concern.
In the old days it was virgins and bloodthirst, but these days it's more about parties and dramatic gestures.
Everyone is trying to maintain their image and work out how to stay ahead of the pack.
Terrible people to work for, though.
Always coming up with crazy, convoluted plans to outdo each other. It's a nightmare to keep track of.
You worked for vampires?
Err. No.
So I hear.

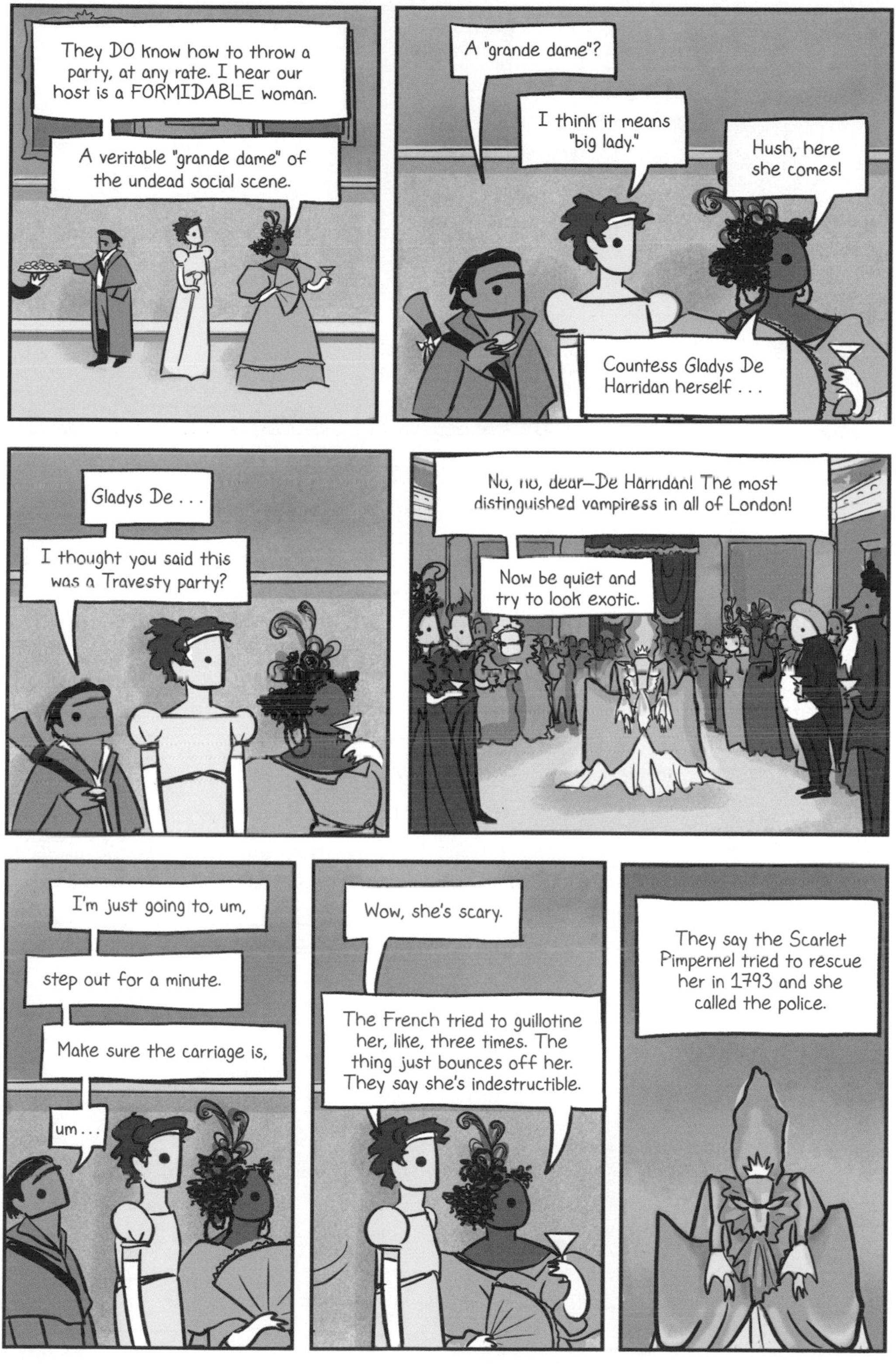
They DO know how to throw a party, at any rate. I hear our host is a FORMIDABLE woman.
A veritable "grande dame" of the undead social scene.
A "grande dame"?
I think it means "big lady."
Hush, here she comes!
Countess Gladys De Harridan herself . . .
Gladys De . . .
I thought you said this was a Travesty party?
No, no, dear—De Harridan! The most distinguished vampiress in all of London!
Now be quiet and try to look exotic.
I'm just going to, um,
step out for a minute.
Make sure the carriage is,
um . . .
Wow, she's scary.
The French tried to guillotine her, like, three times. The thing just bounces off her. They say she's indestructible.
They say the Scarlet Pimpernel tried to rescue her in 1793 and she called the police.

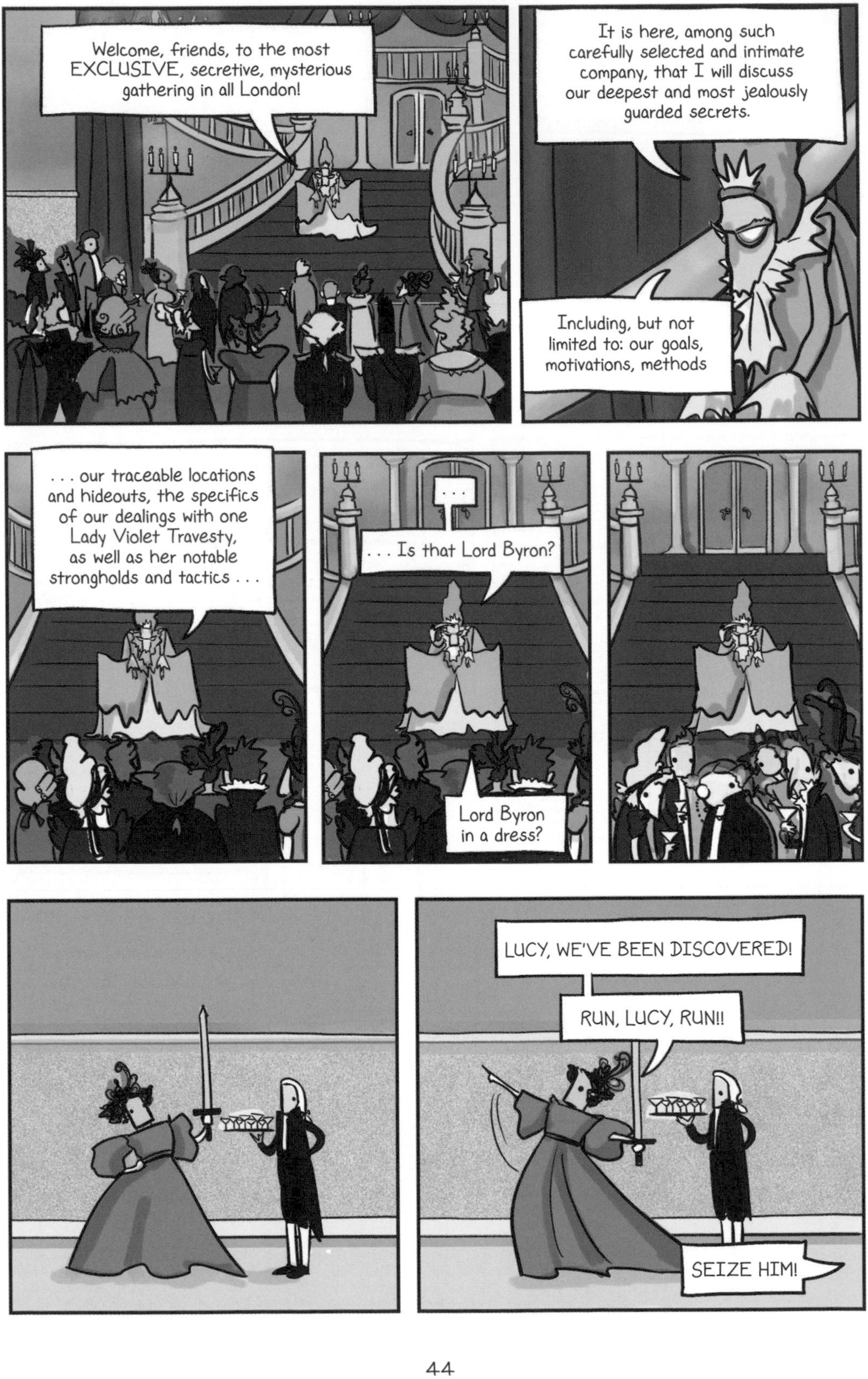

Welcome, friends, to the most EXCLUSIVE, secretive, mysterious gathering in all London!
It is here, among such carefully selected and intimate company, that I will discuss our deepest and most jealously guarded secrets.
Including, but not limited to: our goals, motivations, methods
. . . our traceable locations and hideouts, the specifics of our dealings with one Lady Violet Travesty, as well as her notable strongholds and tactics . . .
. . .
. . . Is that Lord Byron?
Lord Byron in a dress?
LUCY, WE'VE BEEN DISCOVERED!
RUN, LUCY, RUN!!
SEIZE HIM!

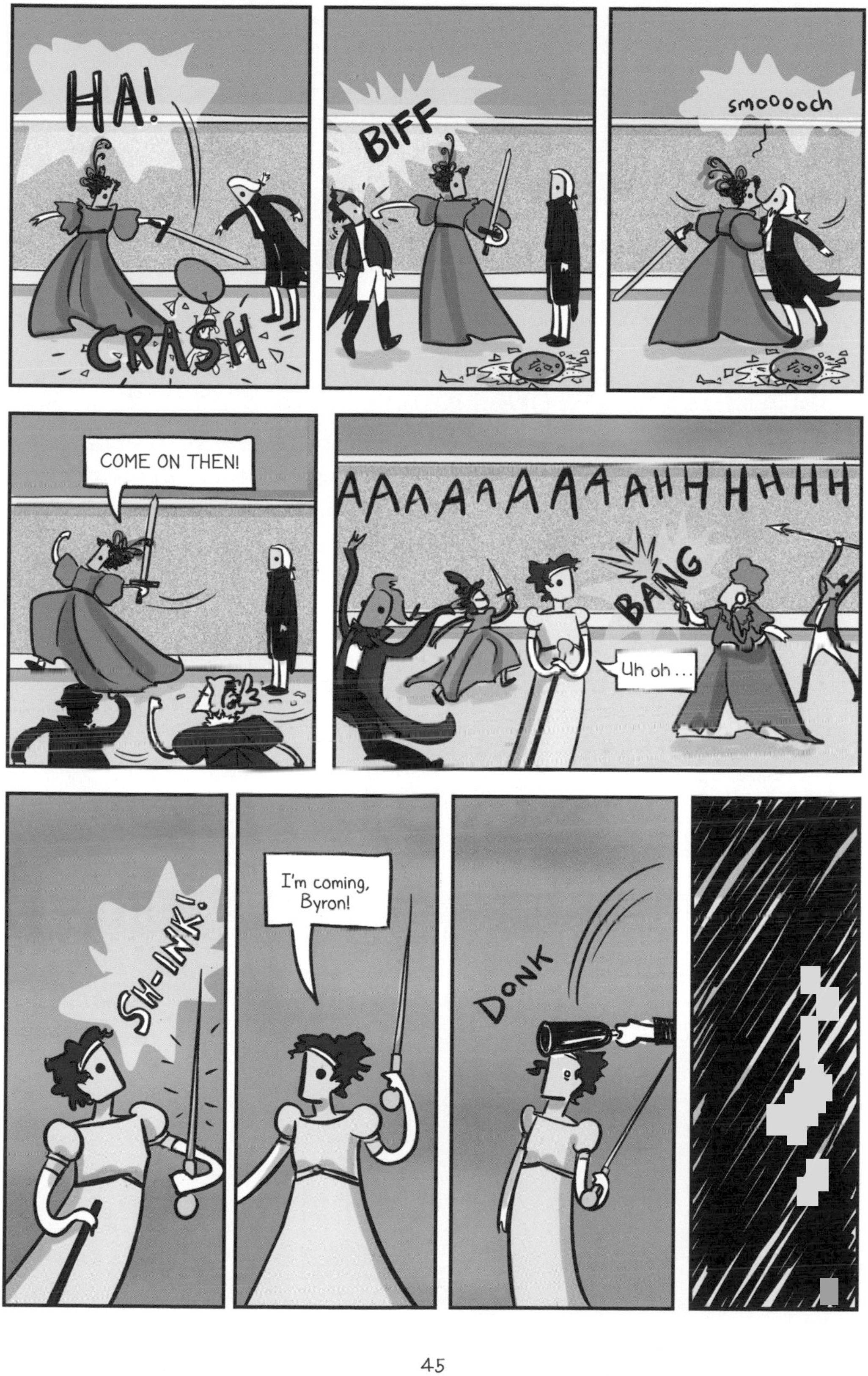
HA!
CRASH
BIFF
smooooch
COME ON THEN!
AAAAAAAAAHHHHHH
BANG
Uh oh . . .
SH-IINK!
I'm coming, Byron!
DONK

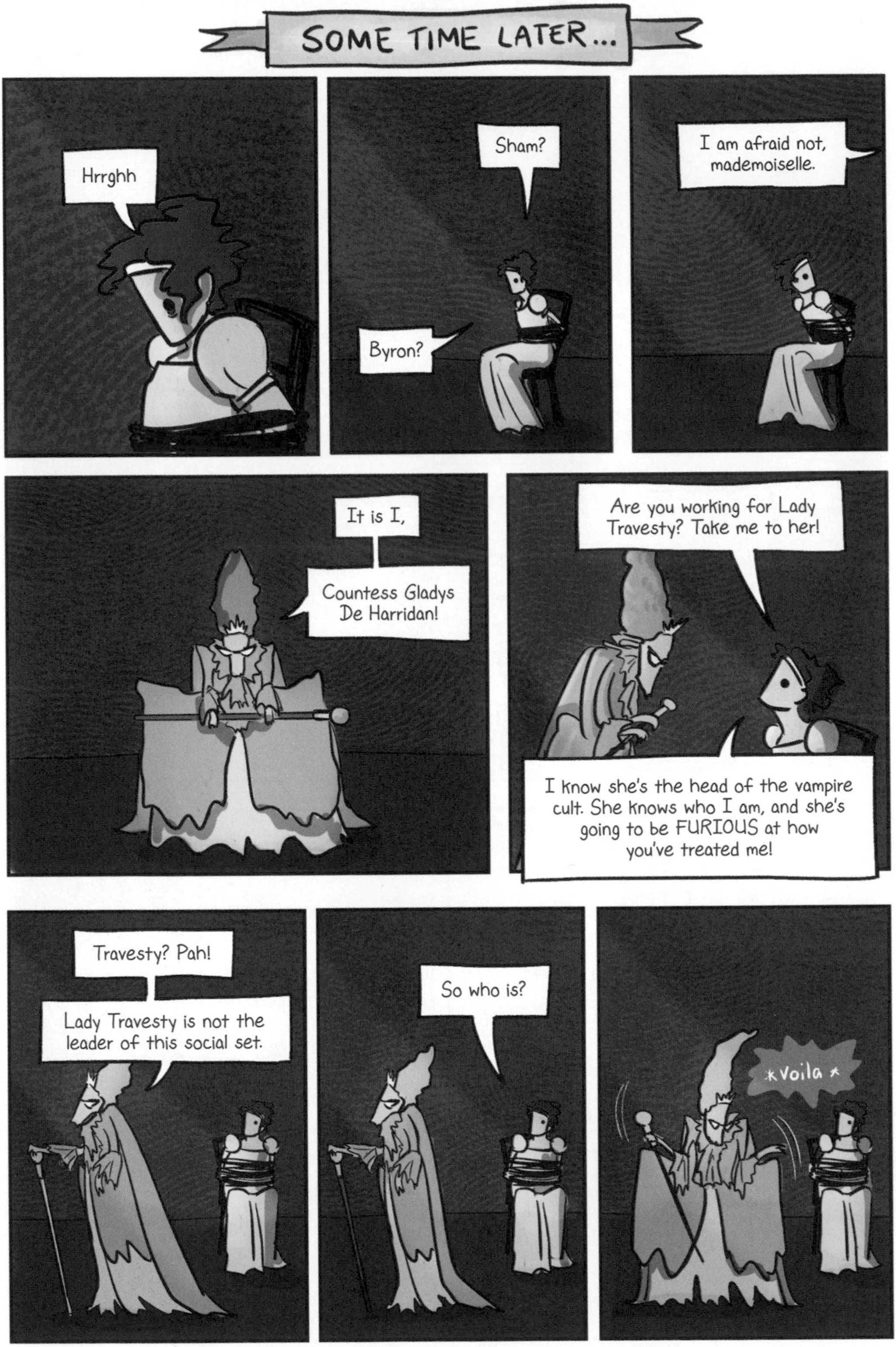
SOME TIME LATER...
Hrrghh
Sham?
Byron?
I am afraid not, mademoiselle.
It is I,
Countess Gladys De Harridan!
Are you working for Lady Travesty? Take me to her!
I know she's the head of the vampire cult. She knows who I am, and she's going to be FURIOUS at how you've treated me!
Travesty? Pah!
Lady Travesty is not the leader of this social set.
So who is?
Voila

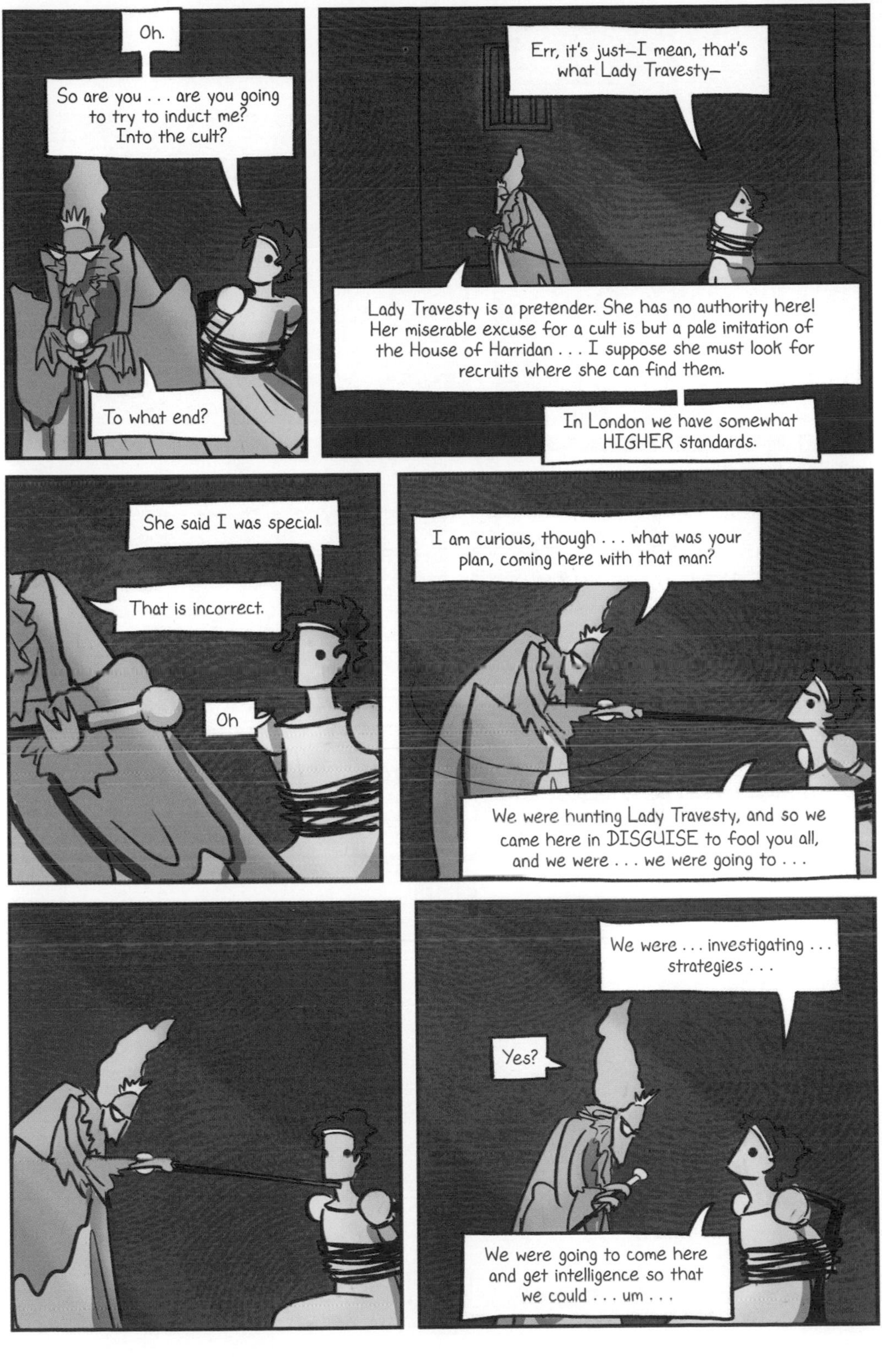
Oh.
So are you . . . are you going to try to induct me? Into the cult?
To what end?
Err, it's just—I mean, that's what Lady Travesty—
Lady Travesty is a pretender. She has no authority here! Her miserable excuse for a cult is but a pale imitation of the House of Harridan . . . I suppose she must look for recruits where she can find them.
In London we have somewhat HIGHER standards.
She said I was special.
That is incorrect.
Oh
I am curious, though . . . what was your plan, coming here with that man?
We were hunting Lady Travesty, and so we came here in DISGUISE to fool you all, and we were . . . we were going to . . .
We were . . . investigating . . . strategies . . .
Yes?
We were going to come here and get intelligence so that we could . . . um . . .

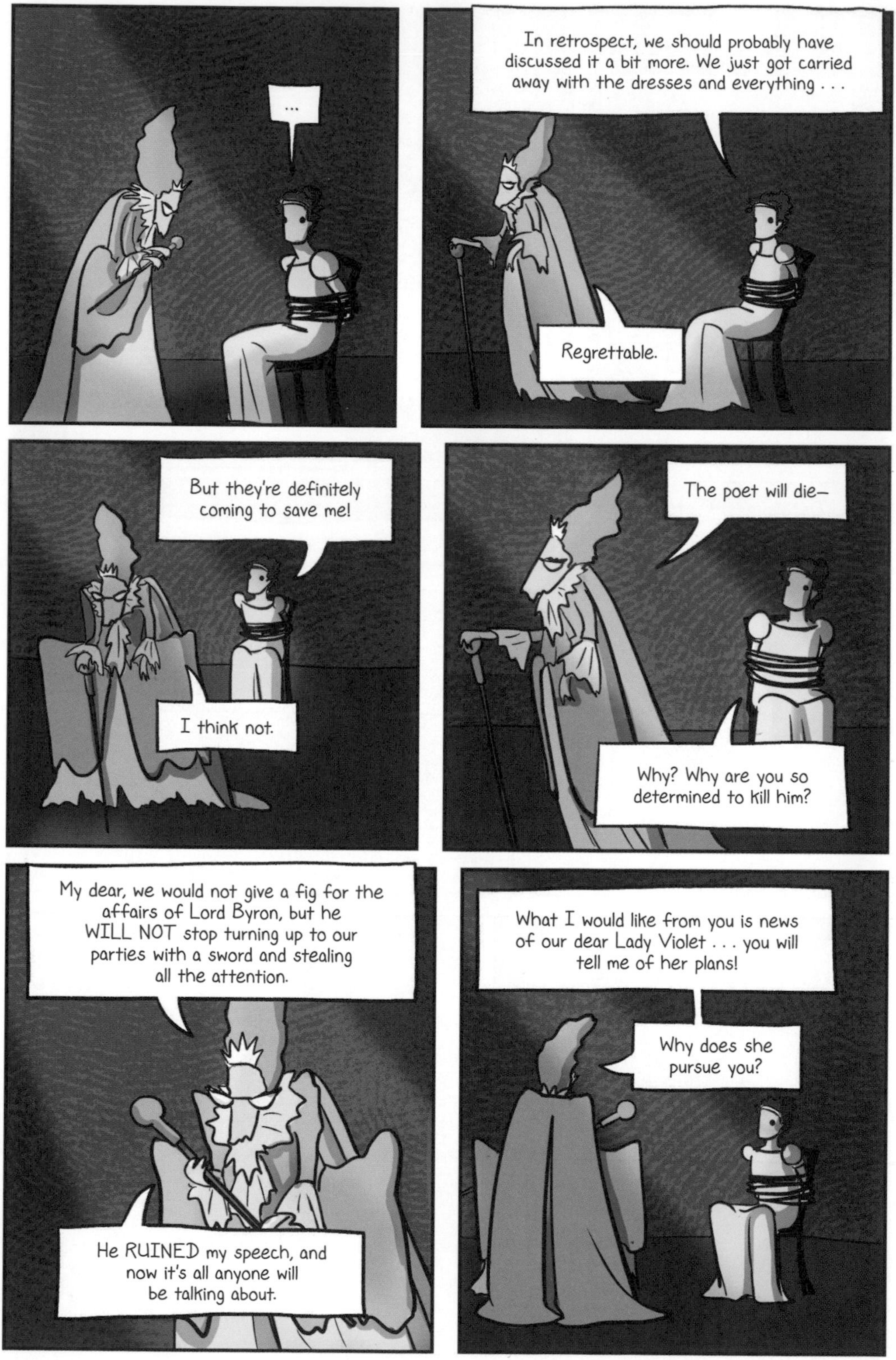
. . .
In retrospect, we should probably have discussed it a bit more. We just got carried away with the dresses and everything . . .
Regrettable.
But they're definitely coming to save me!
I think not.
The poet will die—
Why? Why are you so determined to kill him?
My dear, we would not give a fig for the affairs of Lord Byron, but he WILL NOT stop turning up to our parties with a sword and stealing all the attention.
He RUINED my speech, and now it's all anyone will be talking about.
What I would like from you is news of our dear Lady Violet . . . you will tell me of her plans!
Why does she pursue you?

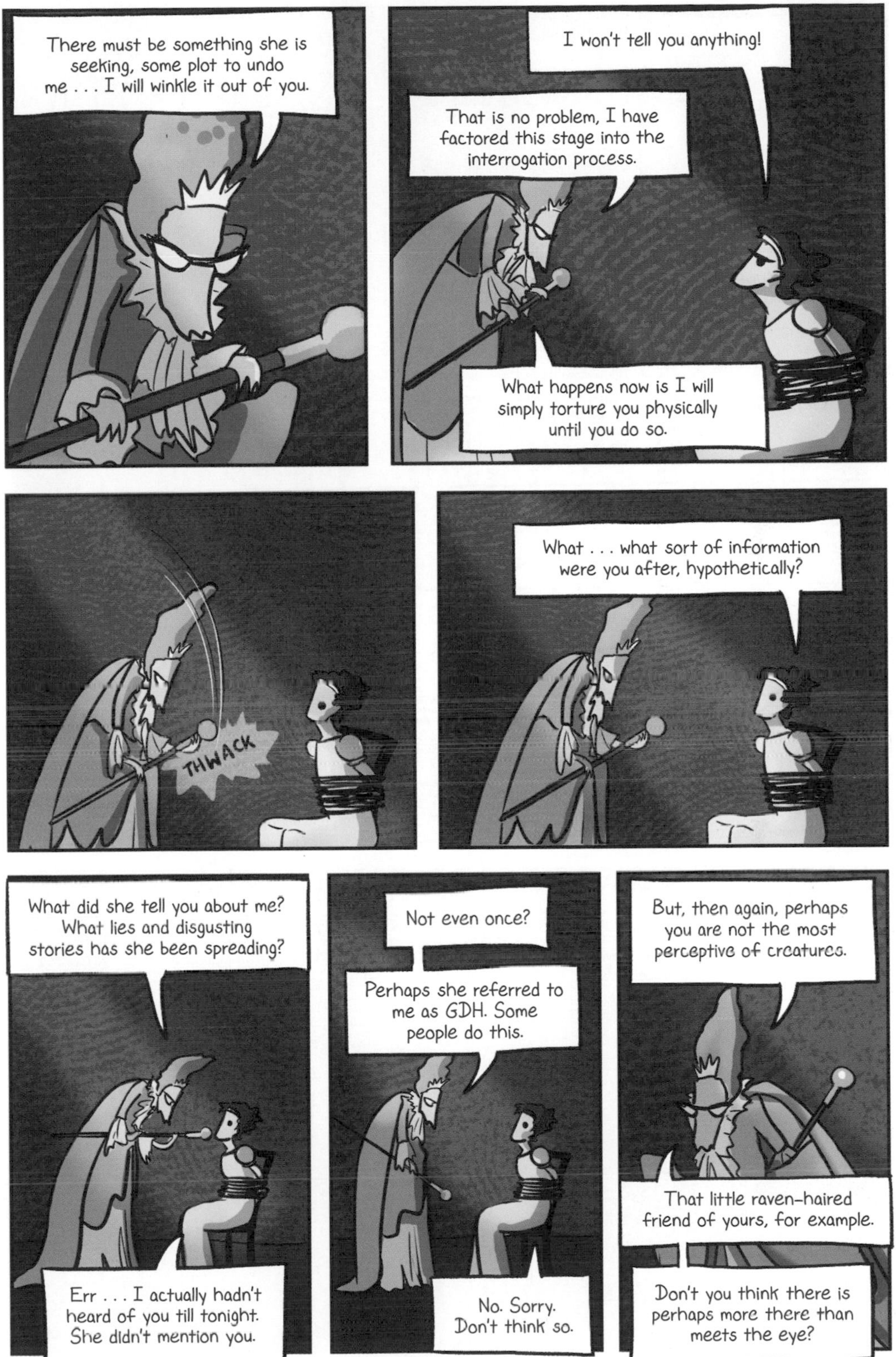
There must be something she is seeking, some plot to undo me . . . I will winkle it out of you.
I won't tell you anything!
That is no problem, I have factored this stage into the interrogation process.
What happens now is I will simply torture you physically until you do so.
THWACK
What . . . what sort of information were you after, hypothetically?
What did she tell you about me? What lies and disgusting stories has she been spreading?
Err . . . I actually hadn't heard of you till tonight. She didn't mention you.
Not even once?
Perhaps she referred to me as GDH. Some people do this.
No. Sorry. Don't think so.
But, then again, perhaps you are not the most perceptive of creatures.
That little raven-haired friend of yours, for example.
Don't you think there is perhaps more there than meets the eye?

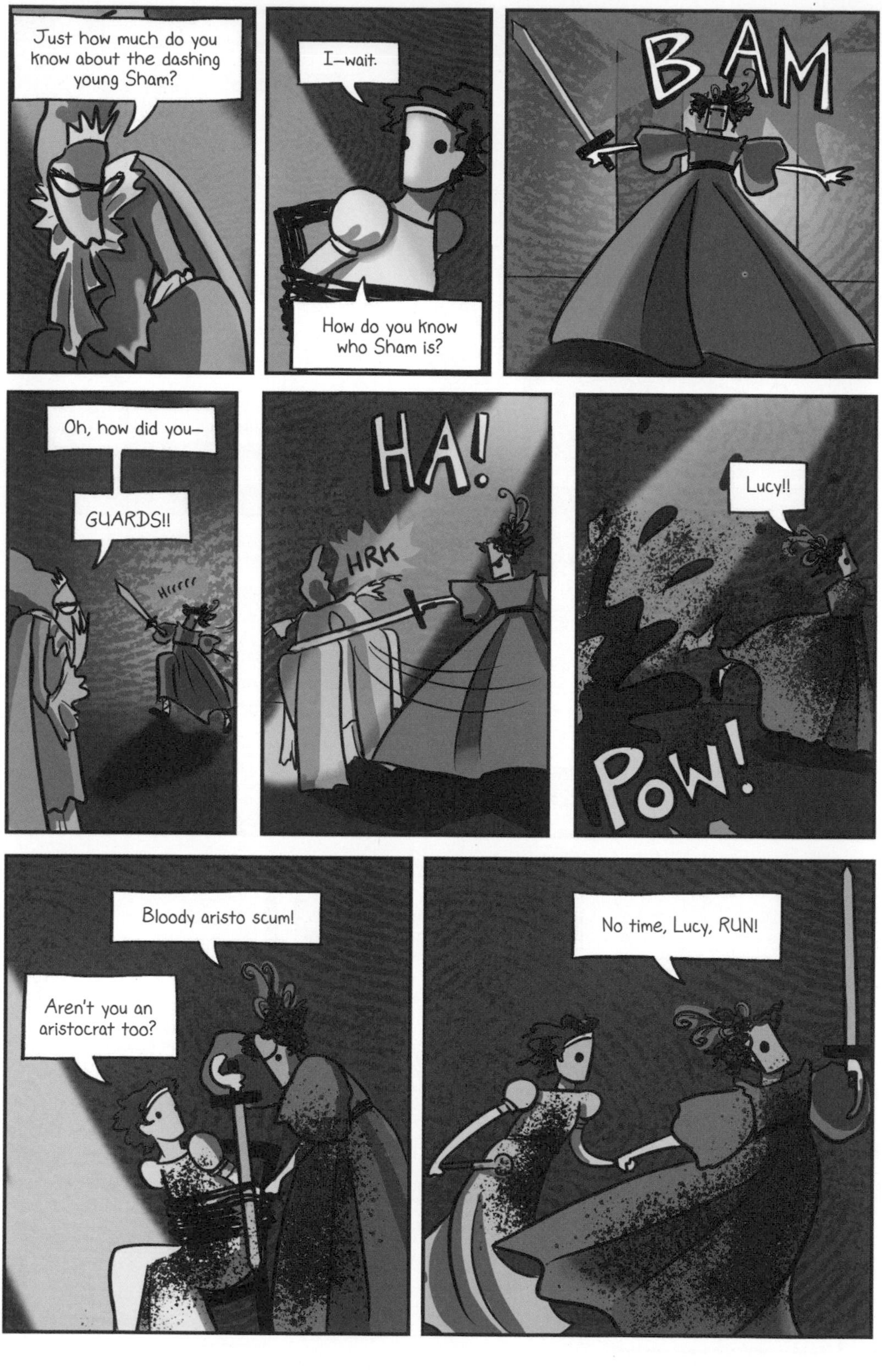
Just how much do you know about the dashing young Sham?
I—wait.
How do you know who Sham is?
BAM
Oh, how did you—
GUARDS!!
HA!
HRK
Lucy!!
POW!
Bloody aristo scum!
Aren't you an aristocrat too?
No time, Lucy, RUN!

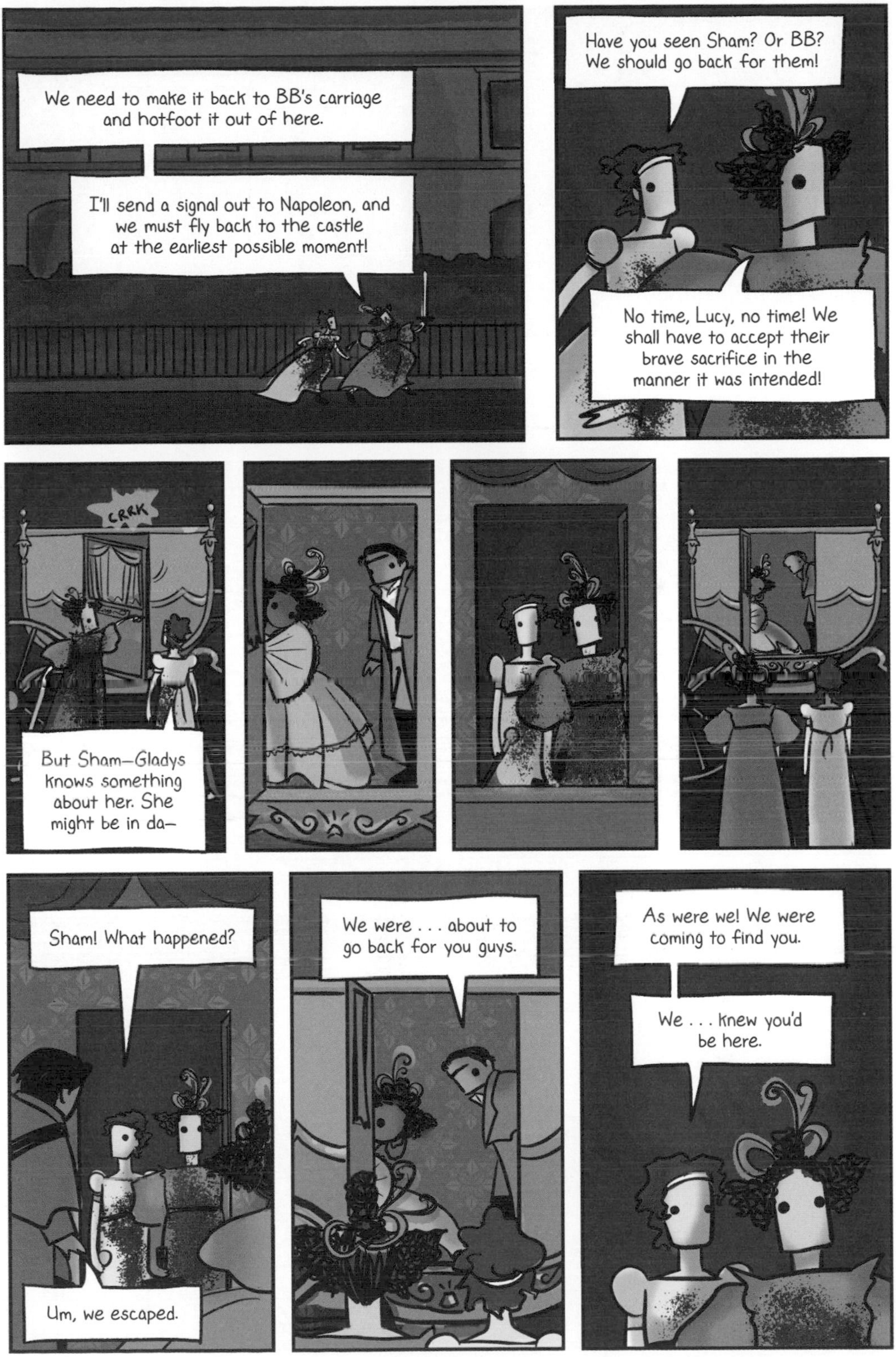
We need to make it back to BB's carriage and hotfoot it out of here.
I'll send a signal out to Napoleon, and we must fly back to the castle at the earliest possible moment!
Have you seen Sham? Or BB? We should go back for them!
No time, Lucy, no time! We shall have to accept their brave sacrifice in the manner it was intended!
CRRK
But Sham—Gladys knows something about her. She might be in da—
Sham! What happened?
Um, we escaped.
We were . . . about to go back for you guys.
As were we! We were coming to find you.
We . . . knew you'd be here.

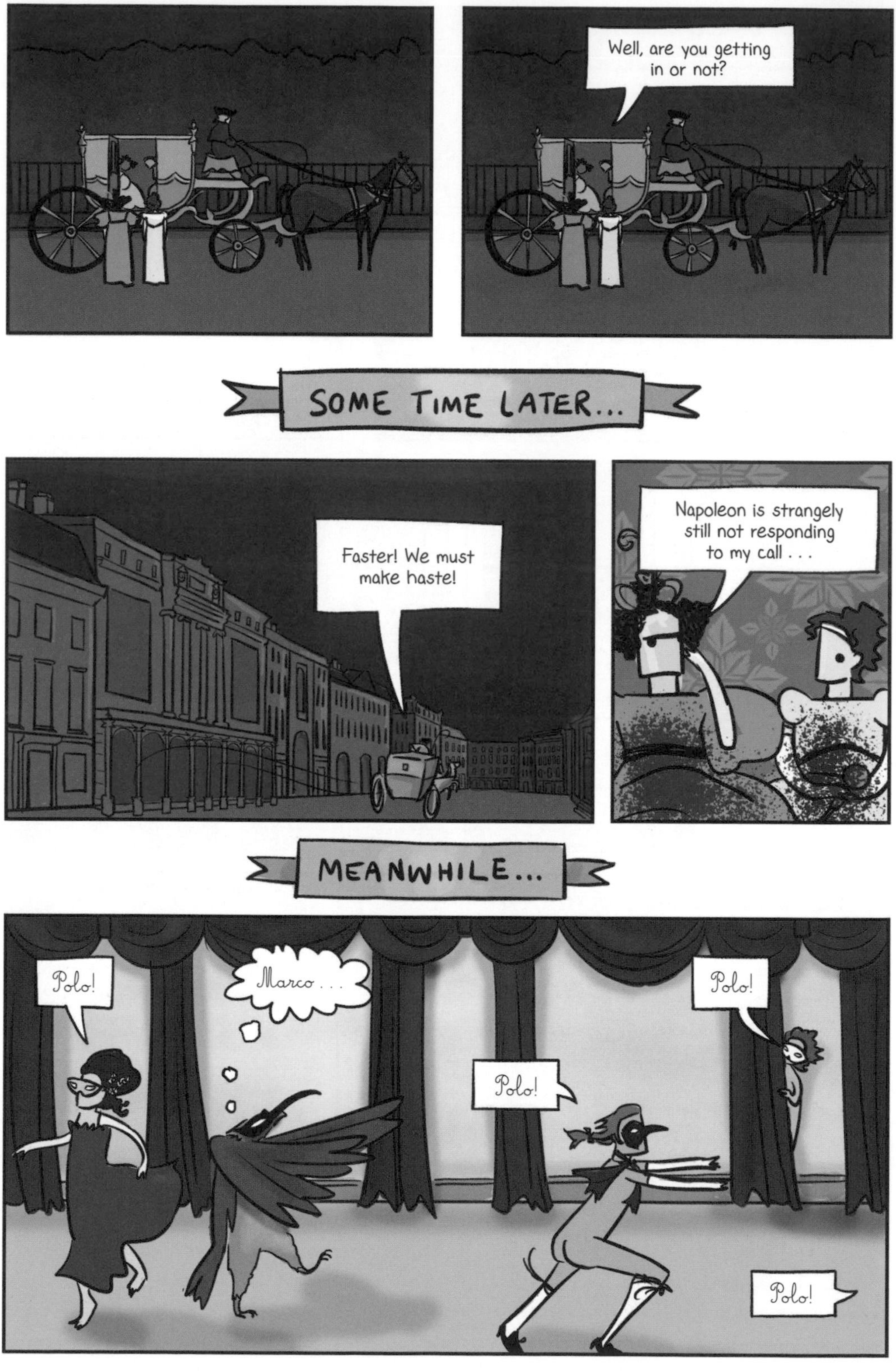
Well, are you getting in or not?
SOME TIME LATER...
Faster! We must make haste!
Napoleon is strangely still not responding to my call . . .
MEANWHILE...
Polo!
Marco . . .
Polo!
Polo!
Polo!

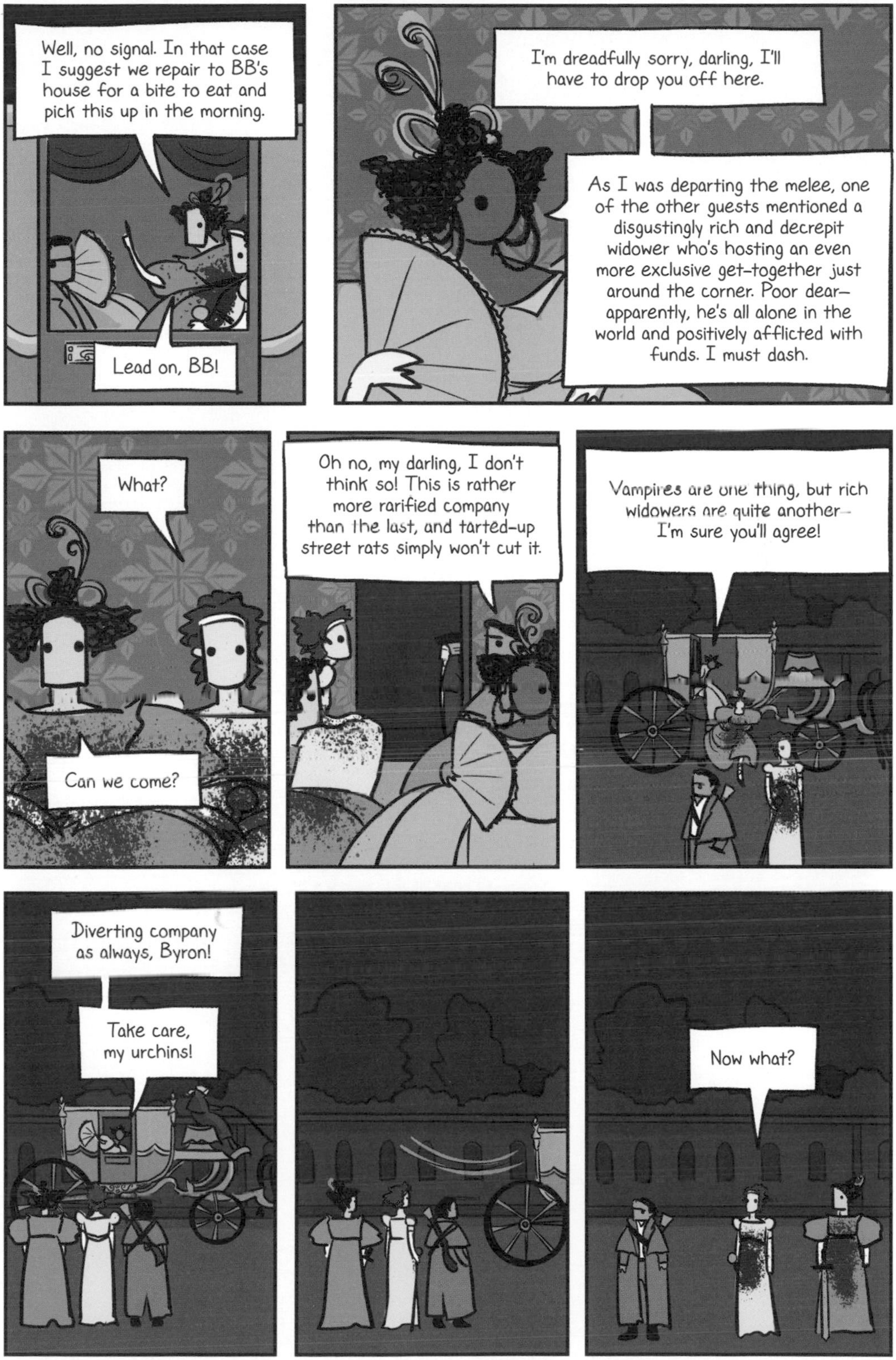

Well, no signal. In that case I suggest we repair to BB's house for a bite to eat and pick this up in the morning.
Lead on, BB!
I'm dreadfully sorry, darling, I'll have to drop you off here.
As I was departing the melee, one of the other guests mentioned a disgustingly rich and decrepit widower who's hosting an even more exclusive get-together just around the corner. Poor dear—apparently, he's all alone in the world and positively afflicted with funds. I must dash.
What?
Can we come?
Oh no, my darling, I don't think so! This is rather more rarified company than the last, and tarted-up street rats simply won't cut it.
Vampires are one thing, but rich widowers are quite another—I'm sure you'll agree!
Diverting company as always, Byron!
Take care, my urchins!
Now what?

CHAPTER IV - THE CLUB

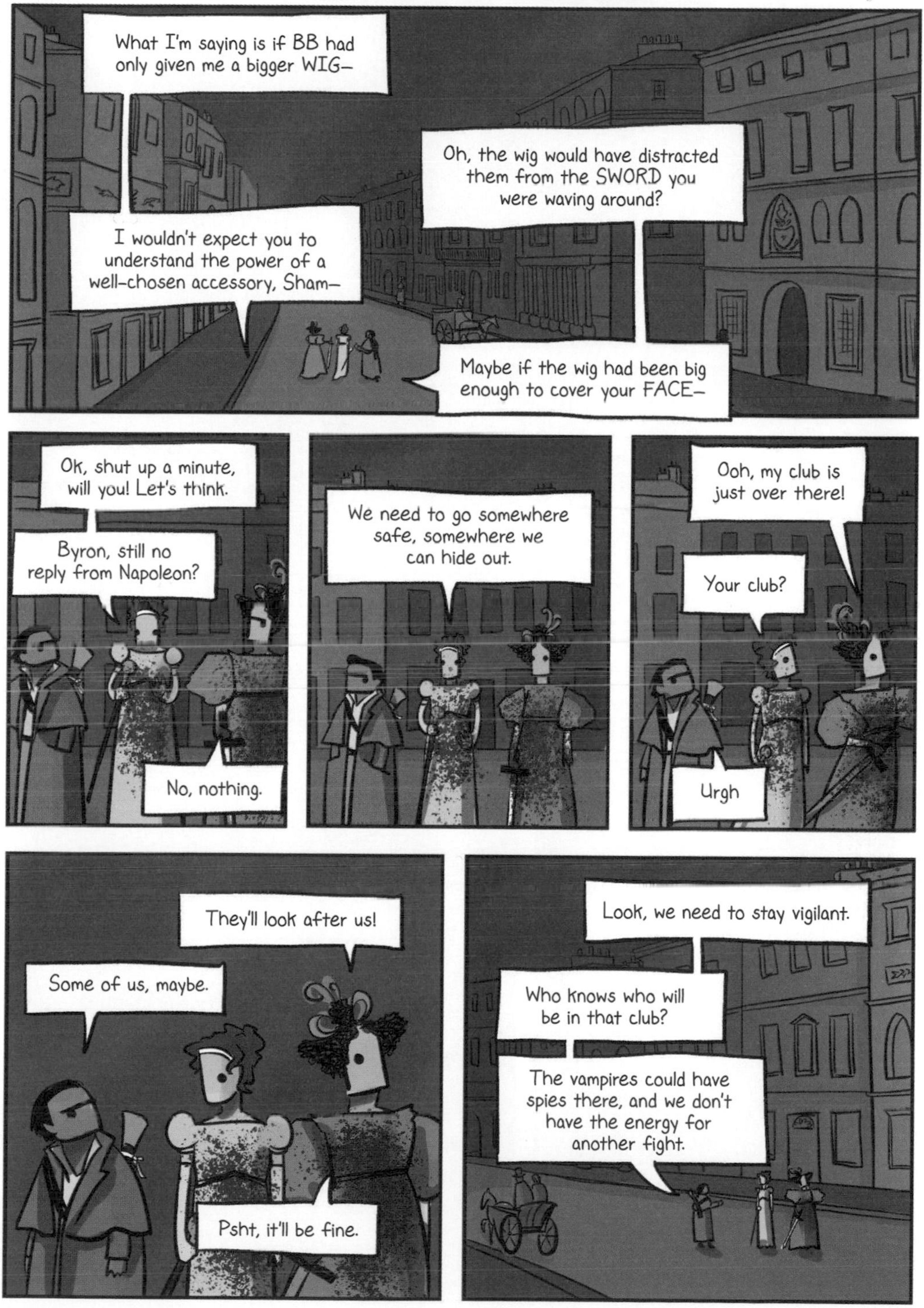
What I'm saying is if BB had only given me a bigger WIG—
I wouldn't expect you to understand the power of a well-chosen accessory, Sham—
Oh, the wig would have distracted them from the SWORD you were waving around?
Maybe if the wig had been big enough to cover your FACE—
Ok, shut up a minute, will you! Let's think.
Byron, still no reply from Napoleon?
No, nothing.
We need to go somewhere safe, somewhere we can hide out.
Ooh, my club is just over there!
Your club?
Urgh
They'll look after us!
Some of us, maybe.
Psht, it'll be fine.
Look, we need to stay vigilant.
Who knows who will be in that club?
The vampires could have spies there, and we don't have the energy for another fight.

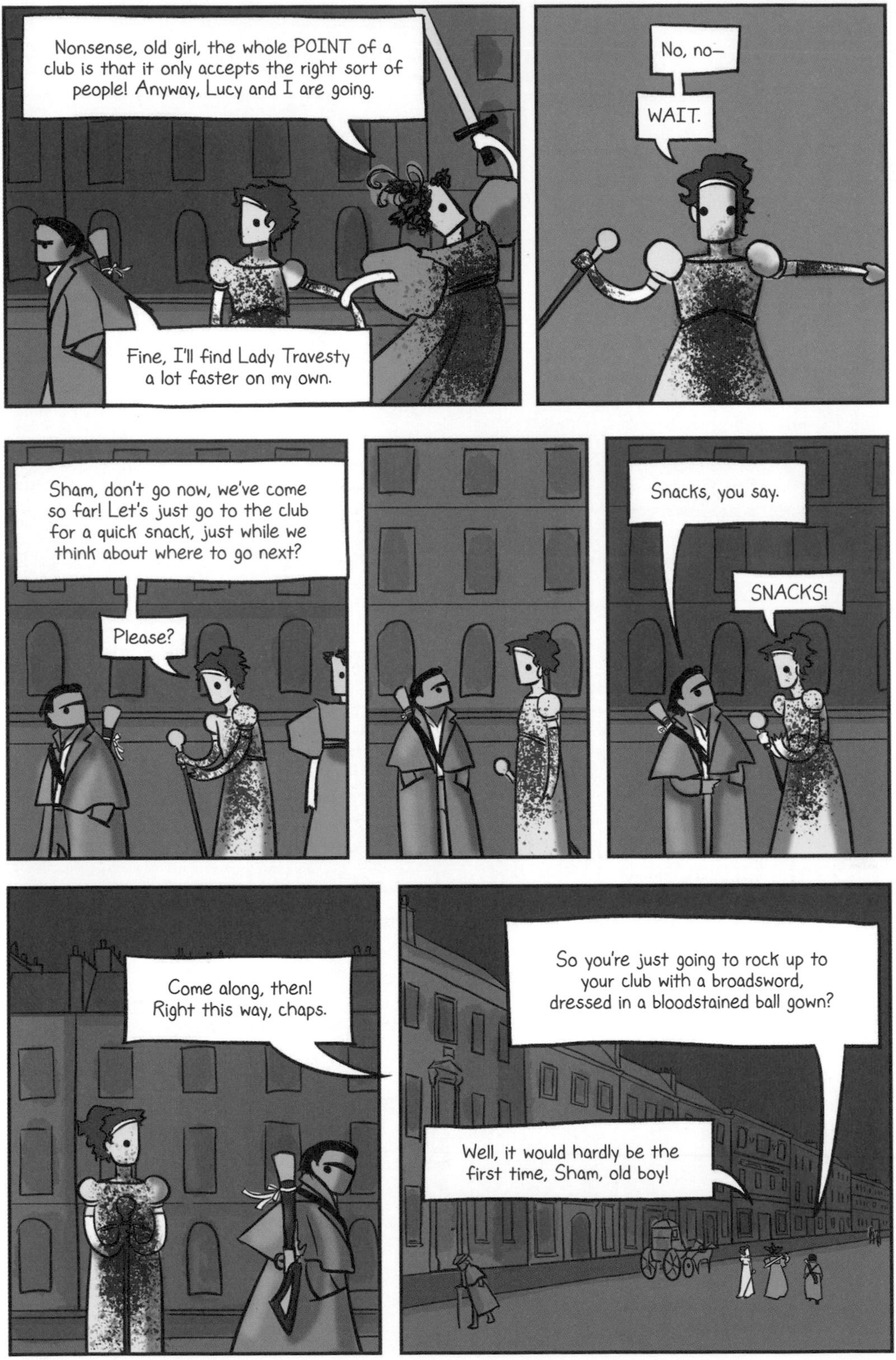
Nonsense, old girl, the whole POINT of a club is that it only accepts the right sort of people! Anyway, Lucy and I are going.
Fine, I'll find Lady Travesty a lot faster on my own.
No, no—
WAIT.
Sham, don't go now, we've come so far! Let's just go to the club for a quick snack, just while we think about where to go next?
Please?
Snacks, you say.
SNACKS!
Come along, then! Right this way, chaps.
So you're just going to rock up to your club with a broadsword, dressed in a bloodstained ball gown?
Well, it would hardly be the first time, Sham, old boy!

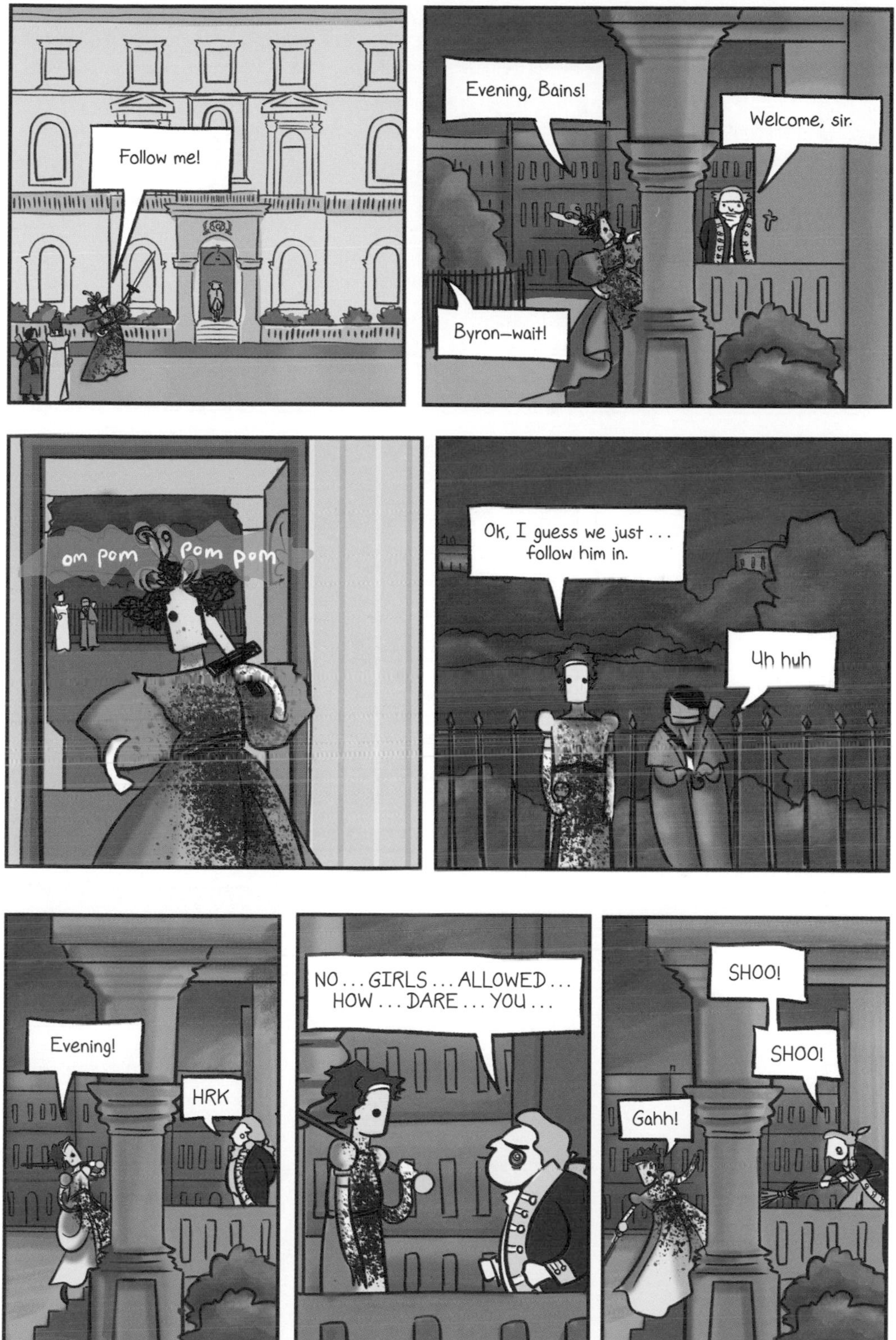
Follow me!
Evening, Bains!
Welcome, sir.
Byron—wait!
om pom pom pom
Ok, I guess we just . . . follow him in.
Uh huh
Evening!
HRK
NO . . . GIRLS . . . ALLOWED . . . HOW . . . DARE . . . YOU . . .
SHOO!
SHOO!
Gahh!

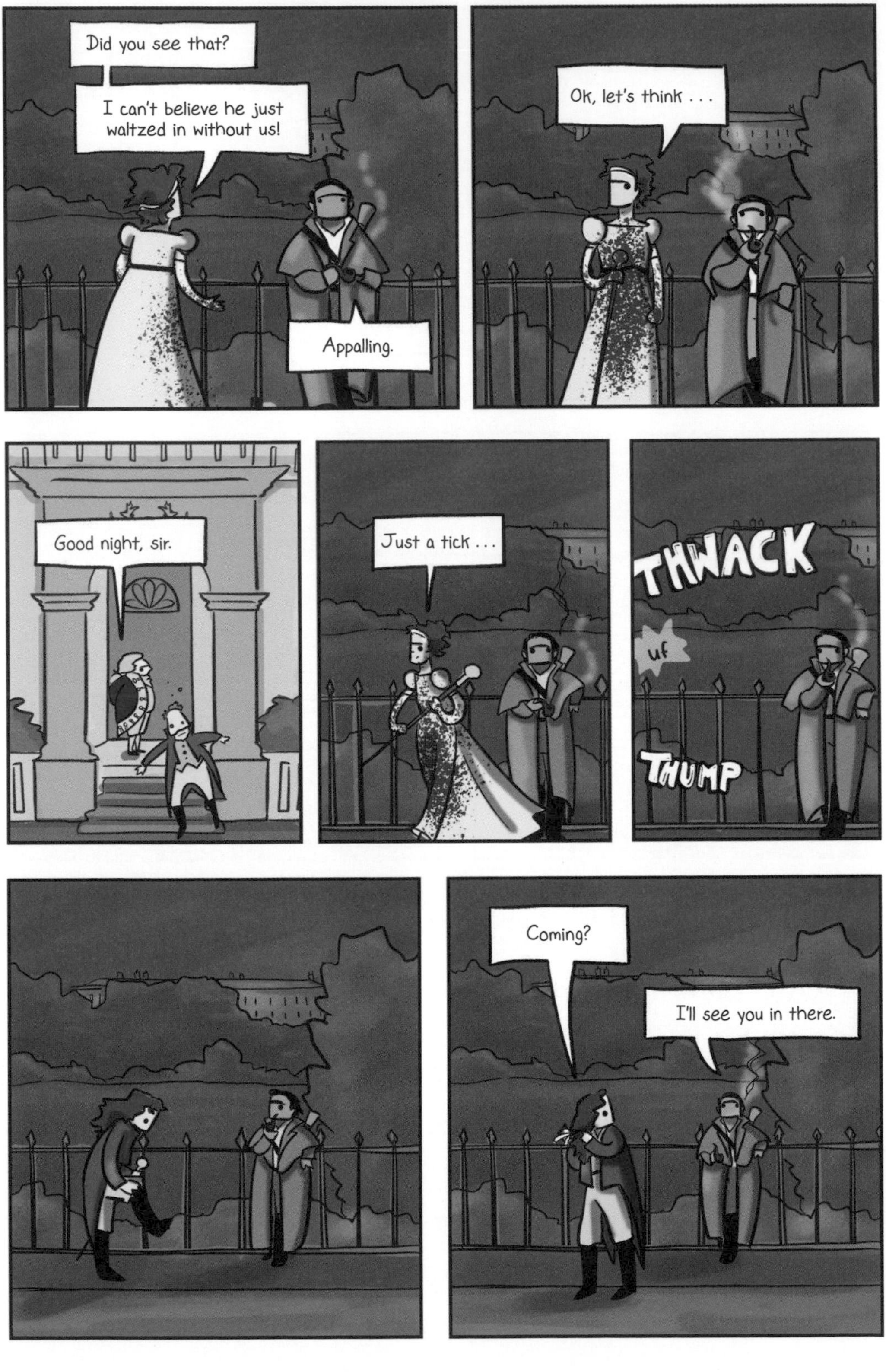
Did you see that?
I can't believe he just waltzed in without us!
Appalling.
Ok, let's think . . .
Good night, sir.
Just a tick . . .
THWACK
uf
THUMP
Coming?
I'll see you in there.

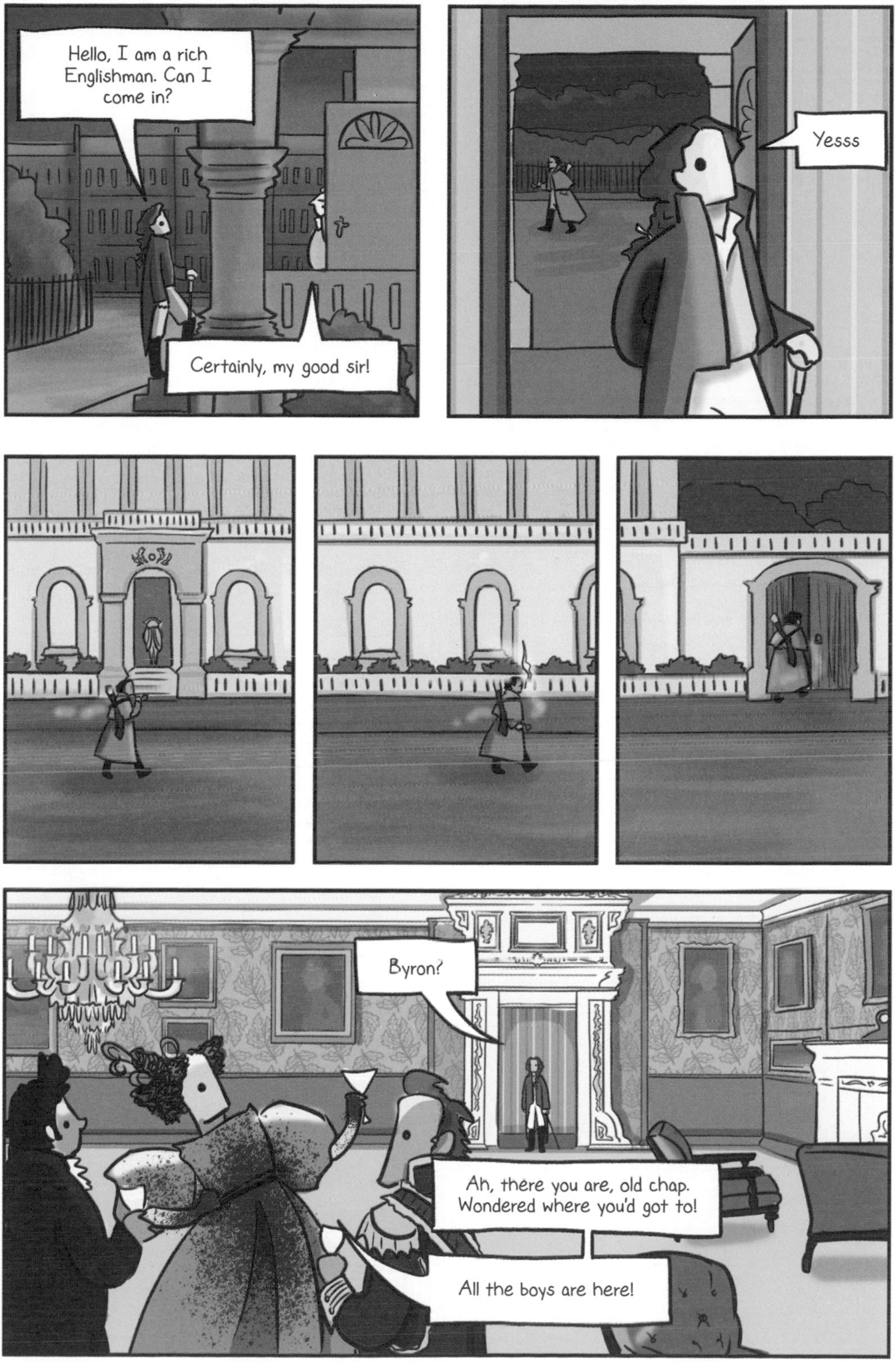
Hello, I am a rich Englishman. Can I come in?
Certainly, my good sir!
Yesss
Byron?
Ah, there you are, old chap. Wondered where you'd got to!
All the boys are here!

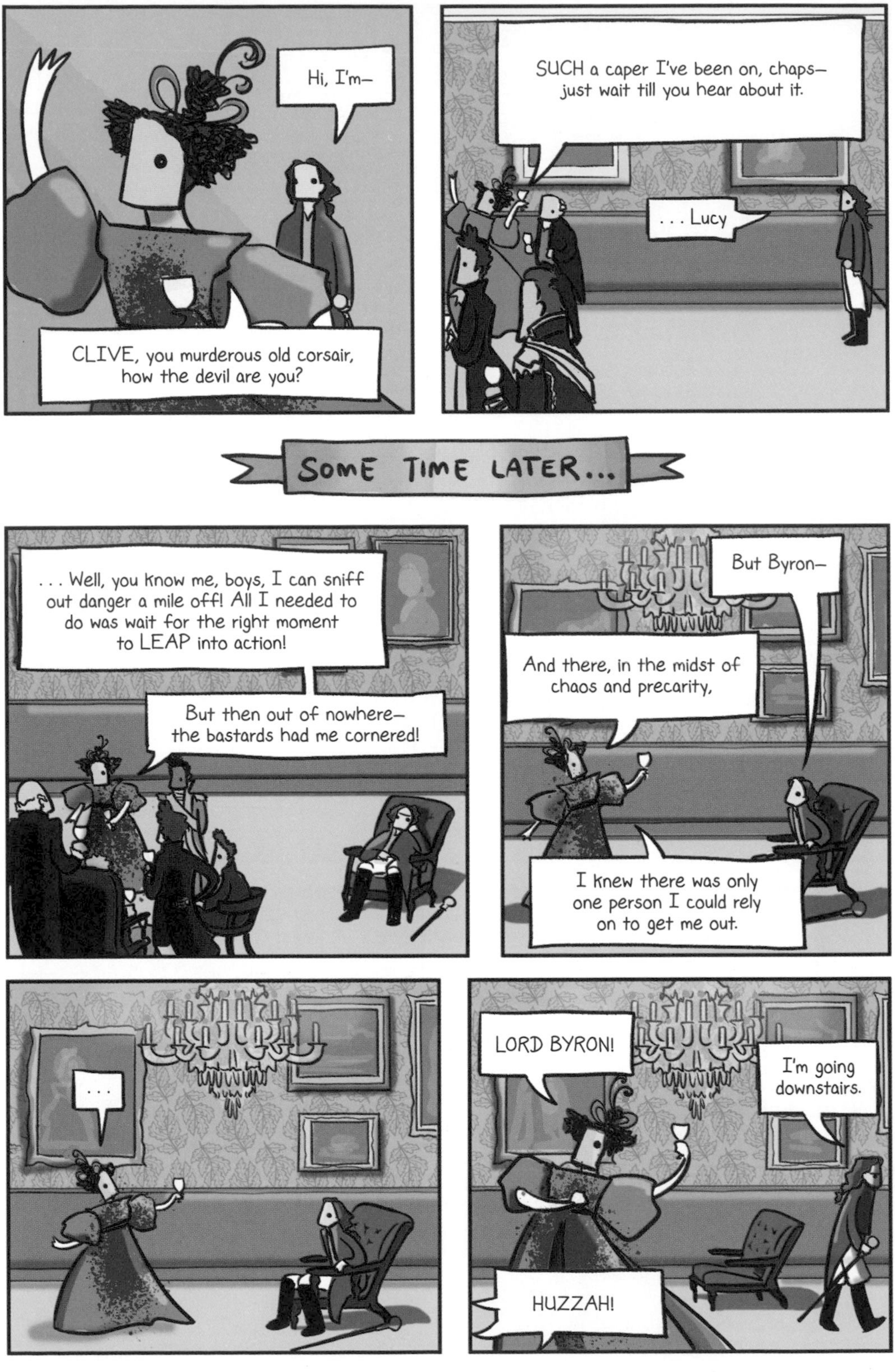
Hi, I'm–
CLIVE, you murderous old corsair, how the devil are you?
SUCH a caper I've been on, chaps– just wait till you hear about it.
. . . Lucy
SOME TIME LATER...
. . . Well, you know me, boys, I can sniff out danger a mile off! All I needed to do was wait for the right moment to LEAP into action!
But then out of nowhere– the bastards had me cornered!
But Byron–
And there, in the midst of chaos and precarity,
I knew there was only one person I could rely on to get me out.
. . .
LORD BYRON!
I'm going downstairs.
HUZZAH!

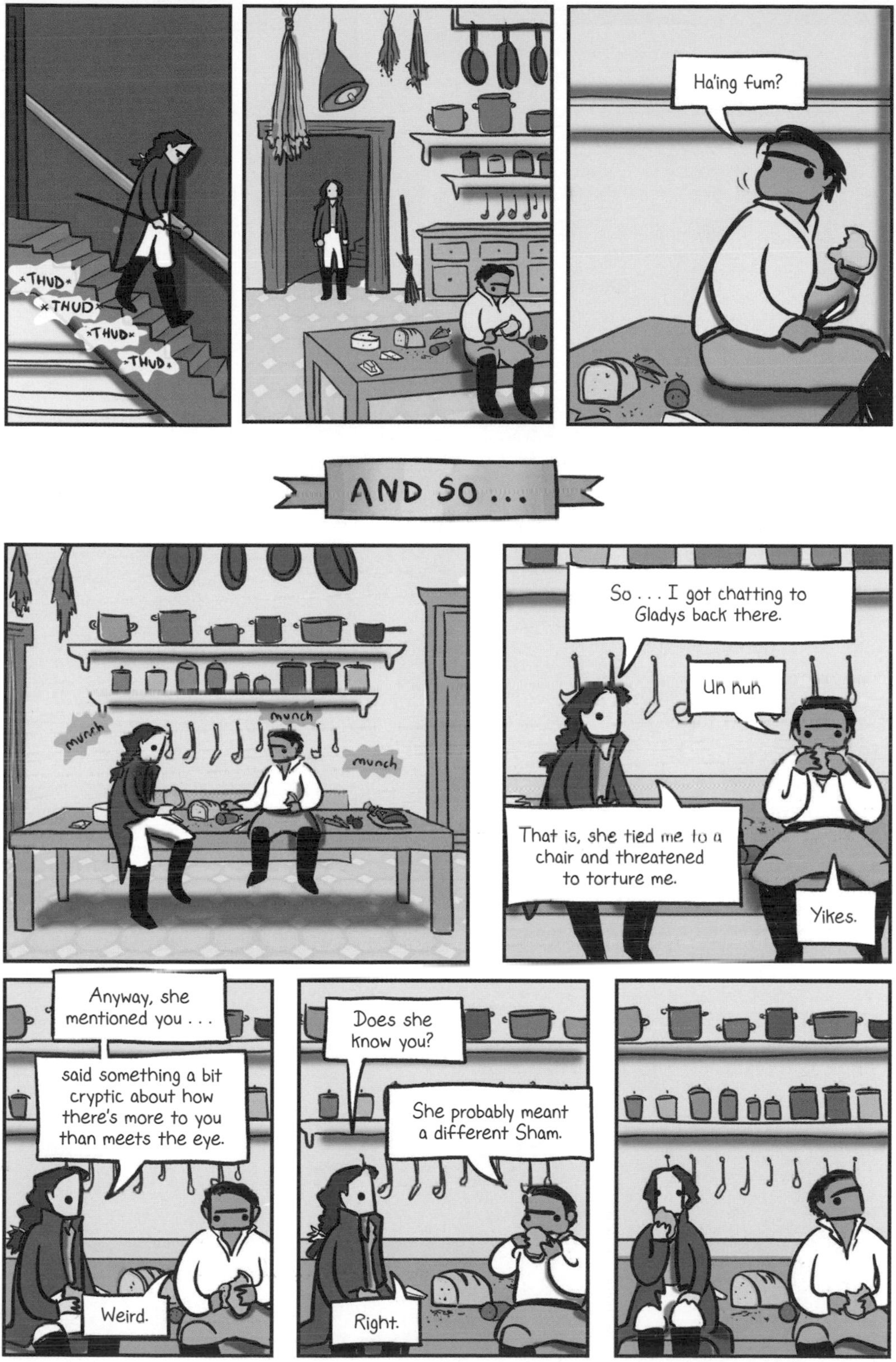

THUD
THUD
THUD
THUD
Ha'ing fum?
AND SO . . .
munch
munch
munch
So . . . I got chatting to Gladys back there.
Uh huh
That is, she tied me to a chair and threatened to torture me.
Yikes.
Anyway, she mentioned you . . .
said something a bit cryptic about how there's more to you than meets the eye.
Weird.
Does she know you?
She probably meant a different Sham.
Right.

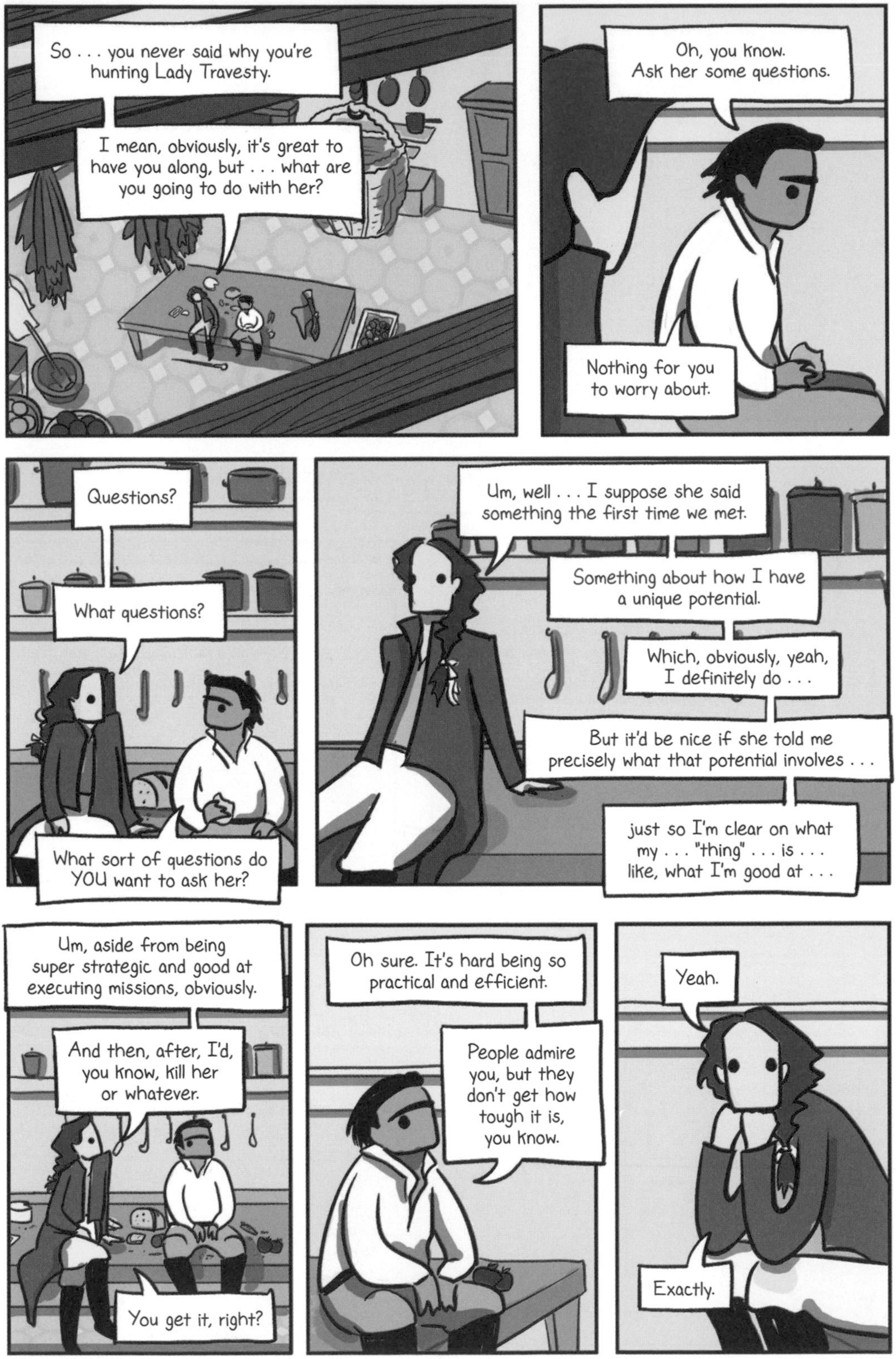
So . . . you never said why you're hunting Lady Travesty.
I mean, obviously, it's great to have you along, but . . . what are you going to do with her?
Oh, you know. Ask her some questions.
Nothing for you to worry about.
Questions?
What questions?
What sort of questions do YOU want to ask her?
Um, well . . . I suppose she said something the first time we met.
Something about how I have a unique potential.
Which, obviously, yeah, I definitely do . . .
But it'd be nice if she told me precisely what that potential involves . . .
just so I'm clear on what my . . . "thing" . . . is . . . like, what I'm good at . . .
Um, aside from being super strategic and good at executing missions, obviously.
And then, after, I'd, you know, kill her or whatever.
You get it, right?
Oh sure. It's hard being so practical and efficient.
People admire you, but they don't get how tough it is, you know.
Yeah.
Exactly.

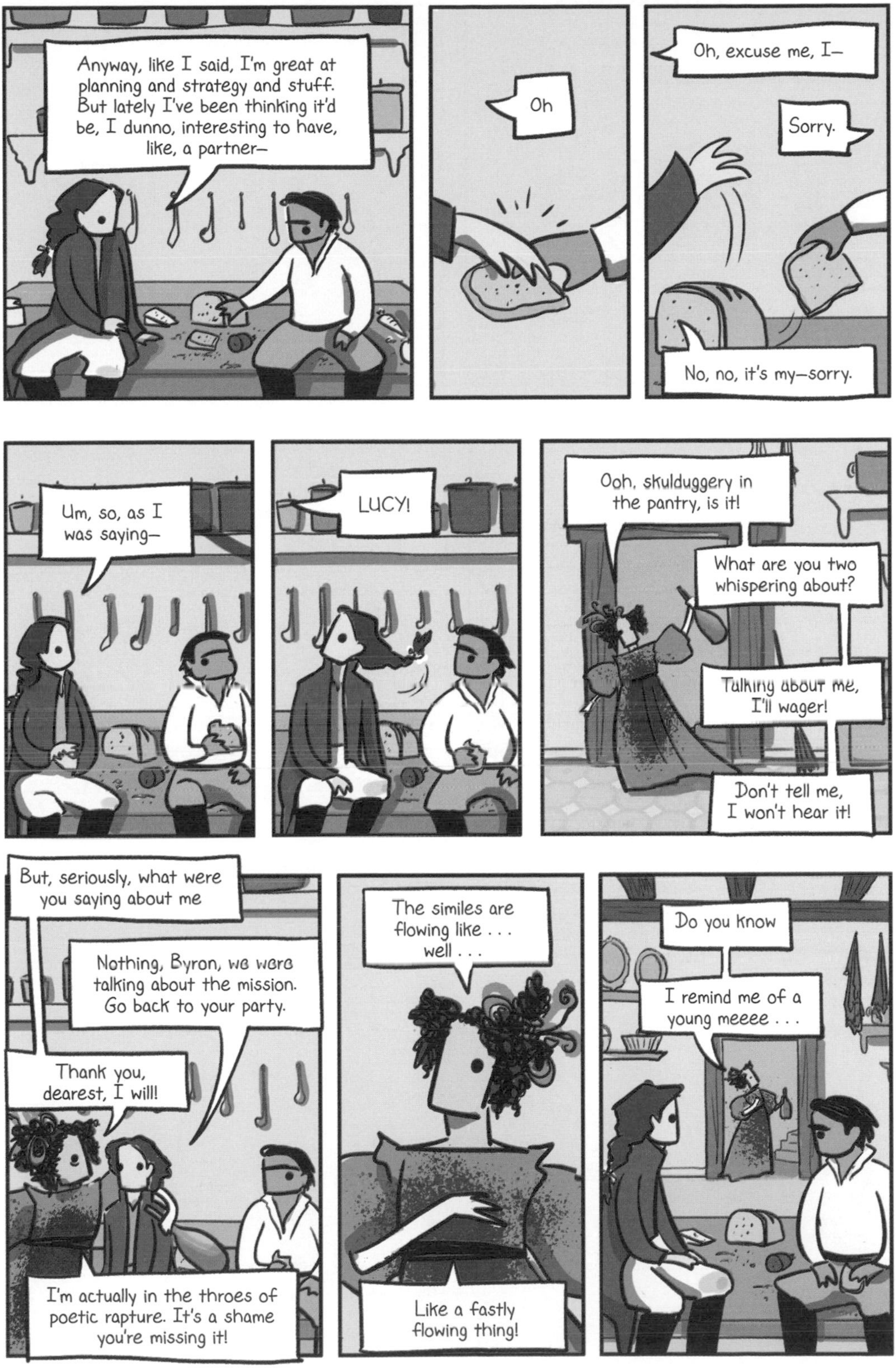
Anyway, like I said, I'm great at planning and strategy and stuff. But lately I've been thinking it'd be, I dunno, interesting to have, like, a partner—
Oh
Oh, excuse me, I—
Sorry.
No, no, it's my—sorry.
Um, so, as I was saying—
LUCY!
Ooh, skulduggery in the pantry, is it!
What are you two whispering about?
Talking about me, I'll wager!
Don't tell me, I won't hear it!
But, seriously, what were you saying about me
Nothing, Byron, we were talking about the mission. Go back to your party.
Thank you, dearest, I will!
I'm actually in the throes of poetic rapture. It's a shame you're missing it!
The similes are flowing like . . . well . . .
Like a fastly flowing thing!
Do you know
I remind me of a young meeee . . .

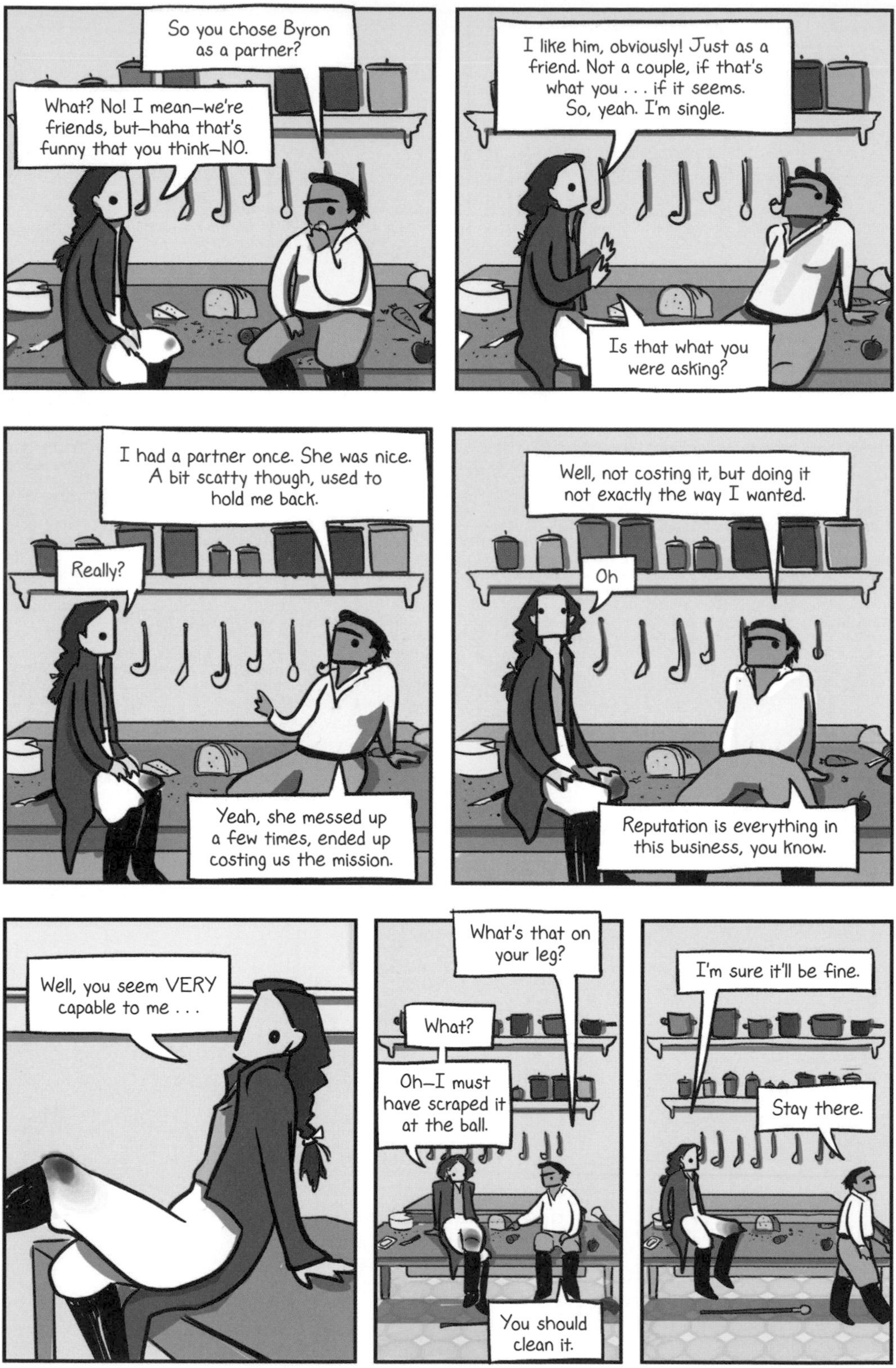
So you chose Byron as a partner?
What? No! I mean—we're friends, but—haha that's funny that you think—NO.
I like him, obviously! Just as a friend. Not a couple, if that's what you . . . if it seems. So, yeah. I'm single.
Is that what you were asking?
I had a partner once. She was nice. A bit scatty though, used to hold me back.
Really?
Yeah, she messed up a few times, ended up costing us the mission.
Well, not costing it, but doing it not exactly the way I wanted.
Oh
Reputation is everything in this business, you know.
Well, you seem VERY capable to me . . .
What's that on your leg?
What?
Oh—I must have scraped it at the ball.
You should clean it.
I'm sure it'll be fine.
Stay there.

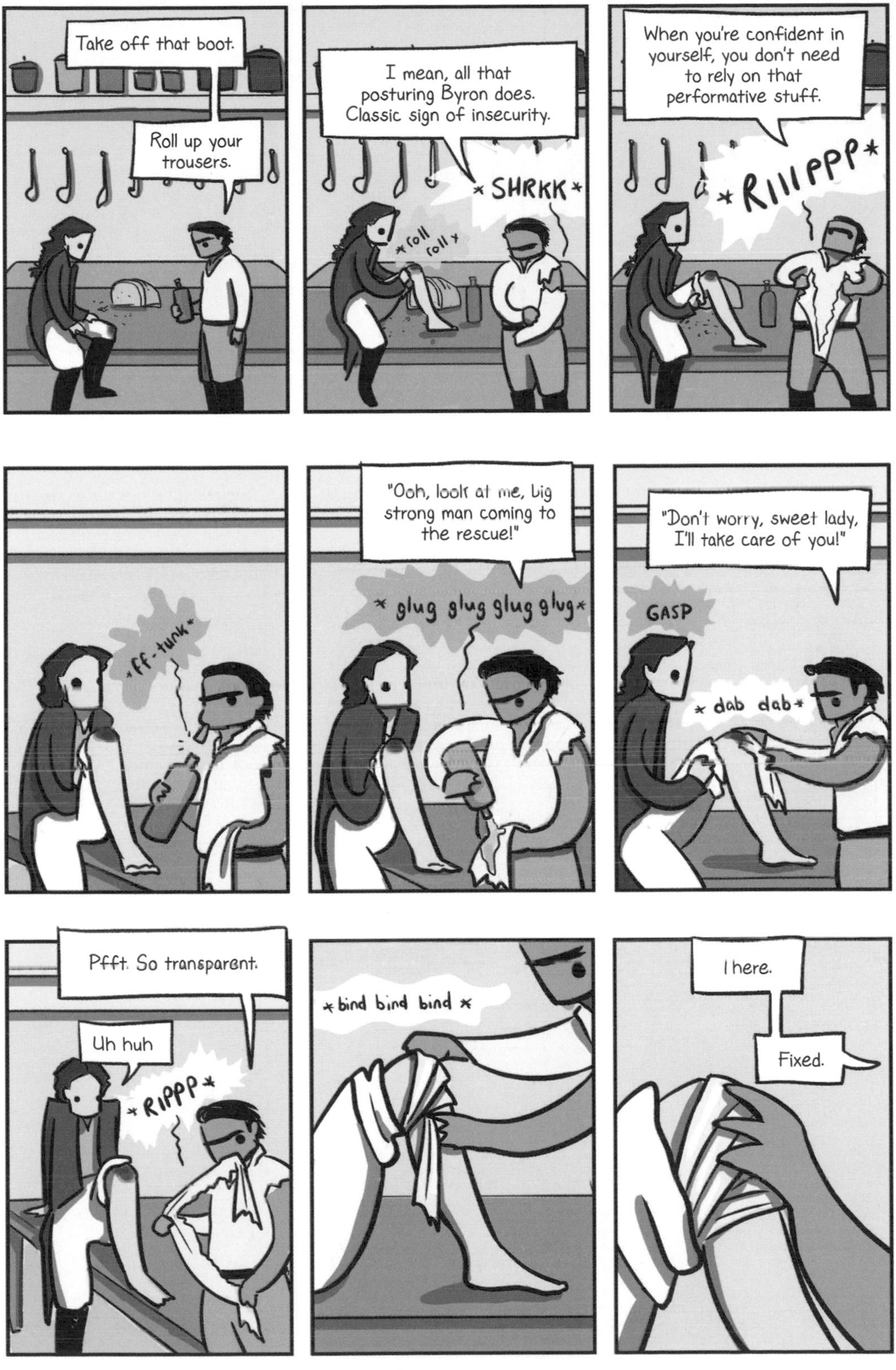
Take off that boot.
Roll up your trousers.
I mean, all that posturing Byron does. Classic sign of insecurity.
roll roll
SHRKK
When you're confident in yourself, you don't need to rely on that performative stuff.
RIIIPPP
ff-tunk
"Ooh, look at me, big strong man coming to the rescue!"
glug glug glug glug
"Don't worry, sweet lady, I'll take care of you!"
GASP
dab dab
Pfft. So transparent.
Uh huh
RIPPP
bind bind bind
There.
Fixed.

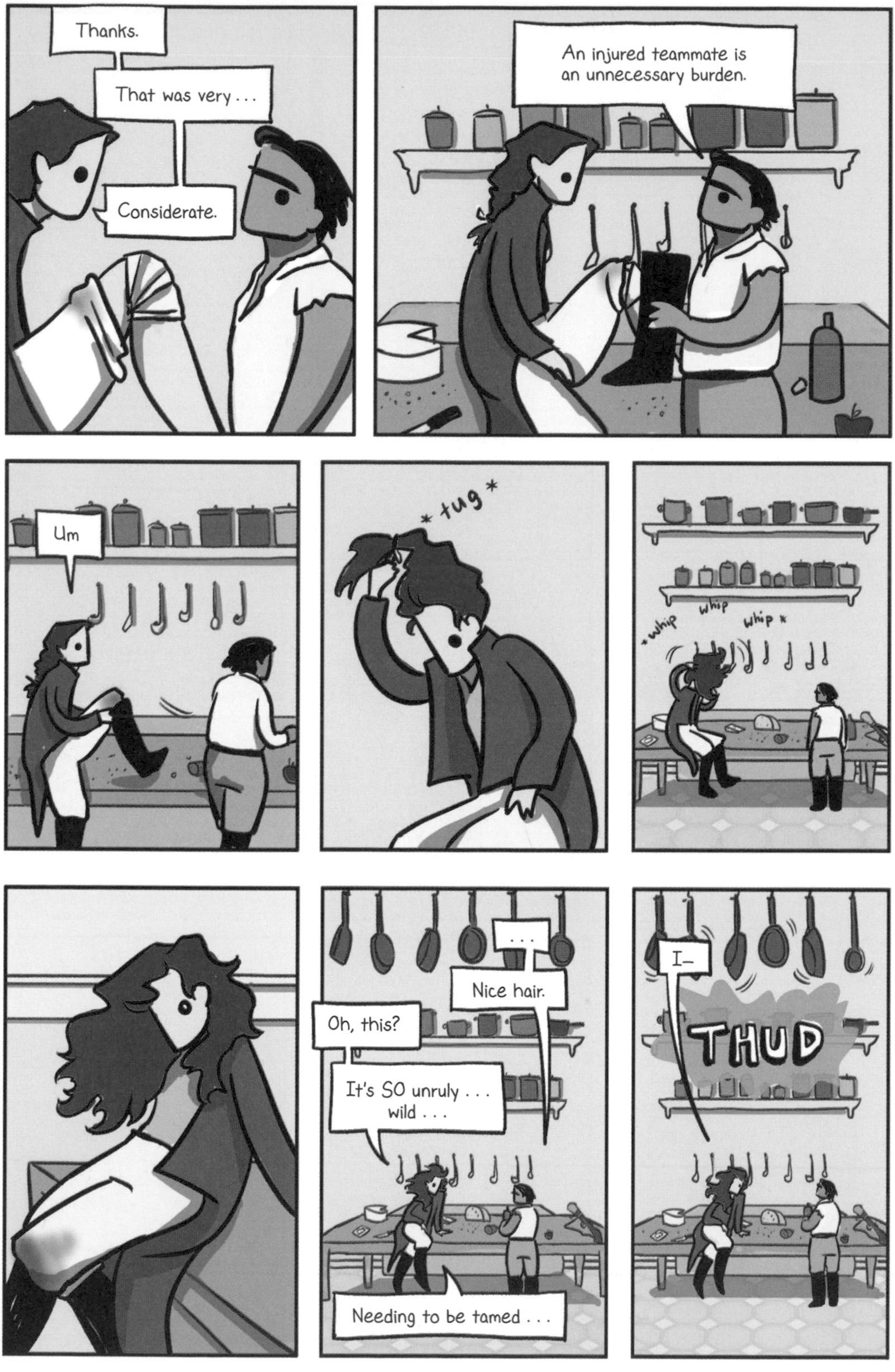

Thanks.
That was very . . .
Considerate.
An injured teammate is an unnecessary burden.
Um
tug
*whip
whip
whip*
Oh, this?
It's SO unruly . . . wild . . .
Needing to be tamed . . .
. . .
Nice hair.
I—
THUD

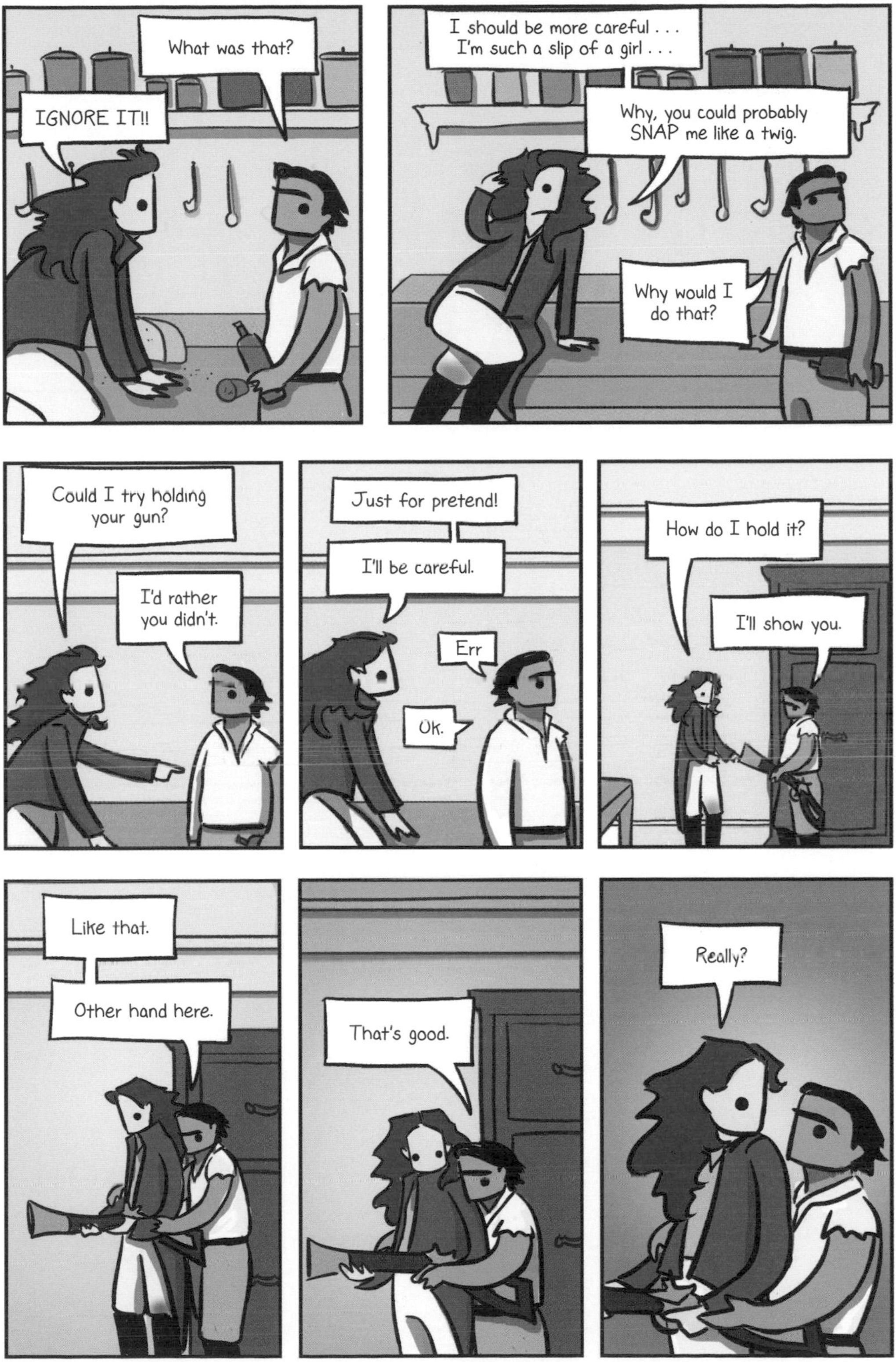
IGNORE IT!!
What was that?
I should be more careful . . . I'm such a slip of a girl . . .
Why, you could probably SNAP me like a twig.
Why would I do that?
Could I try holding your gun?
I'd rather you didn't.
Just for pretend!
I'll be careful.
Err
Ok.
How do I hold it?
I'll show you.
Like that.
Other hand here.
That's good.
Really?

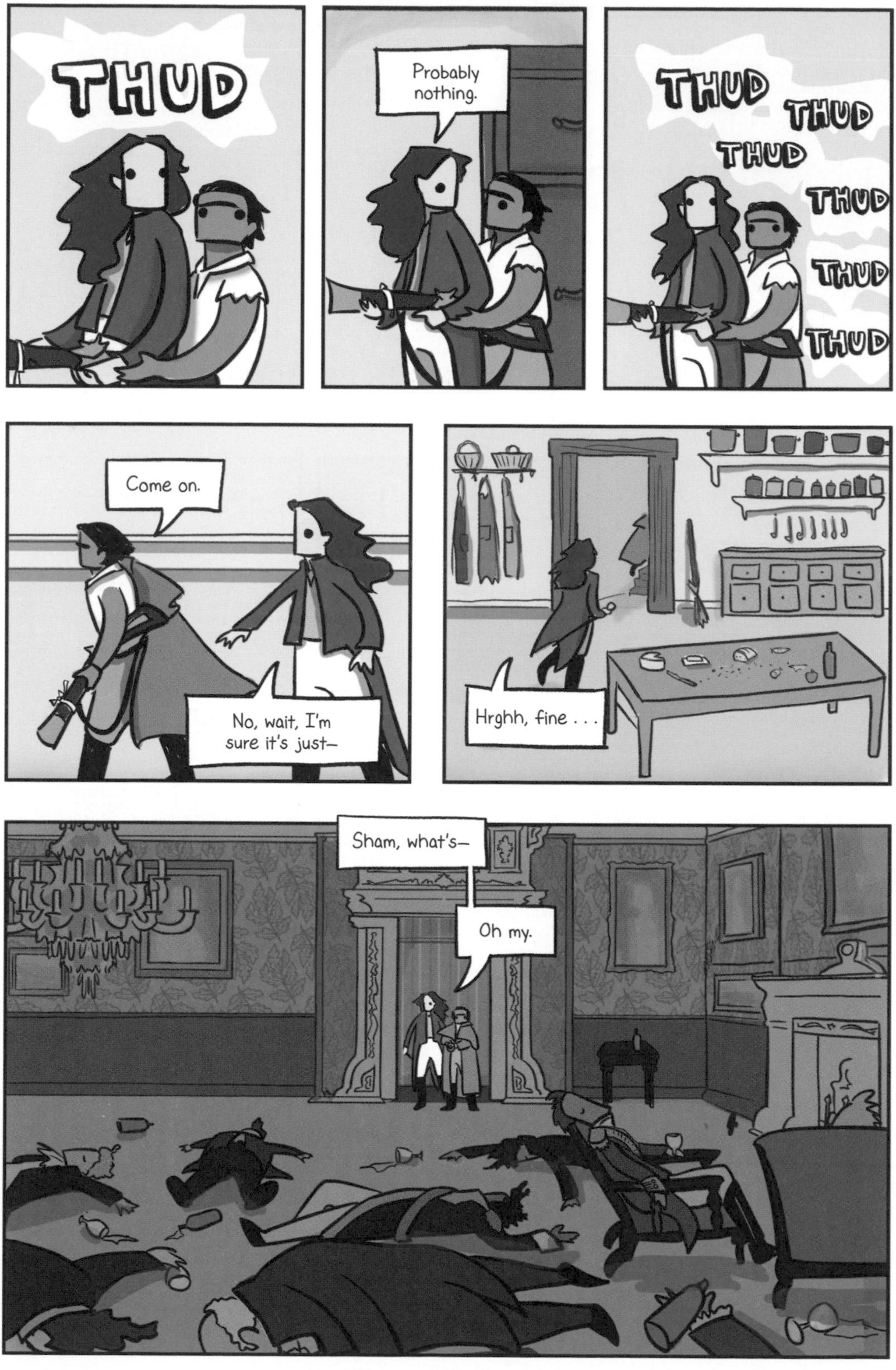
THUD
Probably nothing.
THUD
THUD
THUD
THUD
THUD
THUD
Come on.
No, wait, I'm sure it's just—
Hrghh, fine . . .
Sham, what's—
Oh my.

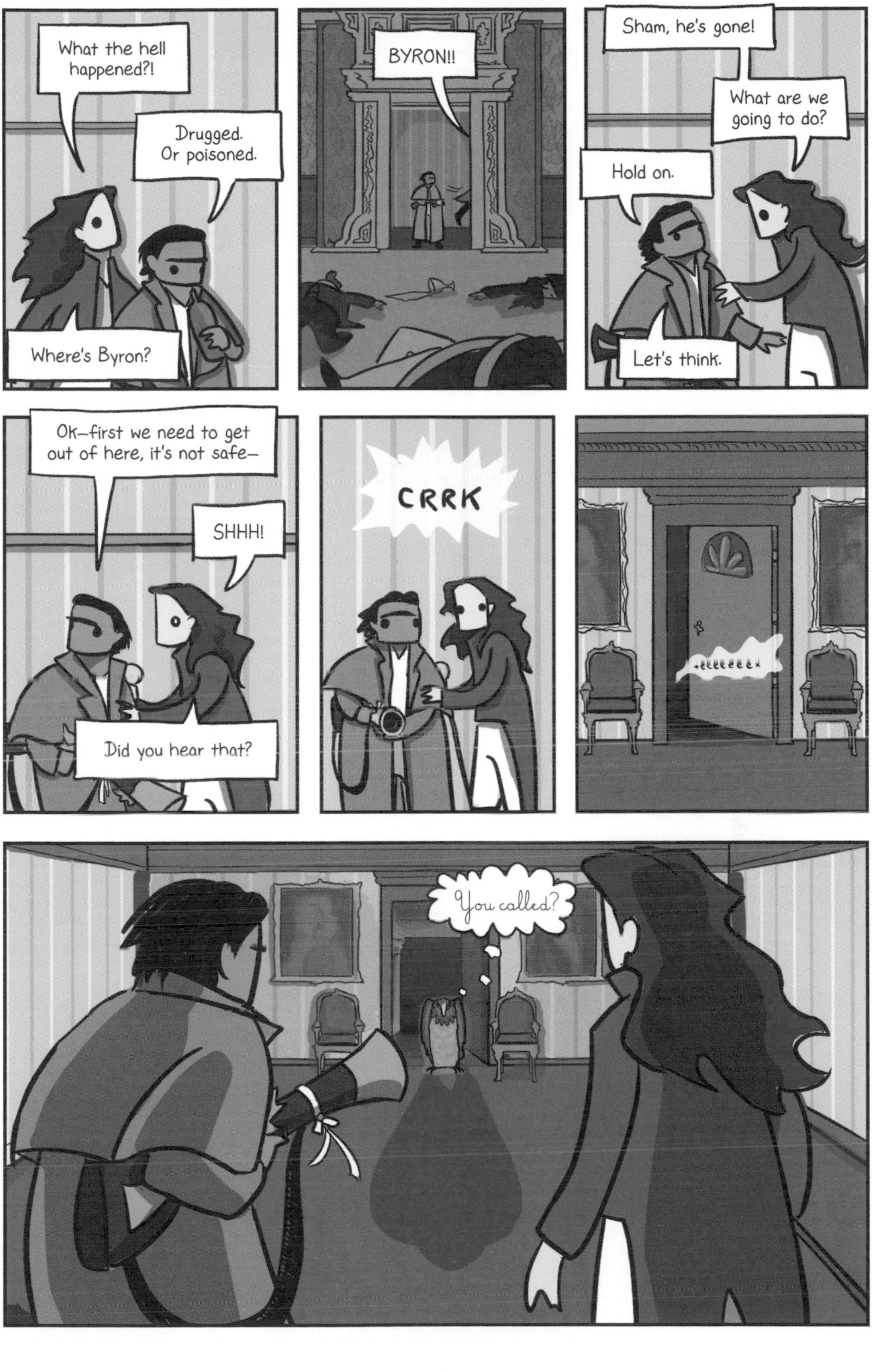
What the hell happened?!
Drugged. Or poisoned.
Where's Byron?
BYRON!!
Sham, he's gone!
What are we going to do?
Hold on.
Let's think.
Ok—first we need to get out of here, it's not safe—
SHHH!
Did you hear that?
CRRK
You called?

CHAPTER V – THE FOREST

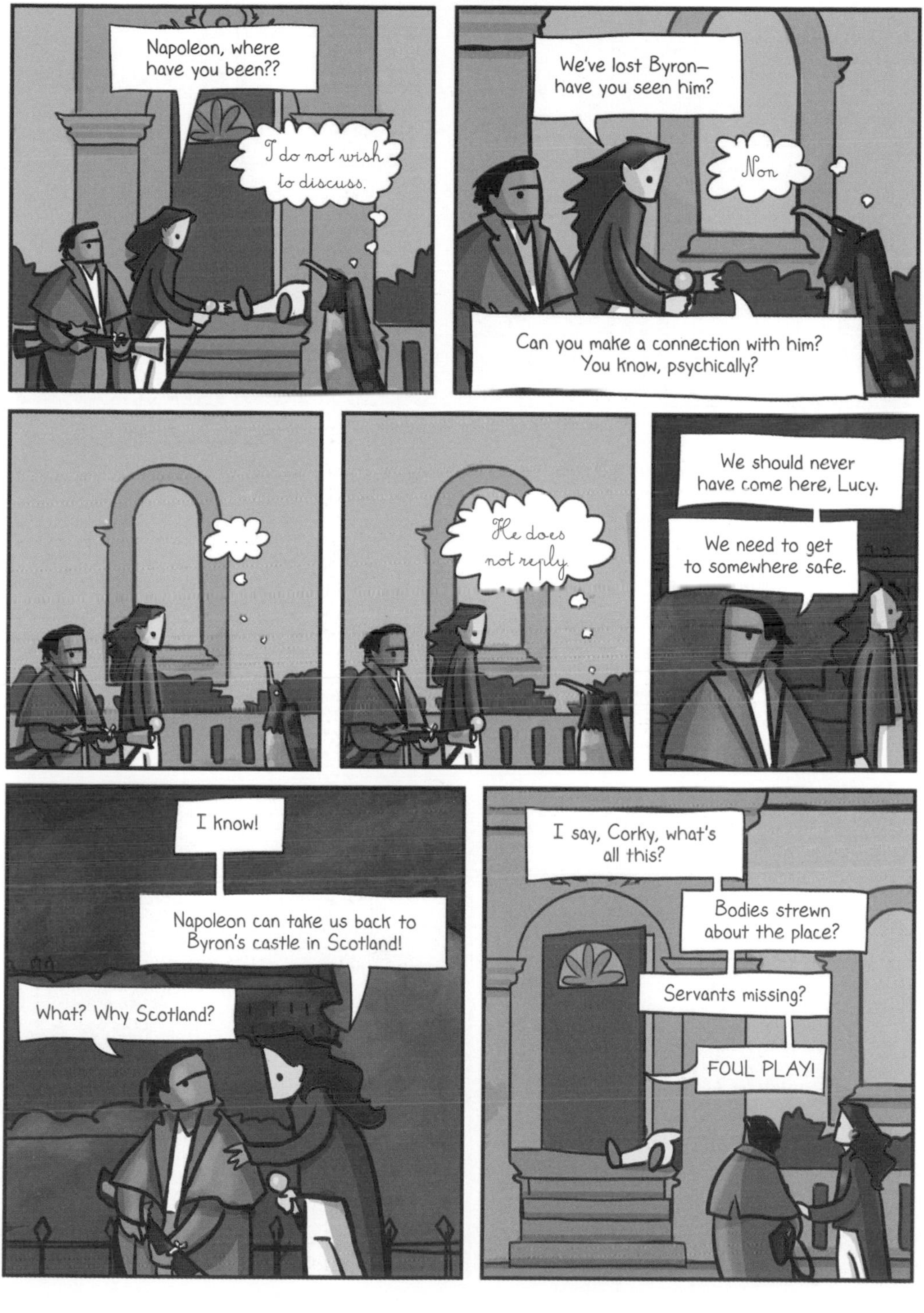
Napoleon, where have you been??
I do not wish to discuss.
We've lost Byron— have you seen him?
Non
Can you make a connection with him? You know, psychically?
. . .
He does not reply.
We should never have come here, Lucy.
We need to get to somewhere safe.
I know!
Napoleon can take us back to Byron's castle in Scotland!
What? Why Scotland?
I say, Corky, what's all this?
Bodies strewn about the place?
Servants missing?
FOUL PLAY!

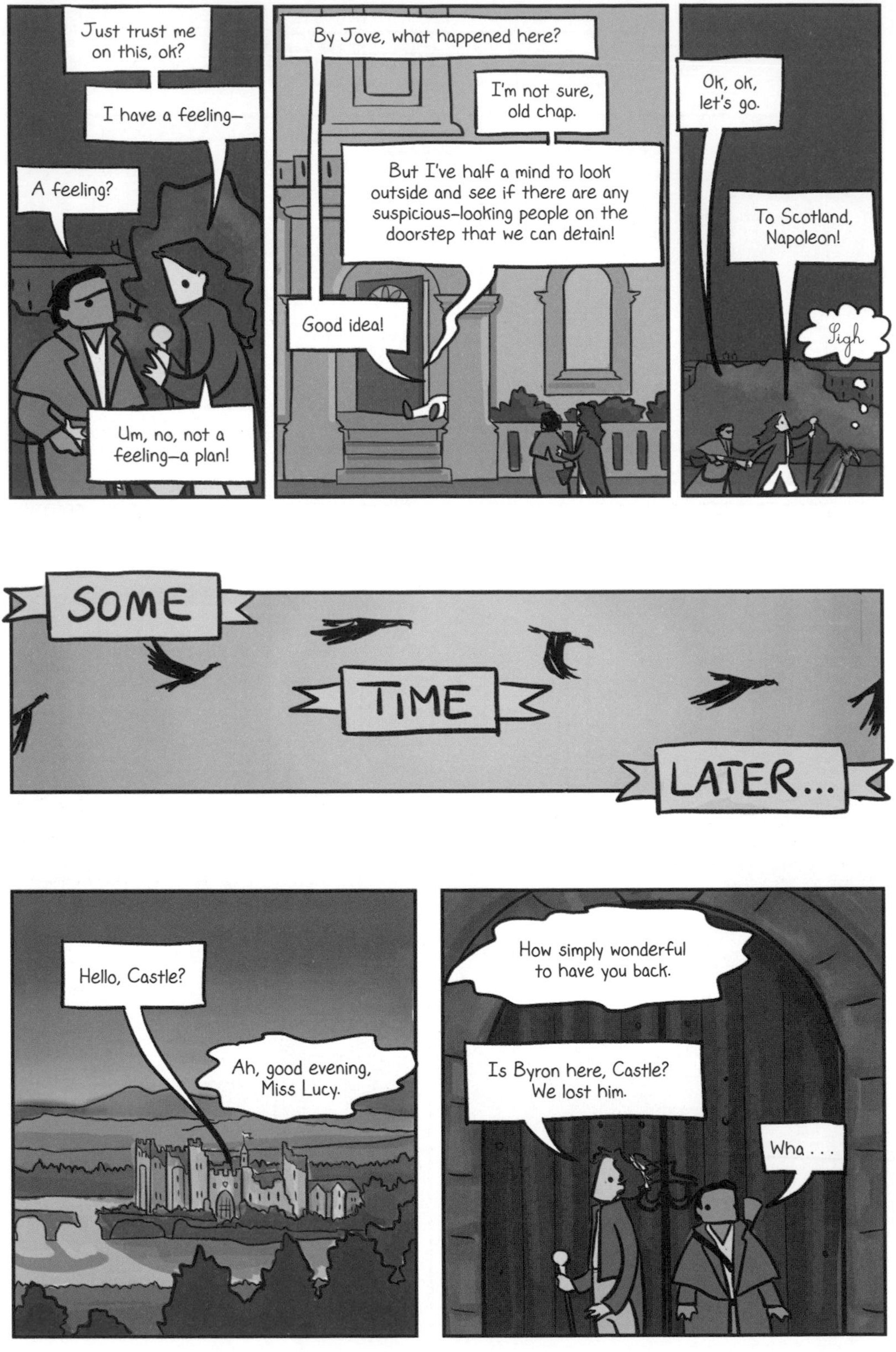
Just trust me on this, ok?
I have a feeling—
A feeling?
Um, no, not a feeling—a plan!
By Jove, what happened here?
I'm not sure, old chap.
But I've half a mind to look outside and see if there are any suspicious-looking people on the doorstep that we can detain!
Good idea!
Ok, ok, let's go.
To Scotland, Napoleon!
Sigh
SOME
TIME
LATER...
Hello, Castle?
Ah, good evening, Miss Lucy.
How simply wonderful to have you back.
Is Byron here, Castle? We lost him.
Wha . . .

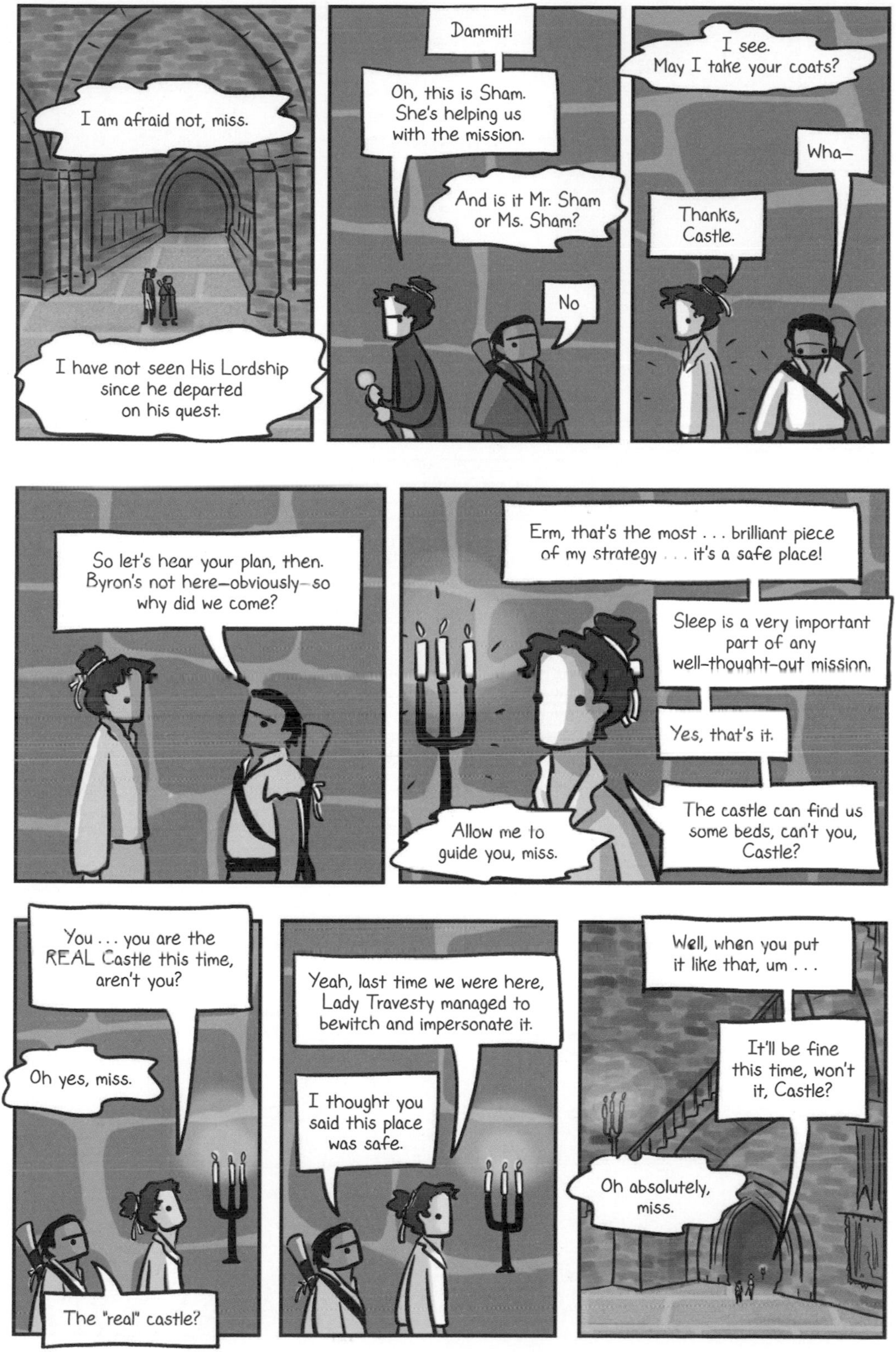
I am afraid not, miss.
I have not seen His Lordship since he departed on his quest.
Dammit!
Oh, this is Sham. She's helping us with the mission.
And is it Mr. Sham or Ms. Sham?
No
I see. May I take your coats?
Wha–
Thanks, Castle.
So let's hear your plan, then. Byron's not here—obviously—so why did we come?
Erm, that's the most . . . brilliant piece of my strategy . . . it's a safe place!
Sleep is a very important part of any well-thought-out mission.
Yes, that's it.
The castle can find us some beds, can't you, Castle?
Allow me to guide you, miss.
You . . . you are the REAL Castle this time, aren't you?
Oh yes, miss.
The "real" castle?
Yeah, last time we were here, Lady Travesty managed to bewitch and impersonate it.
I thought you said this place was safe.
Well, when you put it like that, um . . .
It'll be fine this time, won't it, Castle?
Oh absolutely, miss.

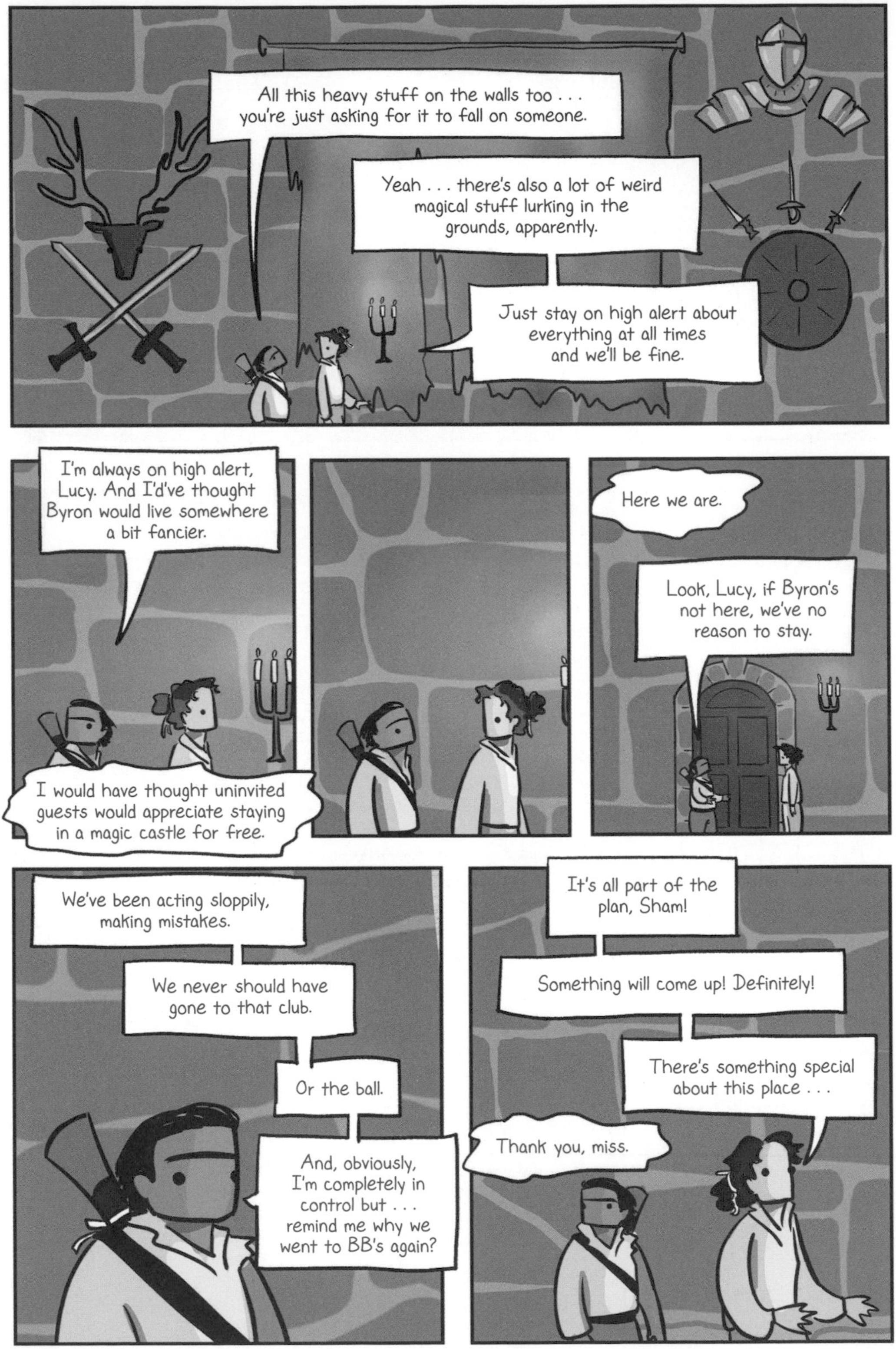
All this heavy stuff on the walls too . . . you're just asking for it to fall on someone.
Yeah . . . there's also a lot of weird magical stuff lurking in the grounds, apparently.
Just stay on high alert about everything at all times and we'll be fine.
I'm always on high alert, Lucy. And I'd've thought Byron would live somewhere a bit fancier.
I would have thought uninvited guests would appreciate staying in a magic castle for free.
Here we are.
Look, Lucy, if Byron's not here, we've no reason to stay.
We've been acting sloppily, making mistakes.
We never should have gone to that club.
Or the ball.
And, obviously, I'm completely in control but . . . remind me why we went to BB's again?
It's all part of the plan, Sham!
Something will come up! Definitely!
There's something special about this place . . .
Thank you, miss.

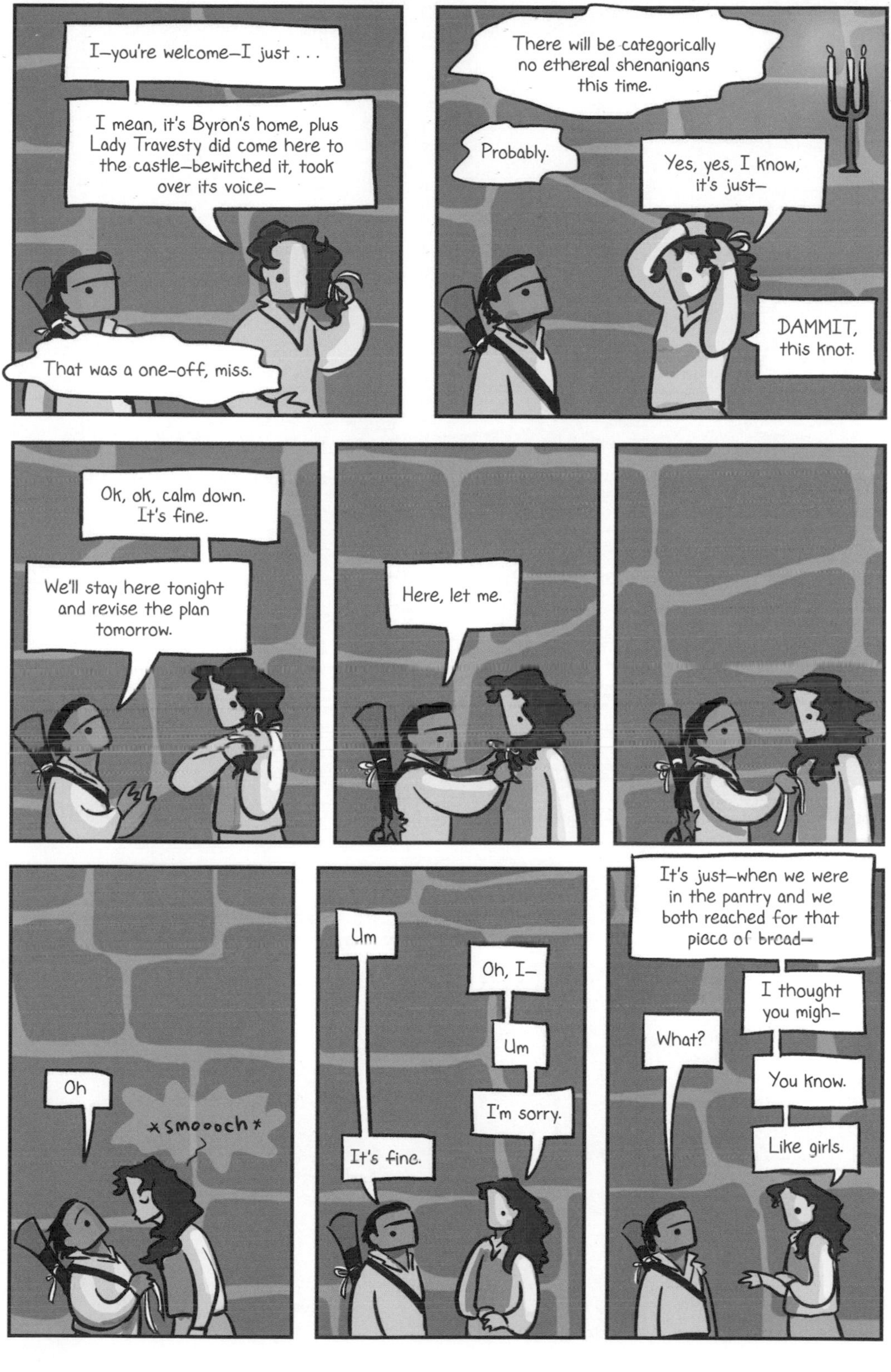

I—you're welcome—I just . . .
I mean, it's Byron's home, plus Lady Travesty did come here to the castle—bewitched it, took over its voice—
That was a one-off, miss.
There will be categorically no ethereal shenanigans this time.
Probably.
Yes, yes, I know, it's just—
DAMMIT, this knot.
Ok, ok, calm down. It's fine.
We'll stay here tonight and revise the plan tomorrow.
Here, let me.
Oh
smoooch
Um
Oh, I—
Um
I'm sorry.
It's fine.
It's just—when we were in the pantry and we both reached for that piece of bread—
I thought you migh—
What?
You know.
Like girls.

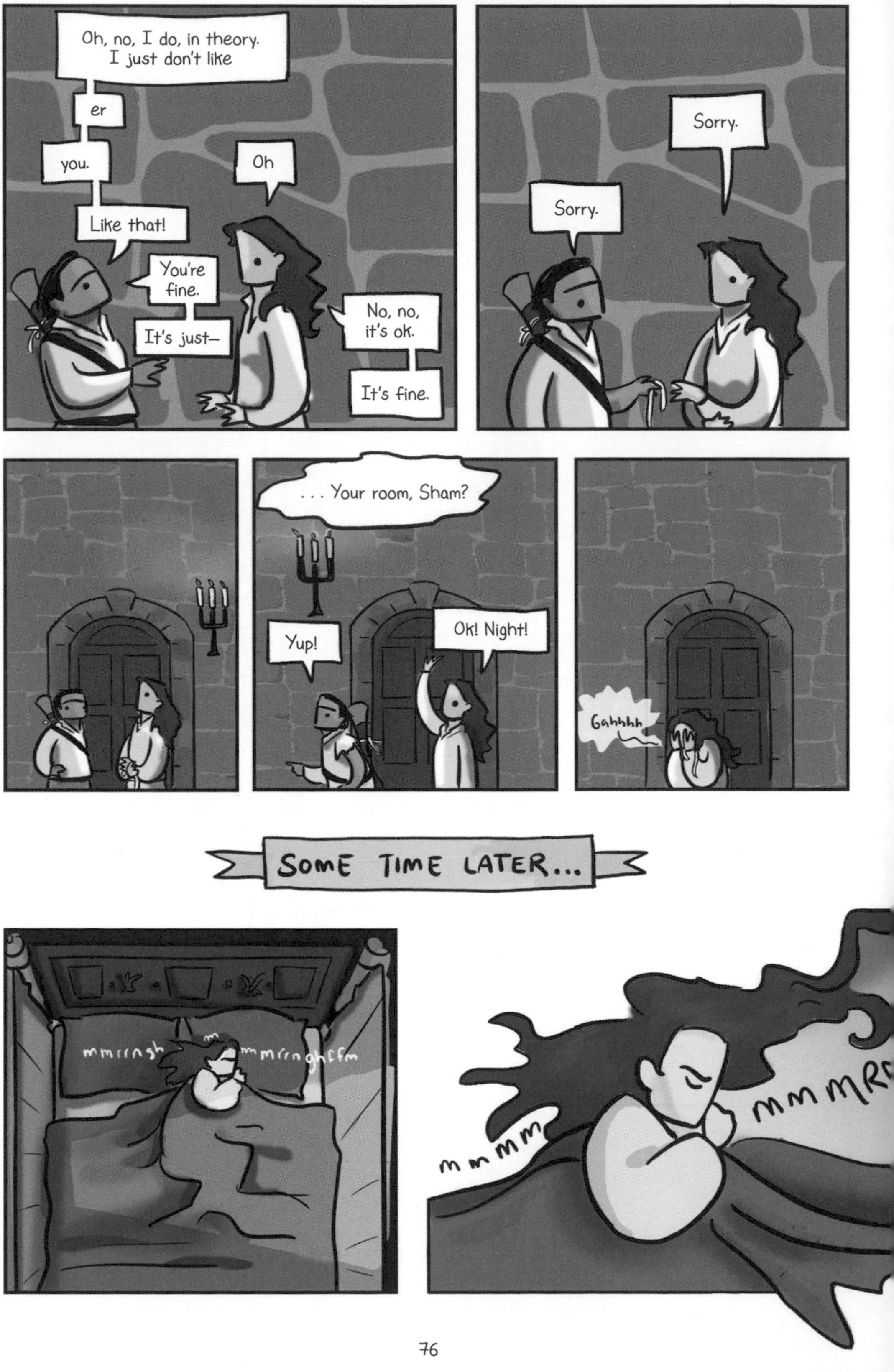
Oh, no, I do, in theory. I just don't like
er
you.
Like that!
Oh
You're fine.
It's just—
No, no, it's ok.
It's fine.
Sorry.
Sorry.
. . . Your room, Sham?
Yup!
Ok! Night!
Gahhhh
SOME TIME LATER...
mmrrngh
mm
mmrrnghffm
mmMM
MMMR

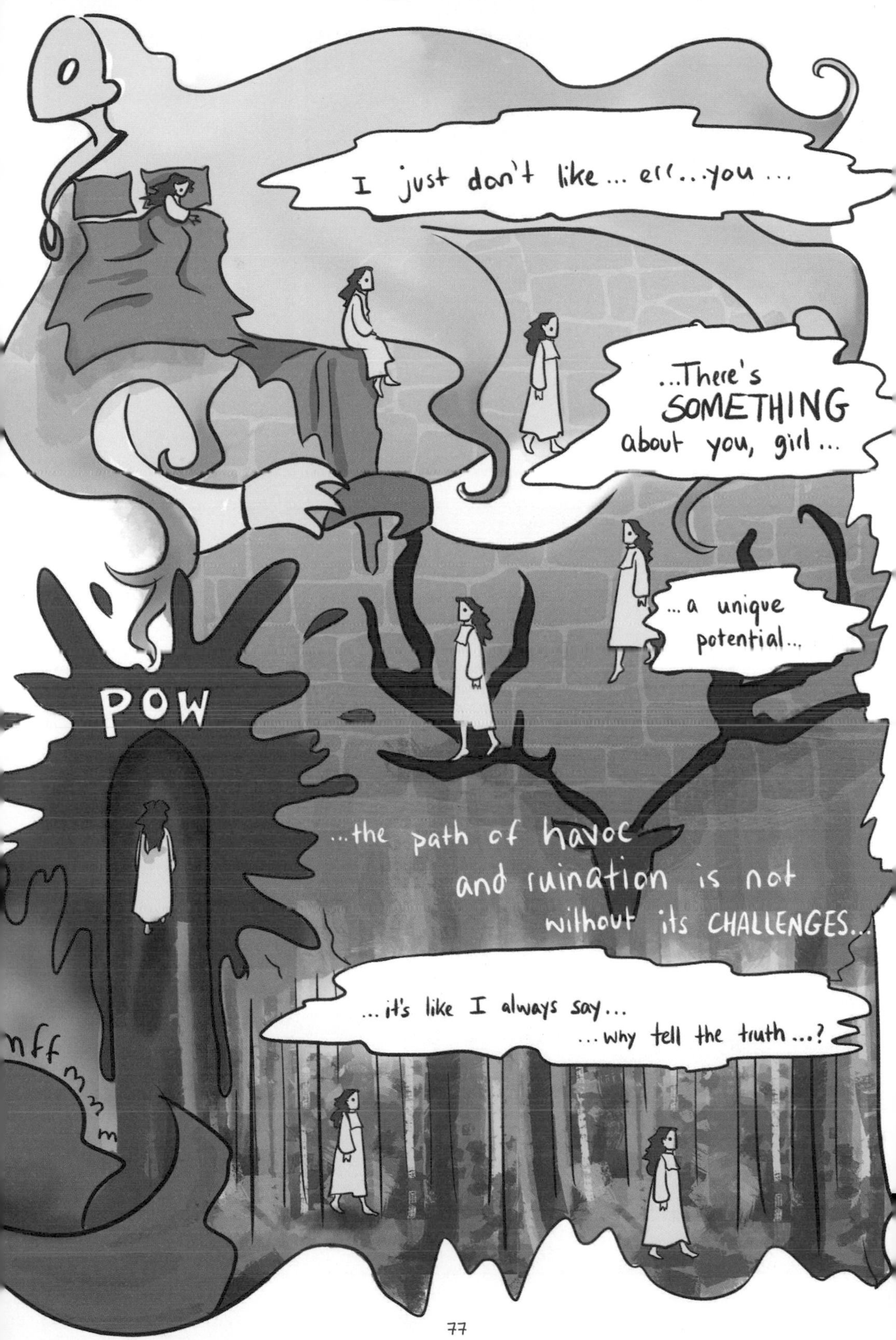
I just don't like... err...you...
...There's SOMETHING about you, girl...
...a unique potential...
POW
...the path of havoc and ruination is not without its CHALLENGES...
...it's like I always say... ...why tell the truth...?
nffmmm

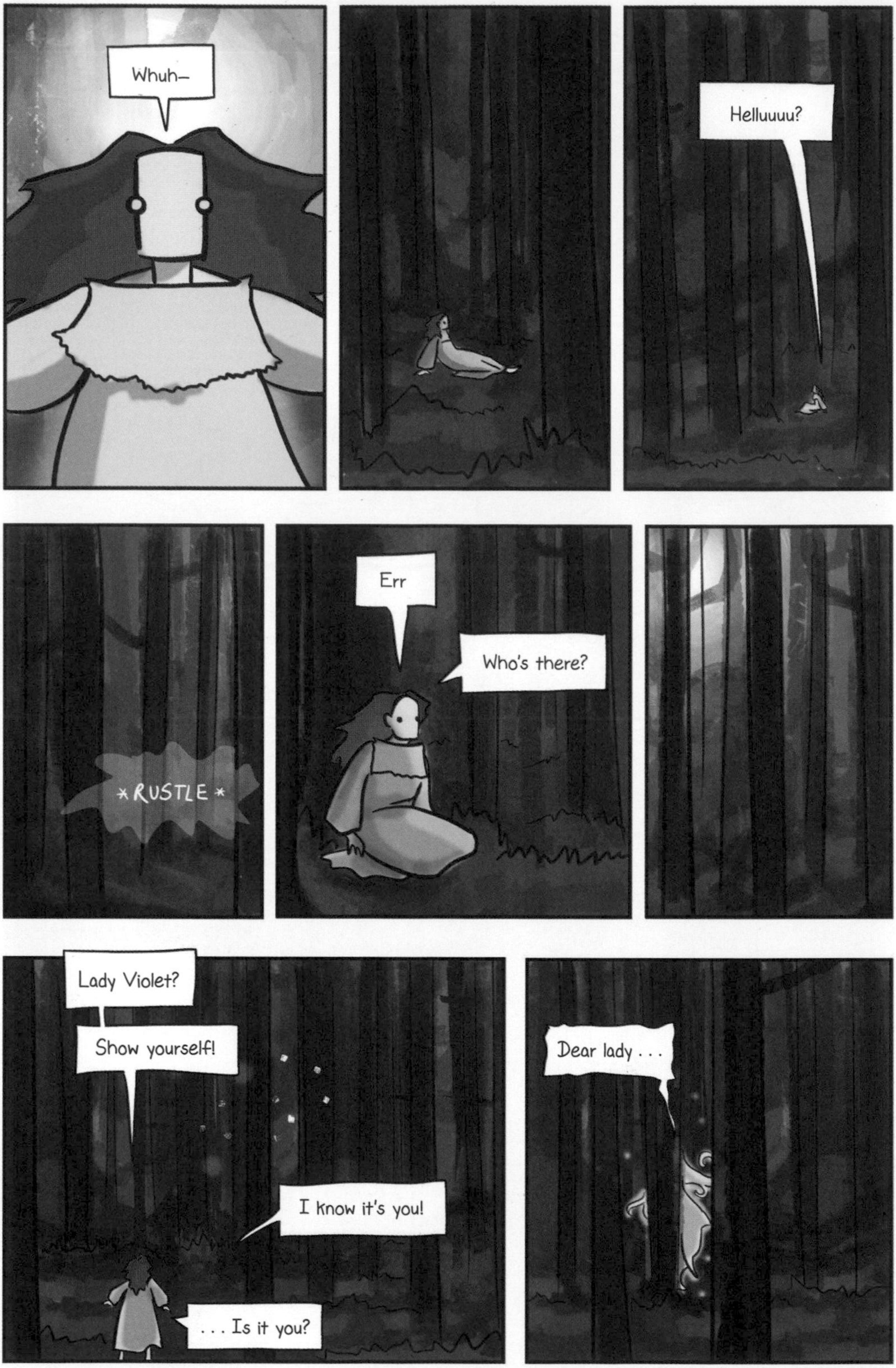
Whuh–
Helluuuu?
RUSTLE
Err
Who's there?
Lady Violet?
Show yourself!
I know it's you!
. . . Is it you?
Dear lady . . .

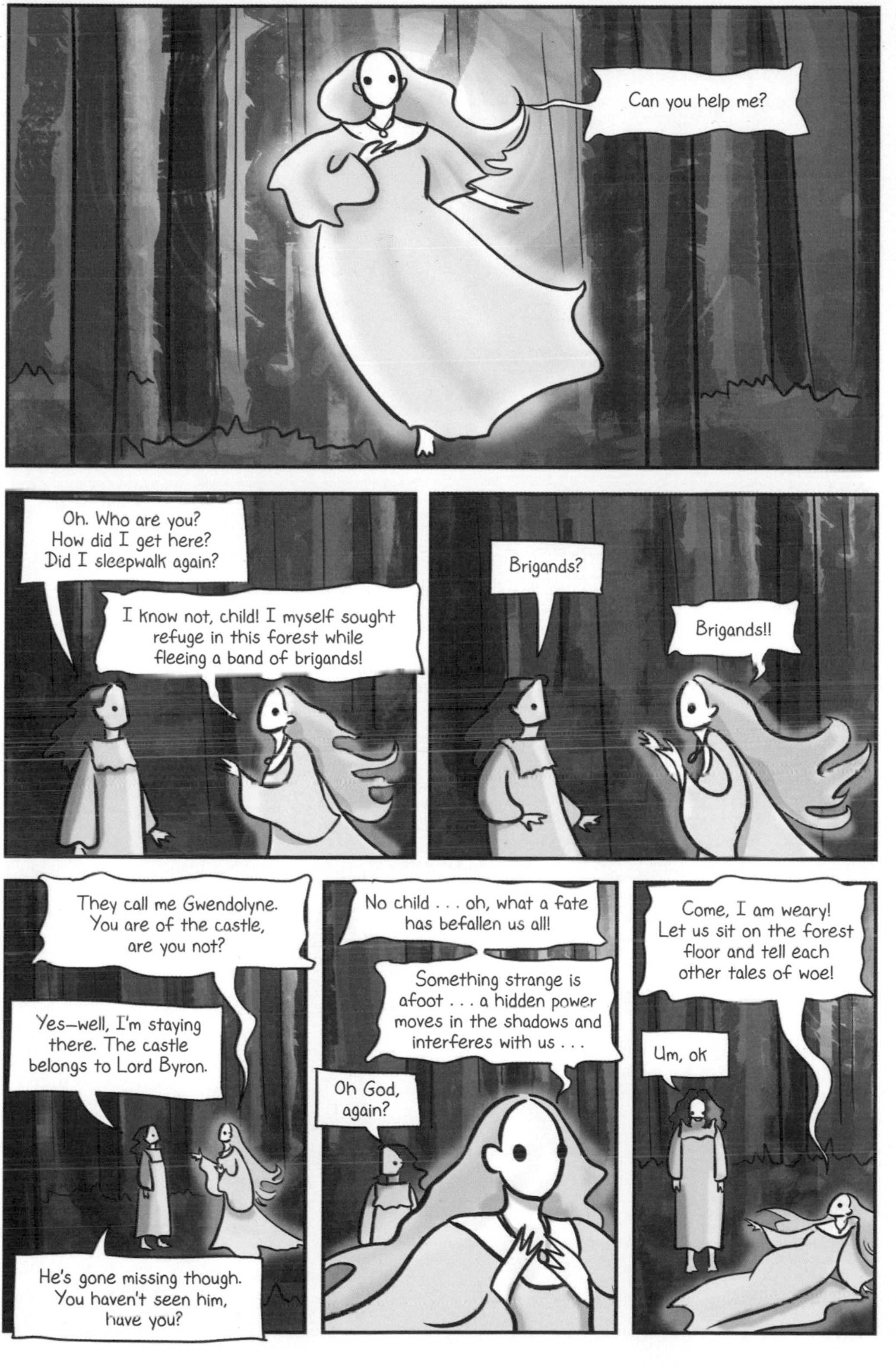
Can you help me?
Oh. Who are you? How did I get here? Did I sleepwalk again?
I know not, child! I myself sought refuge in this forest while fleeing a band of brigands!
Brigands?
Brigands!!
They call me Gwendolyne. You are of the castle, are you not?
Yes—well, I'm staying there. The castle belongs to Lord Byron.
He's gone missing though. You haven't seen him, have you?
No child . . . oh, what a fate has befallen us all!
Something strange is afoot . . . a hidden power moves in the shadows and interferes with us . . .
Oh God, again?
Come, I am weary! Let us sit on the forest floor and tell each other tales of woe!
Um, ok

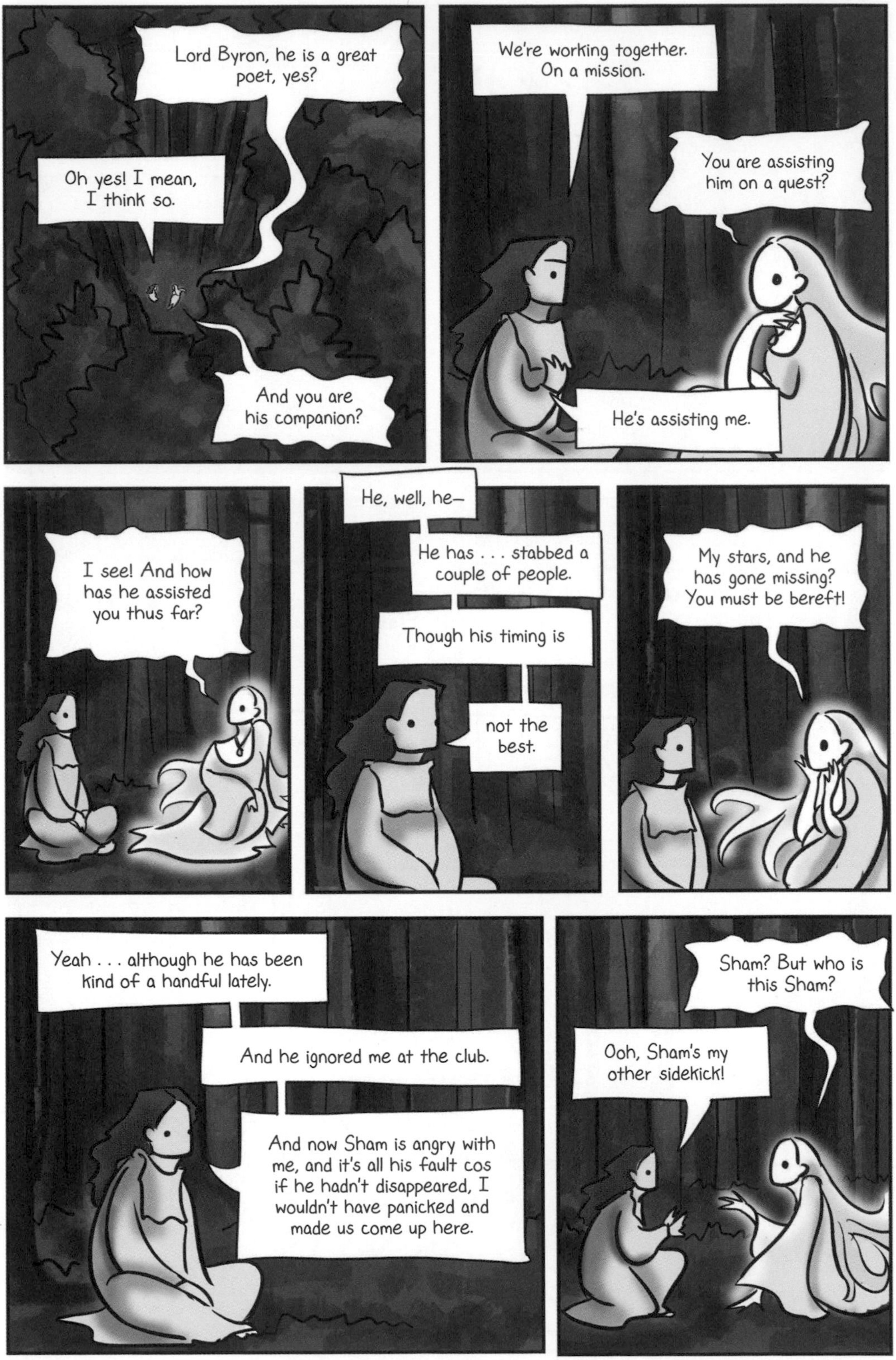
Lord Byron, he is a great poet, yes?
Oh yes! I mean, I think so.
And you are his companion?
We're working together. On a mission.
You are assisting him on a quest?
He's assisting me.
I see! And how has he assisted you thus far?
He, well, he–
He has . . . stabbed a couple of people.
Though his timing is
not the best.
My stars, and he has gone missing? You must be bereft!
Yeah . . . although he has been kind of a handful lately.
And he ignored me at the club.
And now Sham is angry with me, and it's all his fault cos if he hadn't disappeared, I wouldn't have panicked and made us come up here.
Sham? But who is this Sham?
Ooh, Sham's my other sidekick!

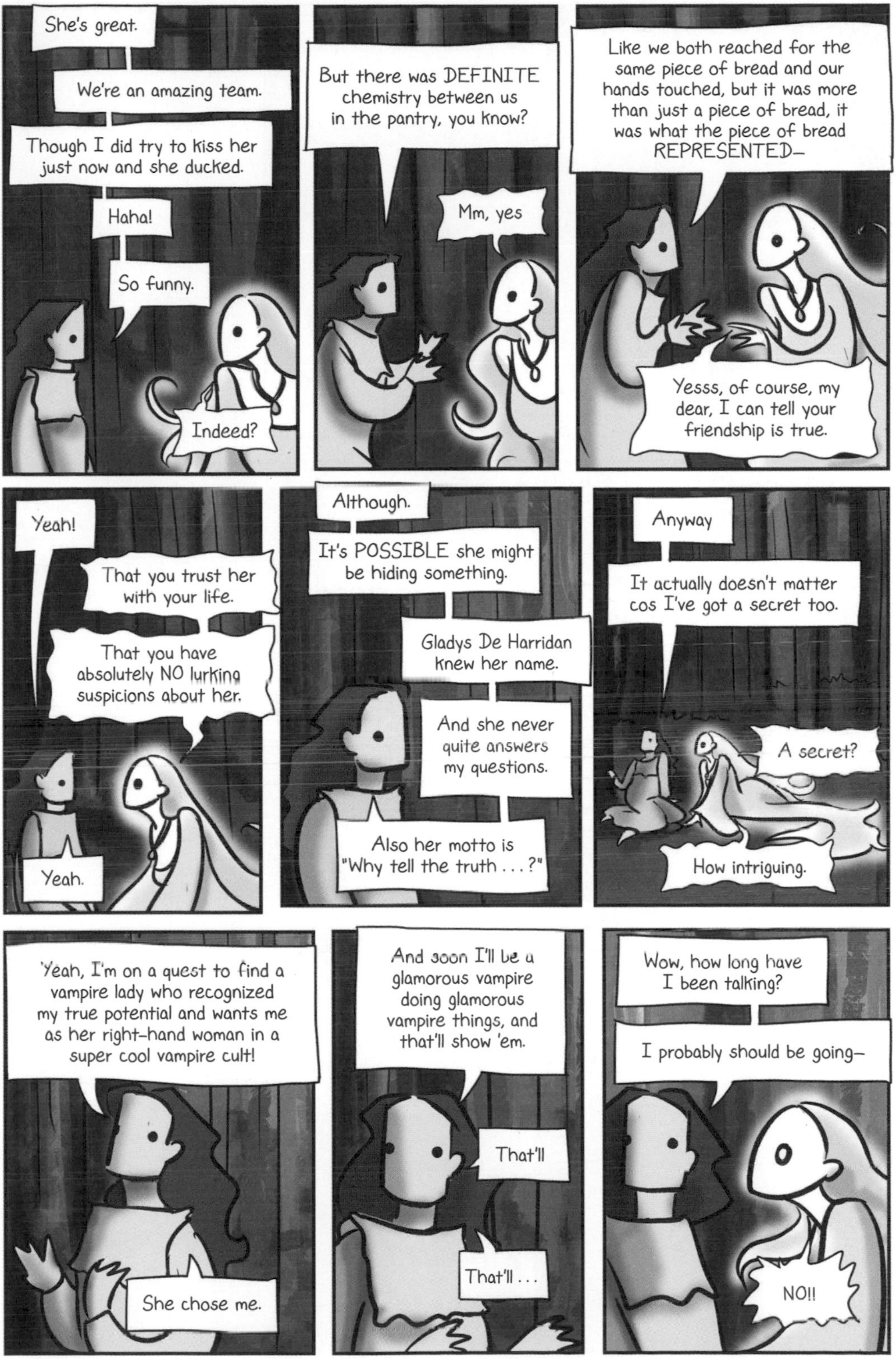
She's great.
We're an amazing team.
Though I did try to kiss her just now and she ducked.
Haha!
So funny.
Indeed?
But there was DEFINITE chemistry between us in the pantry, you know?
Mm, yes
Like we both reached for the same piece of bread and our hands touched, but it was more than just a piece of bread, it was what the piece of bread REPRESENTED—
Yesss, of course, my dear, I can tell your friendship is true.
Yeah!
That you trust her with your life.
That you have absolutely NO lurking suspicions about her.
Yeah.
Although.
It's POSSIBLE she might be hiding something.
Gladys De Harridan knew her name.
And she never quite answers my questions.
Also her motto is "Why tell the truth . . . ?"
Anyway
It actually doesn't matter cos I've got a secret too.
A secret?
How intriguing.
Yeah, I'm on a quest to find a vampire lady who recognized my true potential and wants me as her right-hand woman in a super cool vampire cult!
She chose me.
And soon I'll be a glamorous vampire doing glamorous vampire things, and that'll show 'em.
That'll
That'll . . .
Wow, how long have I been talking?
I probably should be going—
NO!!

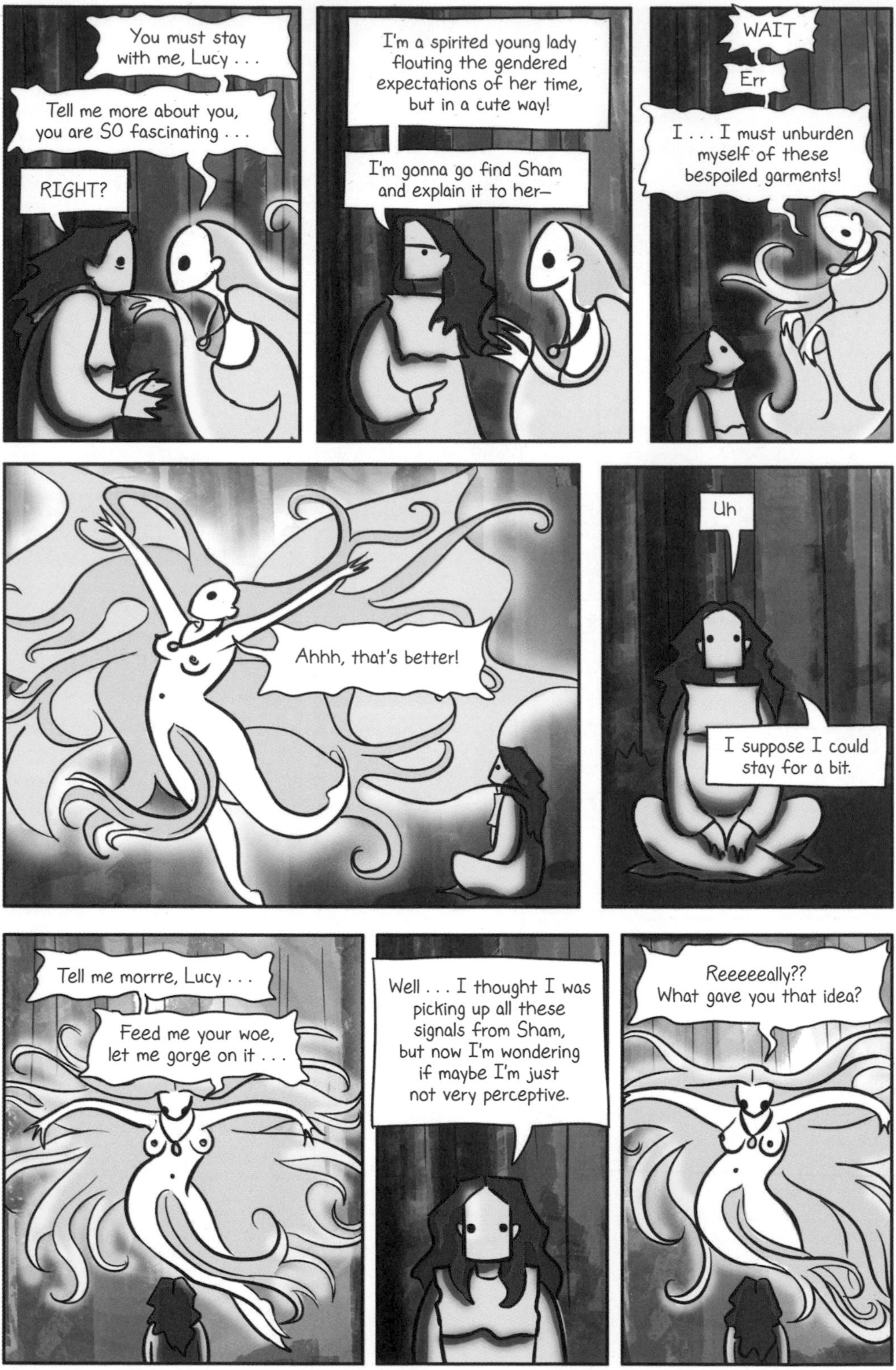
You must stay with me, Lucy . . .
Tell me more about you, you are SO fascinating . . .
RIGHT?
I'm a spirited young lady flouting the gendered expectations of her time, but in a cute way!
I'm gonna go find Sham and explain it to her—
WAIT
Err
I . . . I must unburden myself of these bespoiled garments!
Ahhh, that's better!
Uh
I suppose I could stay for a bit.
Tell me morrre, Lucy . . .
Feed me your woe, let me gorge on it . . .
Well . . . I thought I was picking up all these signals from Sham, but now I'm wondering if maybe I'm just not very perceptive.
Reeeeeally?? What gave you that idea?

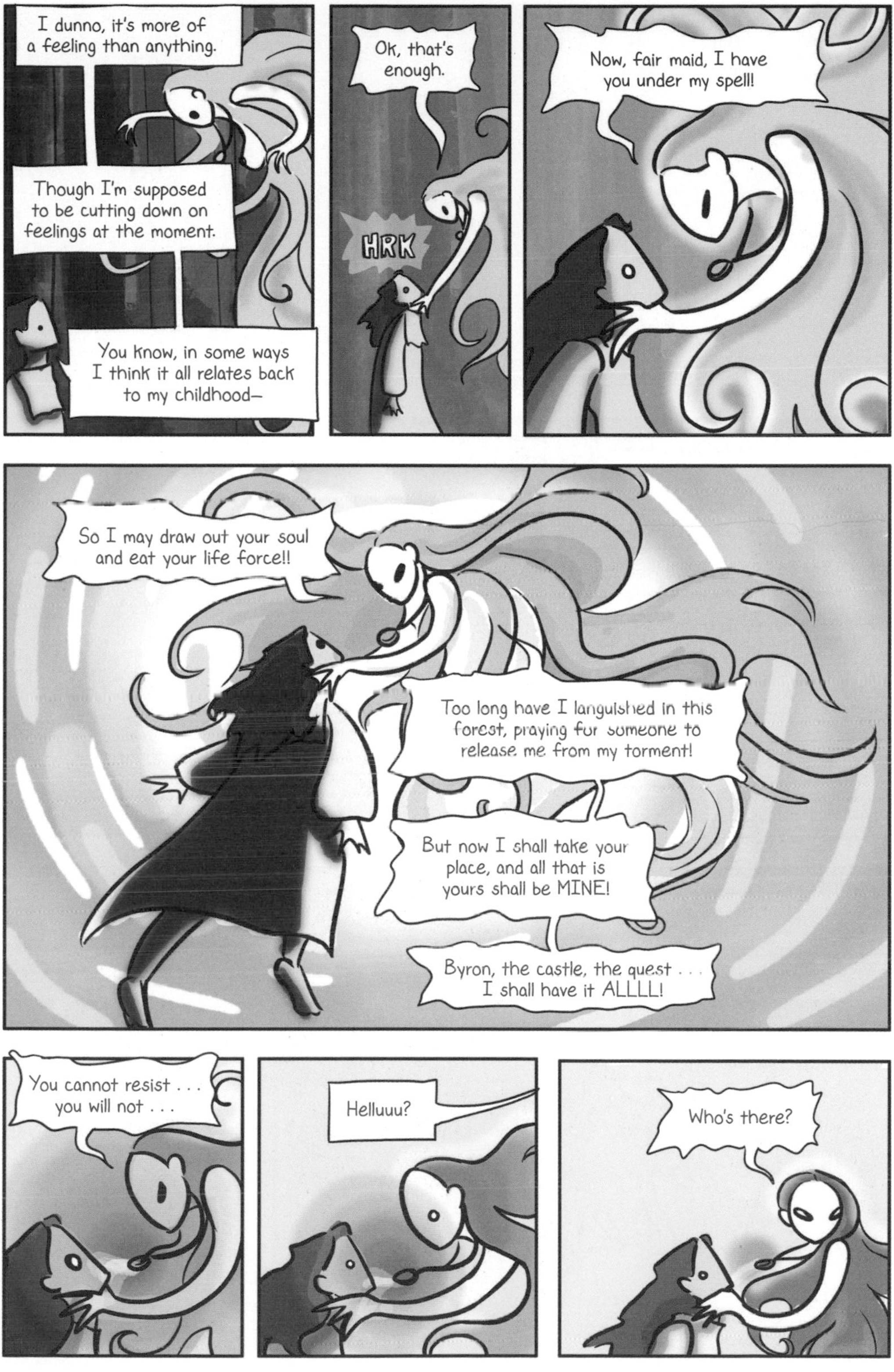

I dunno, it's more of a feeling than anything.
Though I'm supposed to be cutting down on feelings at the moment.
You know, in some ways I think it all relates back to my childhood—
Ok, that's enough.
HRK
Now, fair maid, I have you under my spell!
So I may draw out your soul and eat your life force!!
Too long have I languished in this forest, praying for someone to release me from my torment!
But now I shall take your place, and all that is yours shall be MINE!
Byron, the castle, the quest . . . I shall have it ALLLL!
You cannot resist . . . you will not . . .
Helluuu?
Who's there?

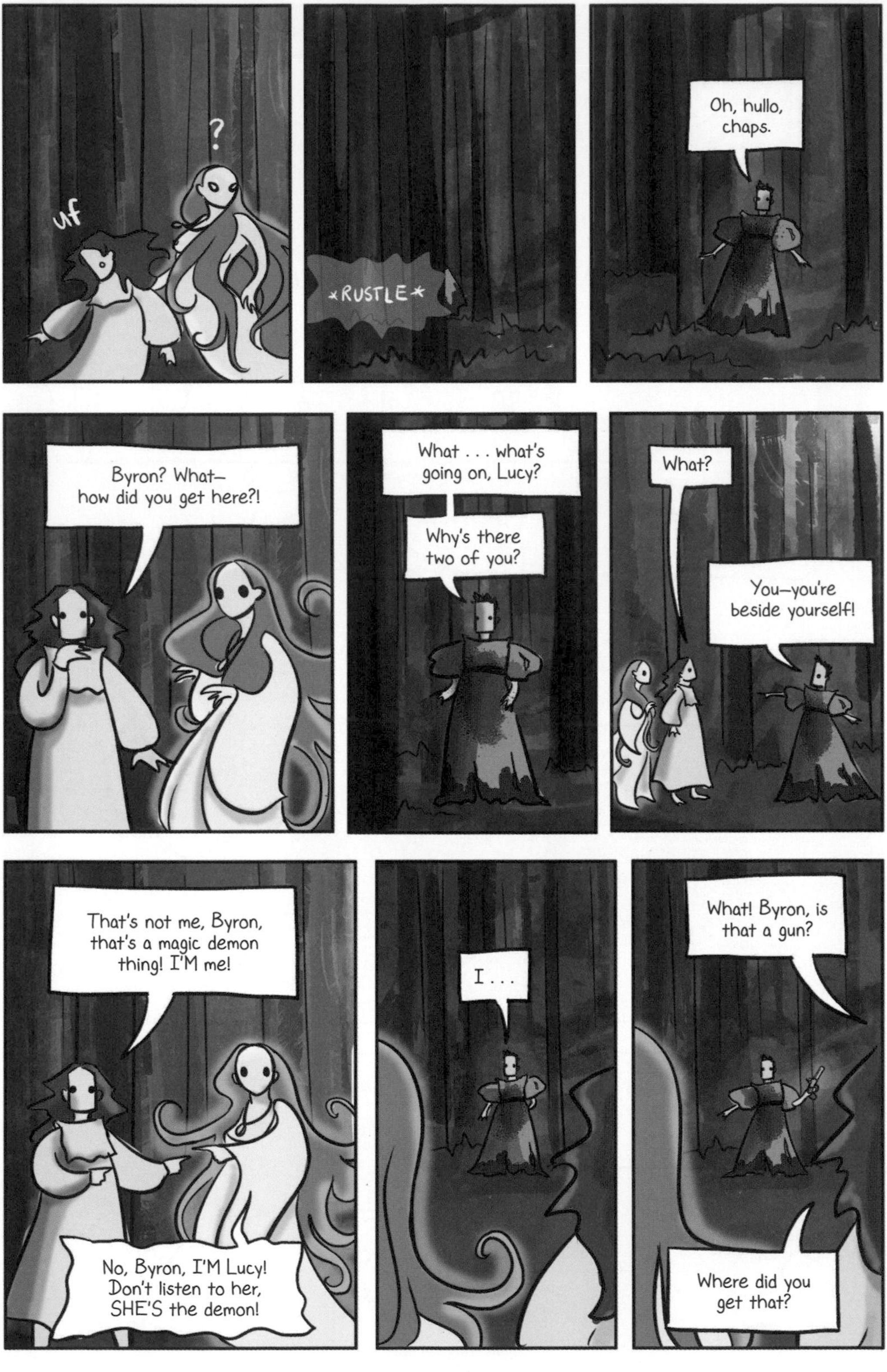
uf
?
RUSTLE
Oh, hullo, chaps.
Byron? What—how did you get here?!
What . . . what's going on, Lucy?
Why's there two of you?
What?
You—you're beside yourself!
That's not me, Byron, that's a magic demon thing! I'M me!
No, Byron, I'M Lucy! Don't listen to her, SHE'S the demon!
I . . .
What! Byron, is that a gun?
Where did you get that?

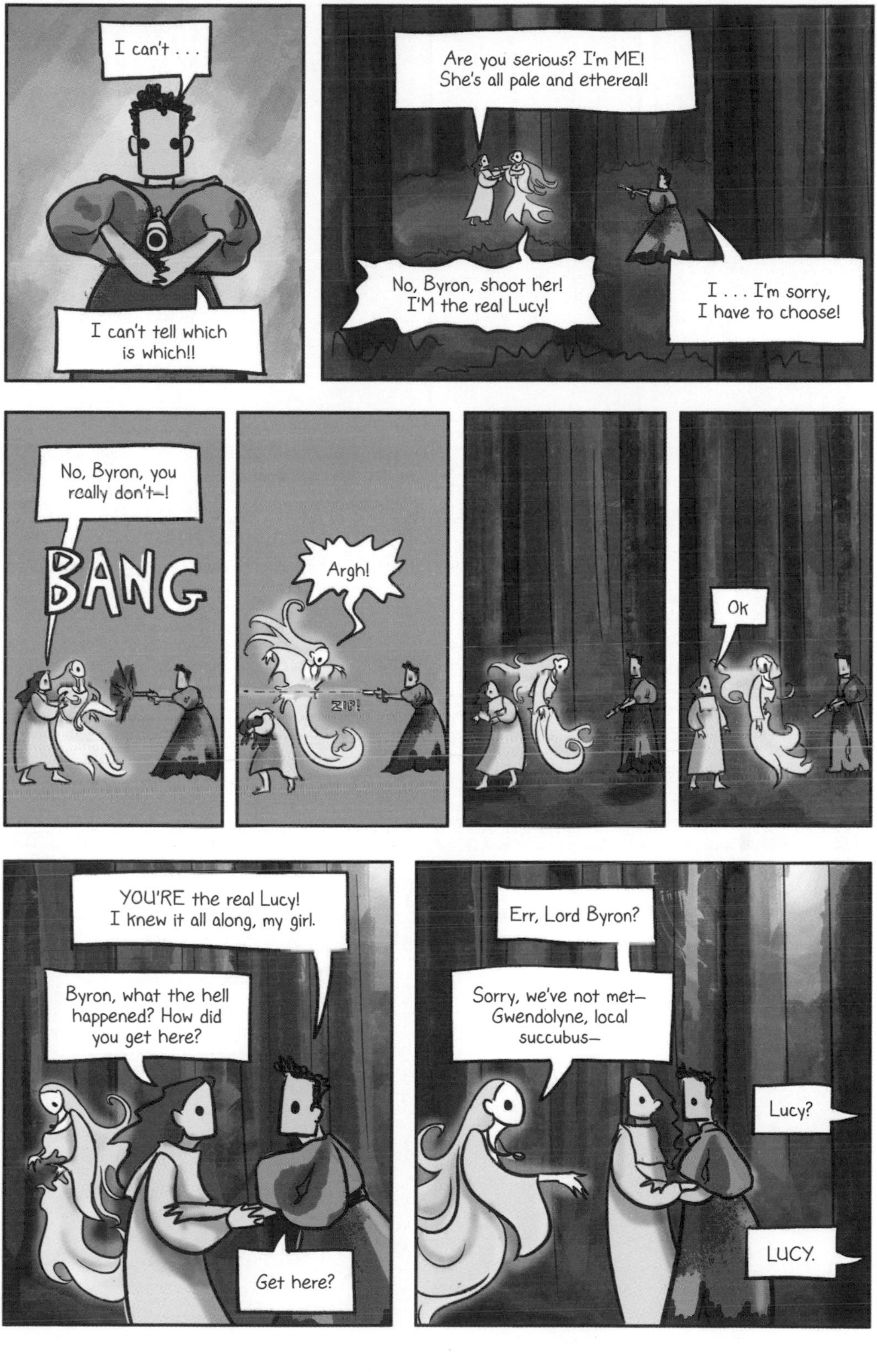

I can't . . .
I can't tell which is which!!
Are you serious? I'm ME! She's all pale and ethereal!
No, Byron, shoot her! I'M the real Lucy!
I . . . I'm sorry, I have to choose!
No, Byron, you really don't—!
BANG
Argh!
ZIP!
Ok
YOU'RE the real Lucy! I knew it all along, my girl.
Byron, what the hell happened? How did you get here?
Get here?
Err, Lord Byron?
Sorry, we've not met— Gwendolyne, local succubus—
Lucy?
LUCY.

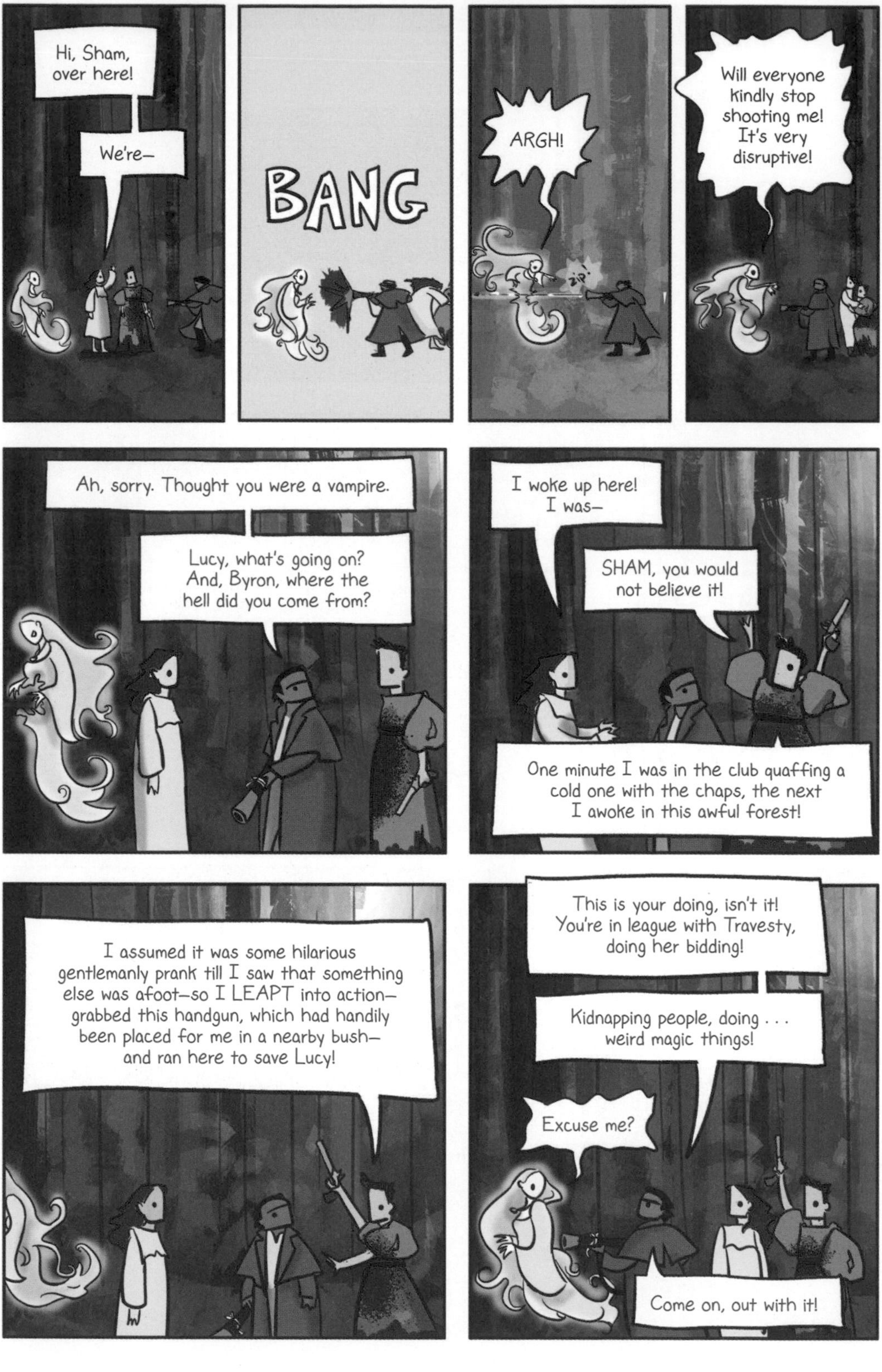
Hi, Sham, over here!
We're–
BANG
ARGH!
ZIP!
Will everyone kindly stop shooting me! It's very disruptive!
Ah, sorry. Thought you were a vampire.
Lucy, what's going on? And, Byron, where the hell did you come from?
I woke up here! I was–
SHAM, you would not believe it!
One minute I was in the club quaffing a cold one with the chaps, the next I awoke in this awful forest!
I assumed it was some hilarious gentlemanly prank till I saw that something else was afoot–so I LEAPT into action–grabbed this handgun, which had handily been placed for me in a nearby bush–and ran here to save Lucy!
This is your doing, isn't it! You're in league with Travesty, doing her bidding!
Kidnapping people, doing . . . weird magic things!
Excuse me?
Come on, out with it!

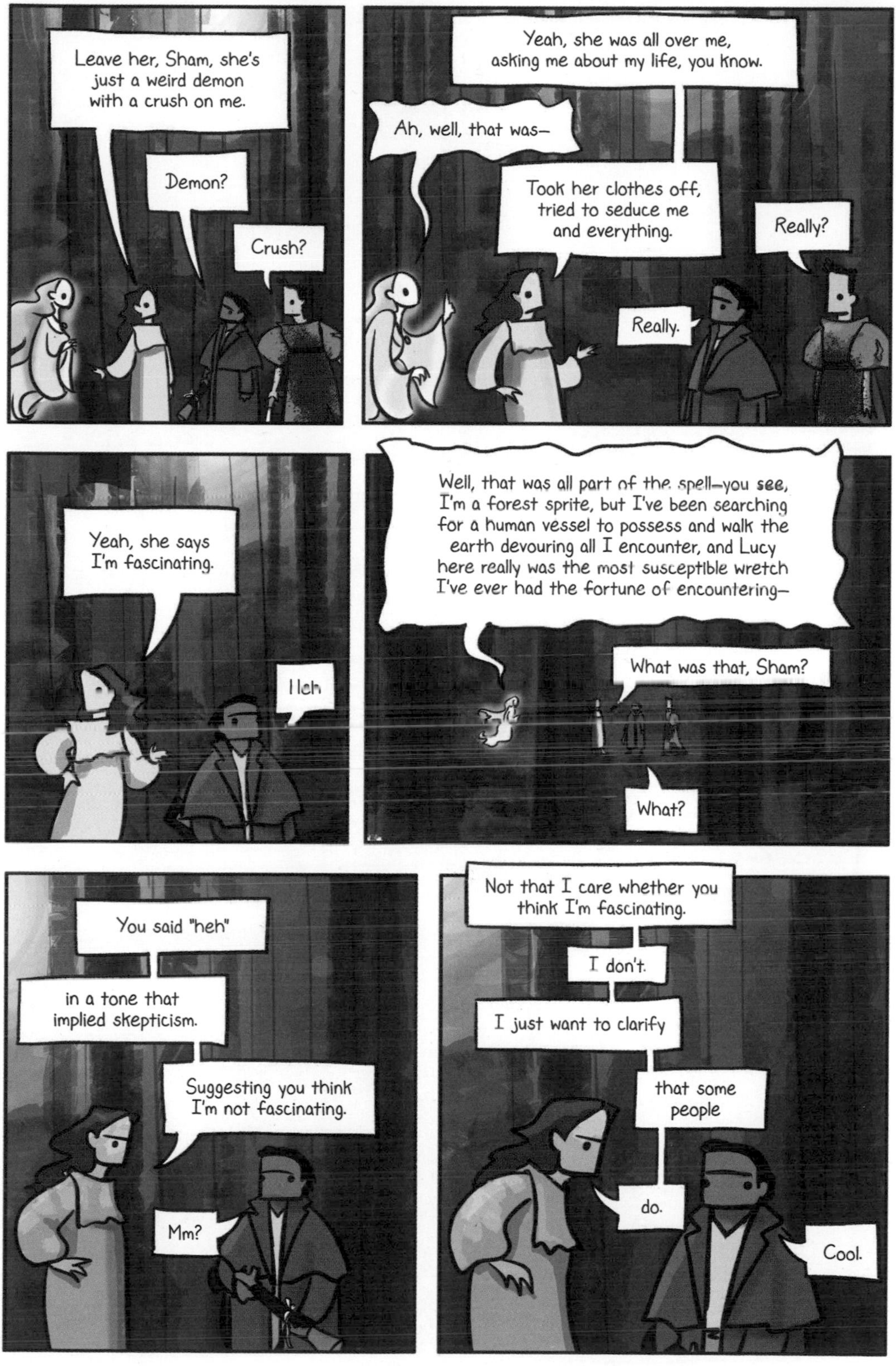

Leave her, Sham, she's just a weird demon with a crush on me.
Demon?
Crush?
Yeah, she was all over me, asking me about my life, you know.
Ah, well, that was–
Took her clothes off, tried to seduce me and everything.
Really?
Really.
Yeah, she says I'm fascinating.
Heh
Well, that was all part of the spell–you see, I'm a forest sprite, but I've been searching for a human vessel to possess and walk the earth devouring all I encounter, and Lucy here really was the most susceptible wretch I've ever had the fortune of encountering–
What was that, Sham?
What?
You said "heh"
in a tone that implied skepticism.
Suggesting you think I'm not fascinating.
Mm?
Not that I care whether you think I'm fascinating.
I don't.
I just want to clarify
that some people
do.
Cool.

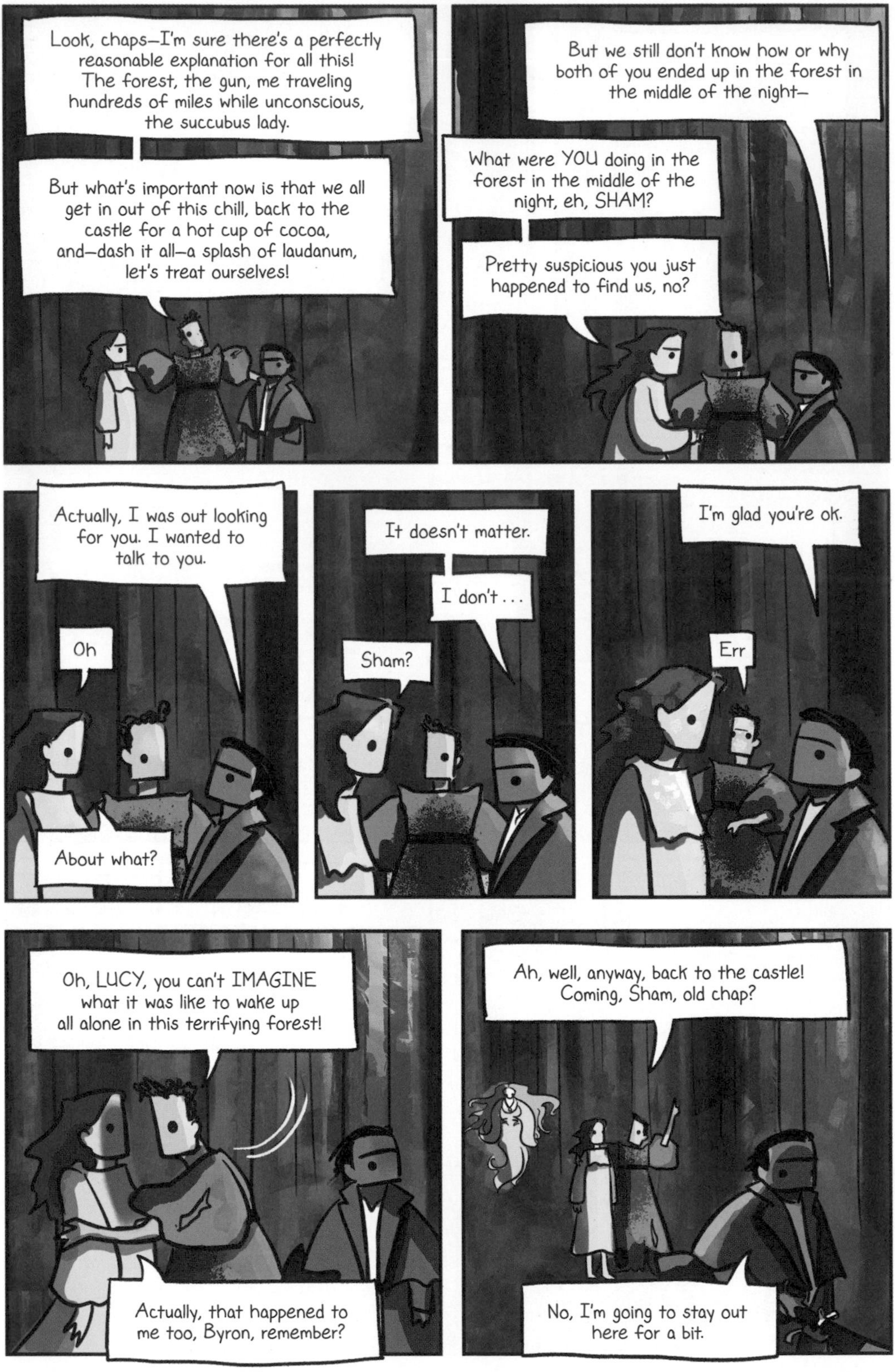
Look, chaps—I'm sure there's a perfectly reasonable explanation for all this! The forest, the gun, me traveling hundreds of miles while unconscious, the succubus lady.
But what's important now is that we all get in out of this chill, back to the castle for a hot cup of cocoa, and—dash it all—a splash of laudanum, let's treat ourselves!
But we still don't know how or why both of you ended up in the forest in the middle of the night—
What were YOU doing in the forest in the middle of the night, eh, SHAM?
Pretty suspicious you just happened to find us, no?
Actually, I was out looking for you. I wanted to talk to you.
Oh
About what?
It doesn't matter.
I don't . . .
Sham?
I'm glad you're ok.
Err
Oh, LUCY, you can't IMAGINE what it was like to wake up all alone in this terrifying forest!
Actually, that happened to me too, Byron, remember?
Ah, well, anyway, back to the castle! Coming, Sham, old chap?
No, I'm going to stay out here for a bit.

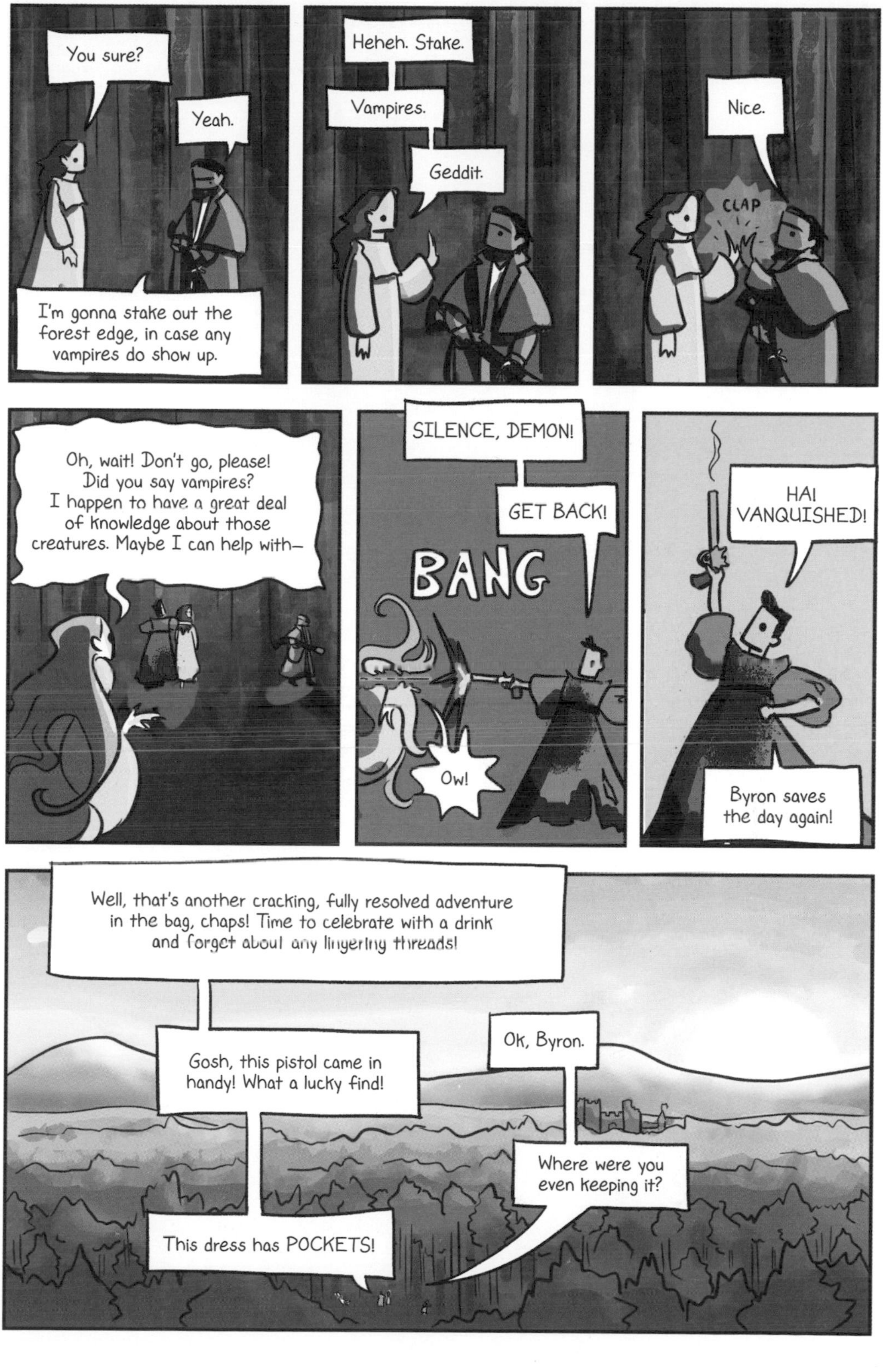

You sure?
Yeah.
I'm gonna stake out the forest edge, in case any vampires do show up.
Heheh. Stake.
Vampires.
Geddit.
Nice.
CLAP
Oh, wait! Don't go, please! Did you say vampires? I happen to have a great deal of knowledge about those creatures. Maybe I can help with—
SILENCE, DEMON!
GET BACK!
BANG
Ow!
HA! VANQUISHED!
Byron saves the day again!
Well, that's another cracking, fully resolved adventure in the bag, chaps! Time to celebrate with a drink and forget about any lingering threads!
Gosh, this pistol came in handy! What a lucky find!
This dress has POCKETS!
Ok, Byron.
Where were you even keeping it?

CHAPTER VI – THE CELLAR

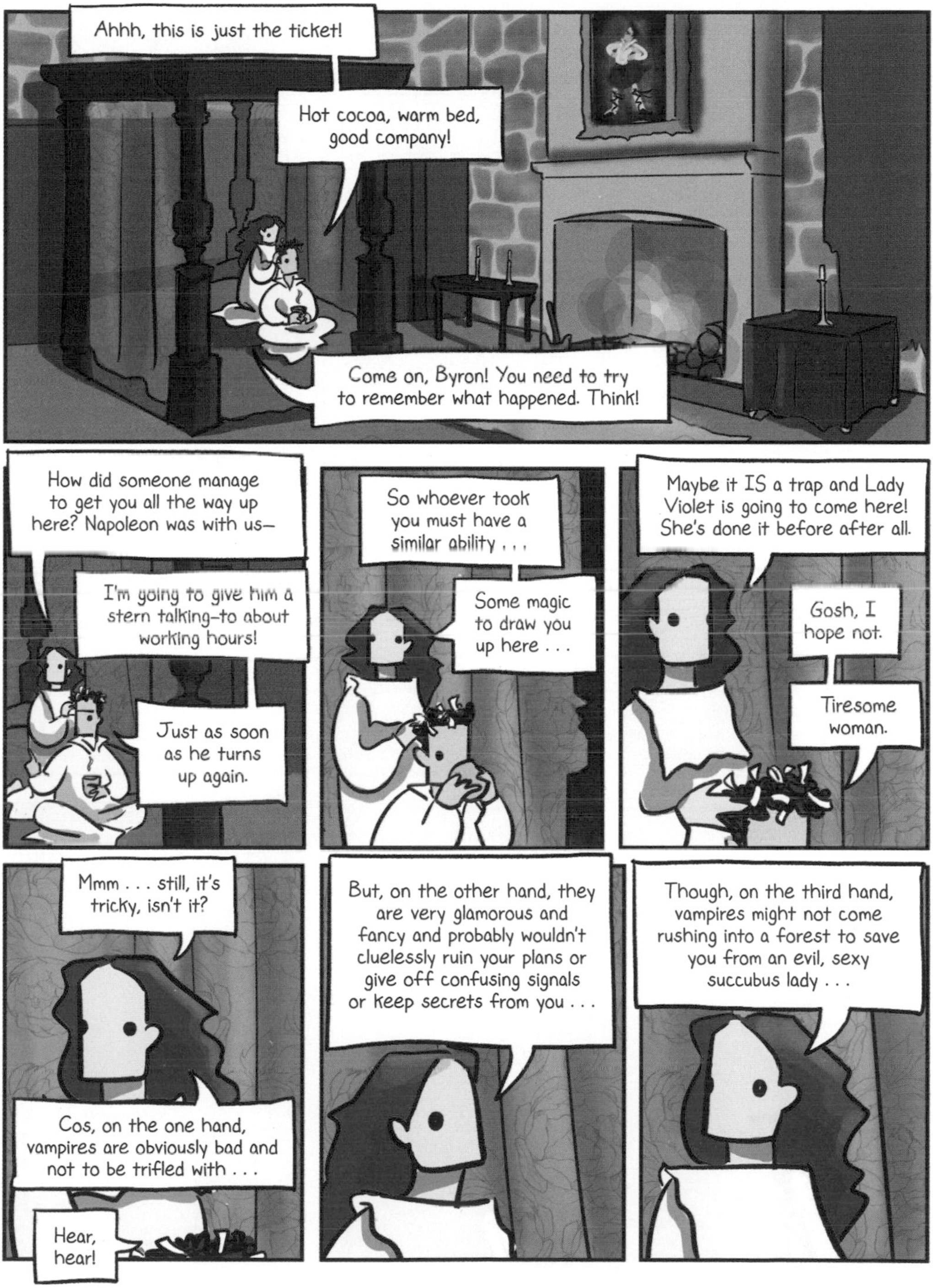
Ahhh, this is just the ticket!
Hot cocoa, warm bed, good company!
Come on, Byron! You need to try to remember what happened. Think!
How did someone manage to get you all the way up here? Napoleon was with us—
I'm going to give him a stern talking-to about working hours!
Just as soon as he turns up again.
So whoever took you must have a similar ability . . .
Some magic to draw you up here . . .
Maybe it IS a trap and Lady Violet is going to come here! She's done it before after all.
Gosh, I hope not.
Tiresome woman.
Mmm . . . still, it's tricky, isn't it?
Cos, on the one hand, vampires are obviously bad and not to be trifled with . . .
Hear, hear!
But, on the other hand, they are very glamorous and fancy and probably wouldn't cluelessly ruin your plans or give off confusing signals or keep secrets from you . . .
Though, on the third hand, vampires might not come rushing into a forest to save you from an evil, sexy succubus lady . . .

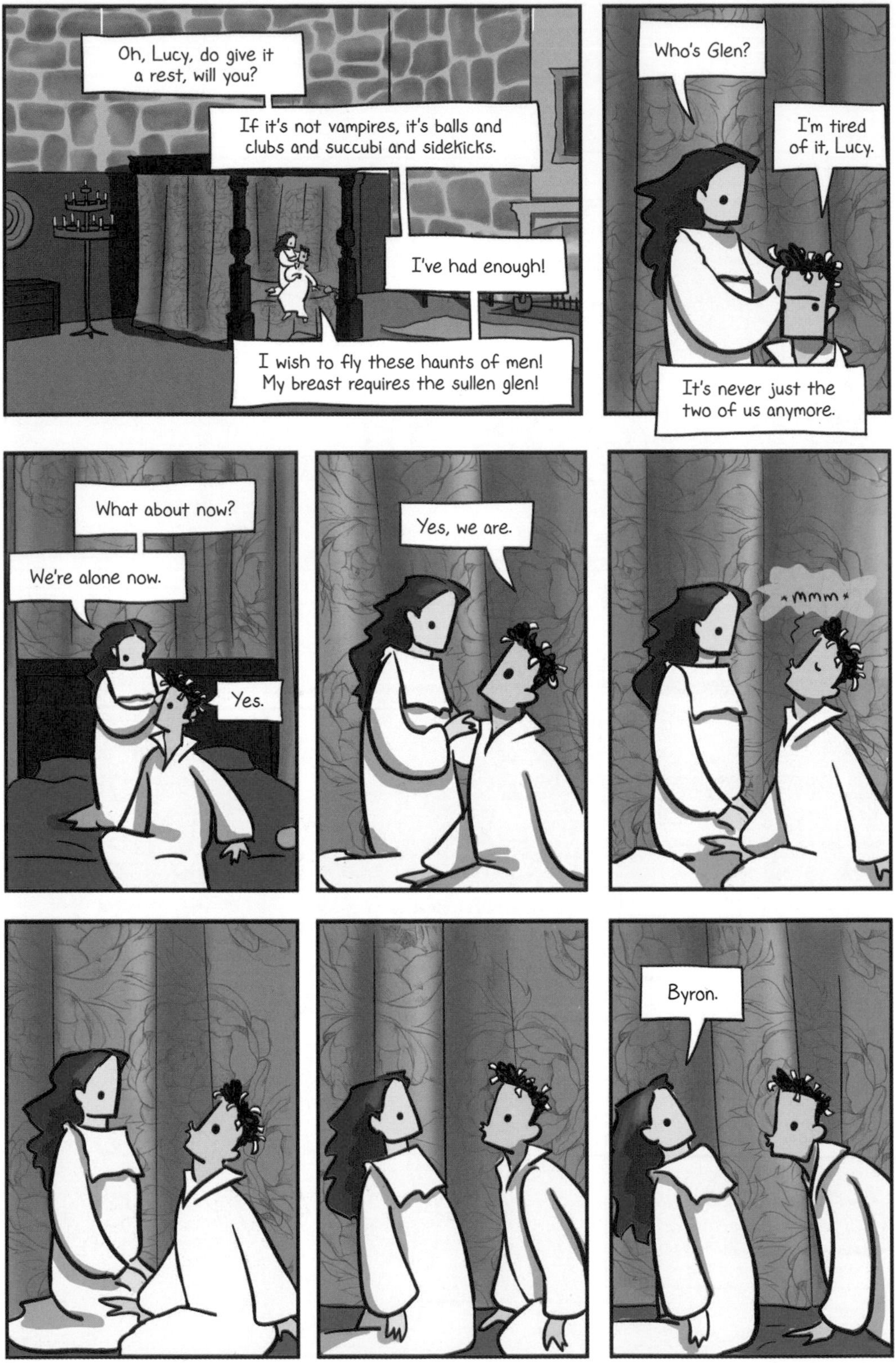
Oh, Lucy, do give it a rest, will you?
If it's not vampires, it's balls and clubs and succubi and sidekicks.
I've had enough!
I wish to fly these haunts of men! My breast requires the sullen glen!
Who's Glen?
I'm tired of it, Lucy.
It's never just the two of us anymore.
What about now?
We're alone now.
Yes.
Yes, we are.
mmm
Byron.

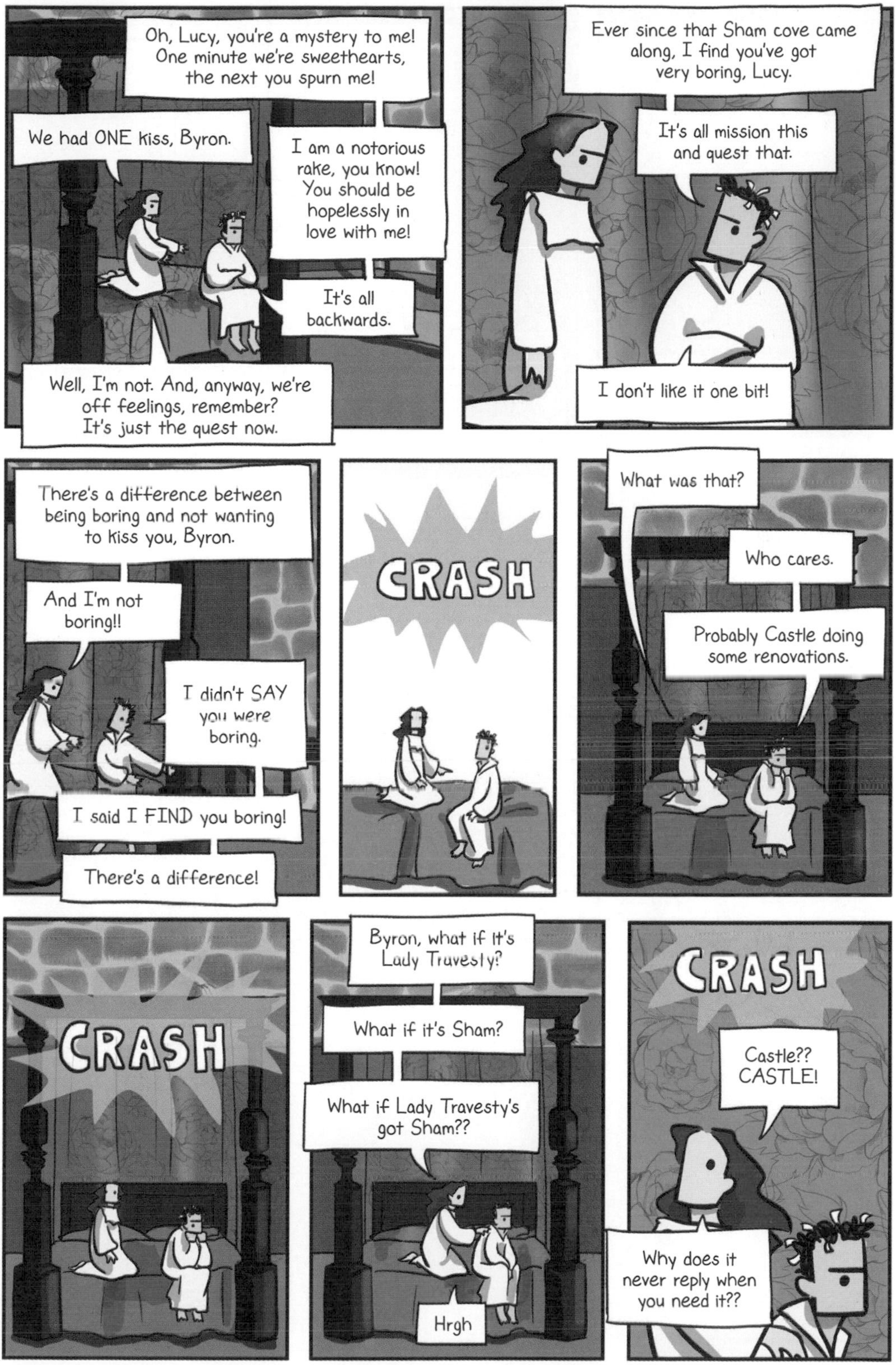

Oh, Lucy, you're a mystery to me! One minute we're sweethearts, the next you spurn me!
We had ONE kiss, Byron.
I am a notorious rake, you know! You should be hopelessly in love with me!
It's all backwards.
Well, I'm not. And, anyway, we're off feelings, remember? It's just the quest now.
Ever since that Sham cove came along, I find you've got very boring, Lucy.
It's all mission this and quest that.
I don't like it one bit!
There's a difference between being boring and not wanting to kiss you, Byron.
And I'm not boring!!
I didn't SAY you were boring.
I said I FIND you boring!
There's a difference!
CRASH
What was that?
Who cares.
Probably Castle doing some renovations.
CRASH
Byron, what if it's Lady Travesty?
What if it's Sham?
What if Lady Travesty's got Sham??
Hrgh
CRASH
Castle?? CASTLE!
Why does it never reply when you need it??

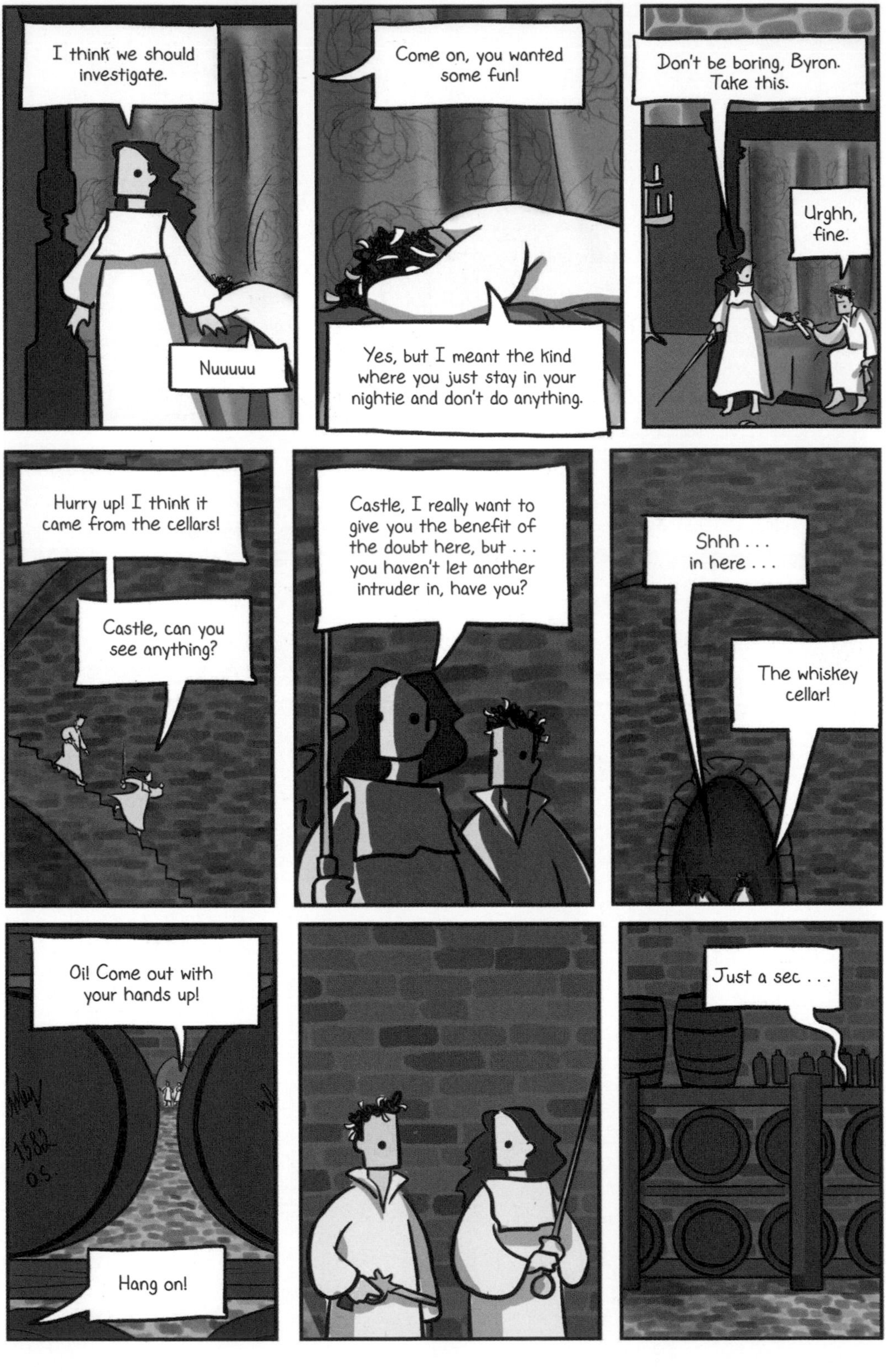
I think we should investigate.
Nuuuuu
Come on, you wanted some fun!
Yes, but I meant the kind where you just stay in your nightie and don't do anything.
Don't be boring, Byron. Take this.
Urghh, fine.
Hurry up! I think it came from the cellars!
Castle, can you see anything?
Castle, I really want to give you the benefit of the doubt here, but . . . you haven't let another intruder in, have you?
Shhh . . . in here . . .
The whiskey cellar!
Oi! Come out with your hands up!
Hang on!
Just a sec . . .

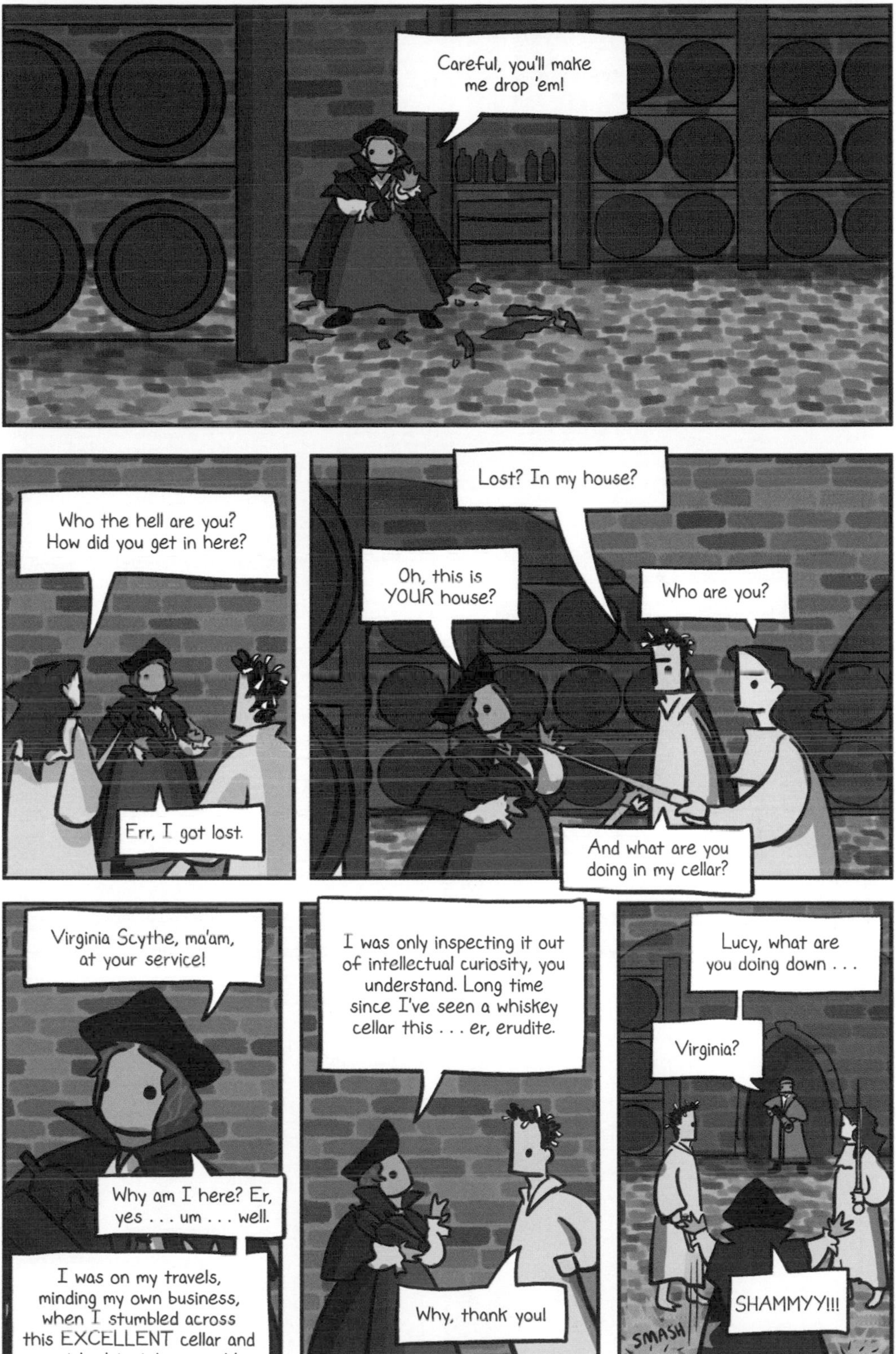
Careful, you'll make me drop 'em!
Who the hell are you? How did you get in here?
Err, I got lost.
Lost? In my house?
Oh, this is YOUR house?
Who are you?
And what are you doing in my cellar?
Virginia Scythe, ma'am, at your service!
Why am I here? Er, yes . . . um . . . well.
I was on my travels, minding my own business, when I stumbled across this EXCELLENT cellar and just had to take a peek!
I was only inspecting it out of intellectual curiosity, you understand. Long time since I've seen a whiskey cellar this . . . er, erudite.
Why, thank you!
Lucy, what are you doing down . . .
Virginia?
SHAMMYY!!!
SMASH

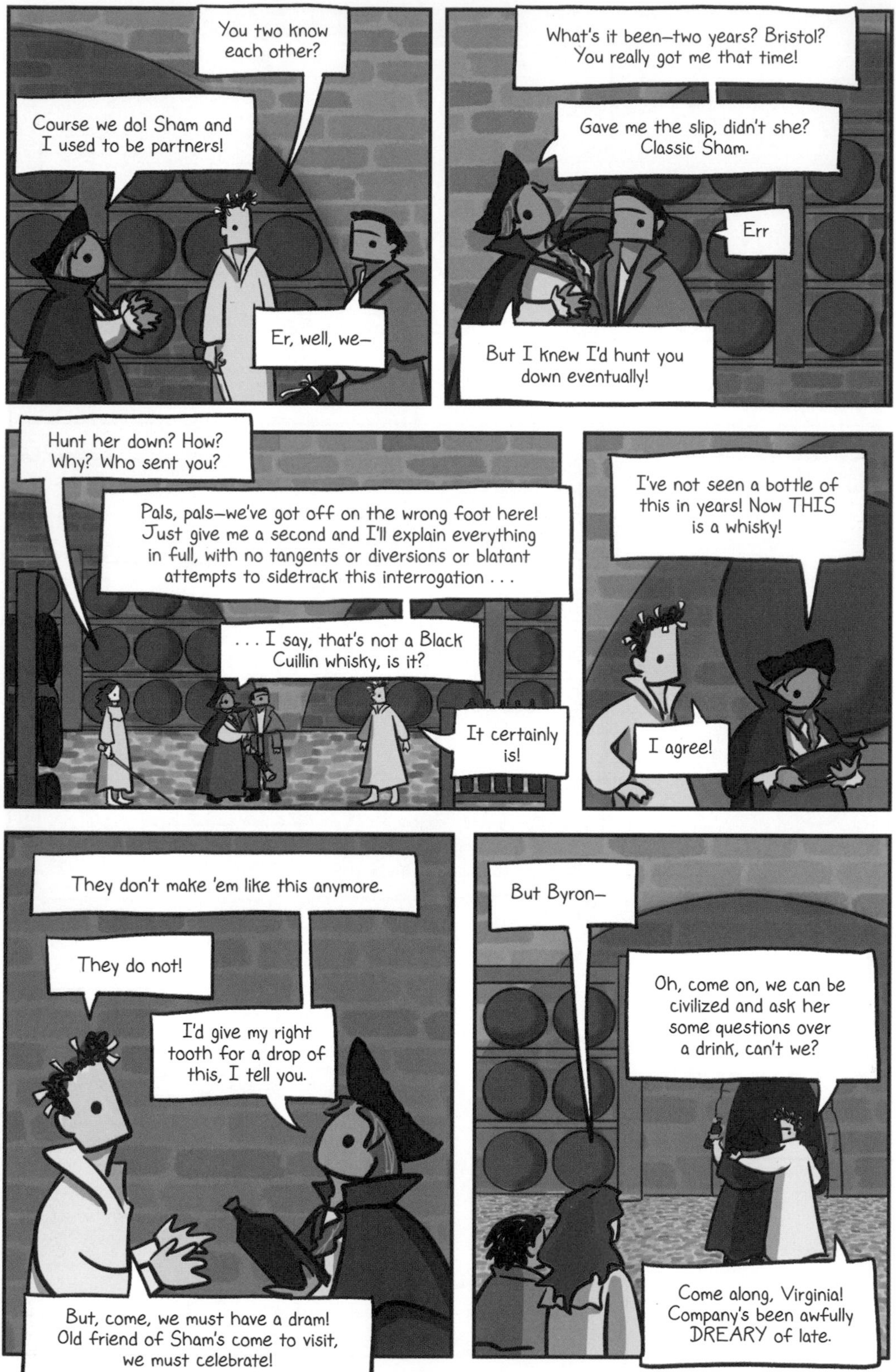
You two know each other?
Course we do! Sham and I used to be partners!
Er, well, we—
What's it been—two years? Bristol? You really got me that time!
Gave me the slip, didn't she? Classic Sham.
Err
But I knew I'd hunt you down eventually!
Hunt her down? How? Why? Who sent you?
Pals, pals—we've got off on the wrong foot here! Just give me a second and I'll explain everything in full, with no tangents or diversions or blatant attempts to sidetrack this interrogation . . .
. . . I say, that's not a Black Cuillin whisky, is it?
It certainly is!
I've not seen a bottle of this in years! Now THIS is a whisky!
I agree!
They don't make 'em like this anymore.
They do not!
I'd give my right tooth for a drop of this, I tell you.
But, come, we must have a dram! Old friend of Sham's come to visit, we must celebrate!
But Byron—
Oh, come on, we can be civilized and ask her some questions over a drink, can't we?
Come along, Virginia! Company's been awfully DREARY of late.

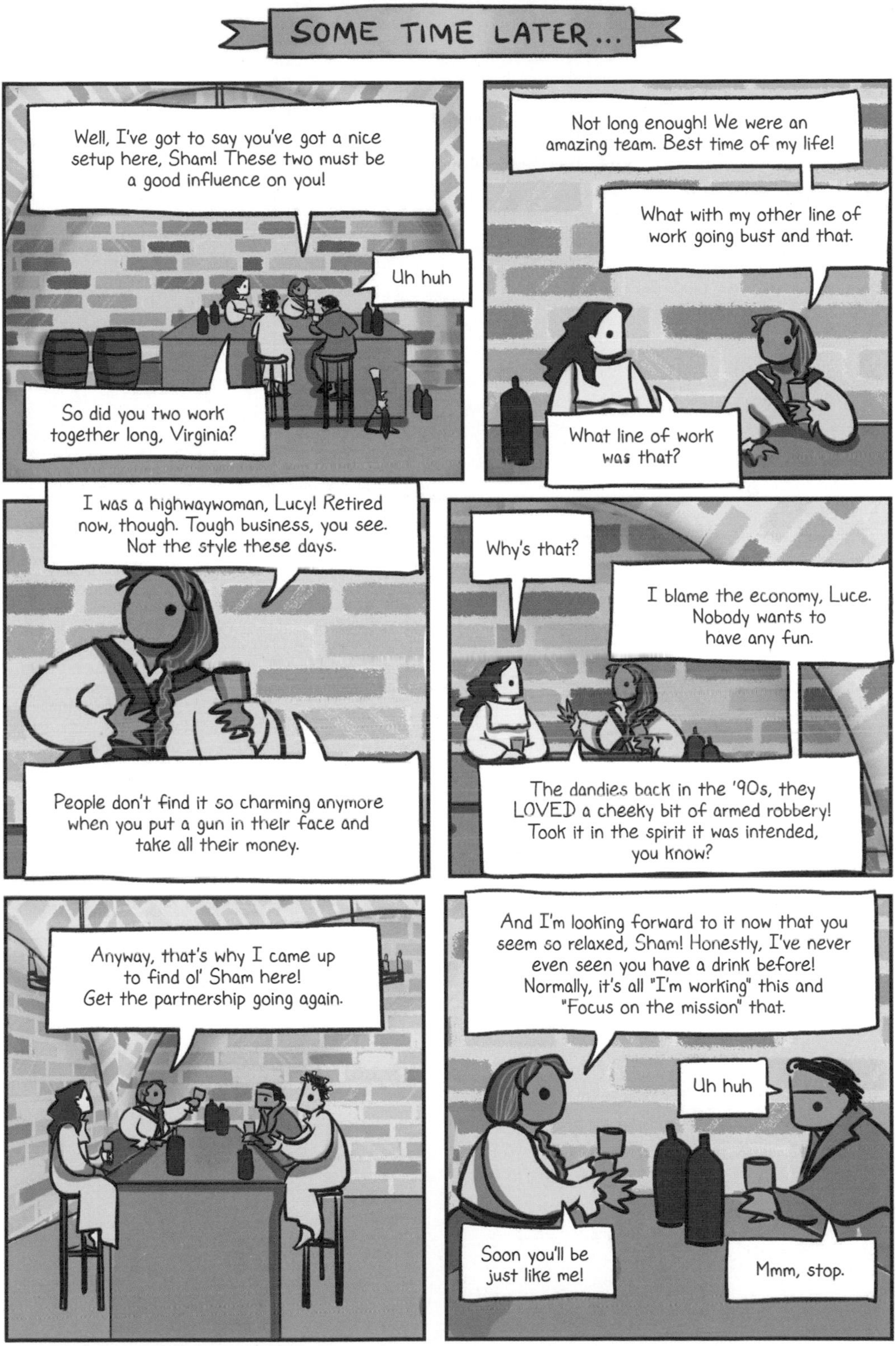
SOME TIME LATER...
Well, I've got to say you've got a nice setup here, Sham! These two must be a good influence on you!
Uh huh
So did you two work together long, Virginia?
Not long enough! We were an amazing team. Best time of my life!
What with my other line of work going bust and that.
What line of work was that?
I was a highwaywoman, Lucy! Retired now, though. Tough business, you see. Not the style these days.
People don't find it so charming anymore when you put a gun in their face and take all their money.
Why's that?
I blame the economy, Luce. Nobody wants to have any fun.
The dandies back in the '90s, they LOVED a cheeky bit of armed robbery! Took it in the spirit it was intended, you know?
Anyway, that's why I came up to find ol' Sham here! Get the partnership going again.
And I'm looking forward to it now that you seem so relaxed, Sham! Honestly, I've never even seen you have a drink before! Normally, it's all "I'm working" this and "Focus on the mission" that.
Uh huh
Soon you'll be just like me!
Mmm, stop.

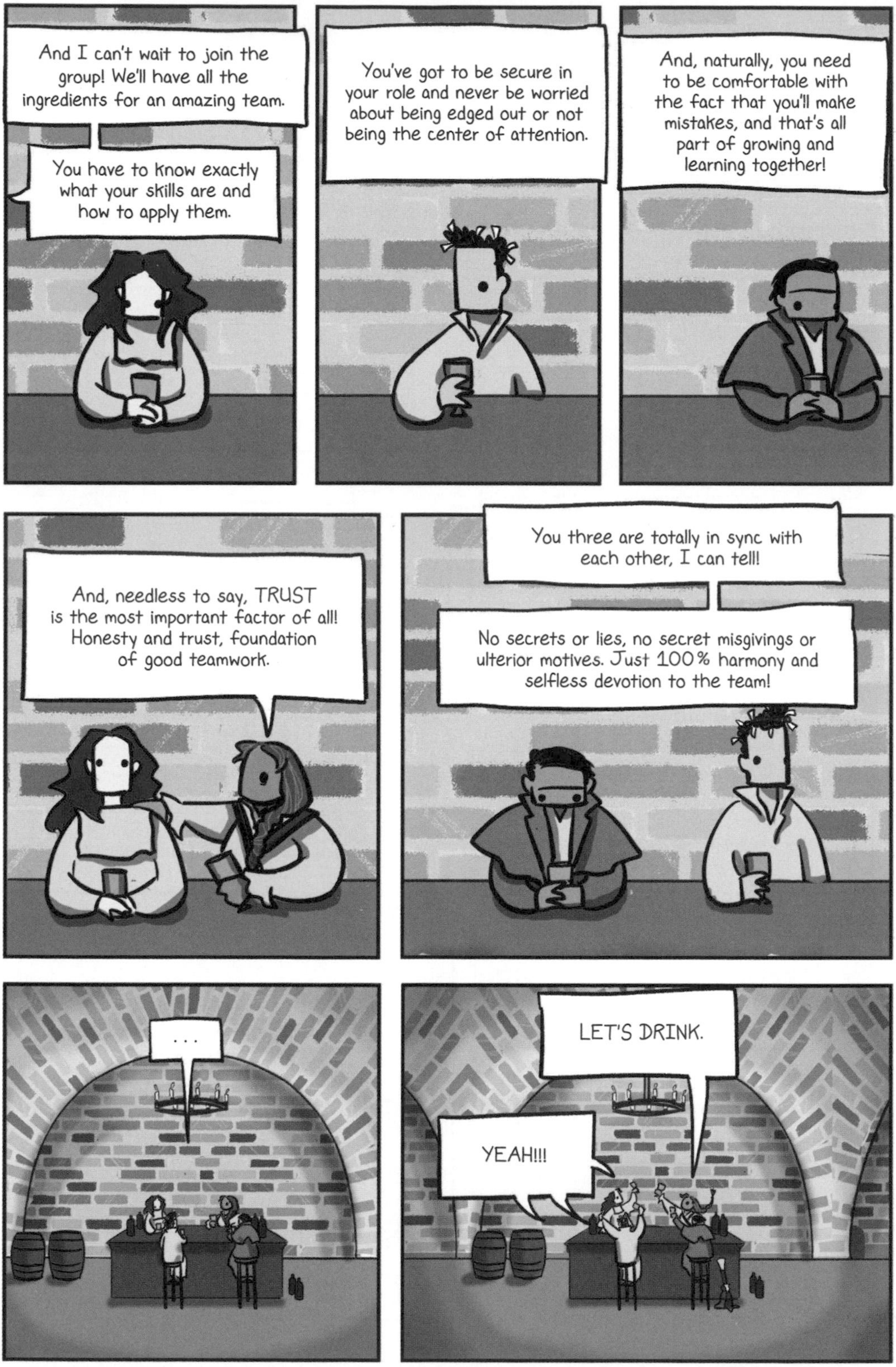
And I can't wait to join the group! We'll have all the ingredients for an amazing team.
You have to know exactly what your skills are and how to apply them.
You've got to be secure in your role and never be worried about being edged out or not being the center of attention.
And, naturally, you need to be comfortable with the fact that you'll make mistakes, and that's all part of growing and learning together!
And, needless to say, TRUST is the most important factor of all! Honesty and trust, foundation of good teamwork.
You three are totally in sync with each other, I can tell!
No secrets or lies, no secret misgivings or ulterior motives. Just 100% harmony and selfless devotion to the team!
. . .
LET'S DRINK.
YEAH!!!

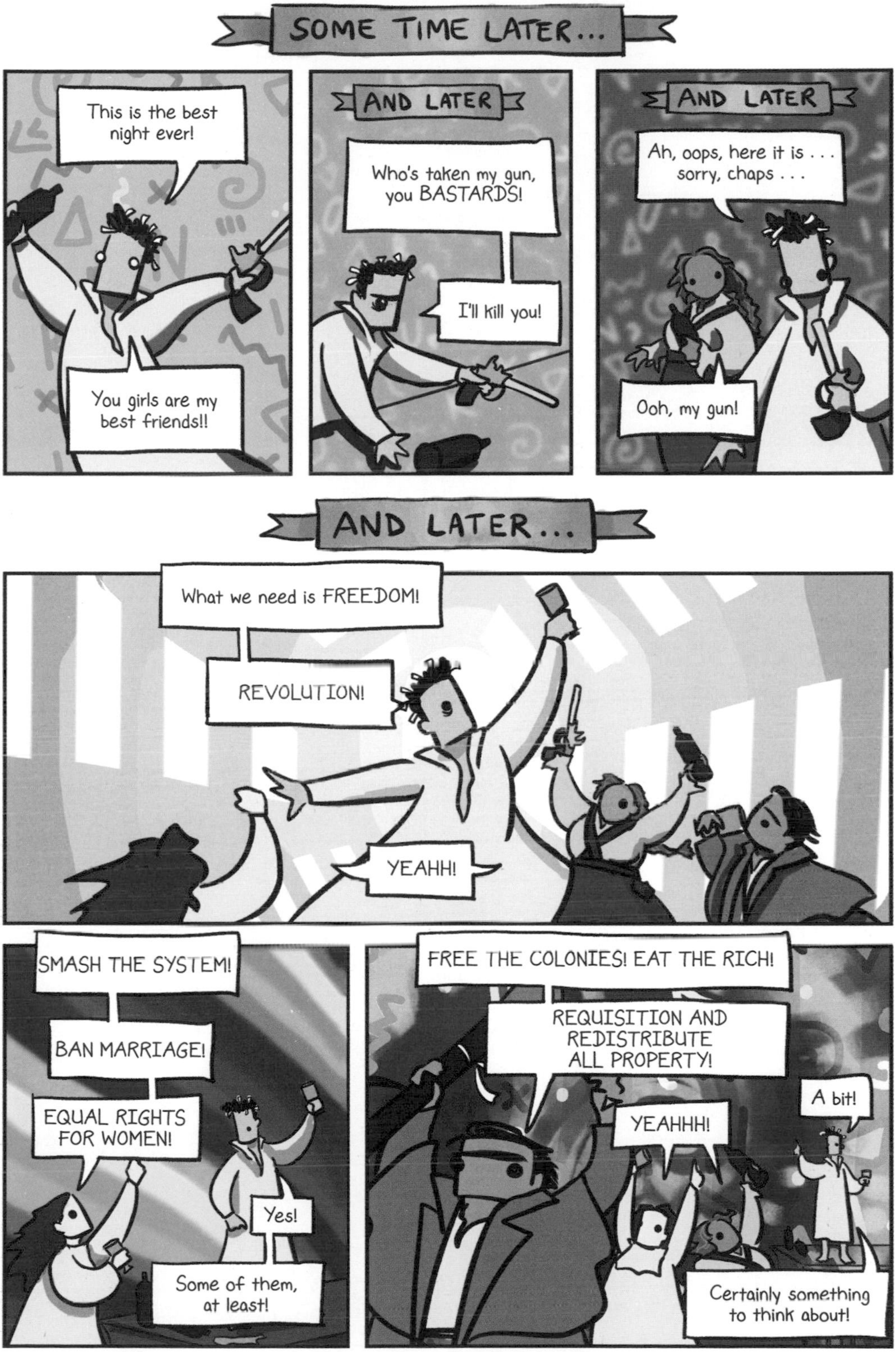
SOME TIME LATER...
This is the best night ever!
You girls are my best friends!!
AND LATER
Who's taken my gun, you BASTARDS!
I'll kill you!
AND LATER
Ah, oops, here it is . . . sorry, chaps . . .
Ooh, my gun!
AND LATER...
What we need is FREEDOM!
REVOLUTION!
YEAHH!
SMASH THE SYSTEM!
BAN MARRIAGE!
EQUAL RIGHTS FOR WOMEN!
Yes!
Some of them, at least!
FREE THE COLONIES! EAT THE RICH!
REQUISITION AND REDISTRIBUTE ALL PROPERTY!
YEAHHH!
A bit!
Certainly something to think about!

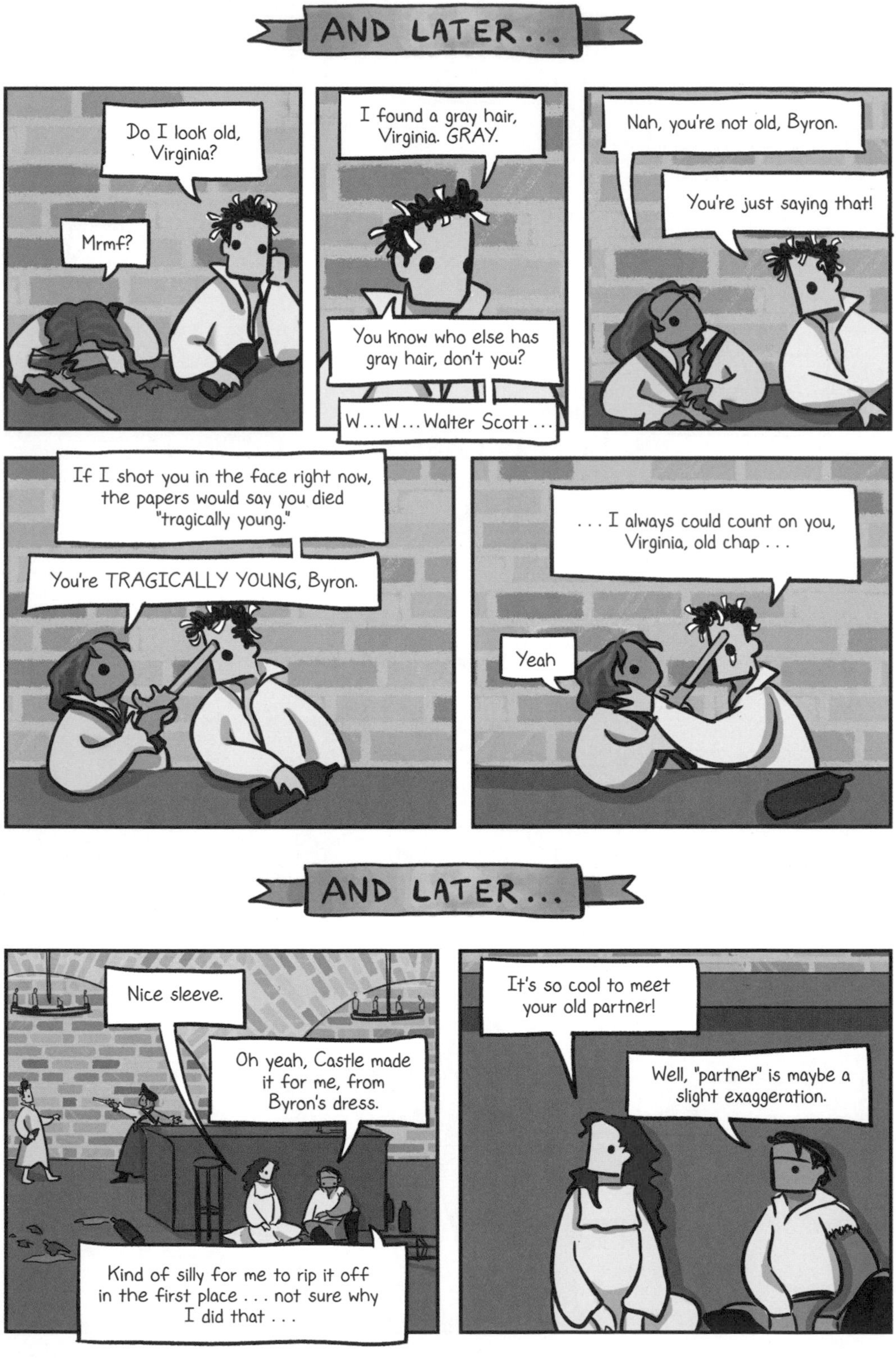
AND LATER . . .
Do I look old, Virginia?
Mrmf?
I found a gray hair, Virginia. GRAY.
You know who else has gray hair, don't you?
W . . . W . . . Walter Scott . . .
Nah, you're not old, Byron.
You're just saying that!
If I shot you in the face right now, the papers would say you died "tragically young."
You're TRAGICALLY YOUNG, Byron.
. . . I always could count on you, Virginia, old chap . . .
Yeah
AND LATER . . .
Nice sleeve.
Oh yeah, Castle made it for me, from Byron's dress.
Kind of silly for me to rip it off in the first place . . . not sure why I did that . . .
It's so cool to meet your old partner!
Well, "partner" is maybe a slight exaggeration.

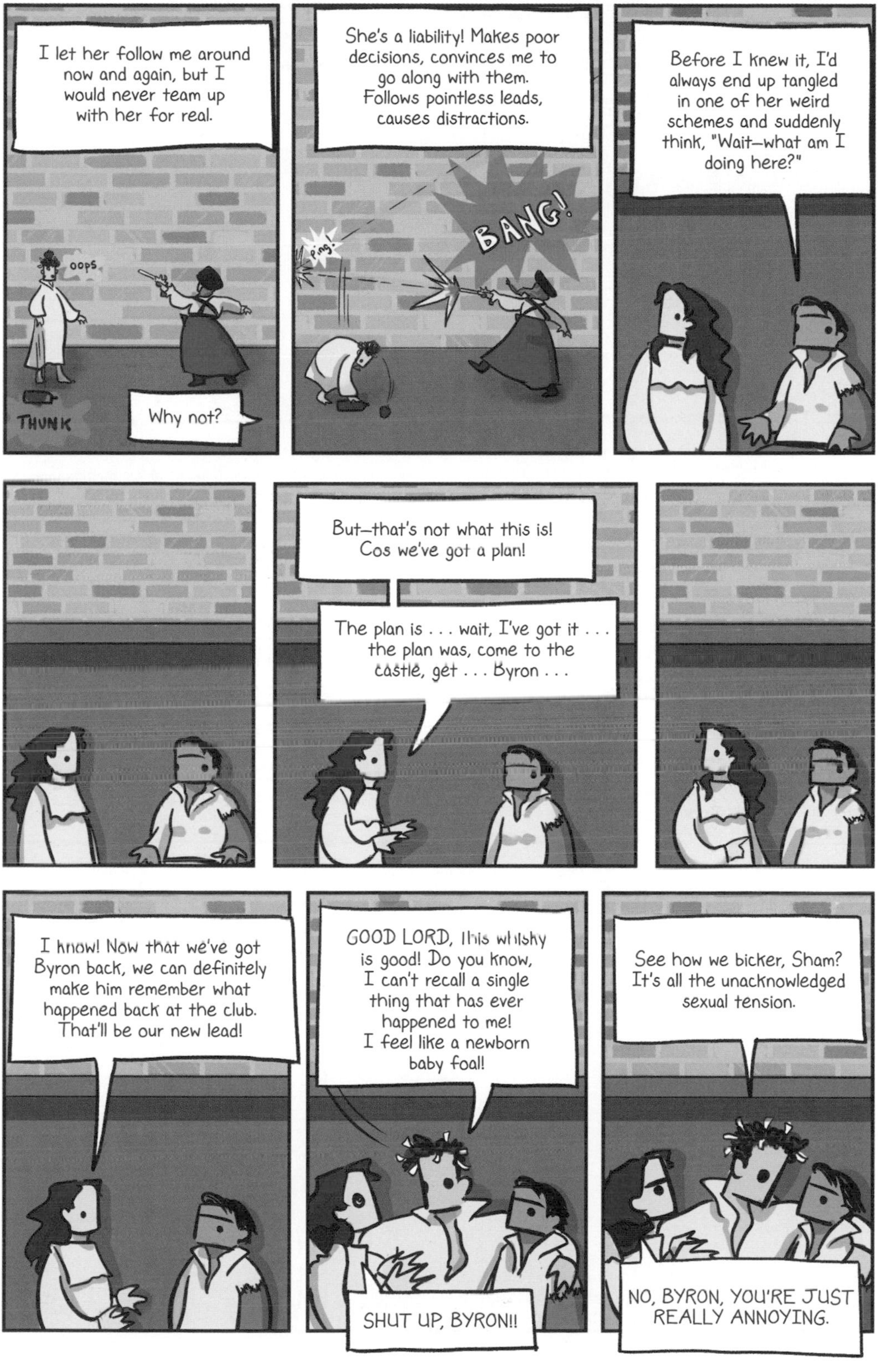
I let her follow me around now and again, but I would never team up with her for real.
oops.
THUNK
Why not?
She's a liability! Makes poor decisions, convinces me to go along with them. Follows pointless leads, causes distractions.
Ping!
BANG!
Before I knew it, I'd always end up tangled in one of her weird schemes and suddenly think, "Wait—what am I doing here?"
But—that's not what this is! Cos we've got a plan!
The plan is . . . wait, I've got it . . . the plan was, come to the castle, get . . . Byron . . .
I know! Now that we've got Byron back, we can definitely make him remember what happened back at the club. That'll be our new lead!
GOOD LORD, this whisky is good! Do you know, I can't recall a single thing that has ever happened to me! I feel like a newborn baby foal!
SHUT UP, BYRON!!
See how we bicker, Sham? It's all the unacknowledged sexual tension.
NO, BYRON, YOU'RE JUST REALLY ANNOYING.

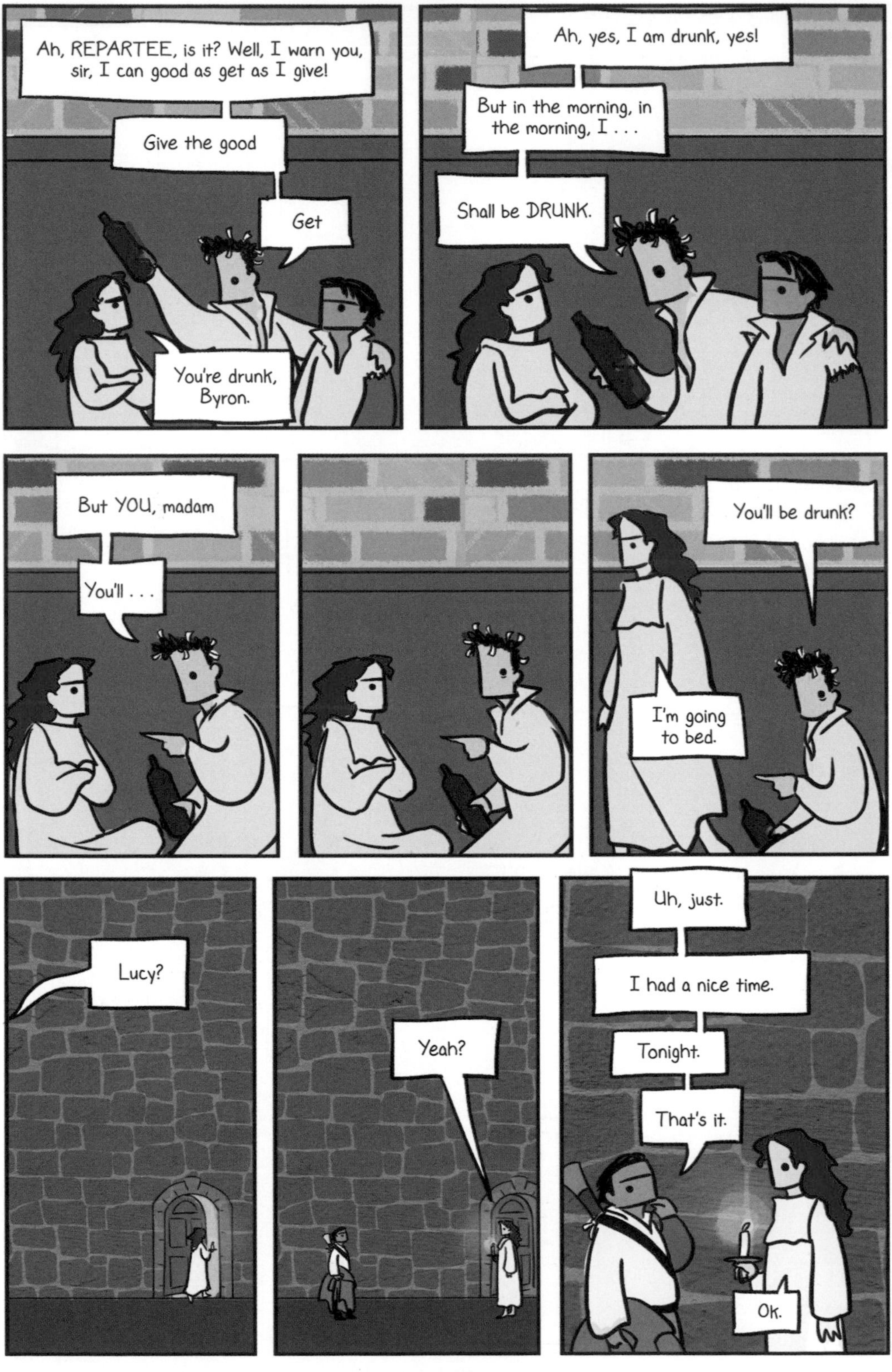
Ah, REPARTEE, is it? Well, I warn you, sir, I can good as get as I give!
Give the good
Get
You're drunk, Byron.
Ah, yes, I am drunk, yes!
But in the morning, in the morning, I . . .
Shall be DRUNK.
But YOU, madam
You'll . . .
You'll be drunk?
I'm going to bed.
Lucy?
Yeah?
Uh, just.
I had a nice time.
Tonight.
That's it.
Ok.

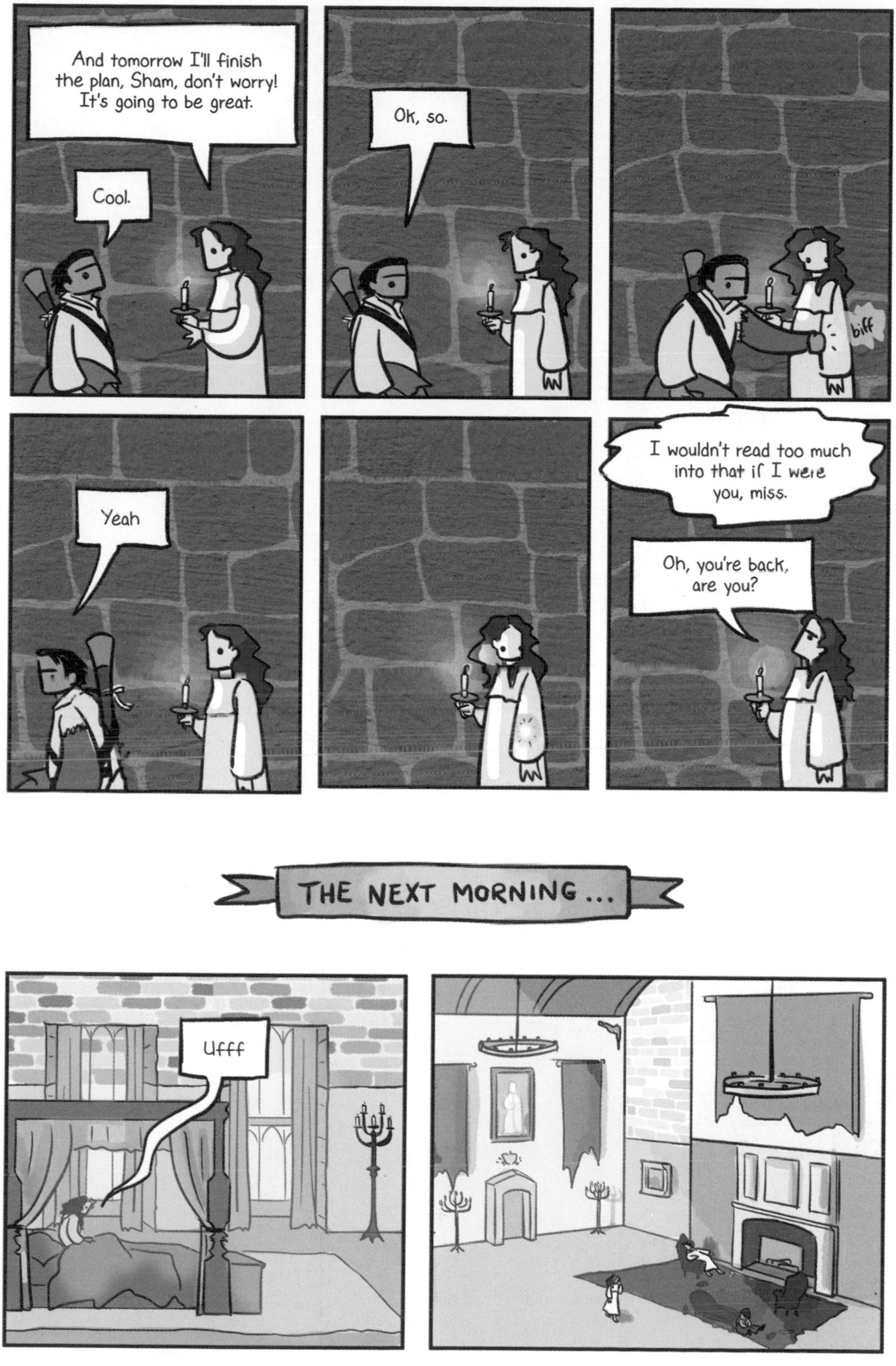
And tomorrow I'll finish the plan, Sham, don't worry! It's going to be great.
Cool.
Ok, so.
biff
Yeah
I wouldn't read too much into that if I were you, miss.
Oh, you're back, are you?
THE NEXT MORNING...
Ufff

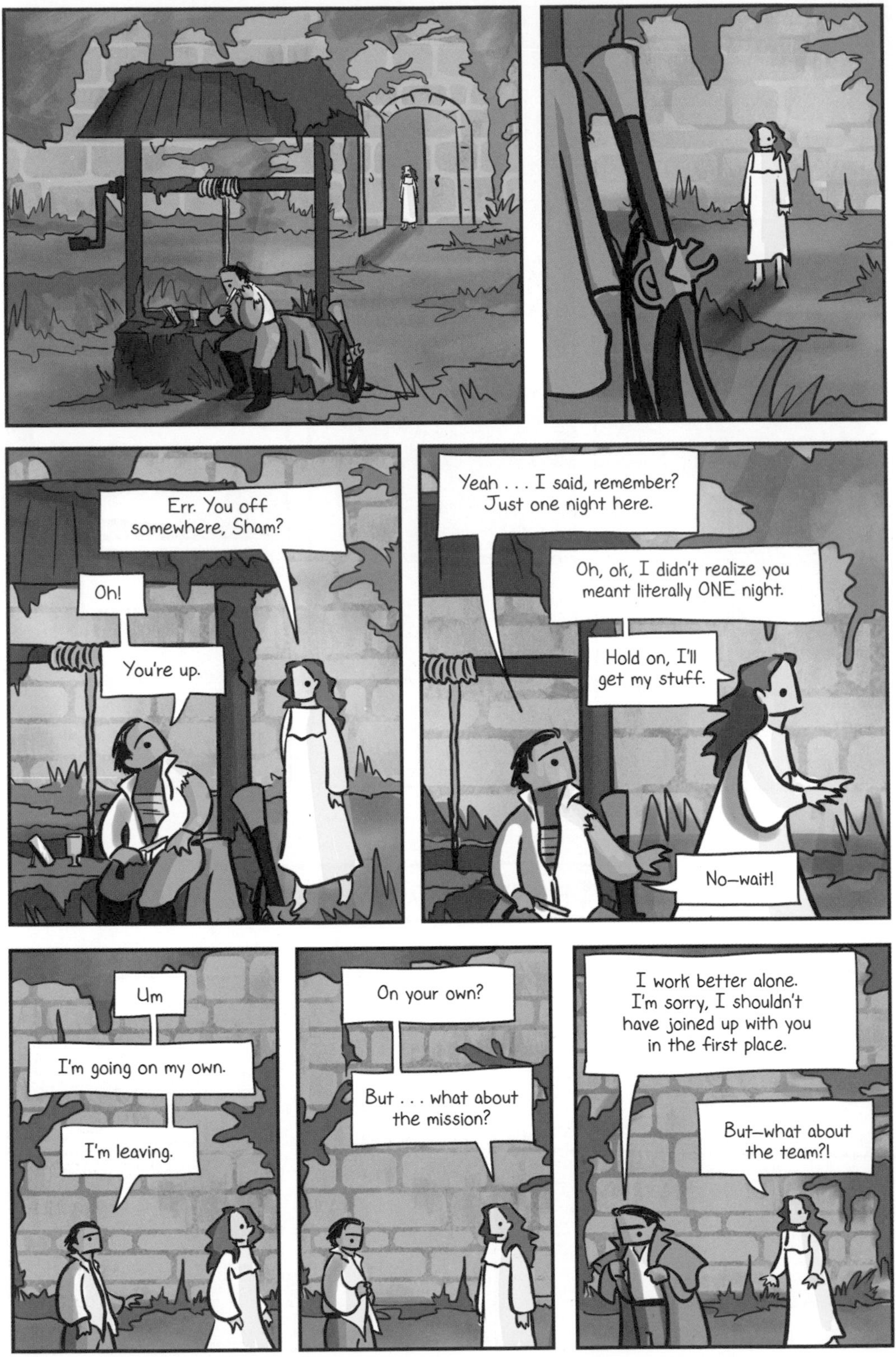
Err. You off somewhere, Sham?
Oh!
You're up.
Yeah . . . I said, remember? Just one night here.
Oh, ok, I didn't realize you meant literally ONE night.
Hold on, I'll get my stuff.
No—wait!
Um
I'm going on my own.
I'm leaving.
On your own?
But . . . what about the mission?
I work better alone. I'm sorry, I shouldn't have joined up with you in the first place.
But—what about the team?!

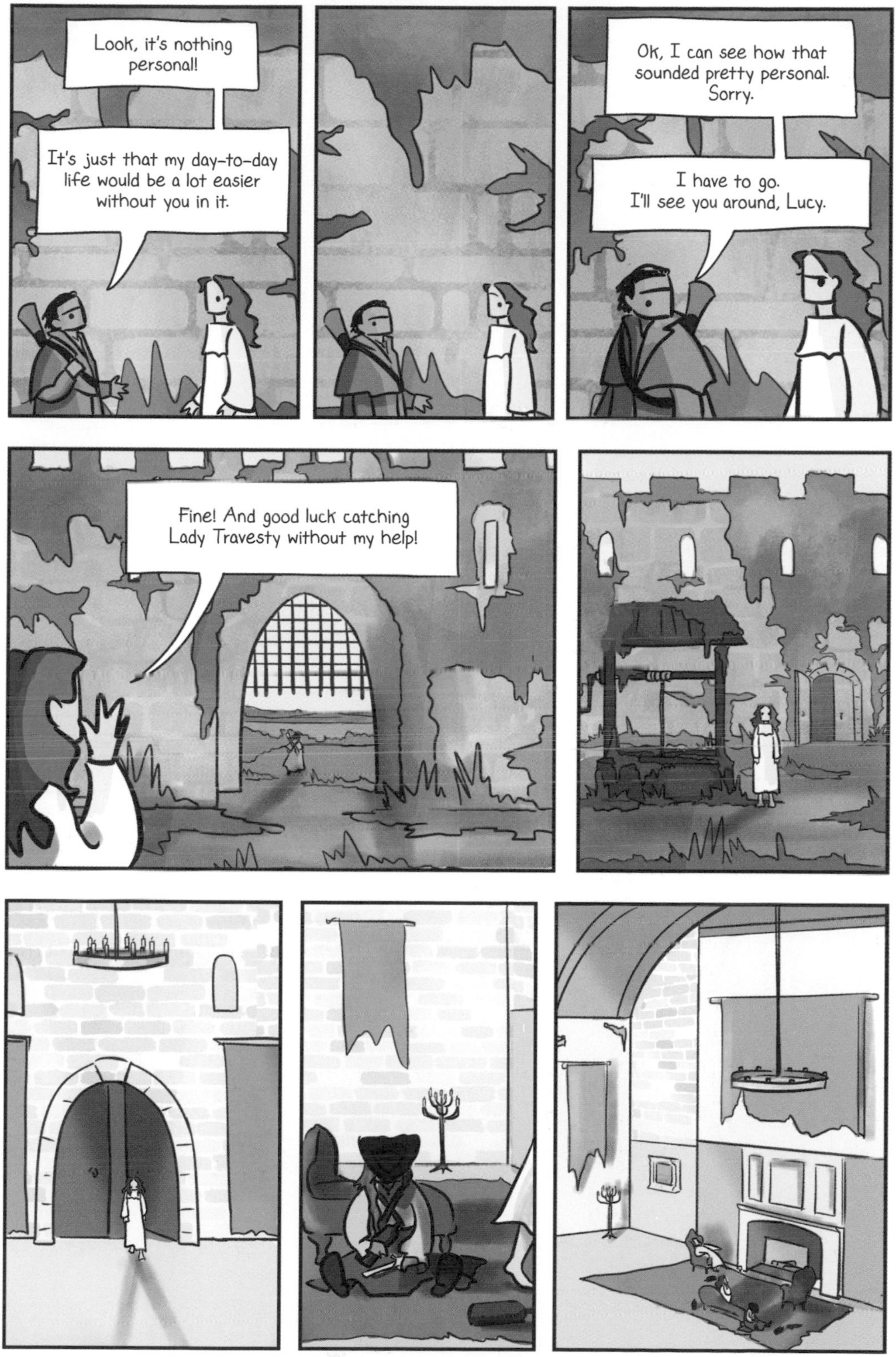
Look, it's nothing personal!
It's just that my day-to-day life would be a lot easier without you in it.
Ok, I can see how that sounded pretty personal. Sorry.
I have to go. I'll see you around, Lucy.
Fine! And good luck catching Lady Travesty without my help!

CHAPTER VII - THE DUNGEON

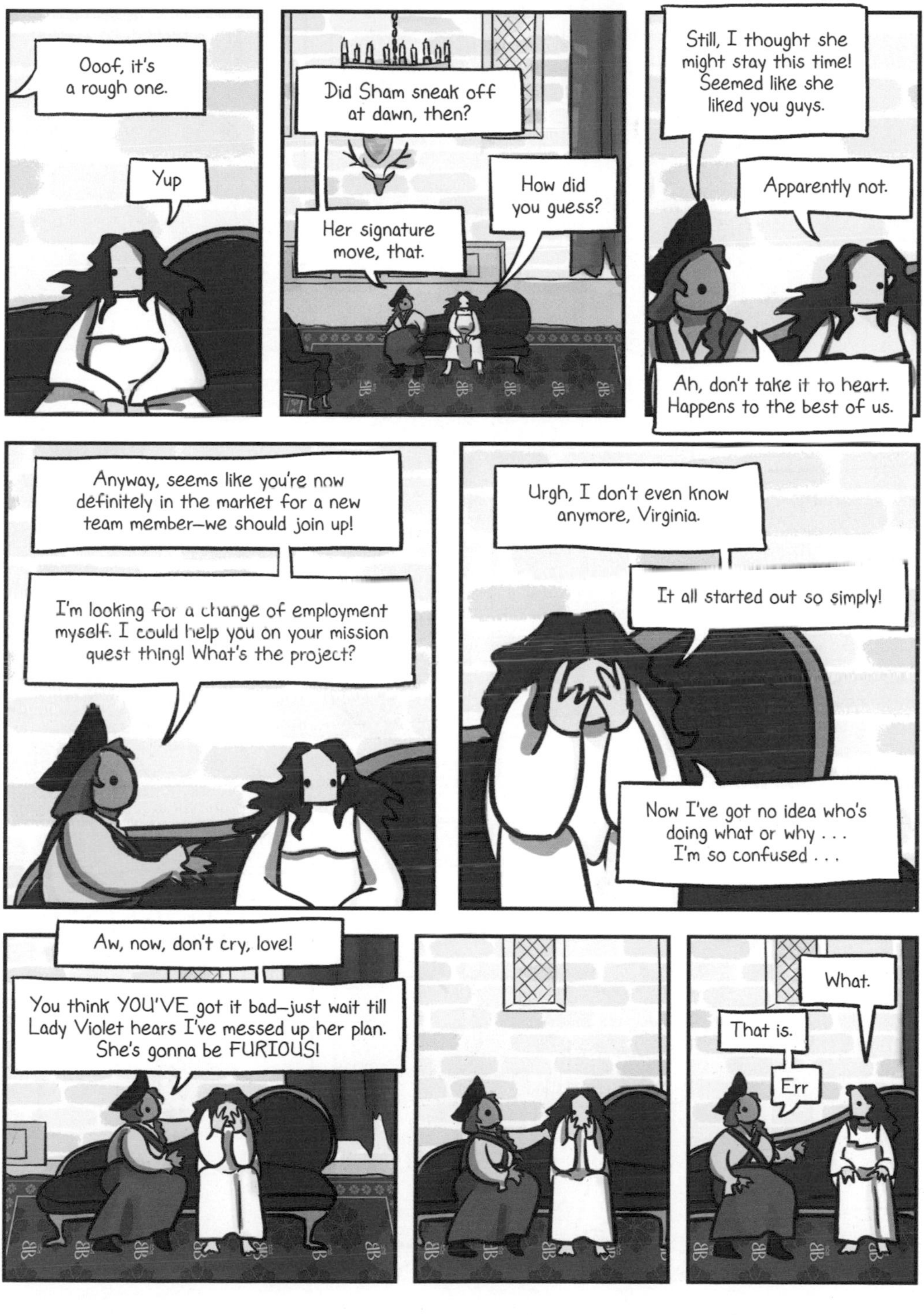
Ooof, it's a rough one.
Yup
Did Sham sneak off at dawn, then?
Her signature move, that.
How did you guess?
Still, I thought she might stay this time! Seemed like she liked you guys.
Apparently not.
Ah, don't take it to heart. Happens to the best of us.
Anyway, seems like you're now definitely in the market for a new team member—we should join up!
I'm looking for a change of employment myself. I could help you on your mission quest thing! What's the project?
Urgh, I don't even know anymore, Virginia.
It all started out so simply!
Now I've got no idea who's doing what or why . . . I'm so confused . . .
Aw, now, don't cry, love!
You think YOU'VE got it bad—just wait till Lady Violet hears I've messed up her plan. She's gonna be FURIOUS!
What.
That is.
Err

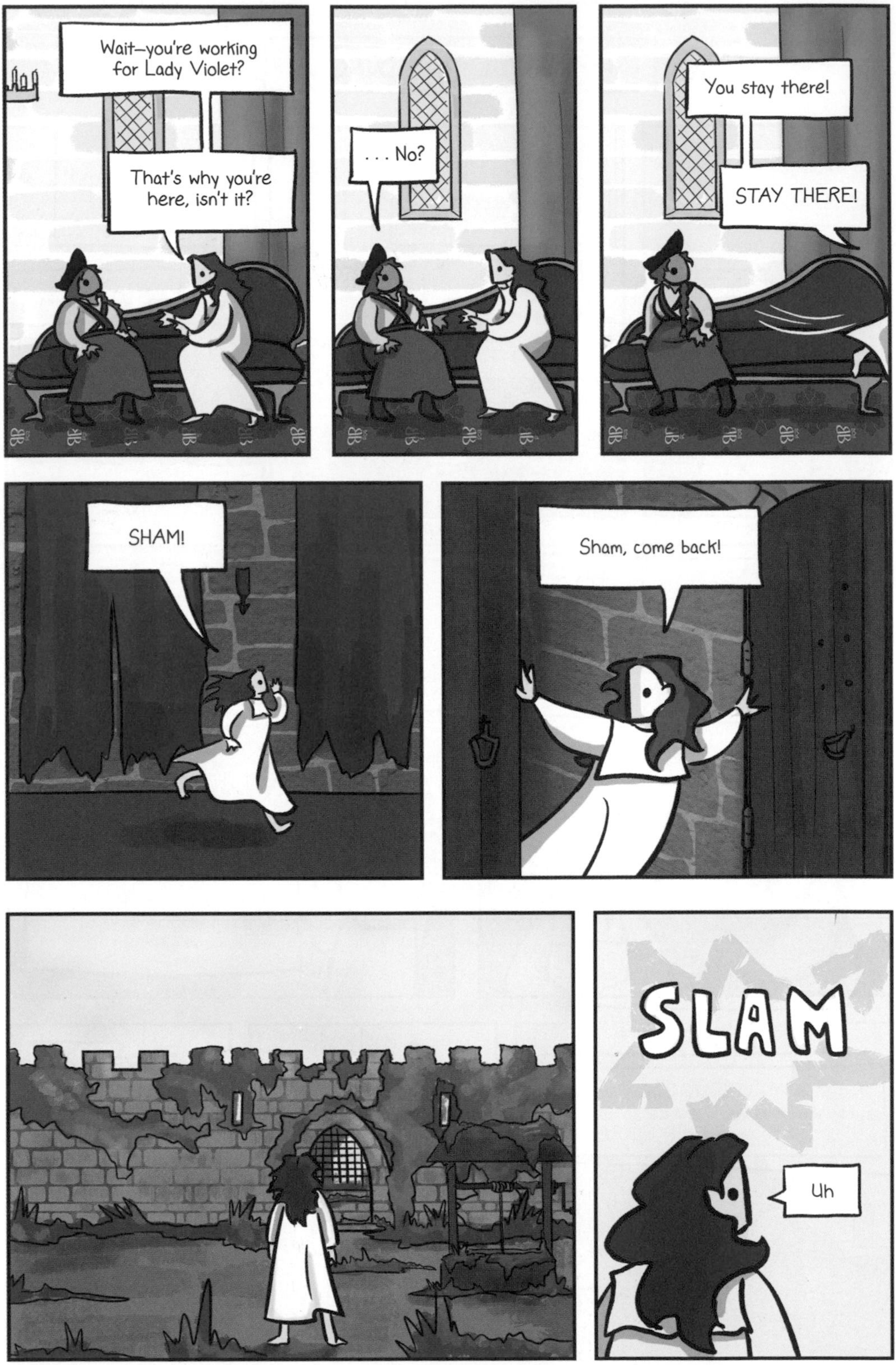
Wait—you're working for Lady Violet?
That's why you're here, isn't it?
. . . No?
You stay there!
STAY THERE!
SHAM!
Sham, come back!
SLAM
Uh

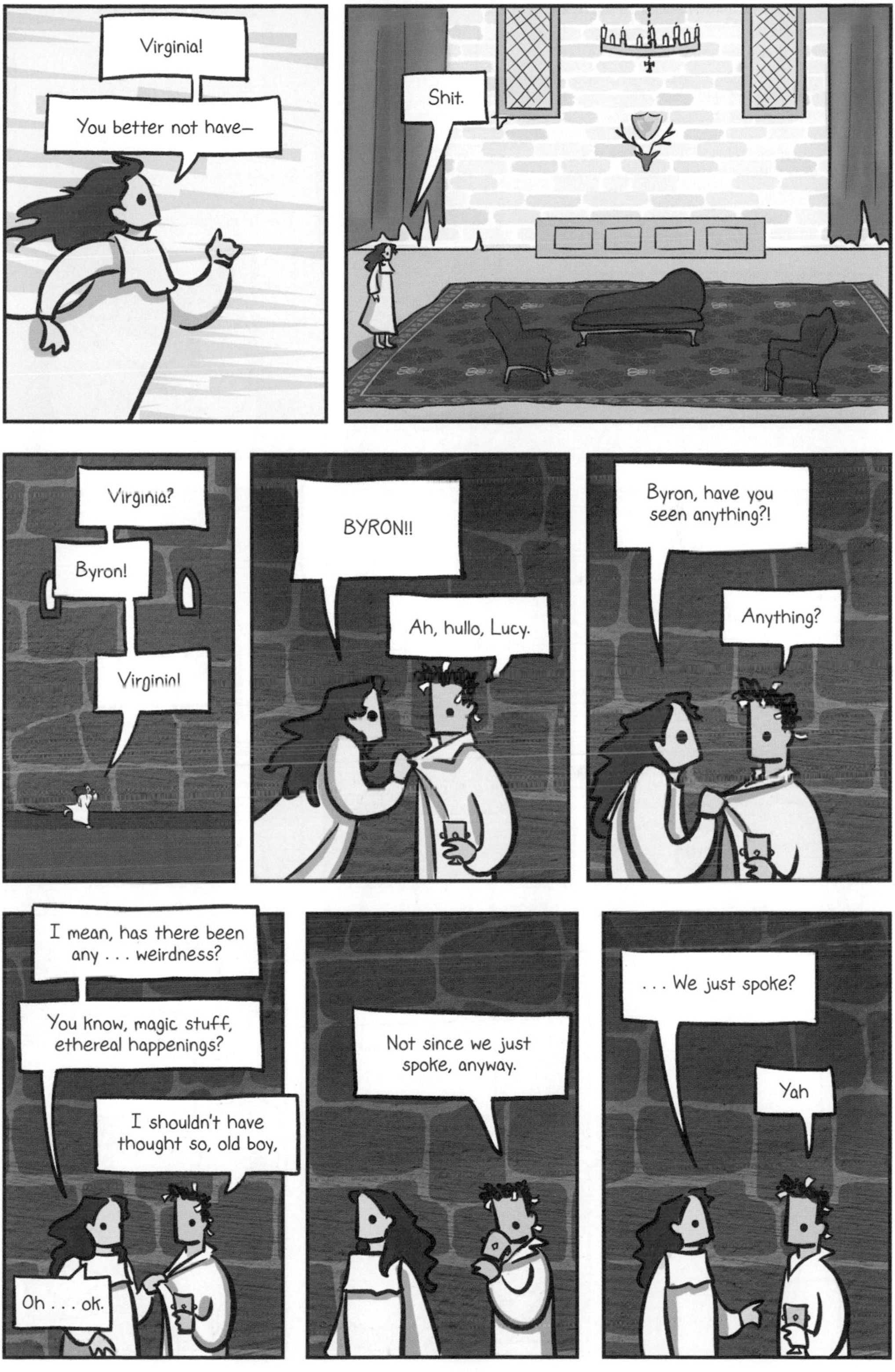
Virginia!
You better not have—
Shit.
Virginia?
Byron!
Virginia!
BYRON!!
Ah, hullo, Lucy.
Byron, have you seen anything?!
Anything?
I mean, has there been any . . . weirdness?
You know, magic stuff, ethereal happenings?
I shouldn't have thought so, old boy,
Oh . . . ok.
Not since we just spoke, anyway.
. . . We just spoke?
Yah

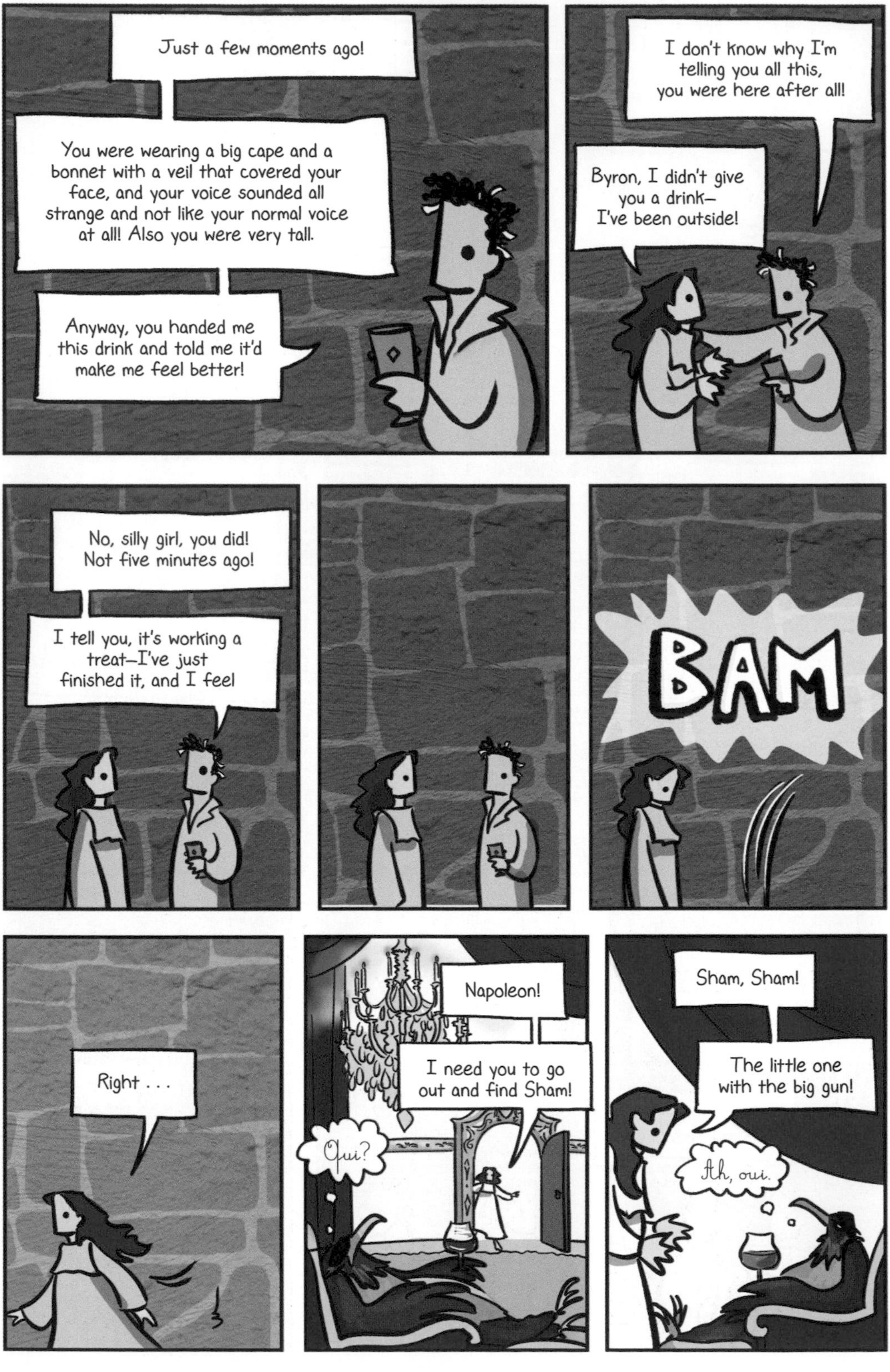

Just a few moments ago!
You were wearing a big cape and a bonnet with a veil that covered your face, and your voice sounded all strange and not like your normal voice at all! Also you were very tall.
Anyway, you handed me this drink and told me it'd make me feel better!
I don't know why I'm telling you all this, you were here after all!
Byron, I didn't give you a drink— I've been outside!
No, silly girl, you did! Not five minutes ago!
I tell you, it's working a treat—I've just finished it, and I feel
BAM
Right . . .
Napoleon!
I need you to go out and find Sham!
Oui?
Sham, Sham!
The little one with the big gun!
Ah, oui.

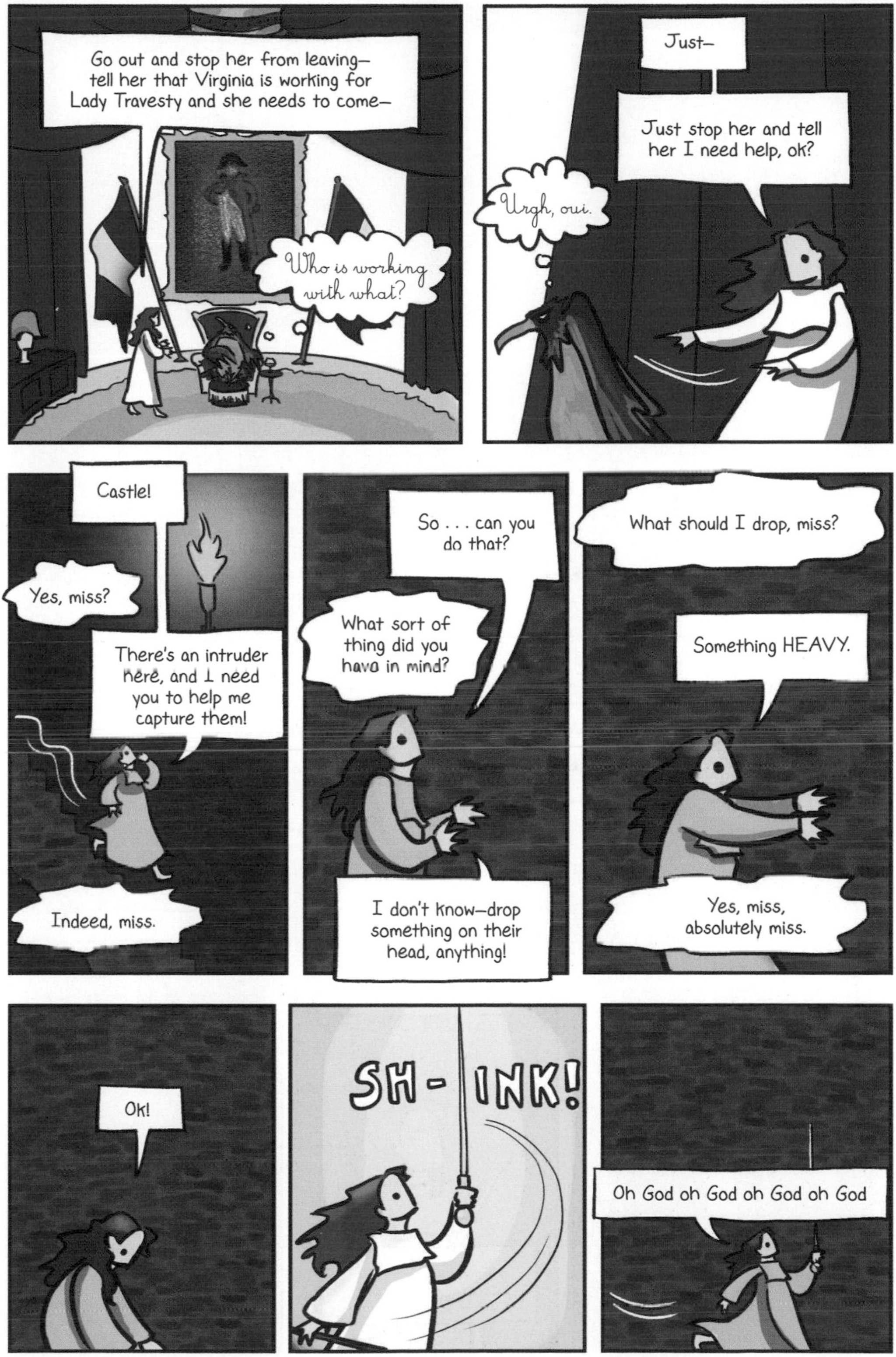

Go out and stop her from leaving—tell her that Virginia is working for Lady Travesty and she needs to come—
Who is working with what?
Just—
Just stop her and tell her I need help, ok?
Urgh, oui.
Castle!
Yes, miss?
There's an intruder here, and I need you to help me capture them!
Indeed, miss.
So . . . can you do that?
What sort of thing did you have in mind?
I don't know—drop something on their head, anything!
What should I drop, miss?
Something HEAVY.
Yes, miss, absolutely miss.
Ok!
SH-INK!
Oh God oh God oh God oh God

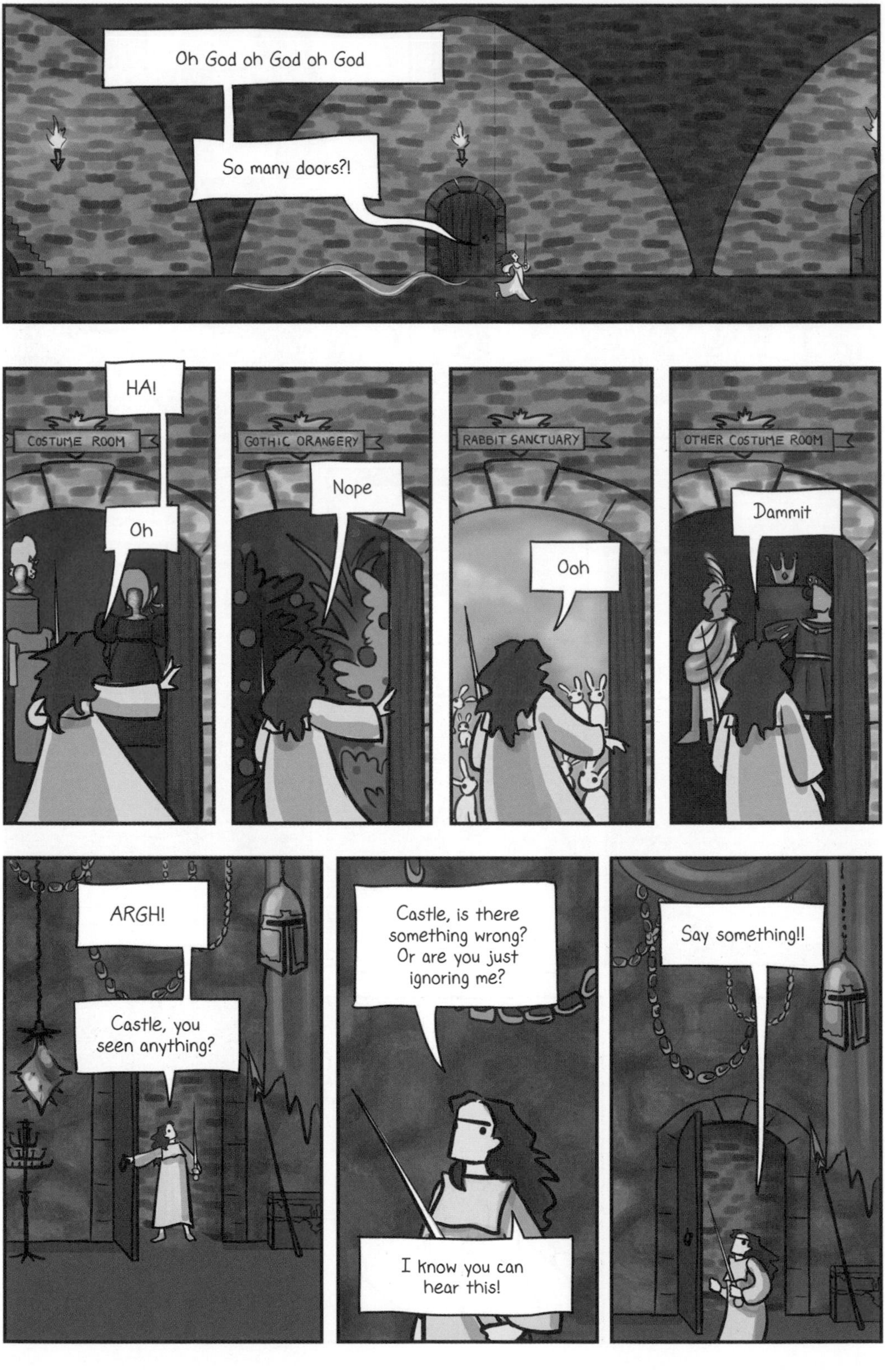
Oh God oh God oh God
So many doors?!
HA!
COSTUME ROOM
Oh
GOTHIC ORANGERY
Nope
RABBIT SANCTUARY
Ooh
OTHER COSTUME ROOM
Dammit
ARGH!
Castle, you seen anything?
Castle, is there something wrong? Or are you just ignoring me?
I know you can hear this!
Say something!!

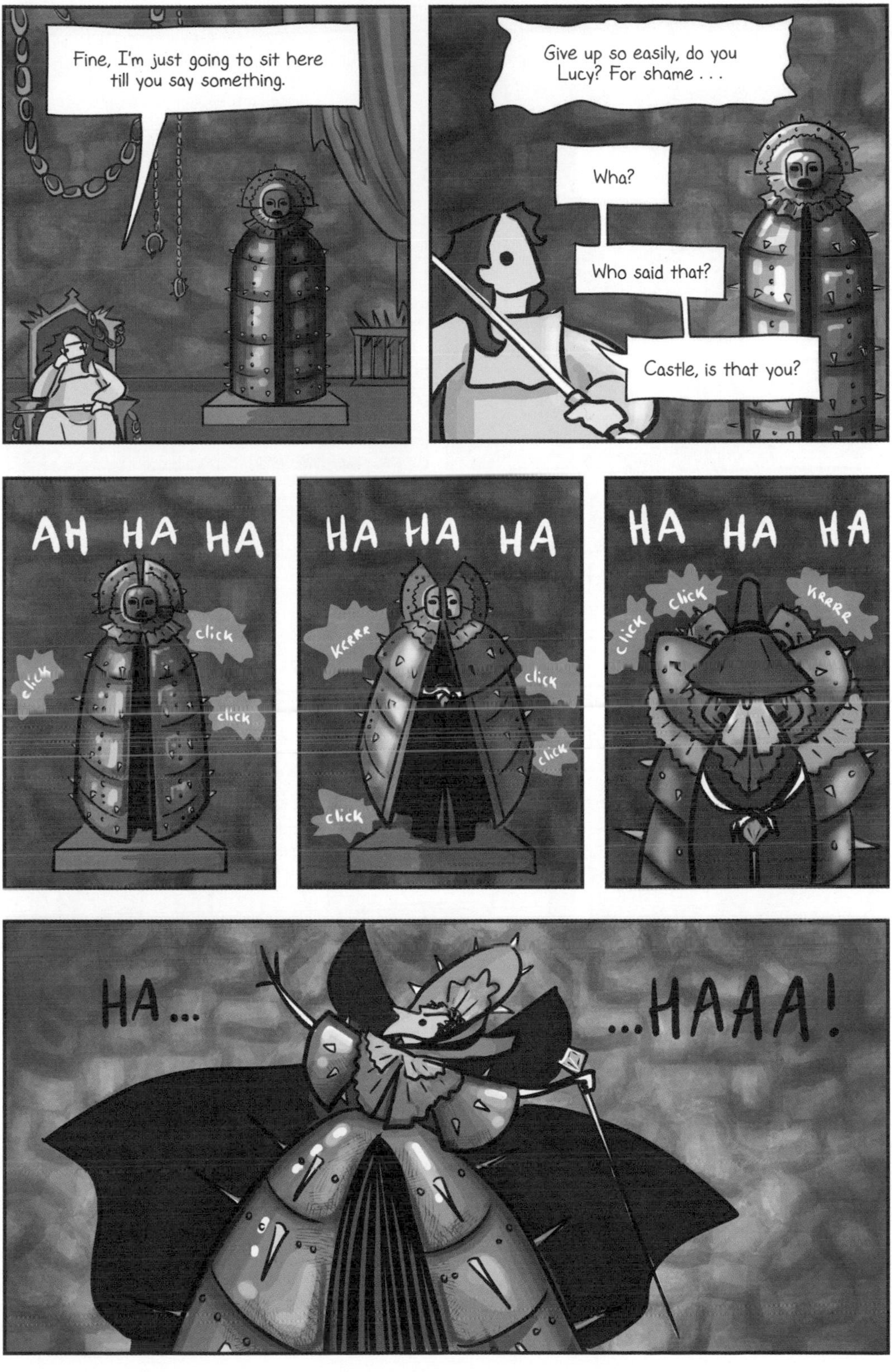
Fine, I'm just going to sit here till you say something.
Give up so easily, do you Lucy? For shame . . .
Wha?
Who said that?
Castle, is that you?
AH HA HA
click
click
click
HA HA HA
KRRRR
click
click
click
HA HA HA
click
click
KRRRR
HA...
...HAAA!

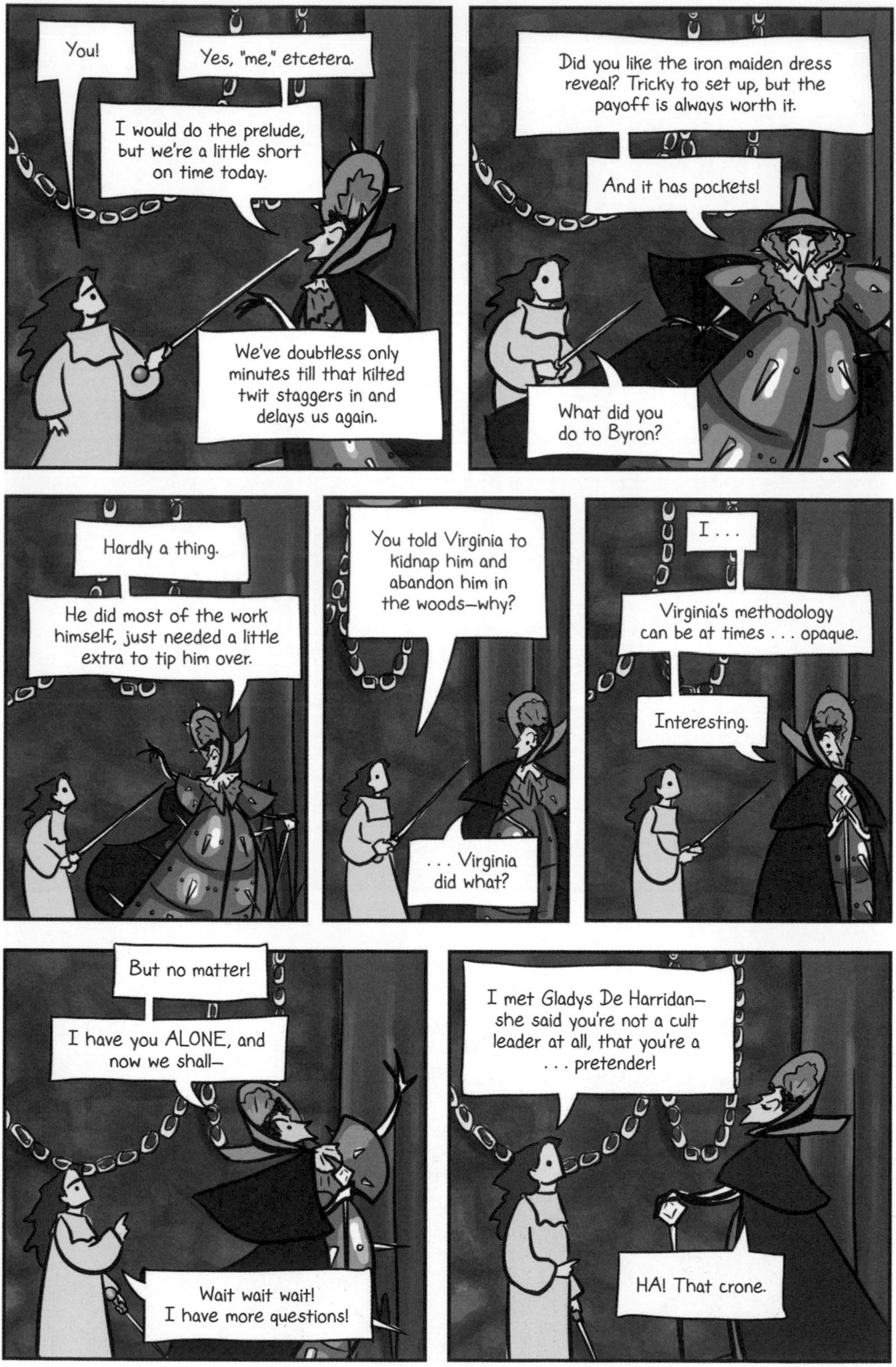
You!
Yes, "me," etcetera.
I would do the prelude, but we're a little short on time today.
We've doubtless only minutes till that kilted twit staggers in and delays us again.
Did you like the iron maiden dress reveal? Tricky to set up, but the payoff is always worth it.
And it has pockets!
What did you do to Byron?
Hardly a thing.
He did most of the work himself, just needed a little extra to tip him over.
You told Virginia to kidnap him and abandon him in the woods—why?
. . . Virginia did what?
I . . .
Virginia's methodology can be at times . . . opaque.
Interesting.
But no matter!
I have you ALONE, and now we shall—
Wait wait wait! I have more questions!
I met Gladys De Harridan—she said you're not a cult leader at all, that you're a . . . pretender!
HA! That crone.

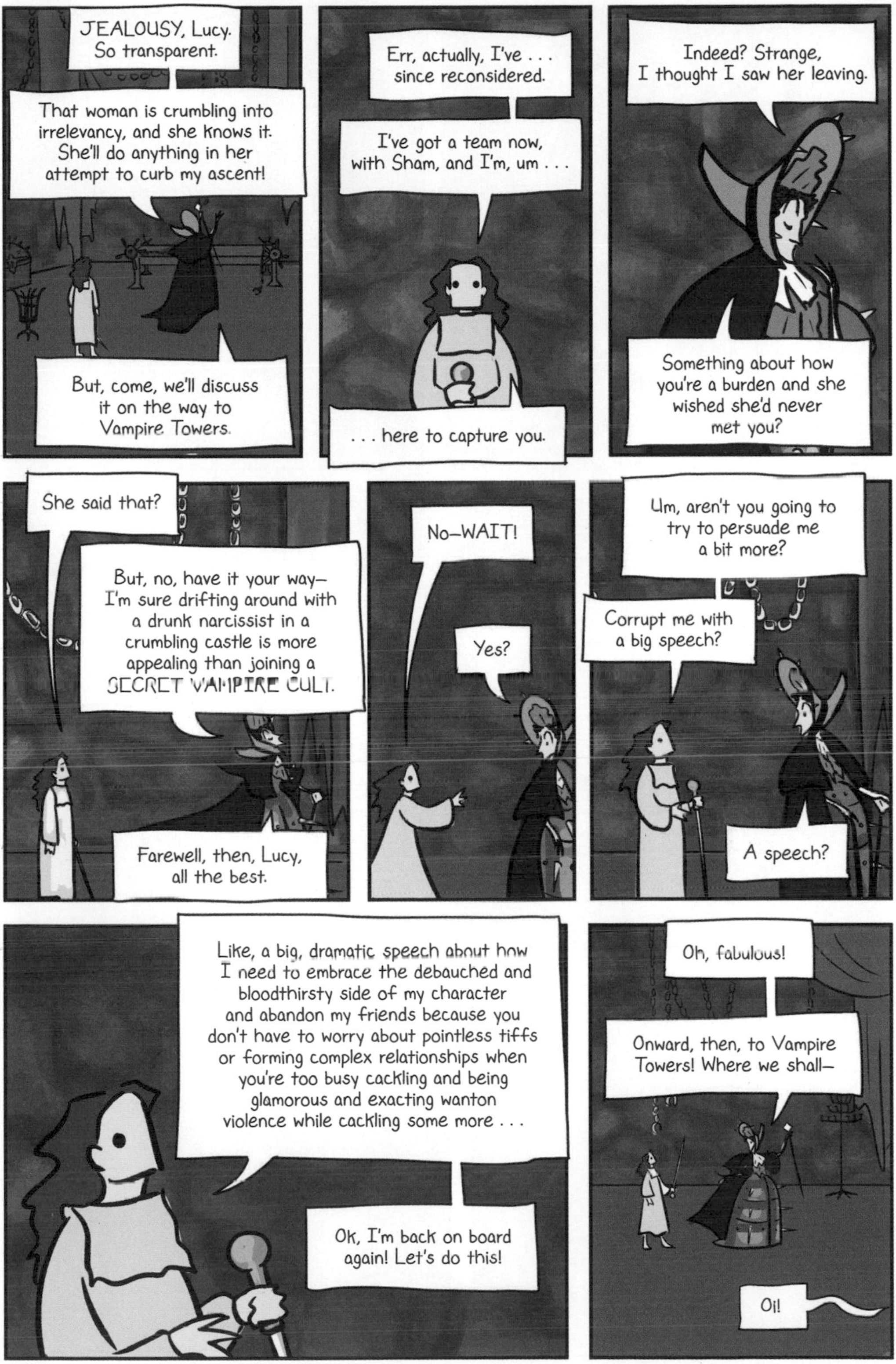
JEALOUSY, Lucy. So transparent.
That woman is crumbling into irrelevancy, and she knows it. She'll do anything in her attempt to curb my ascent!
But, come, we'll discuss it on the way to Vampire Towers.
Err, actually, I've . . . since reconsidered.
I've got a team now, with Sham, and I'm, um . . .
. . . here to capture you.
Indeed? Strange, I thought I saw her leaving.
Something about how you're a burden and she wished she'd never met you?
She said that?
But, no, have it your way— I'm sure drifting around with a drunk narcissist in a crumbling castle is more appealing than joining a SECRET VAMPIRE CULT.
Farewell, then, Lucy, all the best.
No—WAIT!
Yes?
Um, aren't you going to try to persuade me a bit more?
Corrupt me with a big speech?
A speech?
Like, a big, dramatic speech about how I need to embrace the debauched and bloodthirsty side of my character and abandon my friends because you don't have to worry about pointless tiffs or forming complex relationships when you're too busy cackling and being glamorous and exacting wanton violence while cackling some more . . .
Ok, I'm back on board again! Let's do this!
Oh, fabulous!
Onward, then, to Vampire Towers! Where we shall—
Oi!

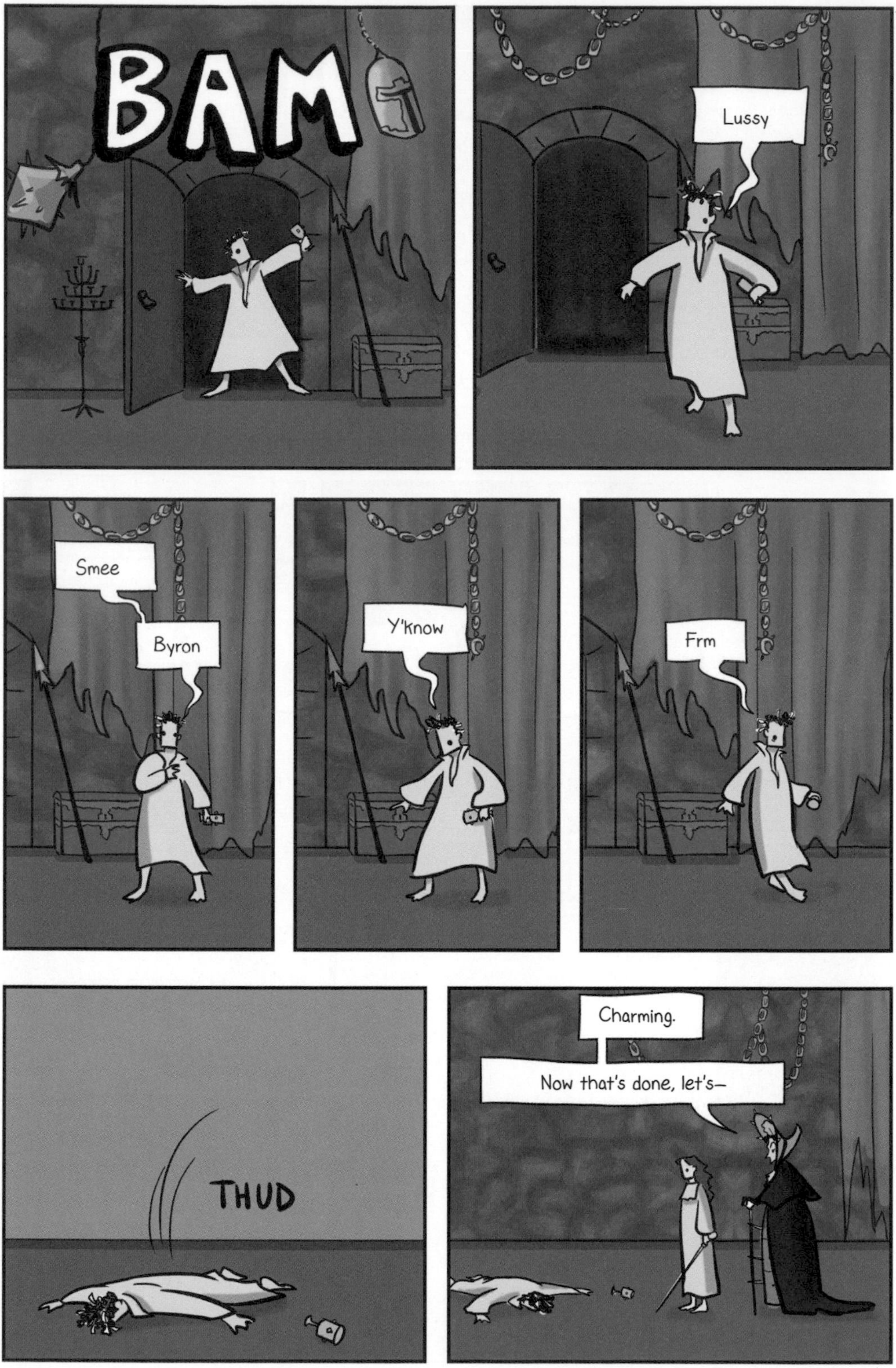
BAM
Lussy
Smee
Byron
Y'know
Frm
THUD
Charming.
Now that's done, let's–

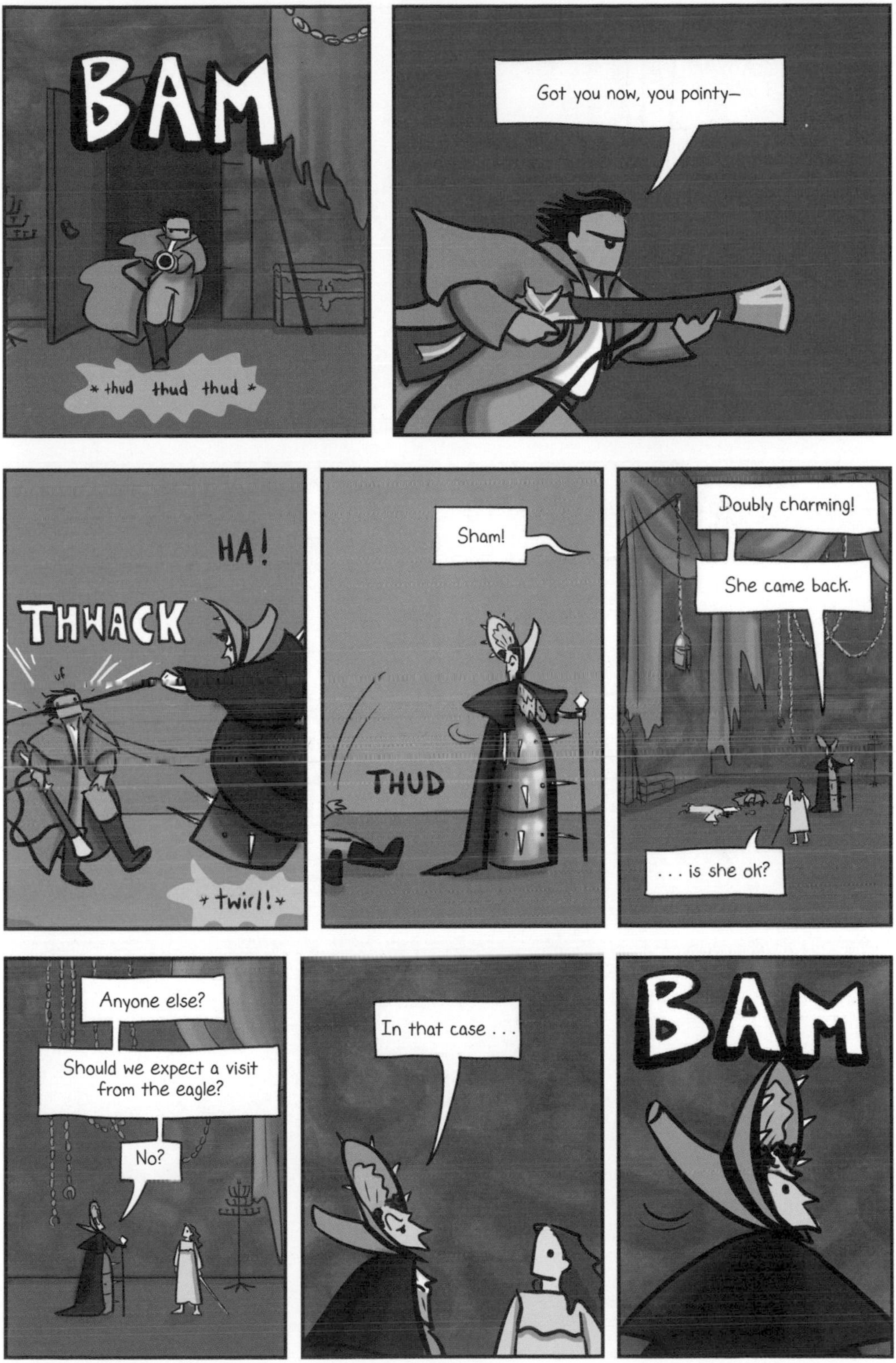

BAM
* thud thud thud *
Got you now, you pointy—
THWACK
HA!
uf
* twirl! *
Sham!
THUD
Doubly charming!
She came back.
. . . is she ok?
Anyone else?
Should we expect a visit from the eagle?
No?
In that case . . .
BAM

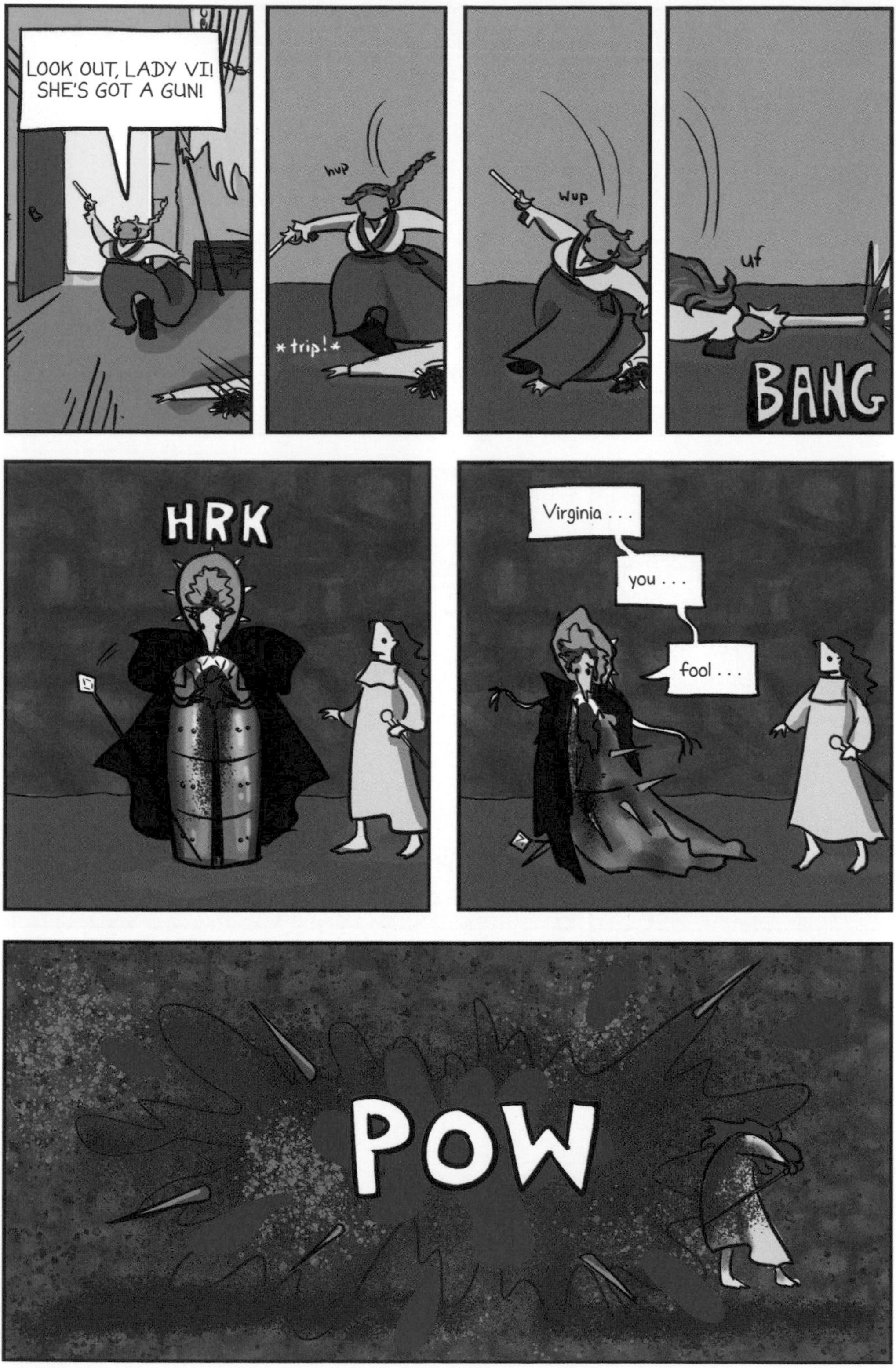
LOOK OUT, LADY VI! SHE'S GOT A GUN!
hup
trip!
wup
uf
BANG
HRK
Virginia . . .
you . . .
fool . . .
POW

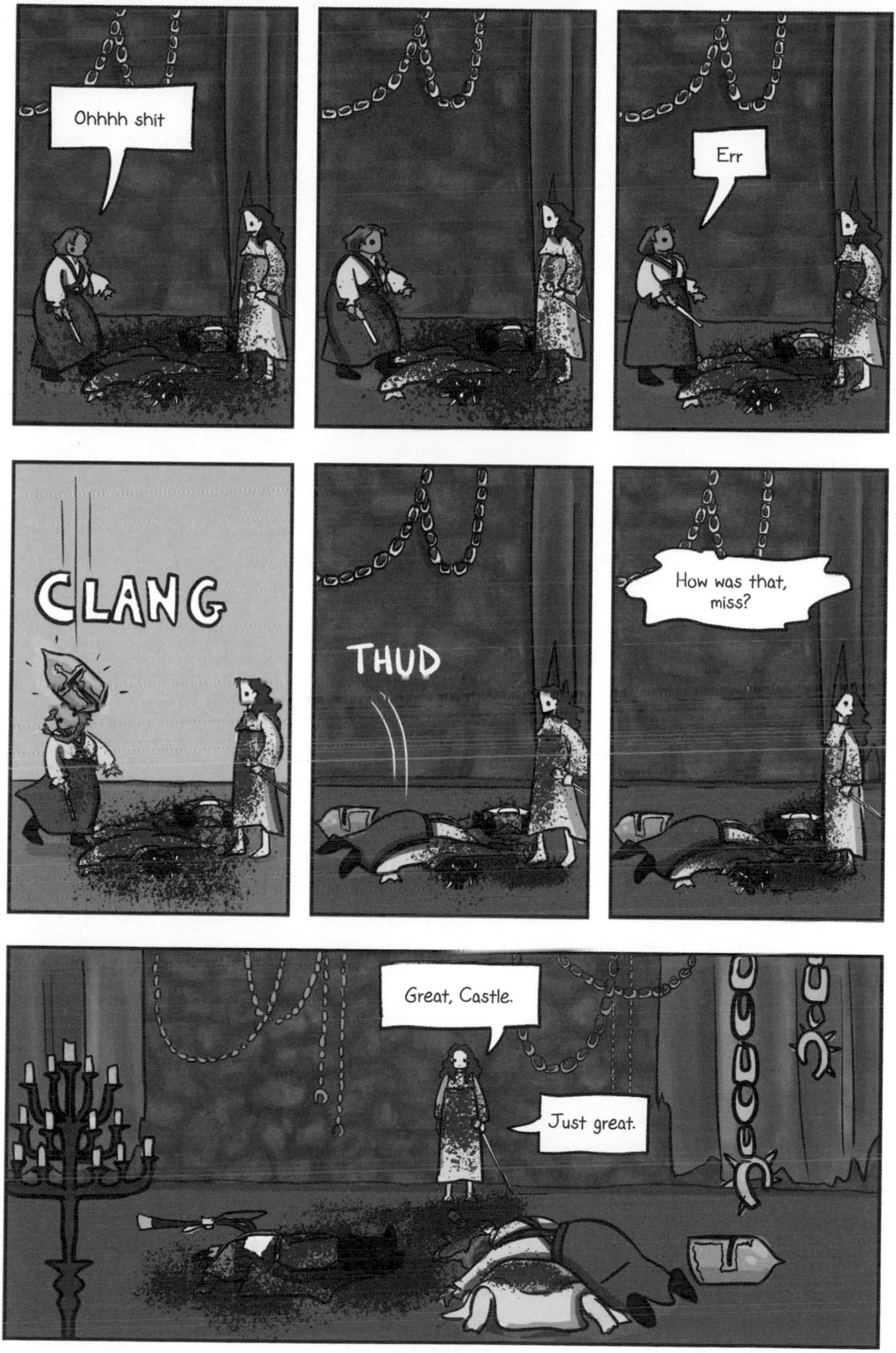
Ohhhh shit
Err
CLANG
THUD
How was that, miss?
Great, Castle.
Just great.

CHAPTER VIII – BATH

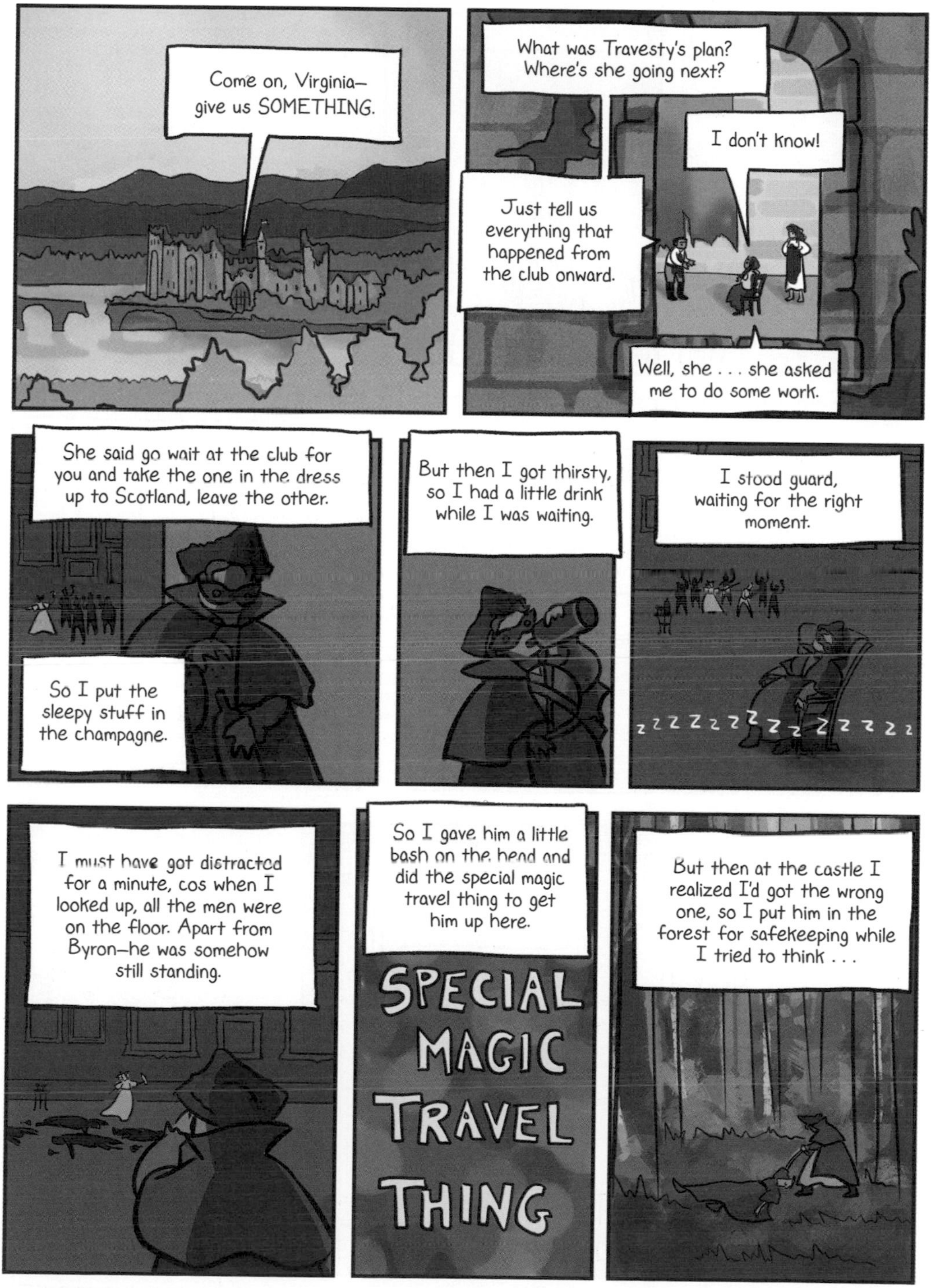
Come on, Virginia–give us SOMETHING.
What was Travesty's plan? Where's she going next?
I don't know!
Just tell us everything that happened from the club onward.
Well, she . . . she asked me to do some work.
She said go wait at the club for you and take the one in the dress up to Scotland, leave the other.
So I put the sleepy stuff in the champagne.
But then I got thirsty, so I had a little drink while I was waiting.
I stood guard, waiting for the right moment.
zzzzzzzzzzzzzz
I must have got distracted for a minute, cos when I looked up, all the men were on the floor. Apart from Byron–he was somehow still standing.
So I gave him a little bash on the head and did the special magic travel thing to get him up here.
SPECIAL MAGIC TRAVEL THING
But then at the castle I realized I'd got the wrong one, so I put him in the forest for safekeeping while I tried to think . . .

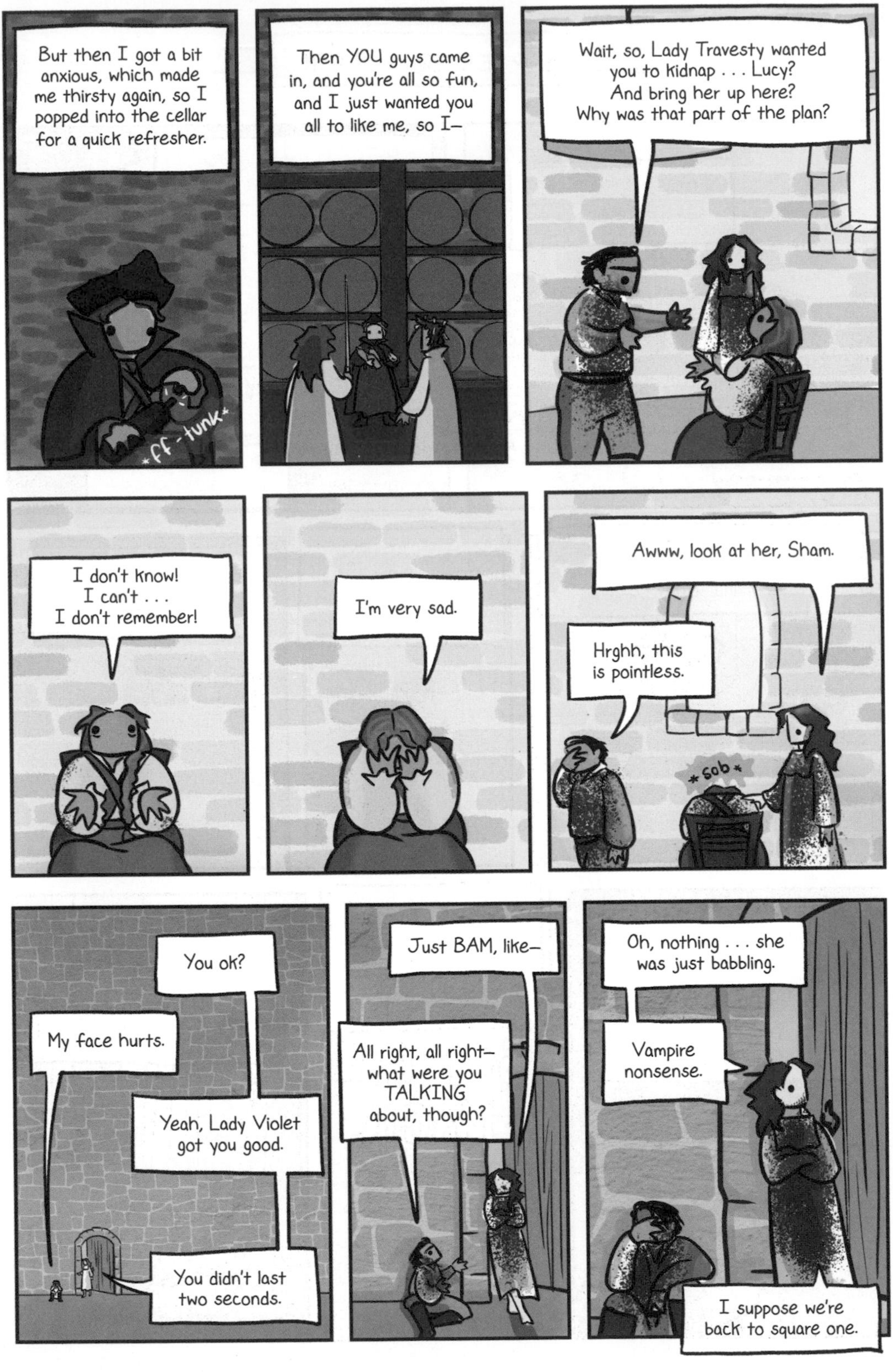
But then I got a bit anxious, which made me thirsty again, so I popped into the cellar for a quick refresher.
ff-tunk
Then YOU guys came in, and you're all so fun, and I just wanted you all to like me, so I—
Wait, so, Lady Travesty wanted you to kidnap . . . Lucy? And bring her up here? Why was that part of the plan?
I don't know! I can't . . . I don't remember!
I'm very sad.
Awww, look at her, Sham.
Hrghh, this is pointless.
sob
You ok?
My face hurts.
Yeah, Lady Violet got you good.
You didn't last two seconds.
Just BAM, like—
All right, all right— what were you TALKING about, though?
Oh, nothing . . . she was just babbling.
Vampire nonsense.
I suppose we're back to square one.

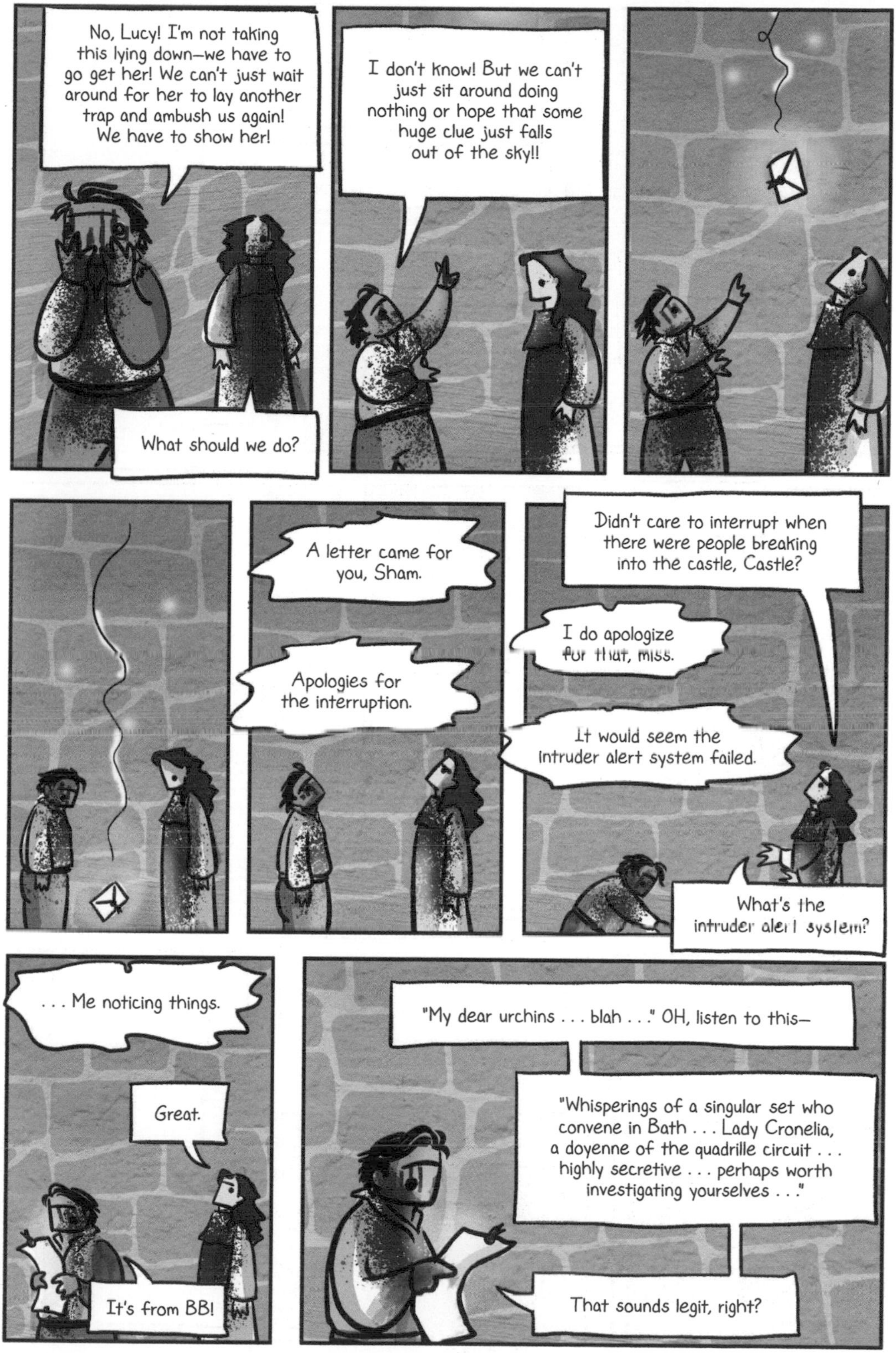
No, Lucy! I'm not taking this lying down—we have to go get her! We can't just wait around for her to lay another trap and ambush us again! We have to show her!
What should we do?
I don't know! But we can't just sit around doing nothing or hope that some huge clue just falls out of the sky!!
A letter came for you, Sham.
Apologies for the interruption.
Didn't care to interrupt when there were people breaking into the castle, Castle?
I do apologize for that, miss.
It would seem the intruder alert system failed.
What's the intruder alert system?
. . . Me noticing things.
Great.
It's from BB!
"My dear urchins . . . blah . . ." OH, listen to this—
"Whisperings of a singular set who convene in Bath . . . Lady Cronelia, a doyenne of the quadrille circuit . . . highly secretive . . . perhaps worth investigating yourselves . . ."
That sounds legit, right?

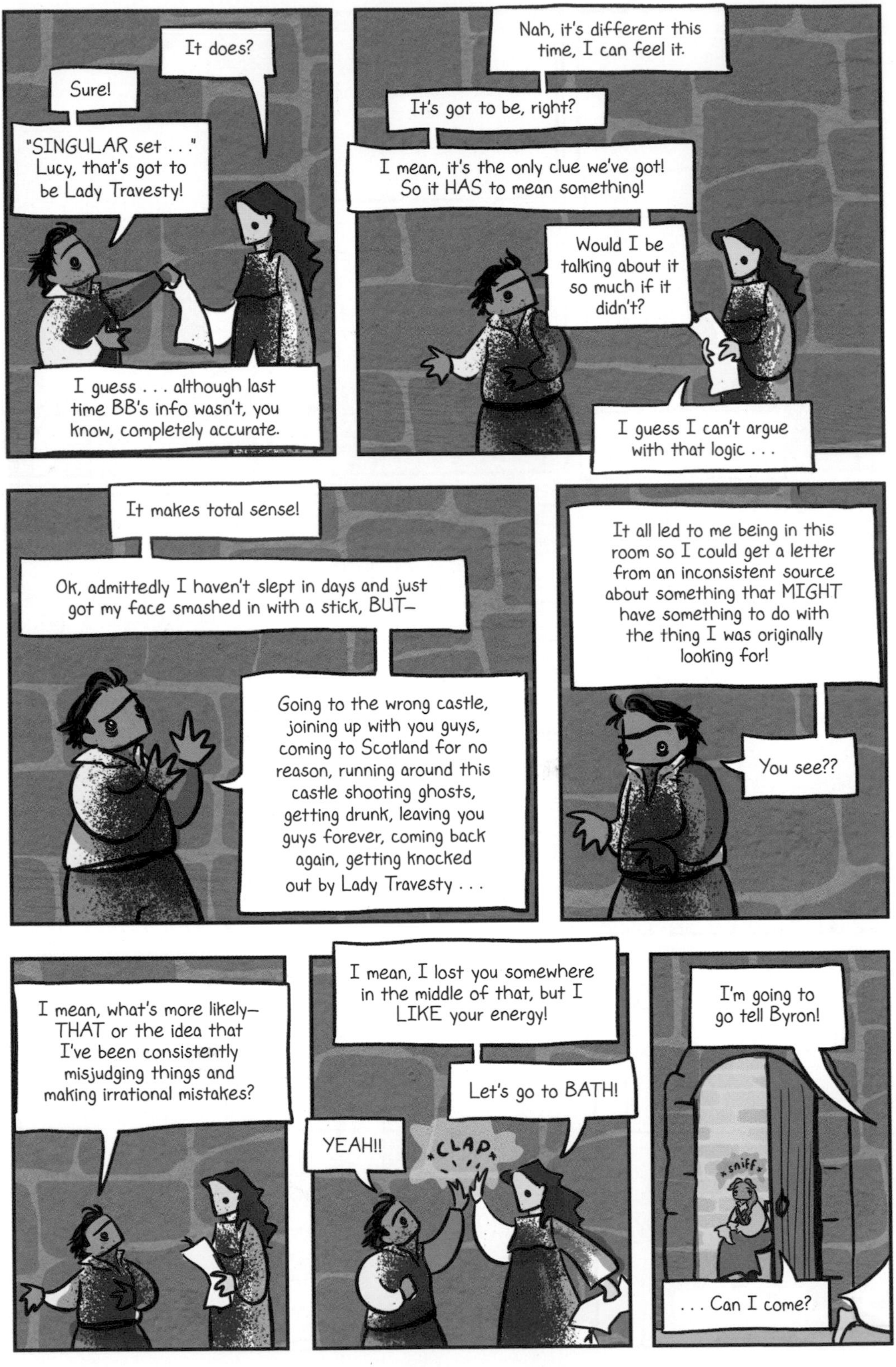

It does?
Sure!
"SINGULAR set . . ." Lucy, that's got to be Lady Travesty!
I guess . . . although last time BB's info wasn't, you know, completely accurate.
Nah, it's different this time, I can feel it.
It's got to be, right?
I mean, it's the only clue we've got! So it HAS to mean something!
Would I be talking about it so much if it didn't?
I guess I can't argue with that logic . . .
It makes total sense!
Ok, admittedly I haven't slept in days and just got my face smashed in with a stick, BUT—
Going to the wrong castle, joining up with you guys, coming to Scotland for no reason, running around this castle shooting ghosts, getting drunk, leaving you guys forever, coming back again, getting knocked out by Lady Travesty . . .
It all led to me being in this room so I could get a letter from an inconsistent source about something that MIGHT have something to do with the thing I was originally looking for!
You see??
I mean, what's more likely— THAT or the idea that I've been consistently misjudging things and making irrational mistakes?
I mean, I lost you somewhere in the middle of that, but I LIKE your energy!
Let's go to BATH!
YEAH!!
CLAP
I'm going to go tell Byron!
sniff
. . . Can I come?

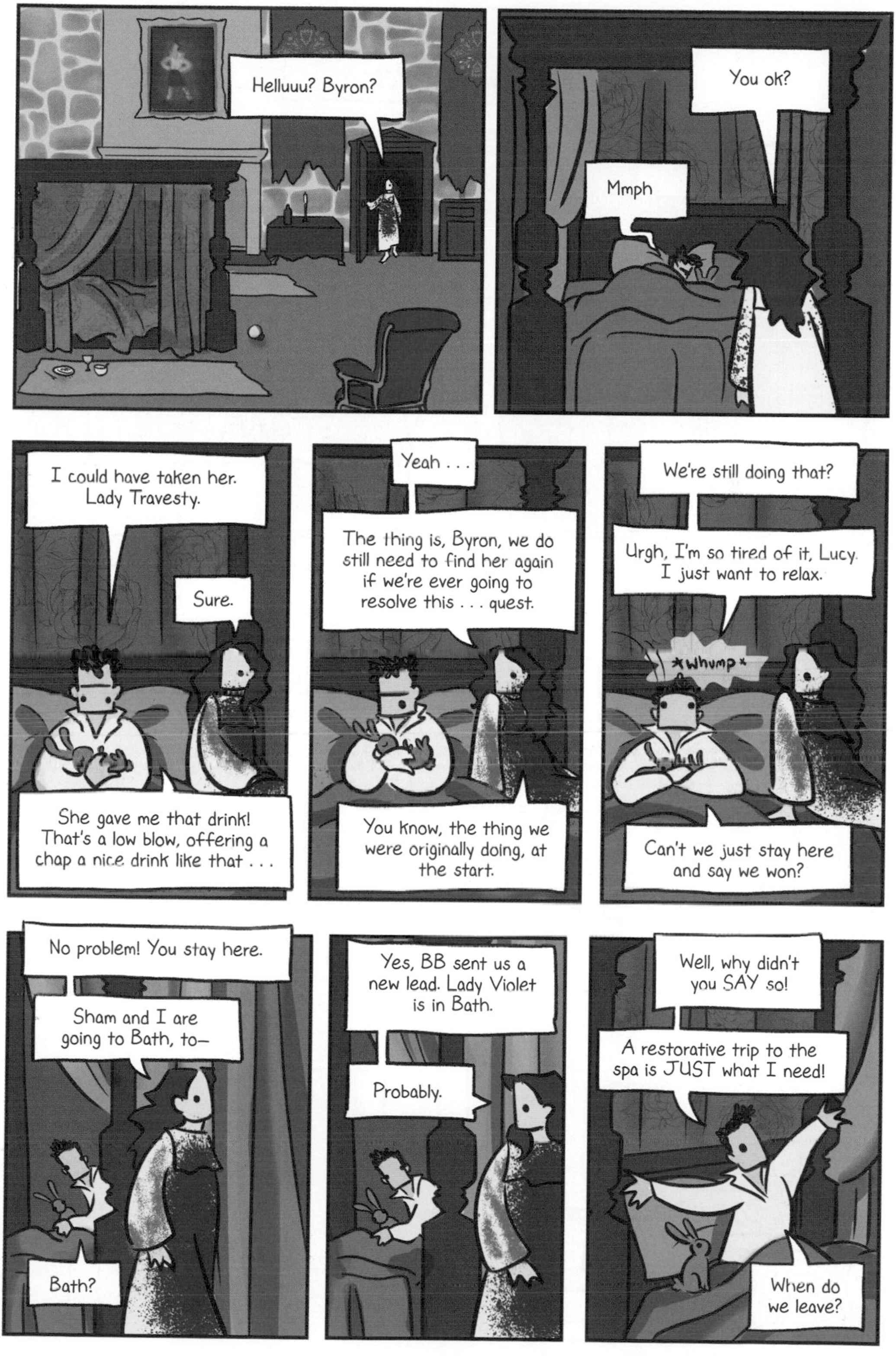
Helluuu? Byron?
You ok?
Mmph
I could have taken her. Lady Travesty.
Sure.
She gave me that drink! That's a low blow, offering a chap a nice drink like that . . .
Yeah . . .
The thing is, Byron, we do still need to find her again if we're ever going to resolve this . . . quest.
You know, the thing we were originally doing, at the start.
We're still doing that?
Urgh, I'm so tired of it, Lucy. I just want to relax.
whump
Can't we just stay here and say we won?
No problem! You stay here.
Sham and I are going to Bath, to—
Bath?
Yes, BB sent us a new lead. Lady Violet is in Bath.
Probably.
Well, why didn't you SAY so!
A restorative trip to the spa is JUST what I need!
When do we leave?

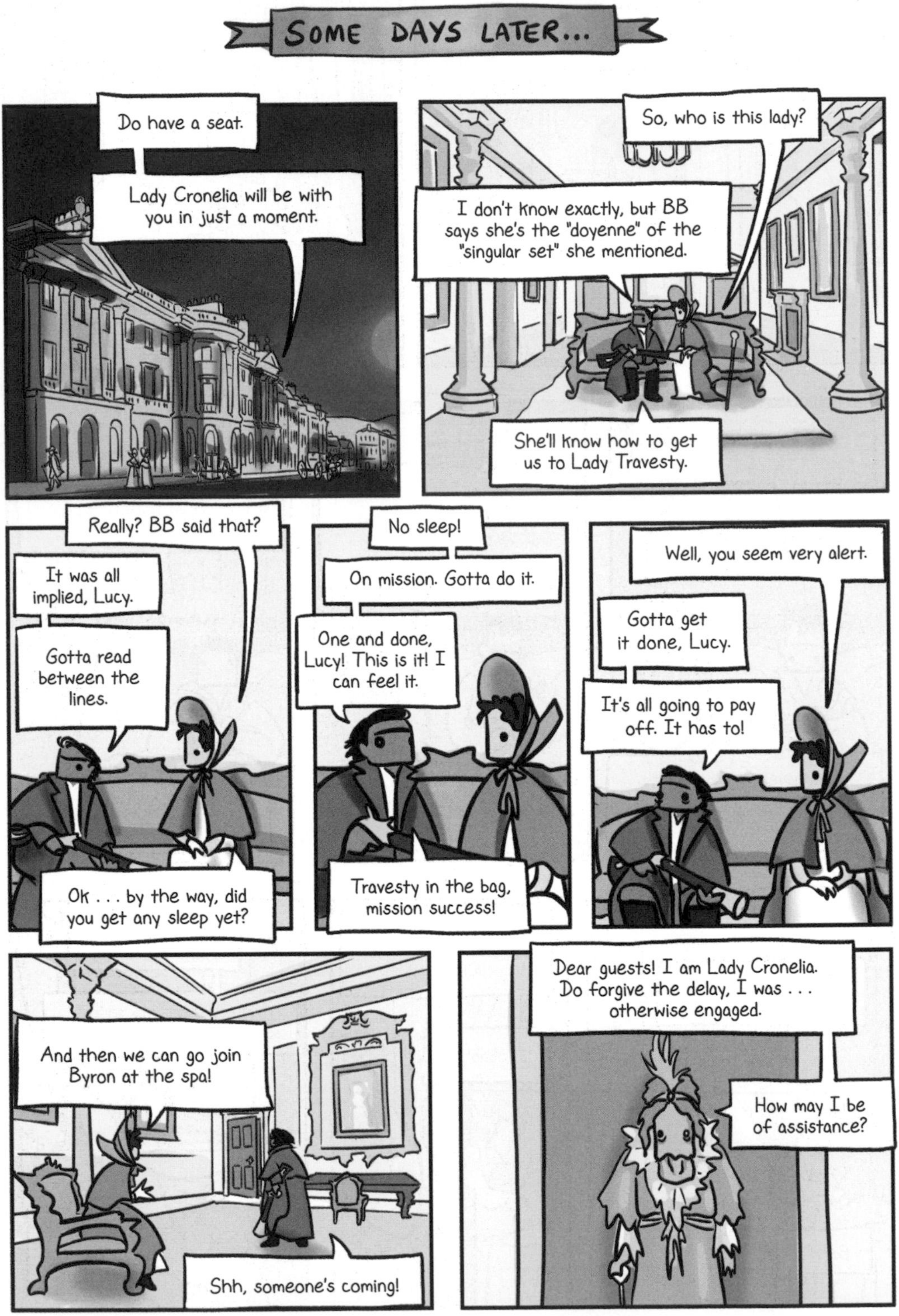
SOME DAYS LATER...
Do have a seat.
Lady Cronelia will be with you in just a moment.
So, who is this lady?
I don't know exactly, but BB says she's the "doyenne" of the "singular set" she mentioned.
She'll know how to get us to Lady Travesty.
Really? BB said that?
It was all implied, Lucy.
Gotta read between the lines.
Ok . . . by the way, did you get any sleep yet?
No sleep!
On mission. Gotta do it.
One and done, Lucy! This is it! I can feel it.
Travesty in the bag, mission success!
Well, you seem very alert.
Gotta get it done, Lucy.
It's all going to pay off. It has to!
And then we can go join Byron at the spa!
Shh, someone's coming!
Dear guests! I am Lady Cronelia. Do forgive the delay, I was . . . otherwise engaged.
How may I be of assistance?

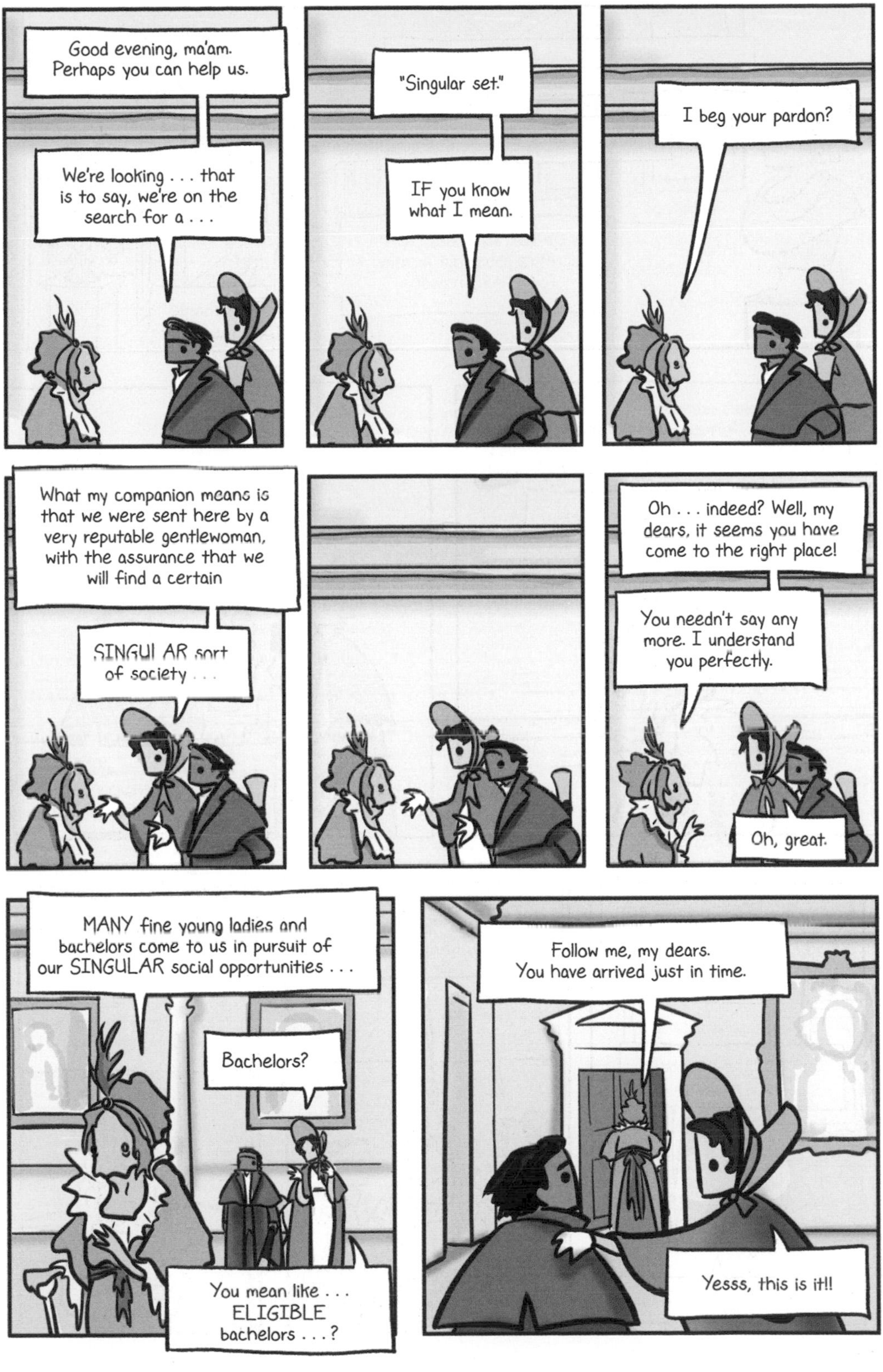

Good evening, ma'am. Perhaps you can help us.
We're looking . . . that is to say, we're on the search for a . . .
"Singular set."
IF you know what I mean.
I beg your pardon?
What my companion means is that we were sent here by a very reputable gentlewoman, with the assurance that we will find a certain
SINGULAR sort of society . . .
Oh . . . indeed? Well, my dears, it seems you have come to the right place!
You needn't say any more. I understand you perfectly.
Oh, great.
MANY fine young ladies and bachelors come to us in pursuit of our SINGULAR social opportunities . . .
Bachelors?
You mean like . . . ELIGIBLE bachelors . . . ?
Follow me, my dears. You have arrived just in time.
Yesss, this is it!!

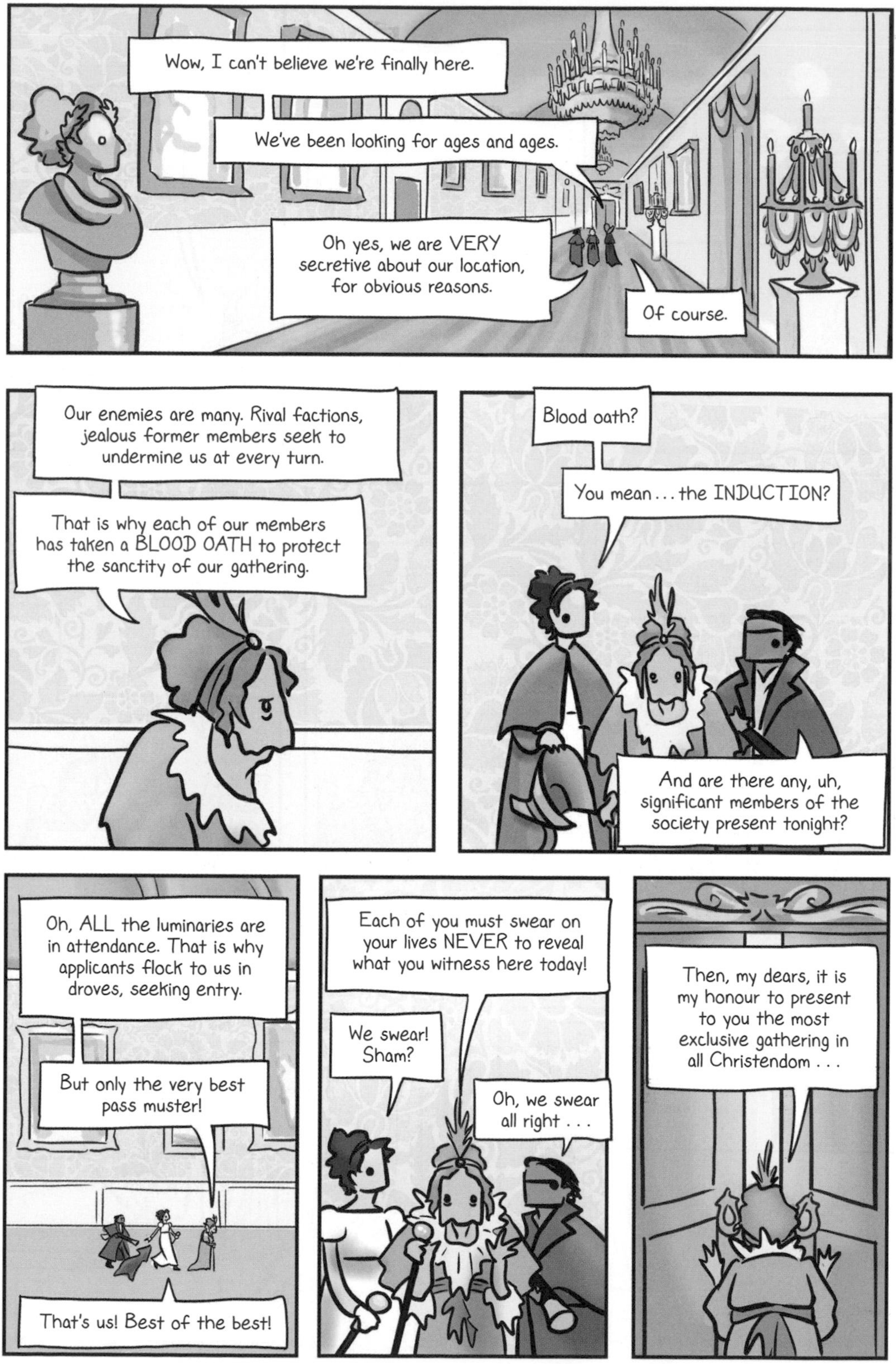

Wow, I can't believe we're finally here.
We've been looking for ages and ages.
Oh yes, we are VERY secretive about our location, for obvious reasons.
Of course.
Our enemies are many. Rival factions, jealous former members seek to undermine us at every turn.
That is why each of our members has taken a BLOOD OATH to protect the sanctity of our gathering.
Blood oath?
You mean . . . the INDUCTION?
And are there any, uh, significant members of the society present tonight?
Oh, ALL the luminaries are in attendance. That is why applicants flock to us in droves, seeking entry.
But only the very best pass muster!
That's us! Best of the best!
Each of you must swear on your lives NEVER to reveal what you witness here today!
We swear! Sham?
Oh, we swear all right . . .
Then, my dears, it is my honour to present to you the most exclusive gathering in all Christendom . . .

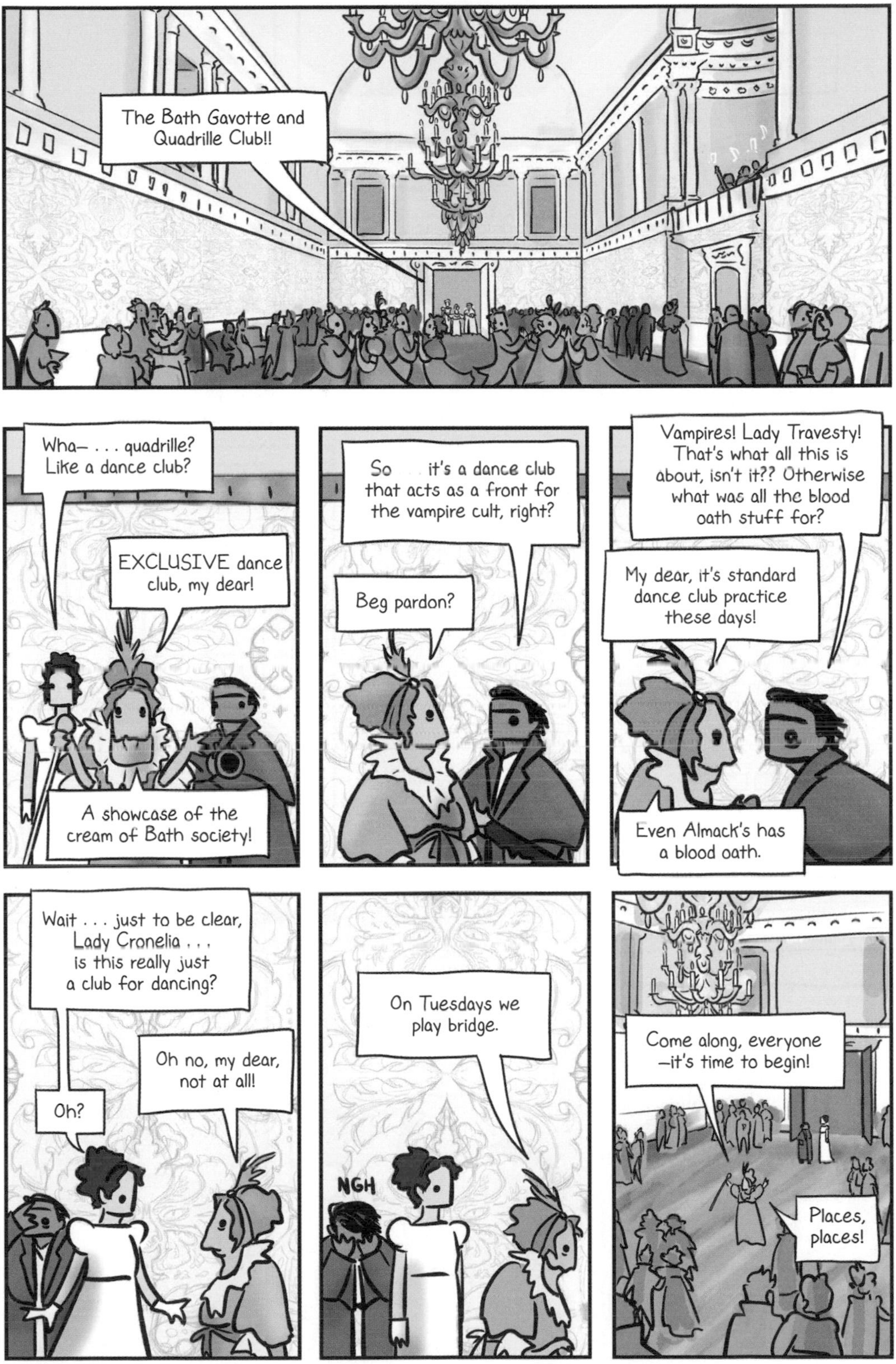

The Bath Gavotte and Quadrille Club!!
Wha– . . . quadrille? Like a dance club?
EXCLUSIVE dance club, my dear!
A showcase of the cream of Bath society!
So . . . it's a dance club that acts as a front for the vampire cult, right?
Beg pardon?
Vampires! Lady Travesty! That's what all this is about, isn't it?? Otherwise what was all the blood oath stuff for?
My dear, it's standard dance club practice these days!
Even Almack's has a blood oath.
Wait . . . just to be clear, Lady Cronelia . . . is this really just a club for dancing?
Oh no, my dear, not at all!
Oh?
On Tuesdays we play bridge.
NGH
Come along, everyone —it's time to begin!
Places, places!

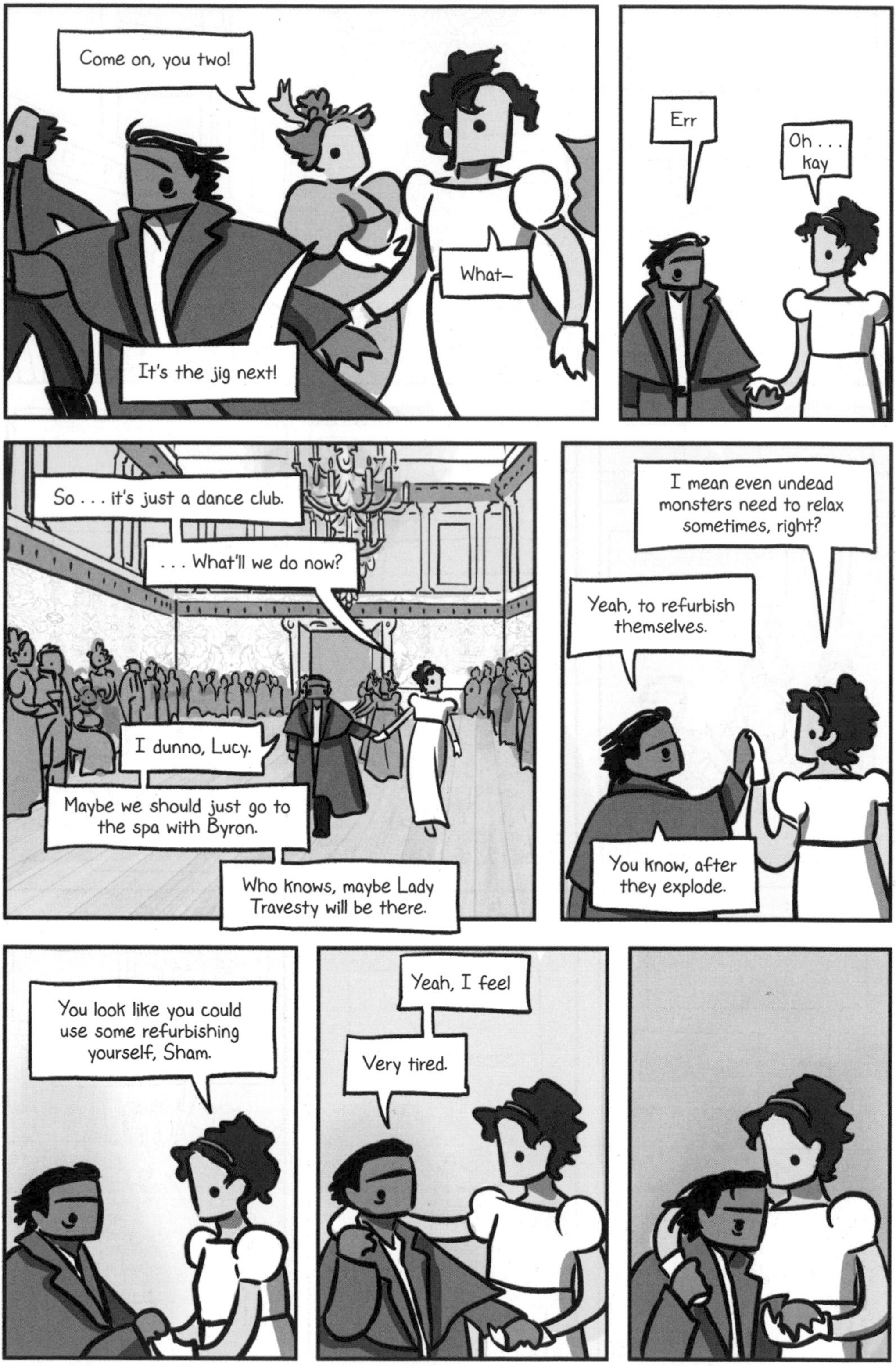

Come on, you two!
It's the jig next!
What–
Err
Oh . . . kay
So . . . it's just a dance club.
. . . What'll we do now?
I dunno, Lucy.
Maybe we should just go to the spa with Byron.
Who knows, maybe Lady Travesty will be there.
I mean even undead monsters need to relax sometimes, right?
Yeah, to refurbish themselves.
You know, after they explode.
You look like you could use some refurbishing yourself, Sham.
Yeah, I feel
Very tired.

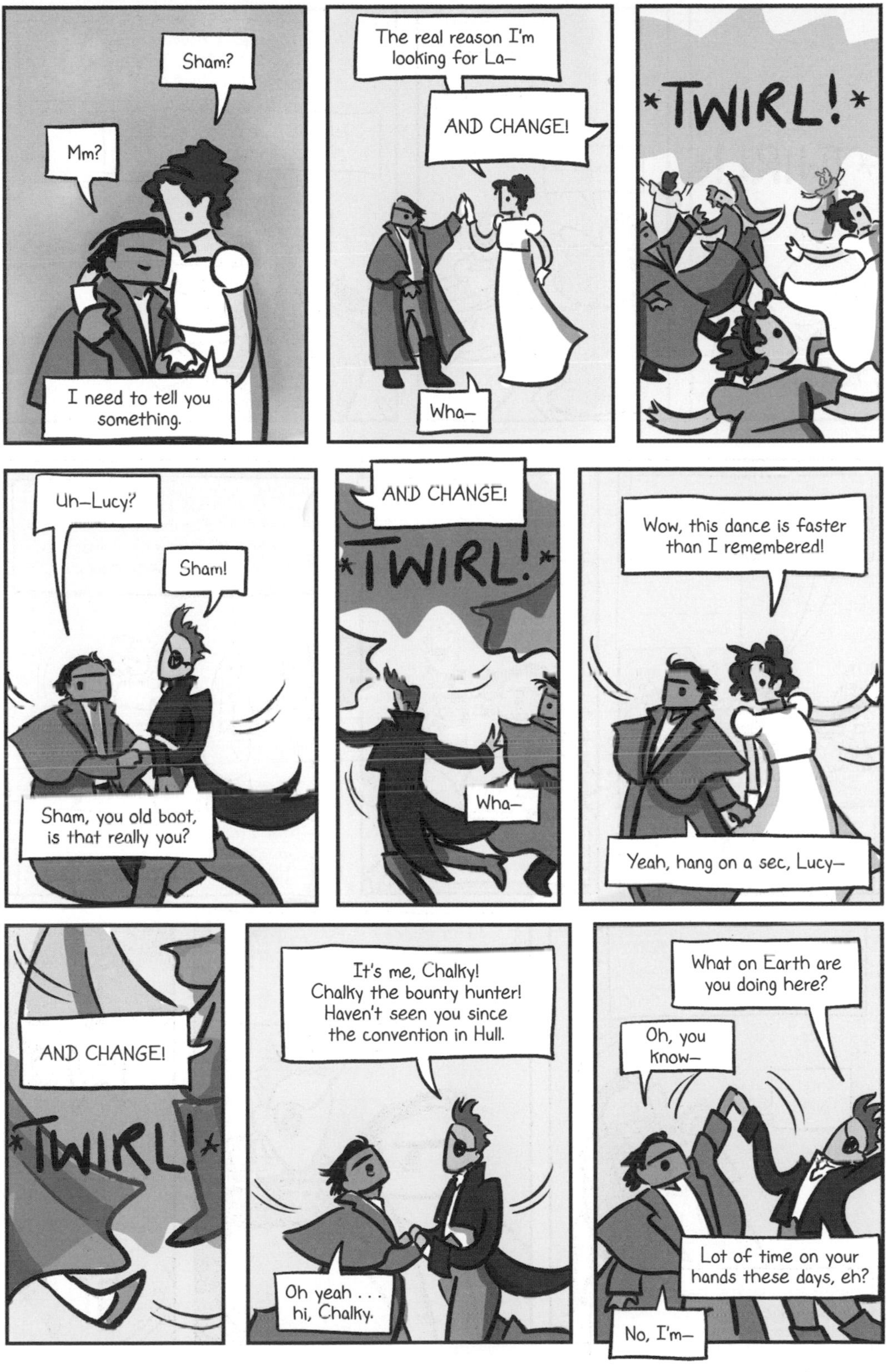
Sham?
Mm?
I need to tell you something.
The real reason I'm looking for La—
AND CHANGE!
Wha—
TWIRL!
Uh—Lucy?
Sham!
Sham, you old boot, is that really you?
AND CHANGE!
TWIRL!
Wha—
Wow, this dance is faster than I remembered!
Yeah, hang on a sec, Lucy—
AND CHANGE!
TWIRL!
It's me, Chalky! Chalky the bounty hunter! Haven't seen you since the convention in Hull.
Oh yeah . . . hi, Chalky.
What on Earth are you doing here?
Oh, you know—
Lot of time on your hands these days, eh?
No, I'm—

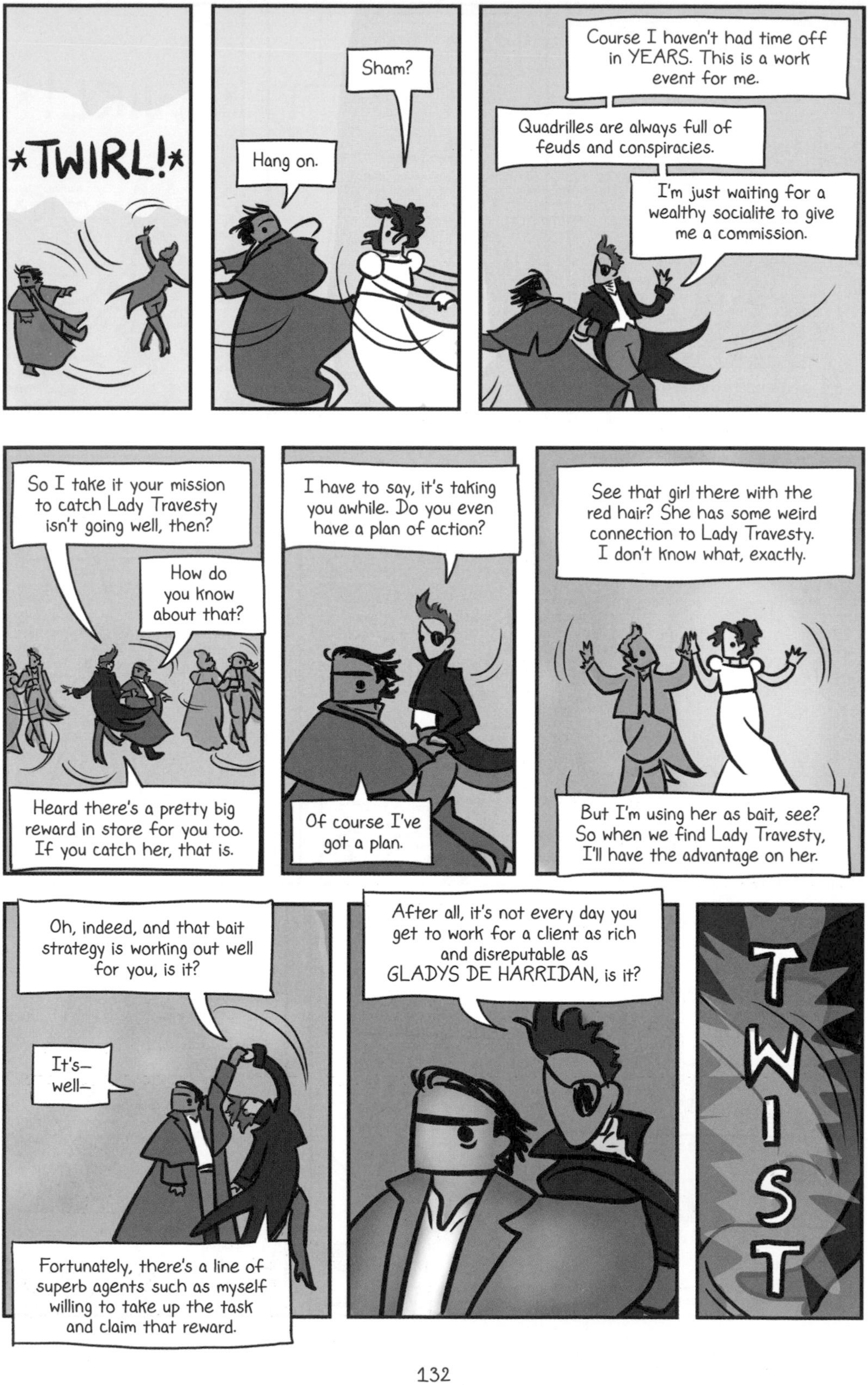

TWIRL!
Hang on.
Sham?
Course I haven't had time off in YEARS. This is a work event for me.
Quadrilles are always full of feuds and conspiracies.
I'm just waiting for a wealthy socialite to give me a commission.
So I take it your mission to catch Lady Travesty isn't going well, then?
How do you know about that?
Heard there's a pretty big reward in store for you too. If you catch her, that is.
I have to say, it's taking you awhile. Do you even have a plan of action?
Of course I've got a plan.
See that girl there with the red hair? She has some weird connection to Lady Travesty. I don't know what, exactly.
But I'm using her as bait, see? So when we find Lady Travesty, I'll have the advantage on her.
Oh, indeed, and that bait strategy is working out well for you, is it?
It's— well—
Fortunately, there's a line of superb agents such as myself willing to take up the task and claim that reward.
After all, it's not every day you get to work for a client as rich and disreputable as GLADYS DE HARRIDAN, is it?
TWIST

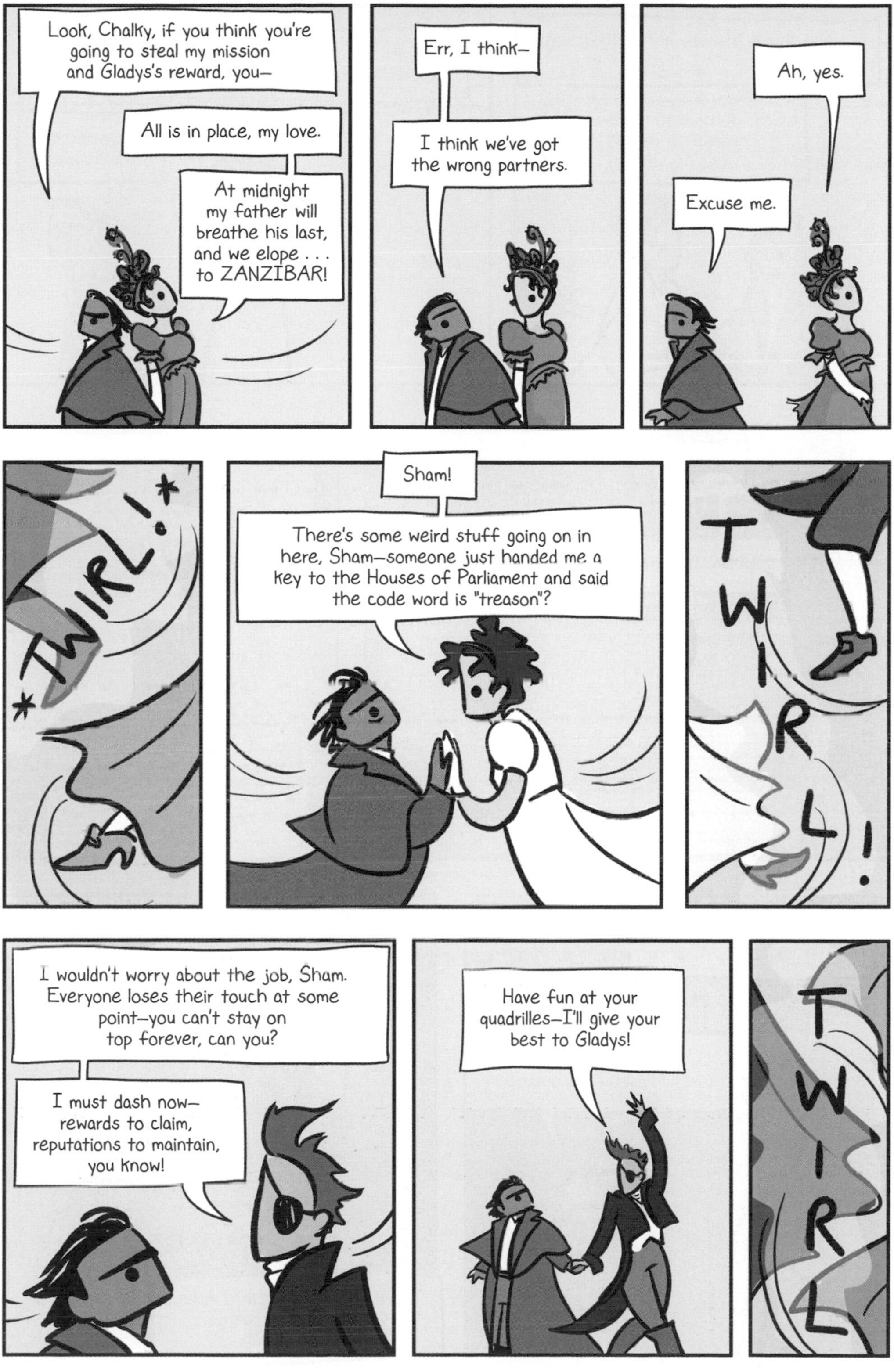

Look, Chalky, if you think you're going to steal my mission and Gladys's reward, you—
All is in place, my love.
At midnight my father will breathe his last, and we elope . . . to ZANZIBAR!
Err, I think—
I think we've got the wrong partners.
Ah, yes.
Excuse me.
TWIRL!
Sham!
There's some weird stuff going on in here, Sham—someone just handed me a key to the Houses of Parliament and said the code word is "treason"?
TWIRL!
I wouldn't worry about the job, Sham. Everyone loses their touch at some point—you can't stay on top forever, can you?
I must dash now—rewards to claim, reputations to maintain, you know!
Have fun at your quadrilles—I'll give your best to Gladys!
TWIRL

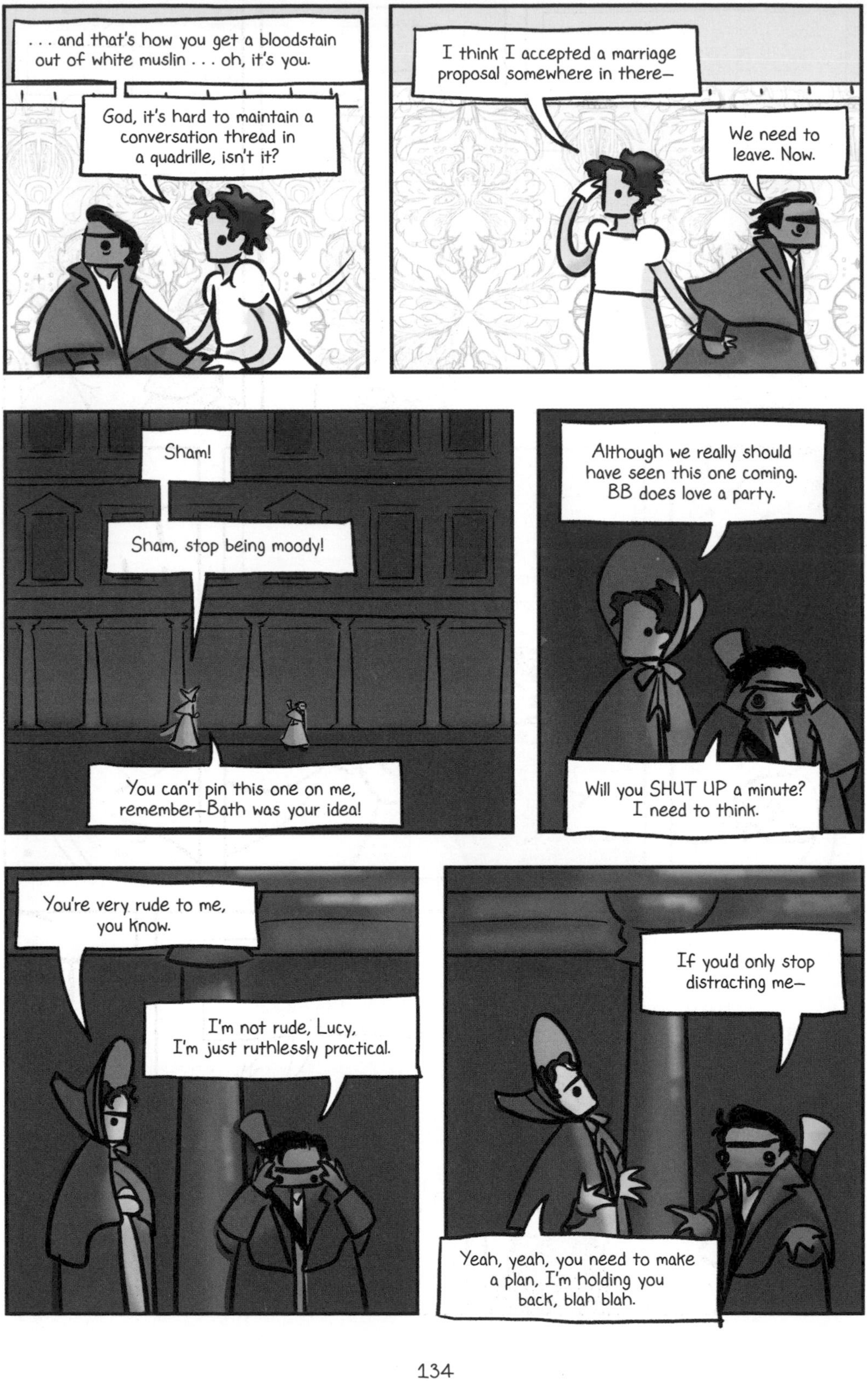

. . . and that's how you get a bloodstain out of white muslin . . . oh, it's you.
God, it's hard to maintain a conversation thread in a quadrille, isn't it?
I think I accepted a marriage proposal somewhere in there–
We need to leave. Now.
Sham!
Sham, stop being moody!
You can't pin this one on me, remember–Bath was your idea!
Although we really should have seen this one coming. BB does love a party.
Will you SHUT UP a minute? I need to think.
You're very rude to me, you know.
I'm not rude, Lucy, I'm just ruthlessly practical.
If you'd only stop distracting me–
Yeah, yeah, you need to make a plan, I'm holding you back, blah blah.

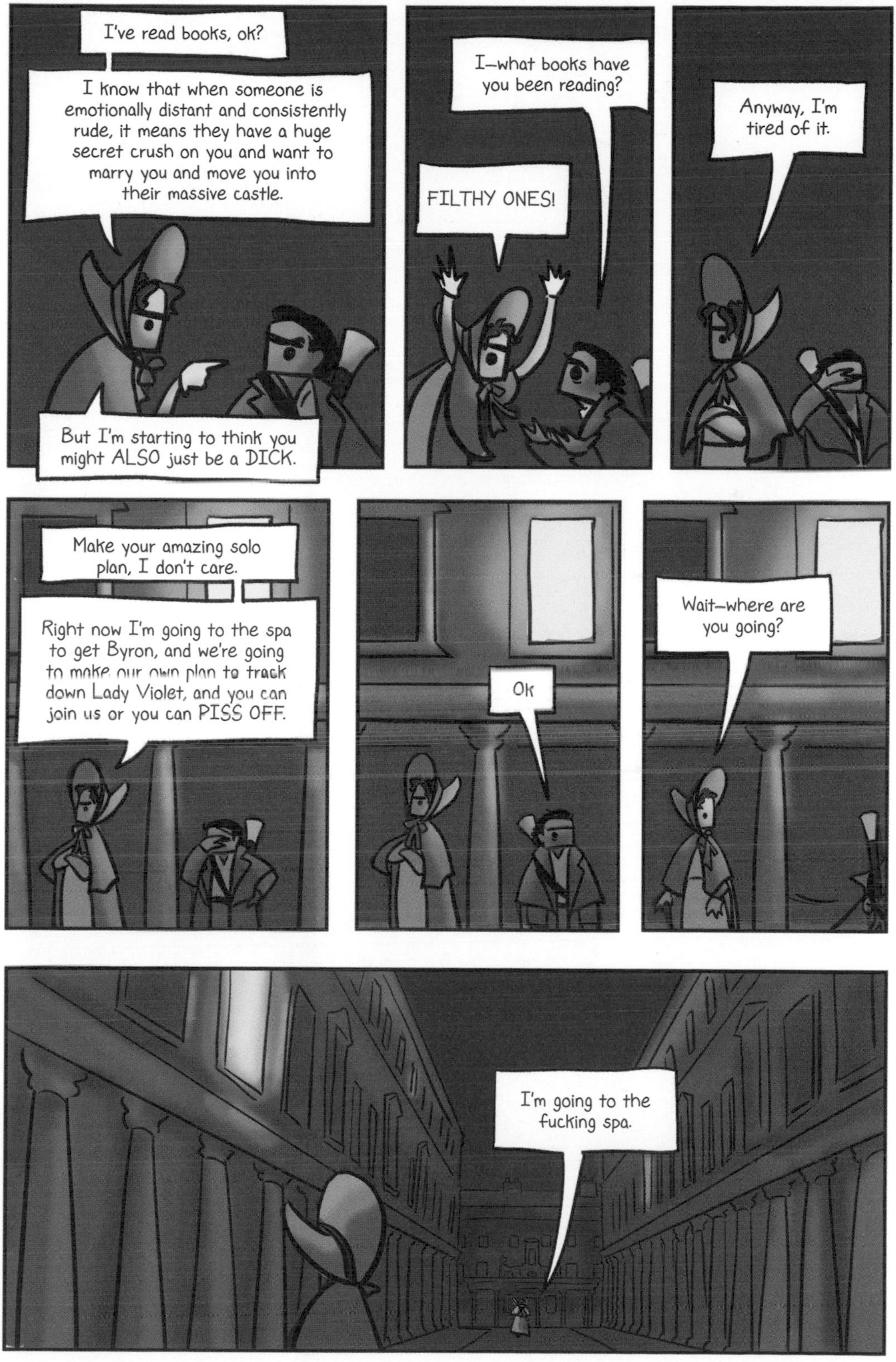
I've read books, ok?
I know that when someone is emotionally distant and consistently rude, it means they have a huge secret crush on you and want to marry you and move you into their massive castle.
But I'm starting to think you might ALSO just be a DICK.
I—what books have you been reading?
FILTHY ONES!
Anyway, I'm tired of it.
Make your amazing solo plan, I don't care.
Right now I'm going to the spa to get Byron, and we're going to make our own plan to track down Lady Violet, and you can join us or you can PISS OFF.
Ok
Wait—where are you going?
I'm going to the fucking spa.

CHAPTER IX - THE TRIP

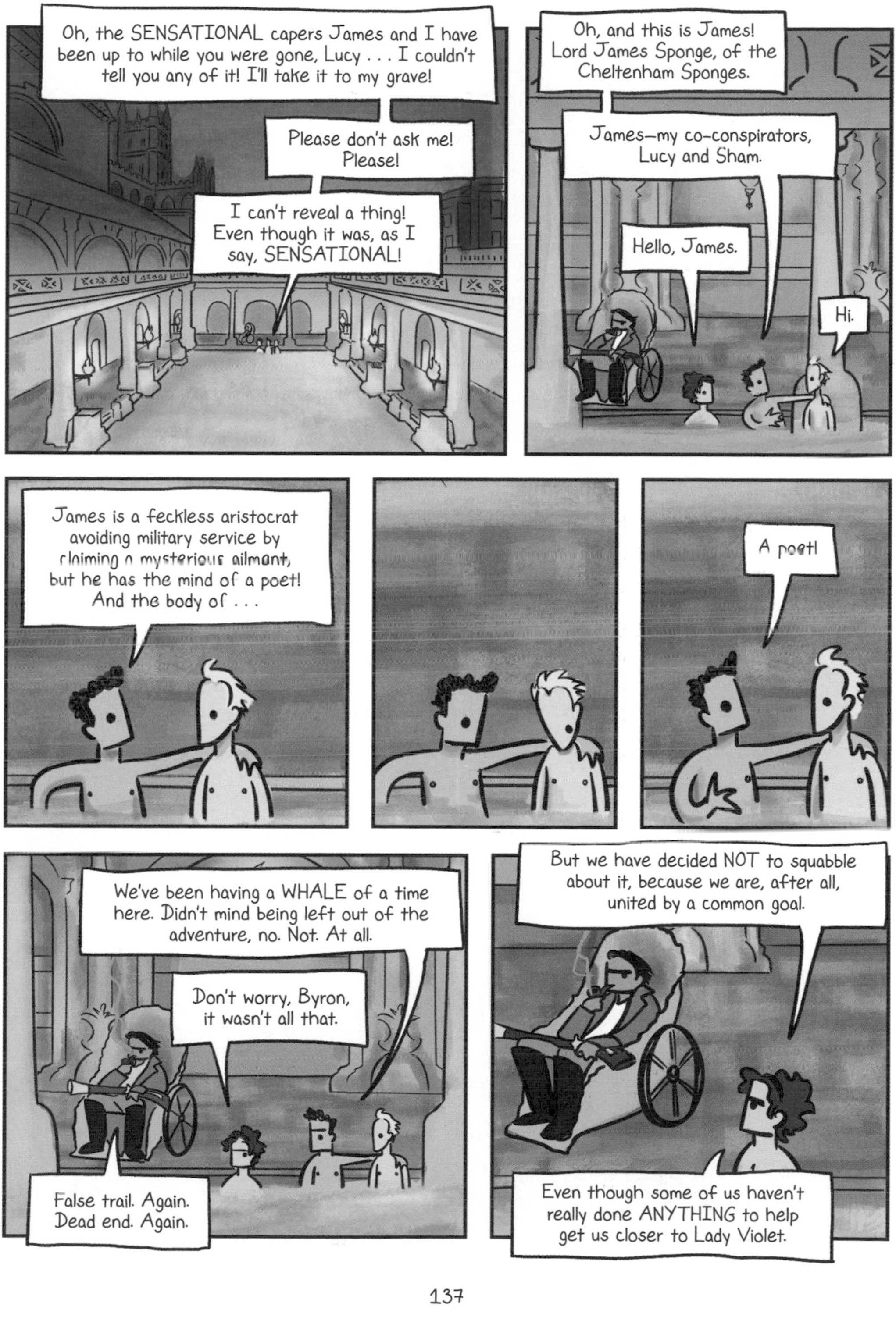
Oh, the SENSATIONAL capers James and I have been up to while you were gone, Lucy . . . I couldn't tell you any of it! I'll take it to my grave!
Please don't ask me! Please!
I can't reveal a thing! Even though it was, as I say, SENSATIONAL!
Oh, and this is James! Lord James Sponge, of the Cheltenham Sponges.
James—my co-conspirators, Lucy and Sham.
Hello, James.
Hi.
James is a feckless aristocrat avoiding military service by claiming a mysterious ailment, but he has the mind of a poet! And the body of . . .
A poet!
We've been having a WHALE of a time here. Didn't mind being left out of the adventure, no. Not. At all.
Don't worry, Byron, it wasn't all that.
False trail. Again. Dead end. Again.
But we have decided NOT to squabble about it, because we are, after all, united by a common goal.
Even though some of us haven't really done ANYTHING to help get us closer to Lady Violet.

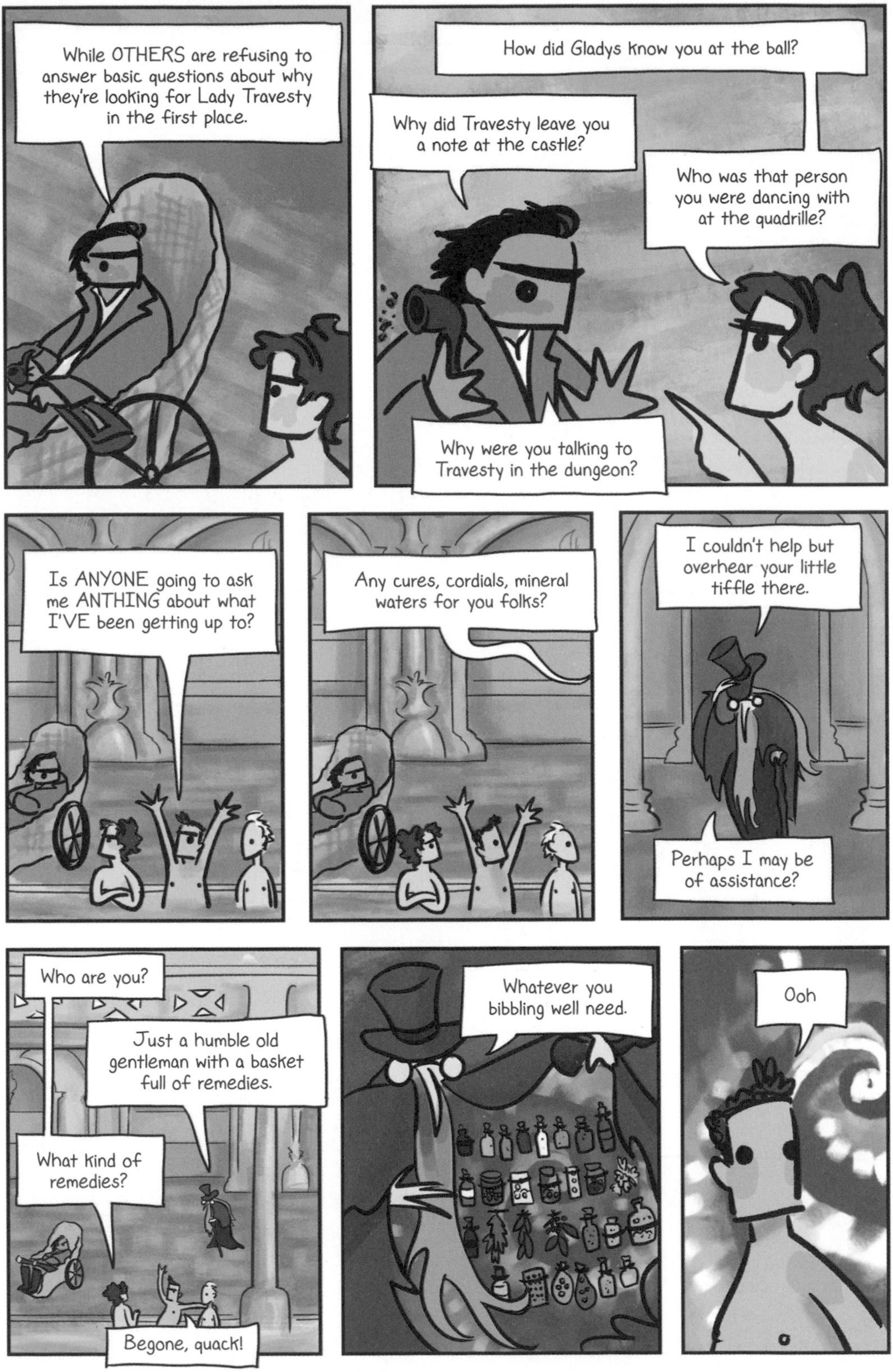
While OTHERS are refusing to answer basic questions about why they're looking for Lady Travesty in the first place.
How did Gladys know you at the ball?
Why did Travesty leave you a note at the castle?
Who was that person you were dancing with at the quadrille?
Why were you talking to Travesty in the dungeon?
Is ANYONE going to ask me ANTHING about what I'VE been getting up to?
Any cures, cordials, mineral waters for you folks?
I couldn't help but overhear your little tiffle there.
Perhaps I may be of assistance?
Who are you?
Just a humble old gentleman with a basket full of remedies.
What kind of remedies?
Begone, quack!
Whatever you bibbling well need.
Ooh

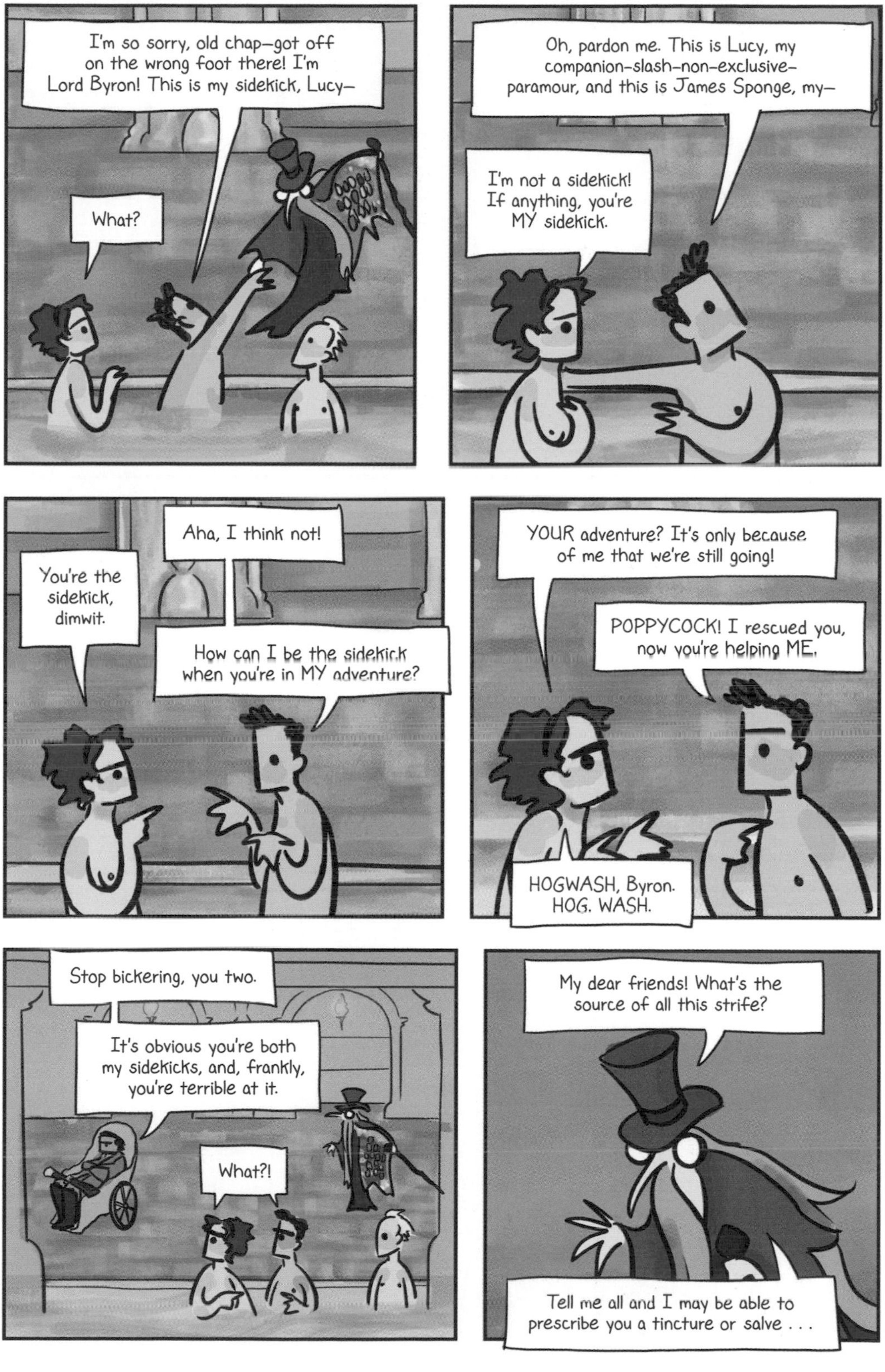
I'm so sorry, old chap—got off on the wrong foot there! I'm Lord Byron! This is my sidekick, Lucy—
What?
Oh, pardon me. This is Lucy, my companion-slash-non-exclusive-paramour, and this is James Sponge, my—
I'm not a sidekick! If anything, you're MY sidekick.
Aha, I think not!
You're the sidekick, dimwit.
How can I be the sidekick when you're in MY adventure?
YOUR adventure? It's only because of me that we're still going!
POPPYCOCK! I rescued you, now you're helping ME.
HOGWASH, Byron. HOG. WASH.
Stop bickering, you two.
It's obvious you're both my sidekicks, and, frankly, you're terrible at it.
What?!
My dear friends! What's the source of all this strife?
Tell me all and I may be able to prescribe you a tincture or salve . . .

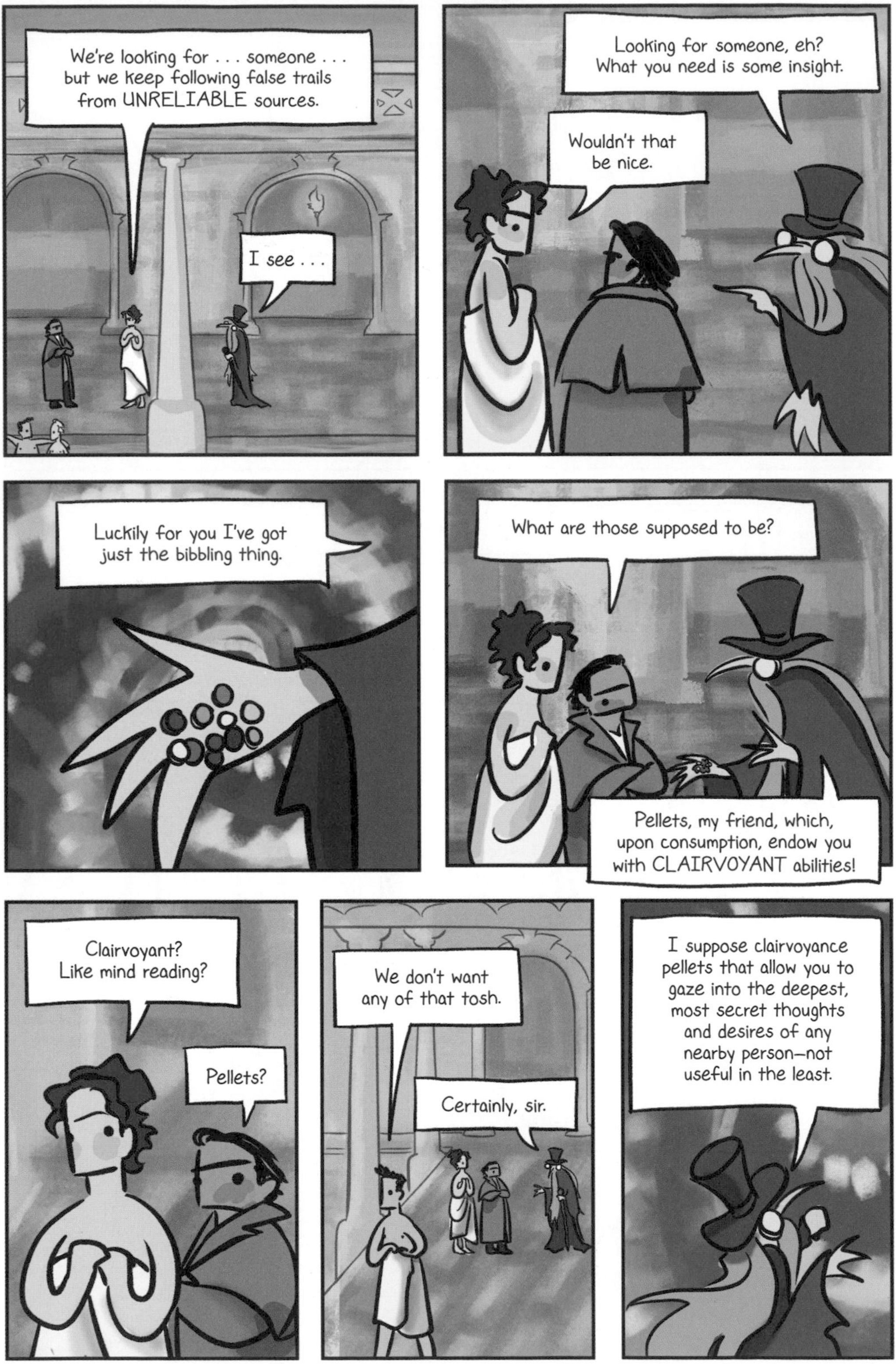
We're looking for . . . someone . . . but we keep following false trails from UNRELIABLE sources.
I see . . .
Looking for someone, eh? What you need is some insight.
Wouldn't that be nice.
Luckily for you I've got just the bibbling thing.
What are those supposed to be?
Pellets, my friend, which, upon consumption, endow you with CLAIRVOYANT abilities!
Clairvoyant? Like mind reading?
Pellets?
We don't want any of that tosh.
Certainly, sir.
I suppose clairvoyance pellets that allow you to gaze into the deepest, most secret thoughts and desires of any nearby person—not useful in the least.

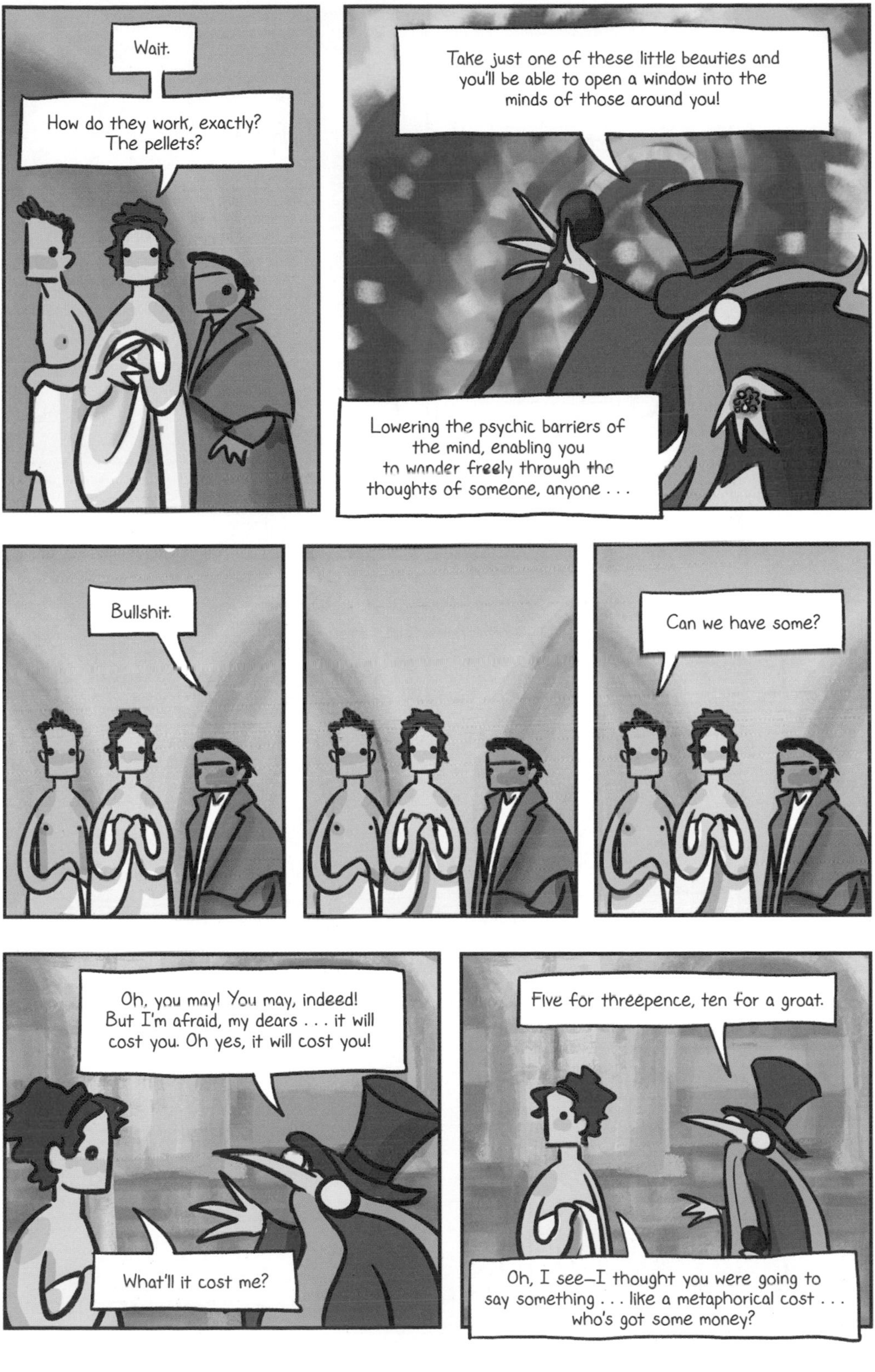
Wait.
How do they work, exactly? The pellets?
Take just one of these little beauties and you'll be able to open a window into the minds of those around you!
Lowering the psychic barriers of the mind, enabling you to wander freely through the thoughts of someone, anyone . . .
Bullshit.
Can we have some?
Oh, you may! You may, indeed! But I'm afraid, my dears . . . it will cost you. Oh yes, it will cost you!
What'll it cost me?
Five for threepence, ten for a groat.
Oh, I see—I thought you were going to say something . . . like a metaphorical cost . . . who's got some money?

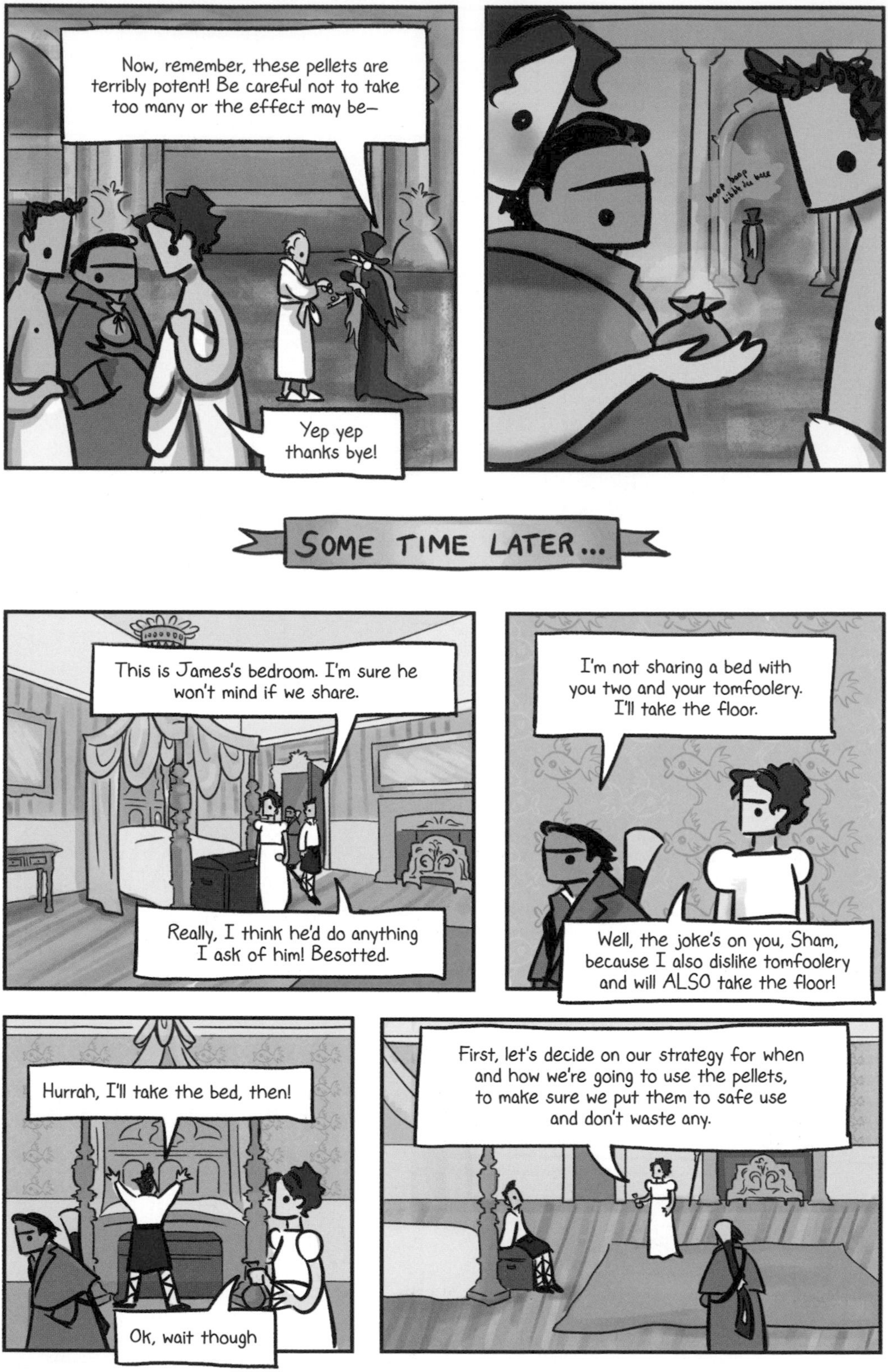

Now, remember, these pellets are terribly potent! Be careful not to take too many or the effect may be—
Yep yep thanks bye!
SOME TIME LATER...
This is James's bedroom. I'm sure he won't mind if we share.
Really, I think he'd do anything I ask of him! Besotted.
I'm not sharing a bed with you two and your tomfoolery. I'll take the floor.
Well, the joke's on you, Sham, because I also dislike tomfoolery and will ALSO take the floor!
Hurrah, I'll take the bed, then!
Ok, wait though
First, let's decide on our strategy for when and how we're going to use the pellets, to make sure we put them to safe use and don't waste any.

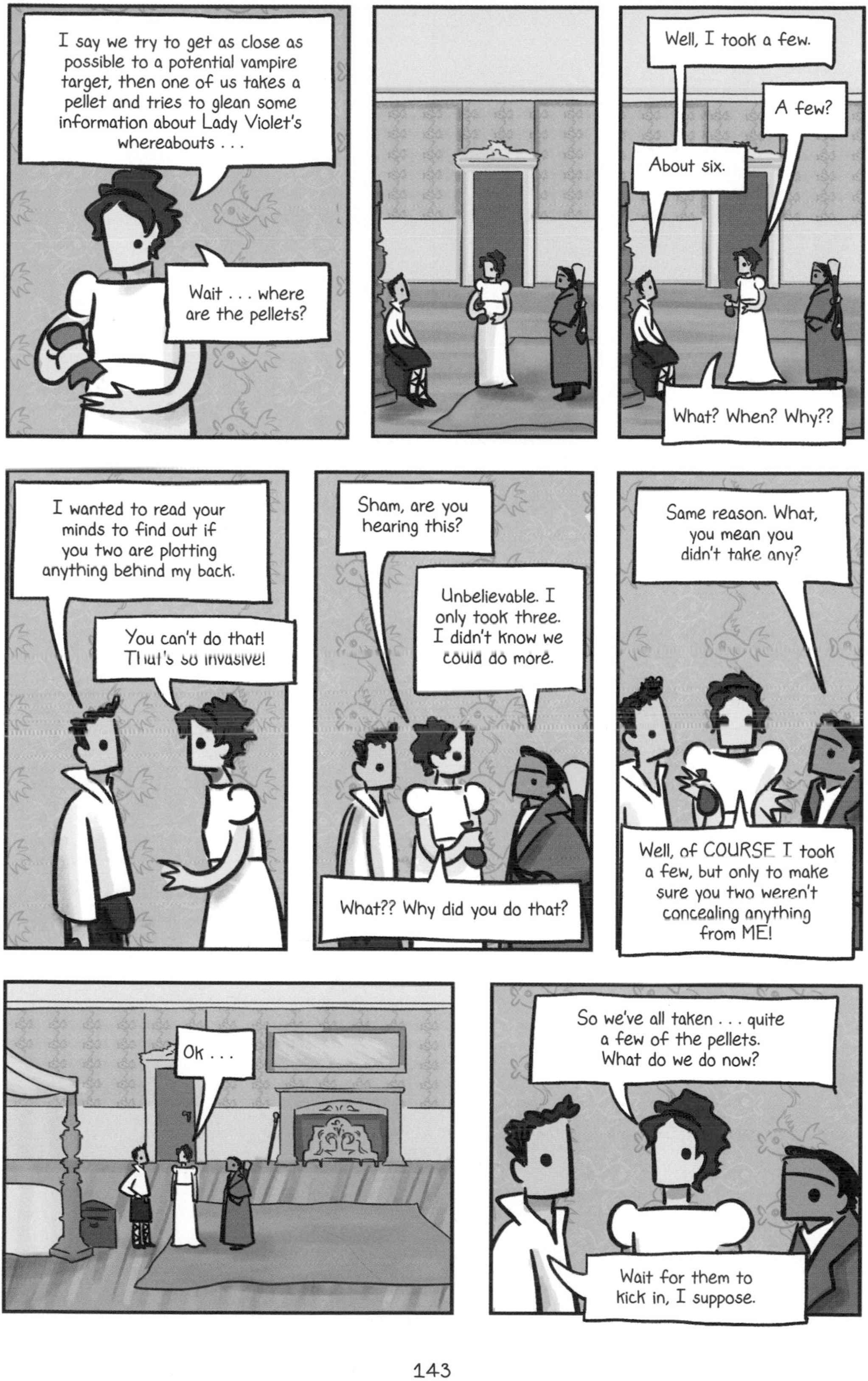

I say we try to get as close as possible to a potential vampire target, then one of us takes a pellet and tries to glean some information about Lady Violet's whereabouts . . .
Wait . . . where are the pellets?
Well, I took a few.
A few?
About six.
What? When? Why??
I wanted to read your minds to find out if you two are plotting anything behind my back.
You can't do that! That's so invasive!
Sham, are you hearing this?
Unbelievable. I only took three. I didn't know we could do more.
What?? Why did you do that?
Same reason. What, you mean you didn't take any?
Well, of COURSE I took a few, but only to make sure you two weren't concealing anything from ME!
Ok . . .
So we've all taken . . . quite a few of the pellets. What do we do now?
Wait for them to kick in, I suppose.

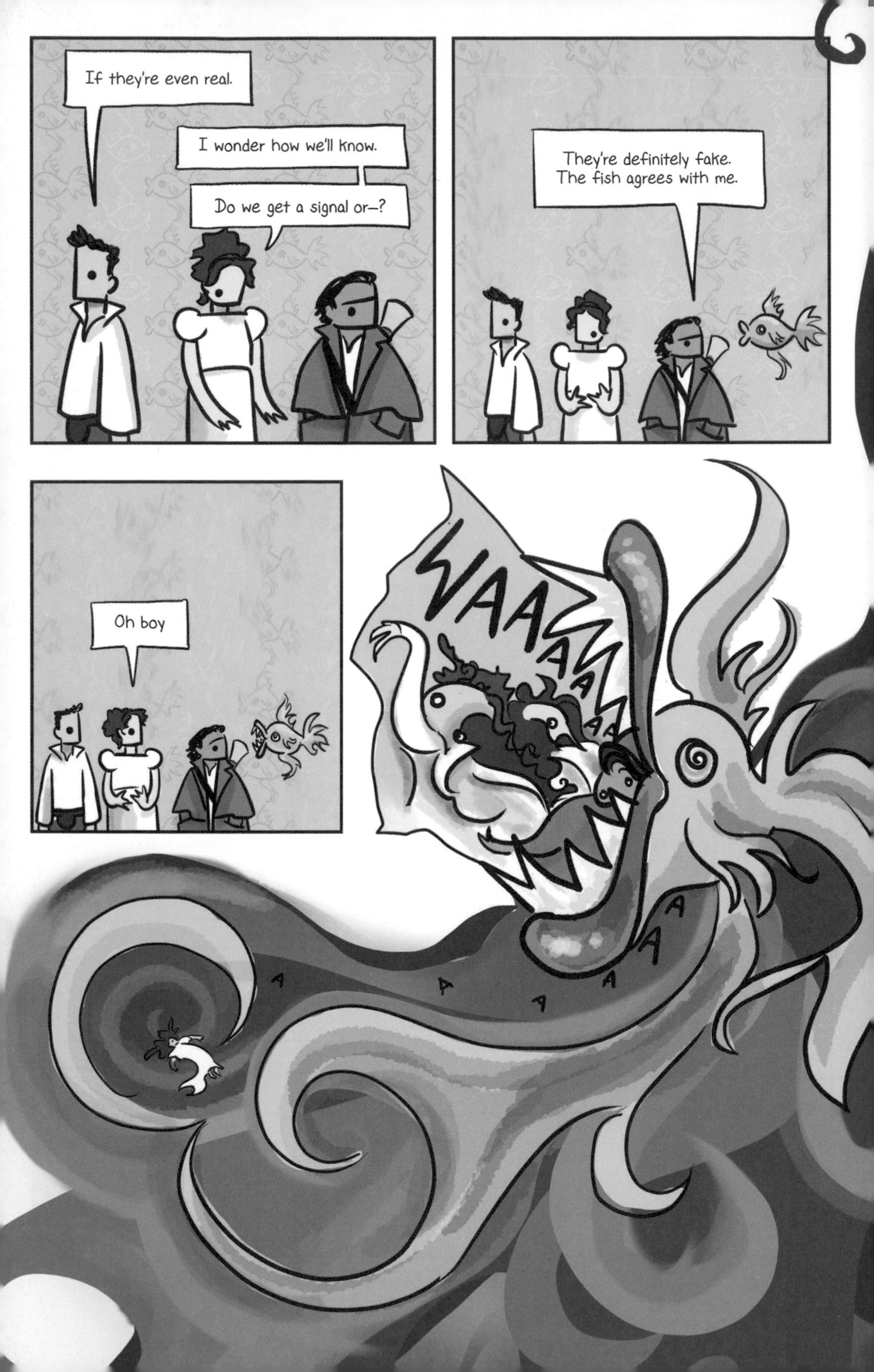

If they're even real.
I wonder how we'll know.
Do we get a signal or–?
They're definitely fake.
The fish agrees with me.
Oh boy
WAAAAAAA
A
A
A
A
A
A
A
A

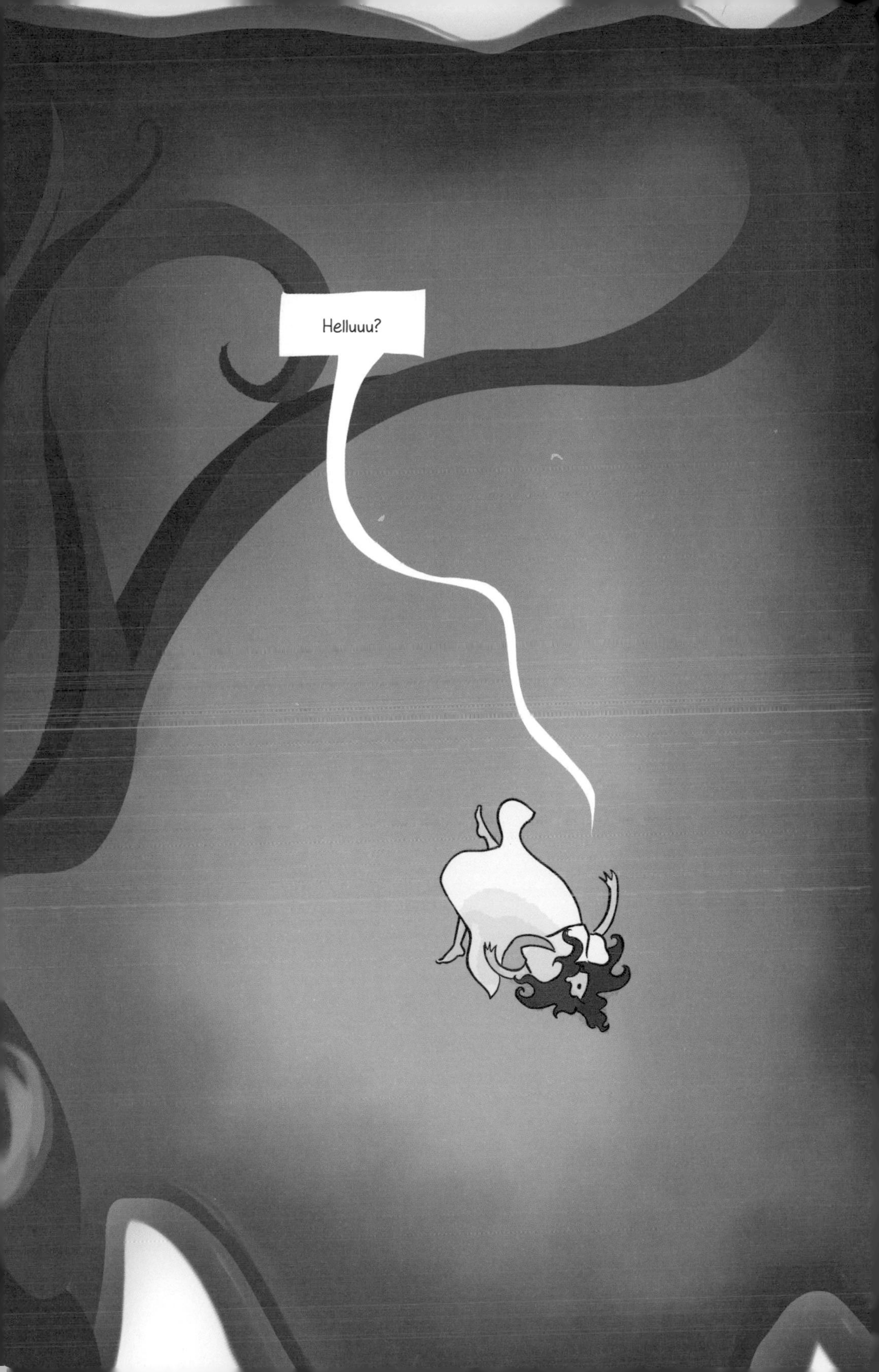
Helluuu?

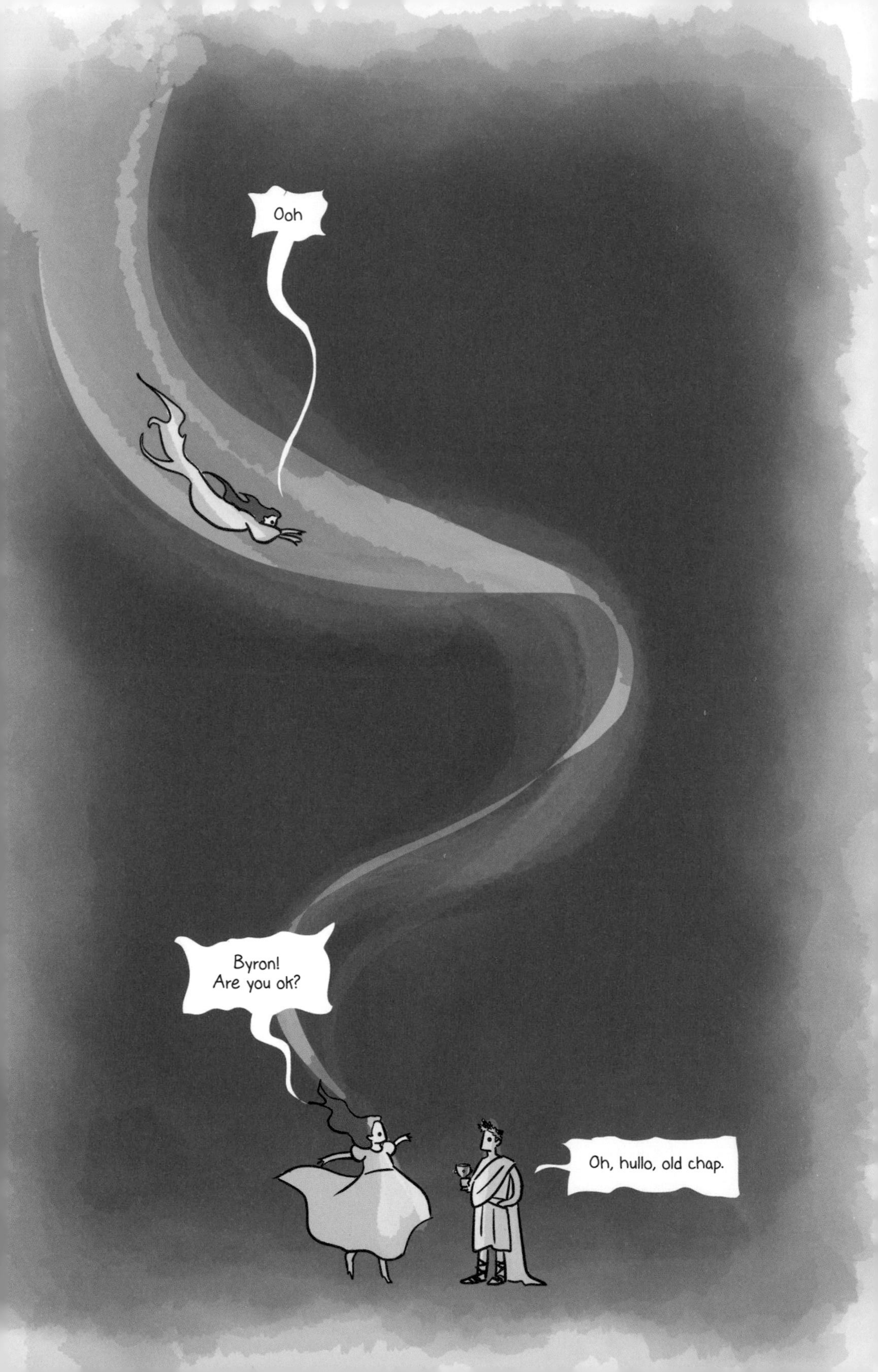
Ooh
Byron! Are you ok?
Oh, hullo, old chap.

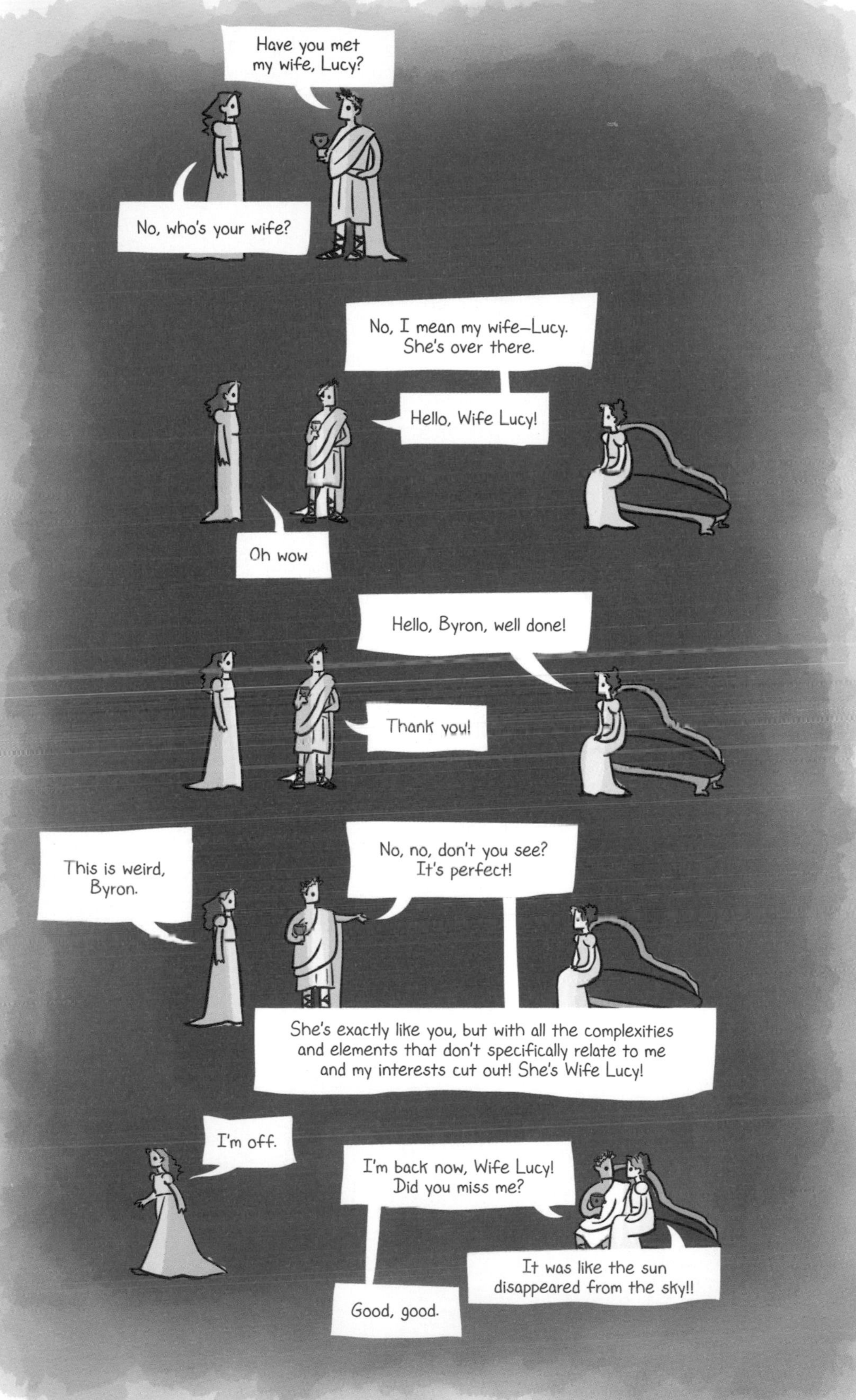
Have you met my wife, Lucy?
No, who's your wife?
No, I mean my wife—Lucy. She's over there.
Hello, Wife Lucy!
Oh wow
Hello, Byron, well done!
Thank you!
This is weird, Byron.
No, no, don't you see? It's perfect!
She's exactly like you, but with all the complexities and elements that don't specifically relate to me and my interests cut out! She's Wife Lucy!
I'm off.
I'm back now, Wife Lucy! Did you miss me?
It was like the sun disappeared from the sky!!
Good, good.

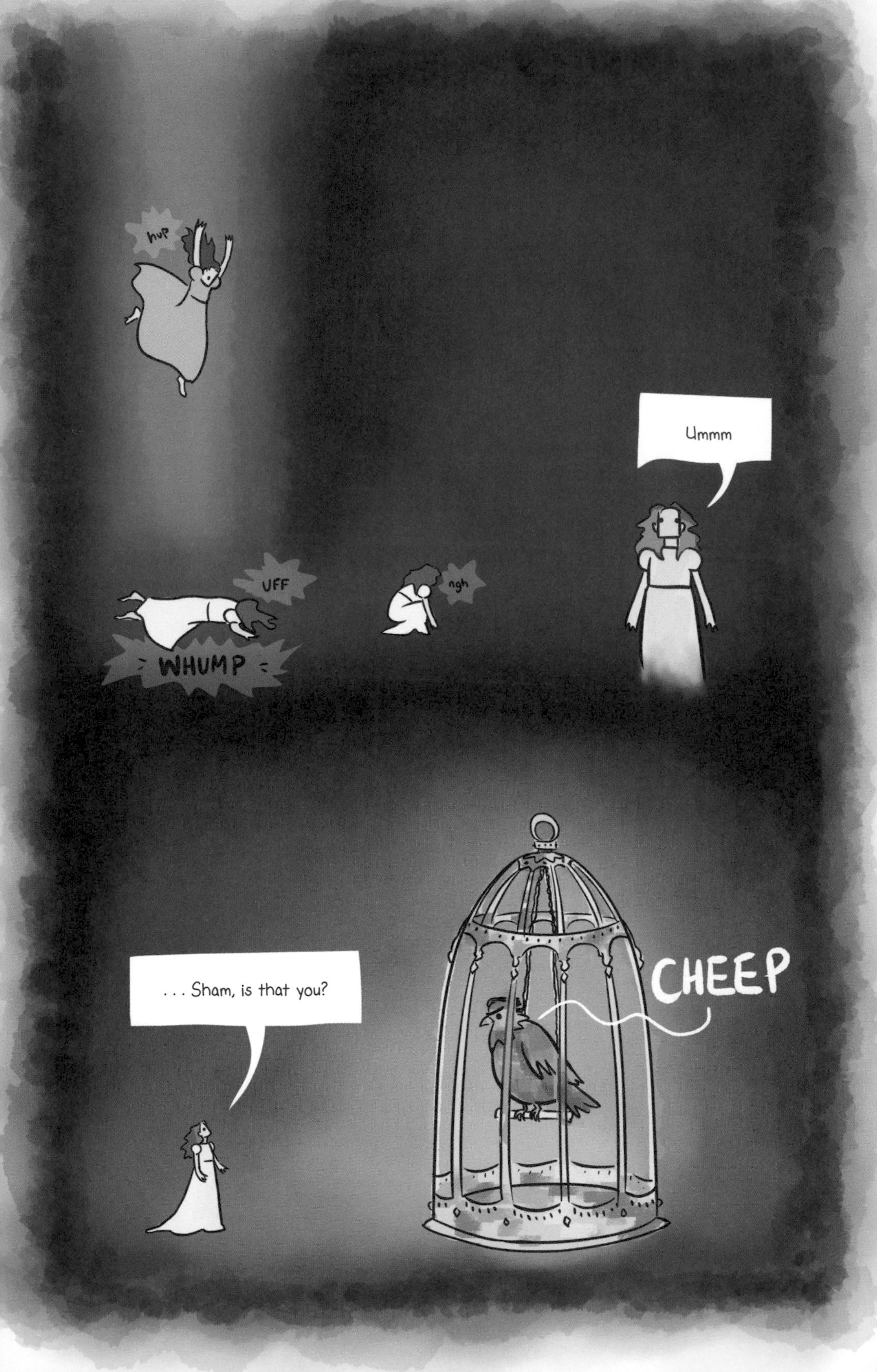
hup
UFF
WHUMP
ngh
Ummm
. . . Sham, is that you?
CHEEP

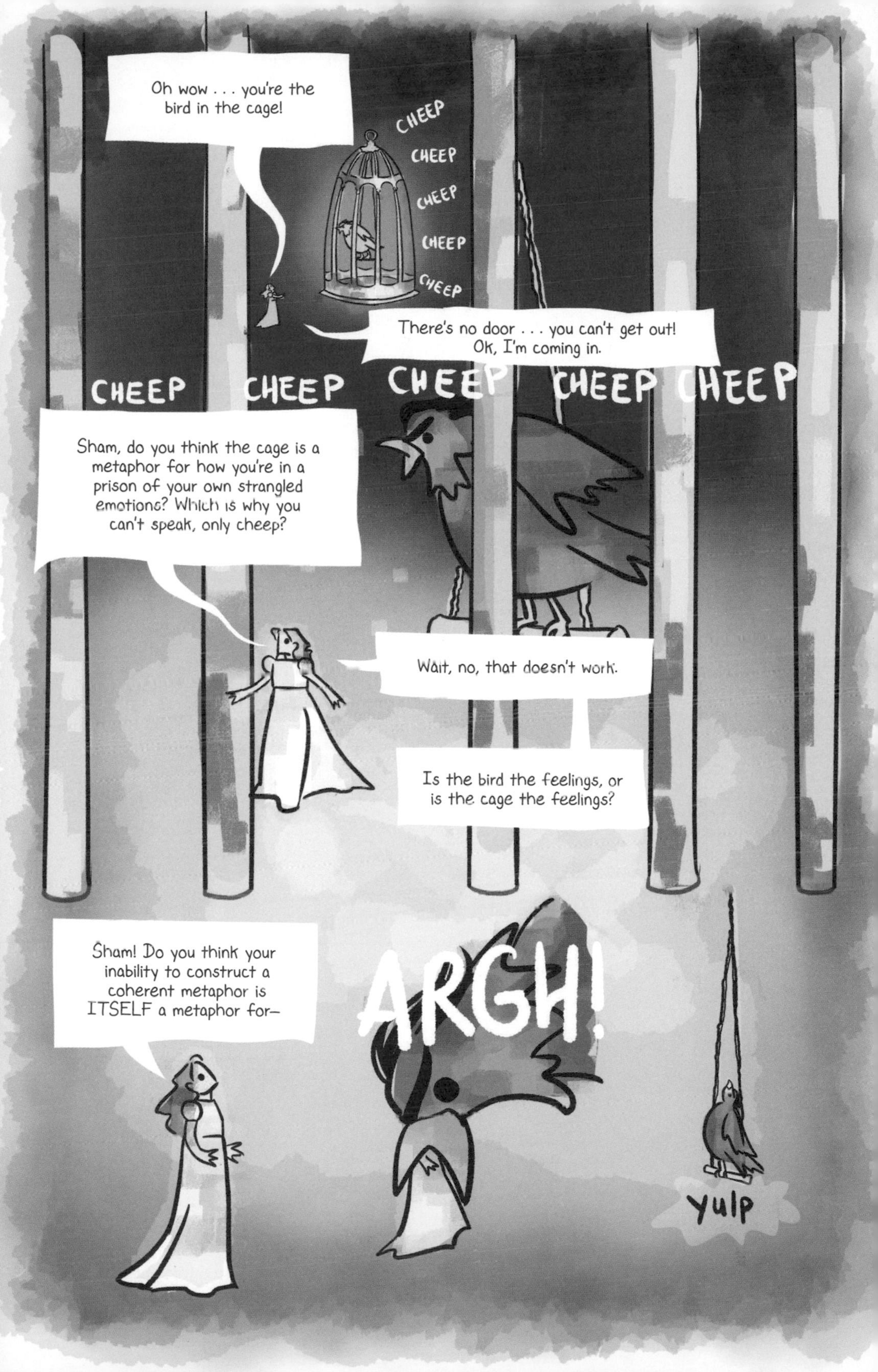
Oh wow . . . you're the bird in the cage!
CHEEP
CHEEP
CHEEP
CHEEP
CHEEP
There's no door . . . you can't get out! Ok, I'm coming in.
CHEEP CHEEP CHEEP CHEEP CHEEP
Sham, do you think the cage is a metaphor for how you're in a prison of your own strangled emotions? Which is why you can't speak, only cheep?
Wait, no, that doesn't work.
Is the bird the feelings, or is the cage the feelings?
Sham! Do you think your inability to construct a coherent metaphor is ITSELF a metaphor for—
ARGH!
yulp

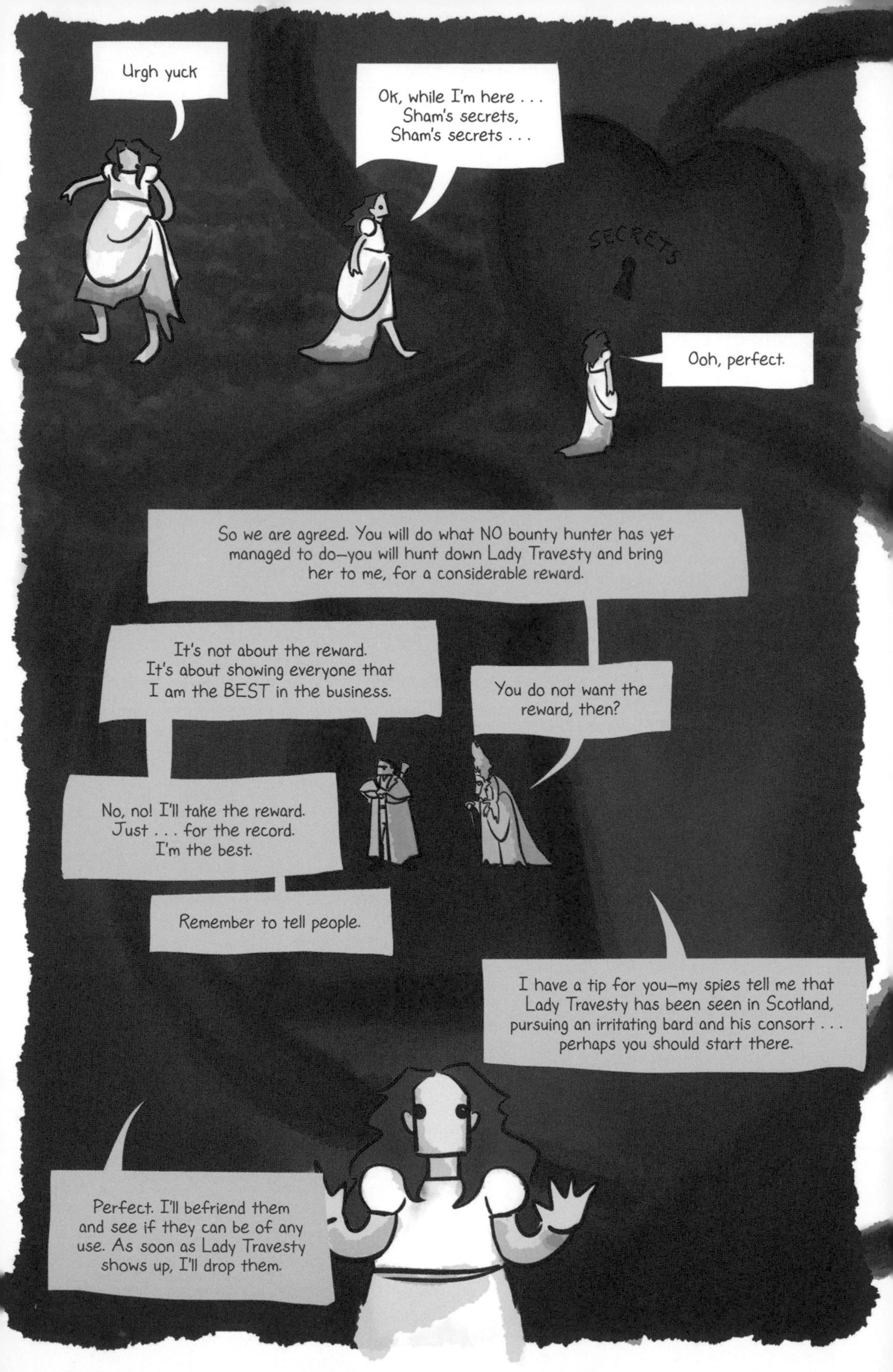
Urgh yuck
Ok, while I'm here . . . Sham's secrets, Sham's secrets . . .
SECRETS
Ooh, perfect.
So we are agreed. You will do what NO bounty hunter has yet managed to do—you will hunt down Lady Travesty and bring her to me, for a considerable reward.
It's not about the reward. It's about showing everyone that I am the BEST in the business.
You do not want the reward, then?
No, no! I'll take the reward. Just . . . for the record. I'm the best.
Remember to tell people.
I have a tip for you—my spies tell me that Lady Travesty has been seen in Scotland, pursuing an irritating bard and his consort . . . perhaps you should start there.
Perfect. I'll befriend them and see if they can be of any use. As soon as Lady Travesty shows up, I'll drop them.

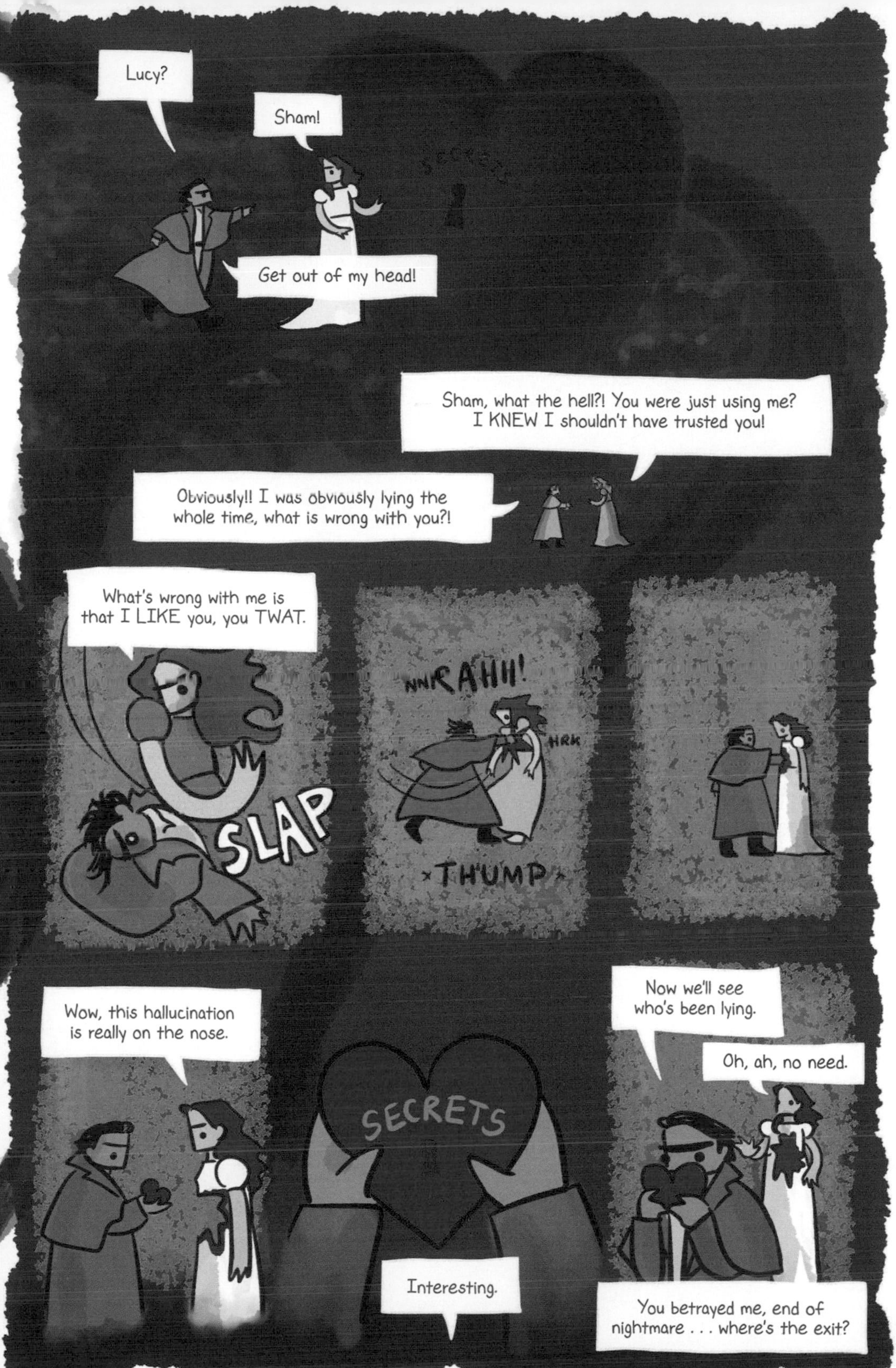
Lucy?
Sham!
SECRETS
Get out of my head!
Sham, what the hell?! You were just using me? I KNEW I shouldn't have trusted you!
Obviously!! I was obviously lying the whole time, what is wrong with you?!
What's wrong with me is that I LIKE you, you TWAT.
SLAP
NNRAHH!
HRK
THUMP
Wow, this hallucination is really on the nose.
SECRETS
Interesting.
Now we'll see who's been lying.
Oh, ah, no need.
You betrayed me, end of nightmare . . . where's the exit?

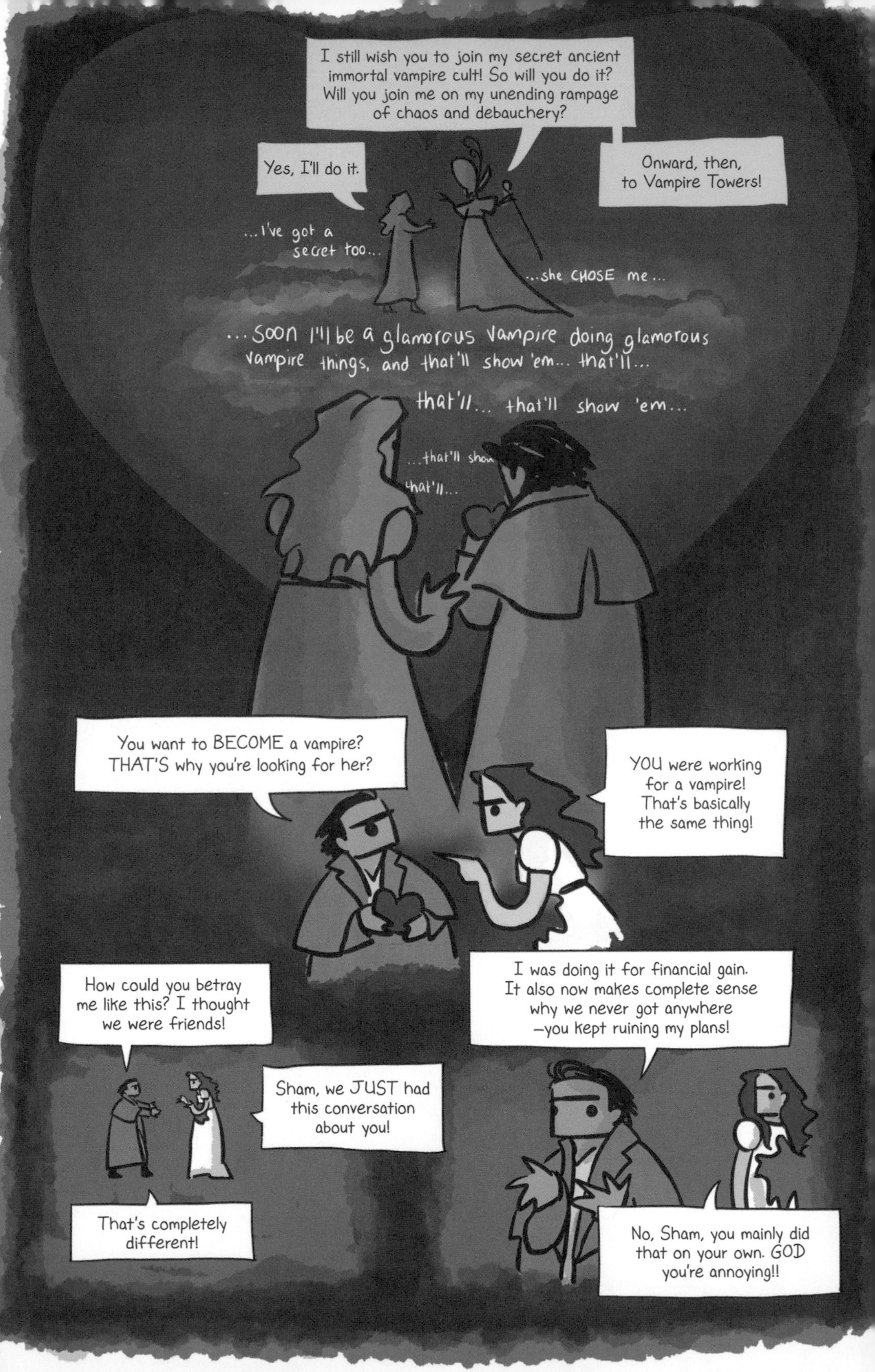
I still wish you to join my secret ancient immortal vampire cult! So will you do it? Will you join me on my unending rampage of chaos and debauchery?
Yes, I'll do it.
Onward, then, to Vampire Towers!
...I've got a secret too...
...she CHOSE me...
...Soon I'll be a glamorous vampire doing glamorous vampire things, and that'll show 'em... that'll...
that'll... that'll show 'em...
...that'll show
that'll...
You want to BECOME a vampire? THAT'S why you're looking for her?
YOU were working for a vampire! That's basically the same thing!
How could you betray me like this? I thought we were friends!
I was doing it for financial gain. It also now makes complete sense why we never got anywhere —you kept ruining my plans!
Sham, we JUST had this conversation about you!
That's completely different!
No, Sham, you mainly did that on your own. GOD you're annoying!!

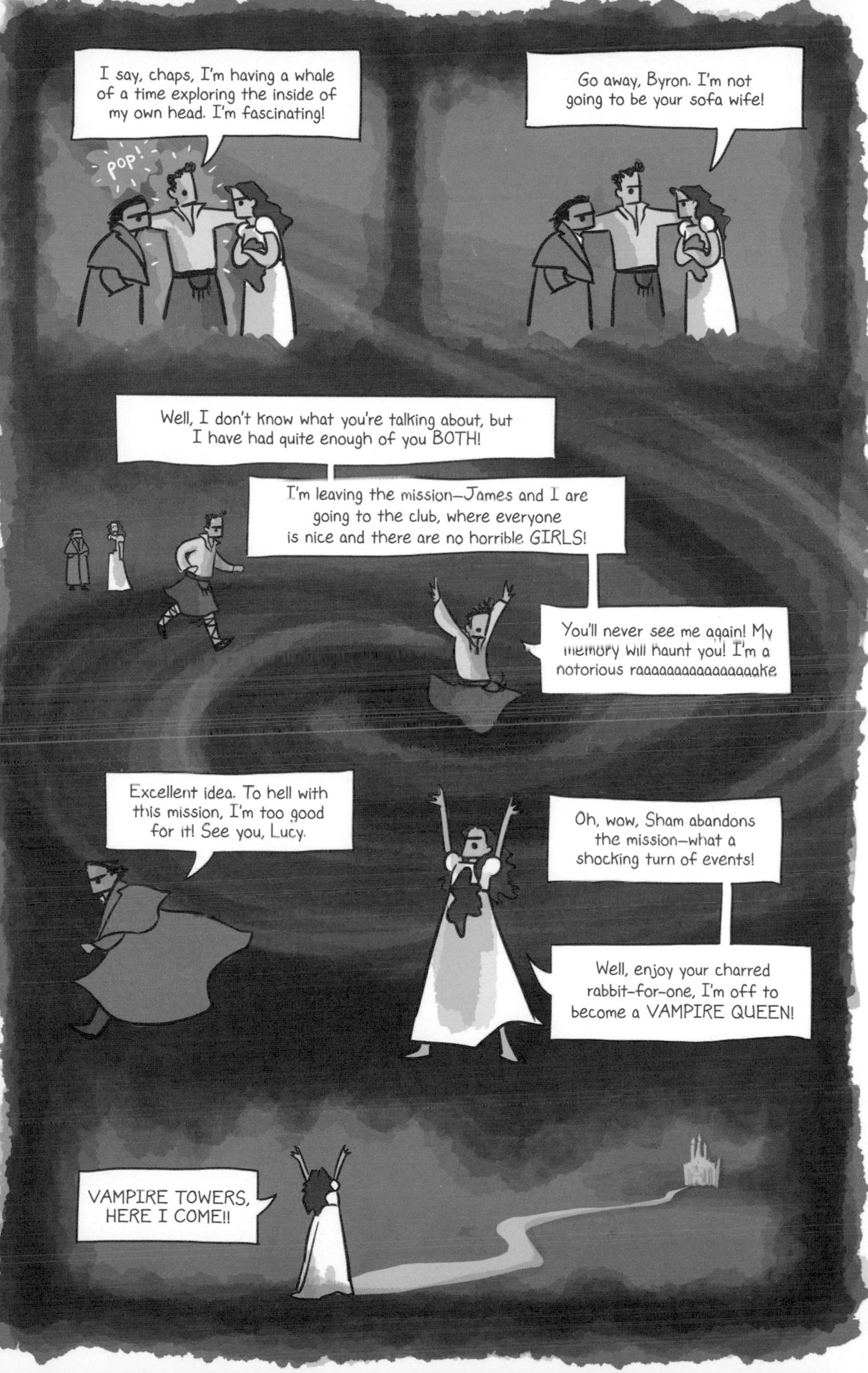
I say, chaps, I'm having a whale of a time exploring the inside of my own head. I'm fascinating!
POP!
Go away, Byron. I'm not going to be your sofa wife!
Well, I don't know what you're talking about, but I have had quite enough of you BOTH!
I'm leaving the mission—James and I are going to the club, where everyone is nice and there are no horrible GIRLS!
You'll never see me again! My memory will haunt you! I'm a notorious raaaaaaaaaaaaaaaake
Excellent idea. To hell with this mission, I'm too good for it! See you, Lucy.
Oh, wow, Sham abandons the mission—what a shocking turn of events!
Well, enjoy your charred rabbit-for-one, I'm off to become a VAMPIRE QUEEN!
VAMPIRE TOWERS, HERE I COME!!

CHAPTER X – VAMPIRE TOWERS

SOME WEEKS LATER...

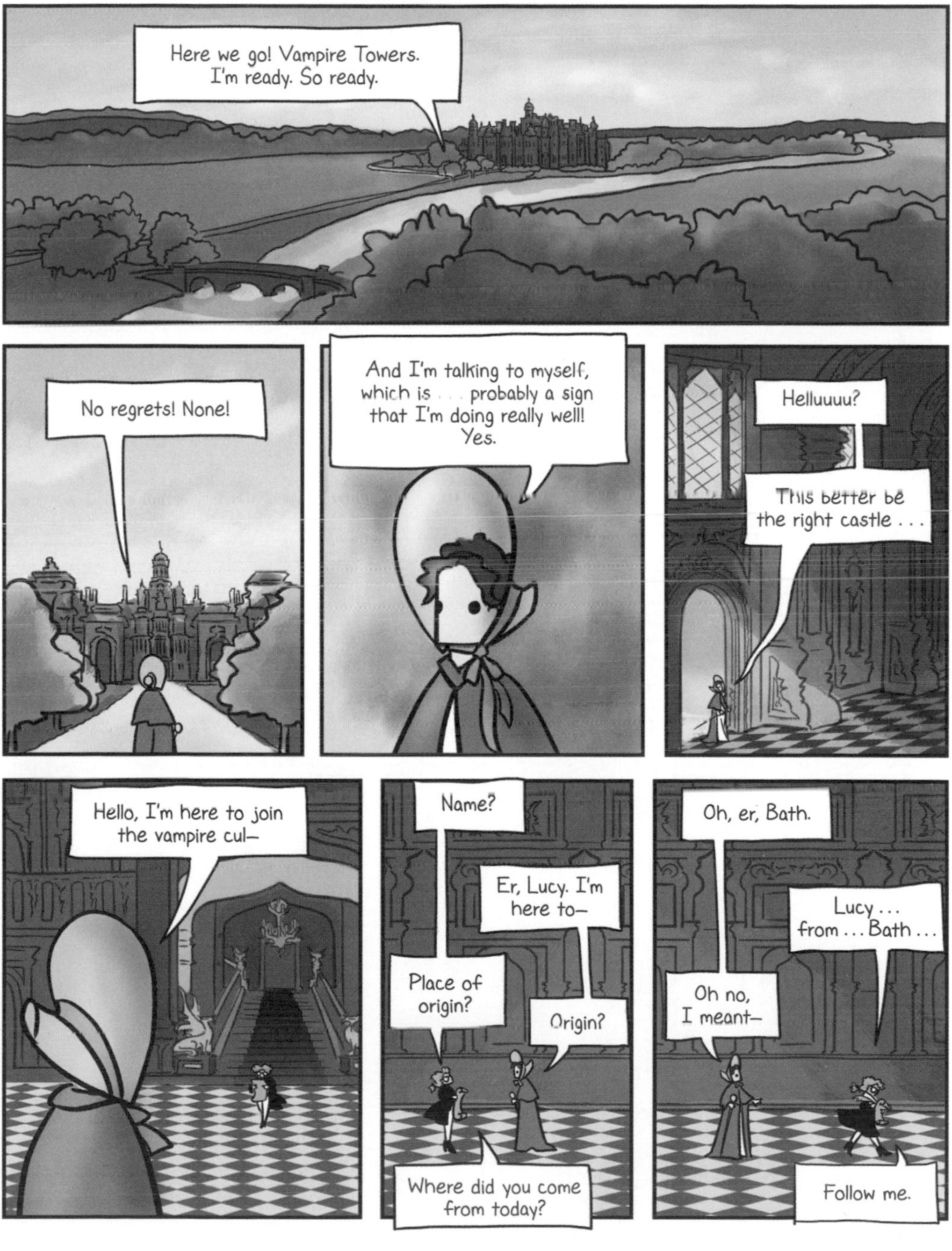
Here we go! Vampire Towers. I'm ready. So ready.
No regrets! None!
And I'm talking to myself, which is . . . probably a sign that I'm doing really well! Yes.
Helluuuu?
This better be the right castle . . .
Hello, I'm here to join the vampire cul–
Name?
Er, Lucy. I'm here to–
Place of origin?
Origin?
Where did you come from today?
Oh, er, Bath.
Lucy . . . from . . . Bath . . .
Oh no, I meant–
Follow me.

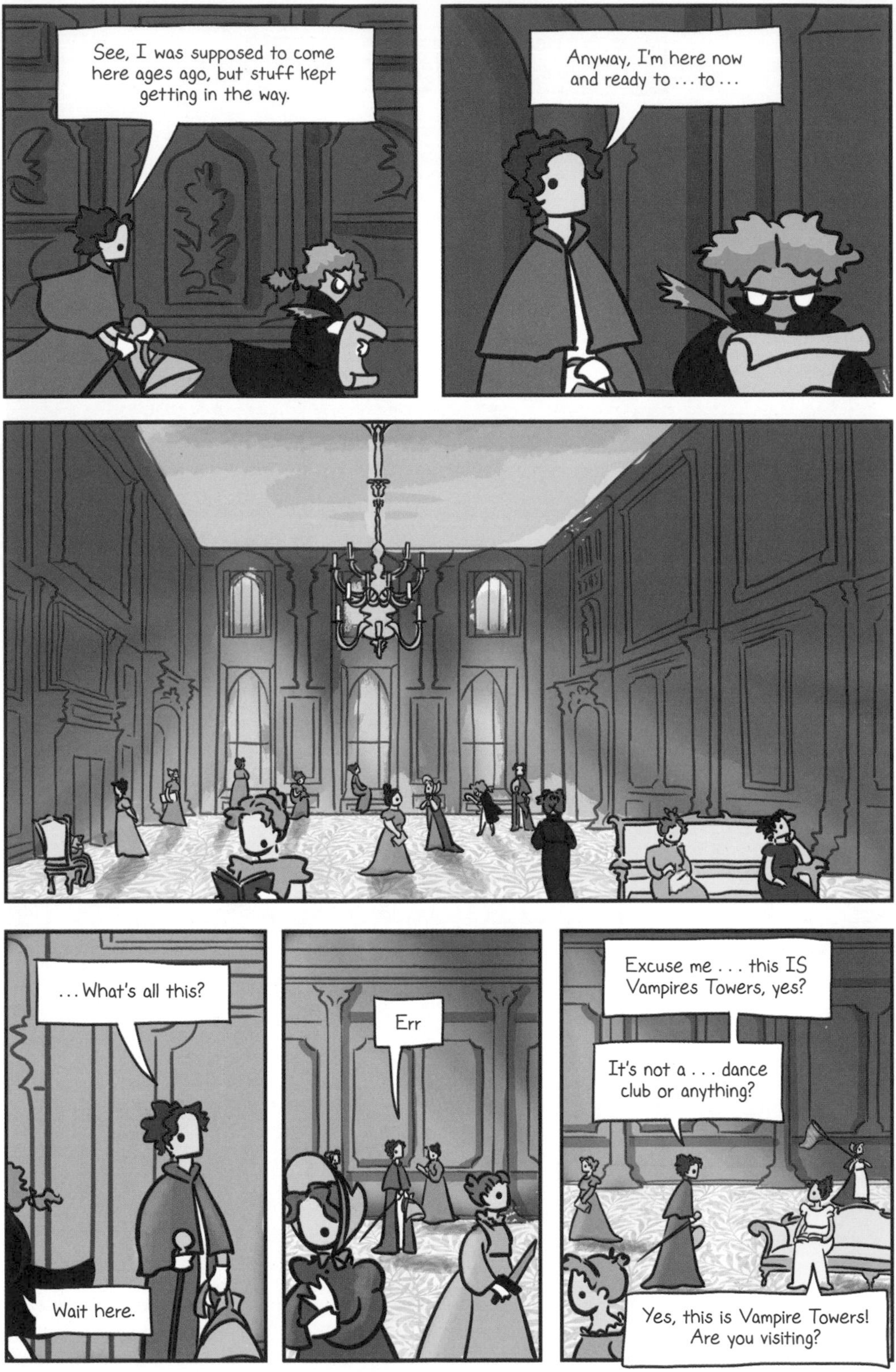

See, I was supposed to come here ages ago, but stuff kept getting in the way.
Anyway, I'm here now and ready to . . . to . . .
. . . What's all this?
Wait here.
Err
Excuse me . . . this IS Vampires Towers, yes?
It's not a . . . dance club or anything?
Yes, this is Vampire Towers! Are you visiting?

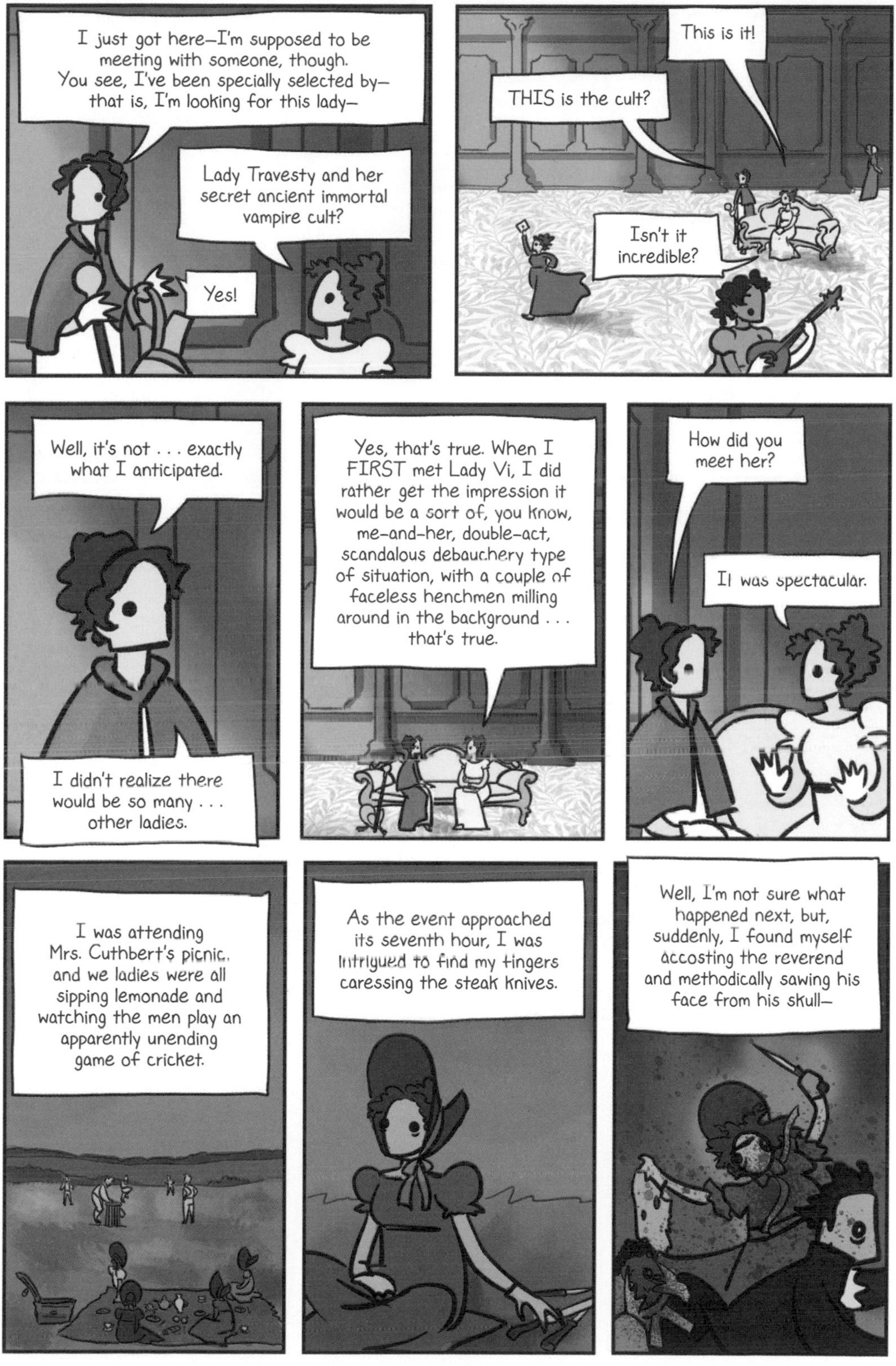
I just got here—I'm supposed to be meeting with someone, though. You see, I've been specially selected by—that is, I'm looking for this lady—
Lady Travesty and her secret ancient immortal vampire cult?
Yes!
This is it!
THIS is the cult?
Isn't it incredible?
Well, it's not . . . exactly what I anticipated.
I didn't realize there would be so many . . . other ladies.
Yes, that's true. When I FIRST met Lady Vi, I did rather get the impression it would be a sort of, you know, me-and-her, double-act, scandalous debauchery type of situation, with a couple of faceless henchmen milling around in the background . . . that's true.
How did you meet her?
It was spectacular.
I was attending Mrs. Cuthbert's picnic, and we ladies were all sipping lemonade and watching the men play an apparently unending game of cricket.
As the event approached its seventh hour, I was intrigued to find my fingers caressing the steak knives.
Well, I'm not sure what happened next, but, suddenly, I found myself accosting the reverend and methodically sawing his face from his skull—

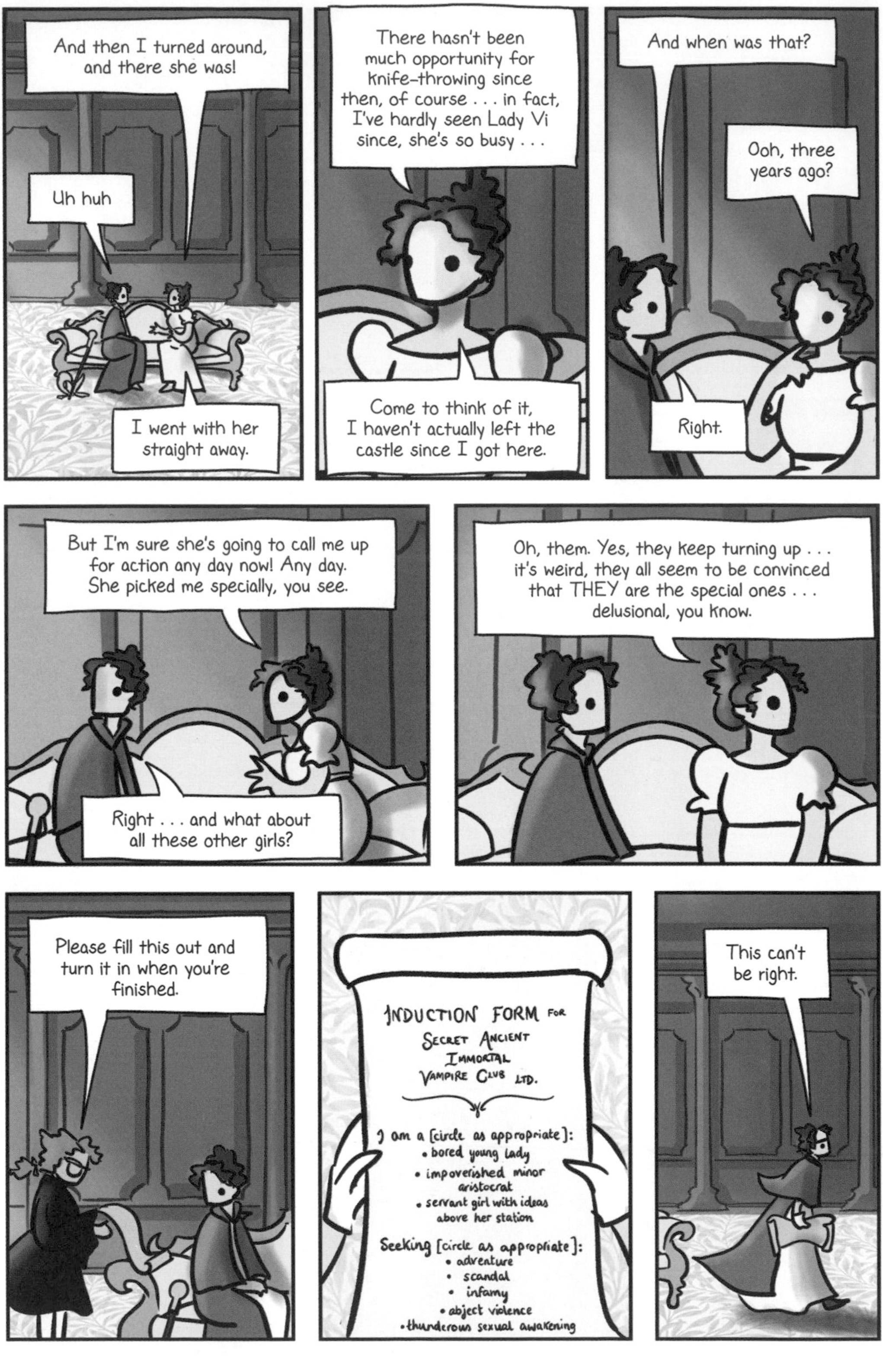
And then I turned around, and there she was!
Uh huh
I went with her straight away.
There hasn't been much opportunity for knife-throwing since then, of course . . . in fact, I've hardly seen Lady Vi since, she's so busy . . .
Come to think of it, I haven't actually left the castle since I got here.
And when was that?
Ooh, three years ago?
Right.
But I'm sure she's going to call me up for action any day now! Any day. She picked me specially, you see.
Right . . . and what about all these other girls?
Oh, them. Yes, they keep turning up . . . it's weird, they all seem to be convinced that THEY are the special ones . . . delusional, you know.
Please fill this out and turn it in when you're finished.
INDUCTION FORM FOR
SECRET ANCIENT IMMORTAL VAMPIRE CLUB LTD.
I am a [circle as appropriate]:
• bored young lady
• impoverished minor aristocrat
• servant girl with ideas above her station
Seeking [circle as appropriate]:
• adventure
• scandal
• infamy
• abject violence
• thunderous sexual awakening
This can't be right.

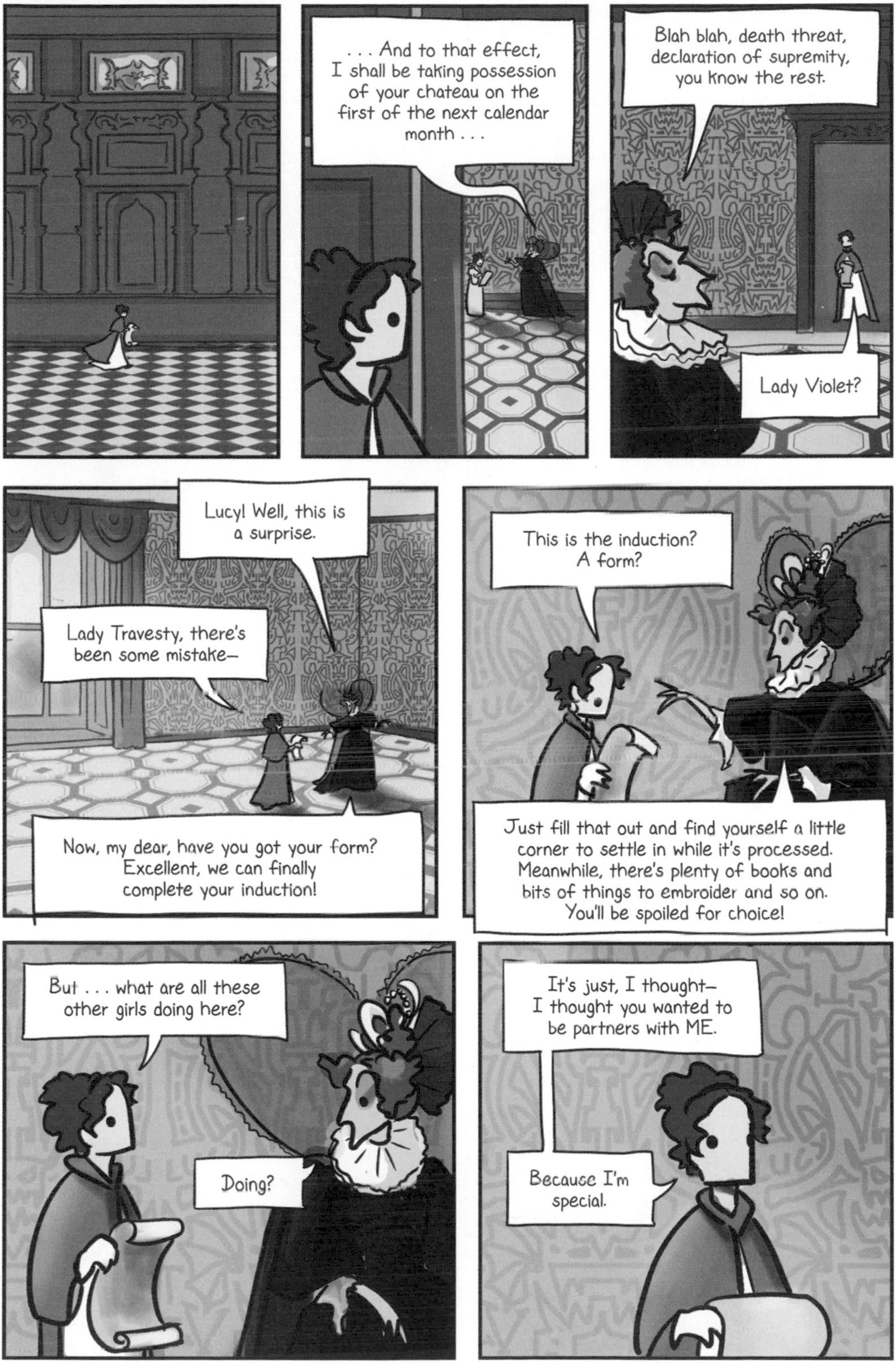
. . . And to that effect, I shall be taking possession of your chateau on the first of the next calendar month . . .
Blah blah, death threat, declaration of supremity, you know the rest.
Lady Violet?
Lucy! Well, this is a surprise.
Lady Travesty, there's been some mistake–
Now, my dear, have you got your form? Excellent, we can finally complete your induction!
This is the induction? A form?
Just fill that out and find yourself a little corner to settle in while it's processed. Meanwhile, there's plenty of books and bits of things to embroider and so on. You'll be spoiled for choice!
But . . . what are all these other girls doing here?
Doing?
It's just, I thought– I thought you wanted to be partners with ME.
Because I'm special.

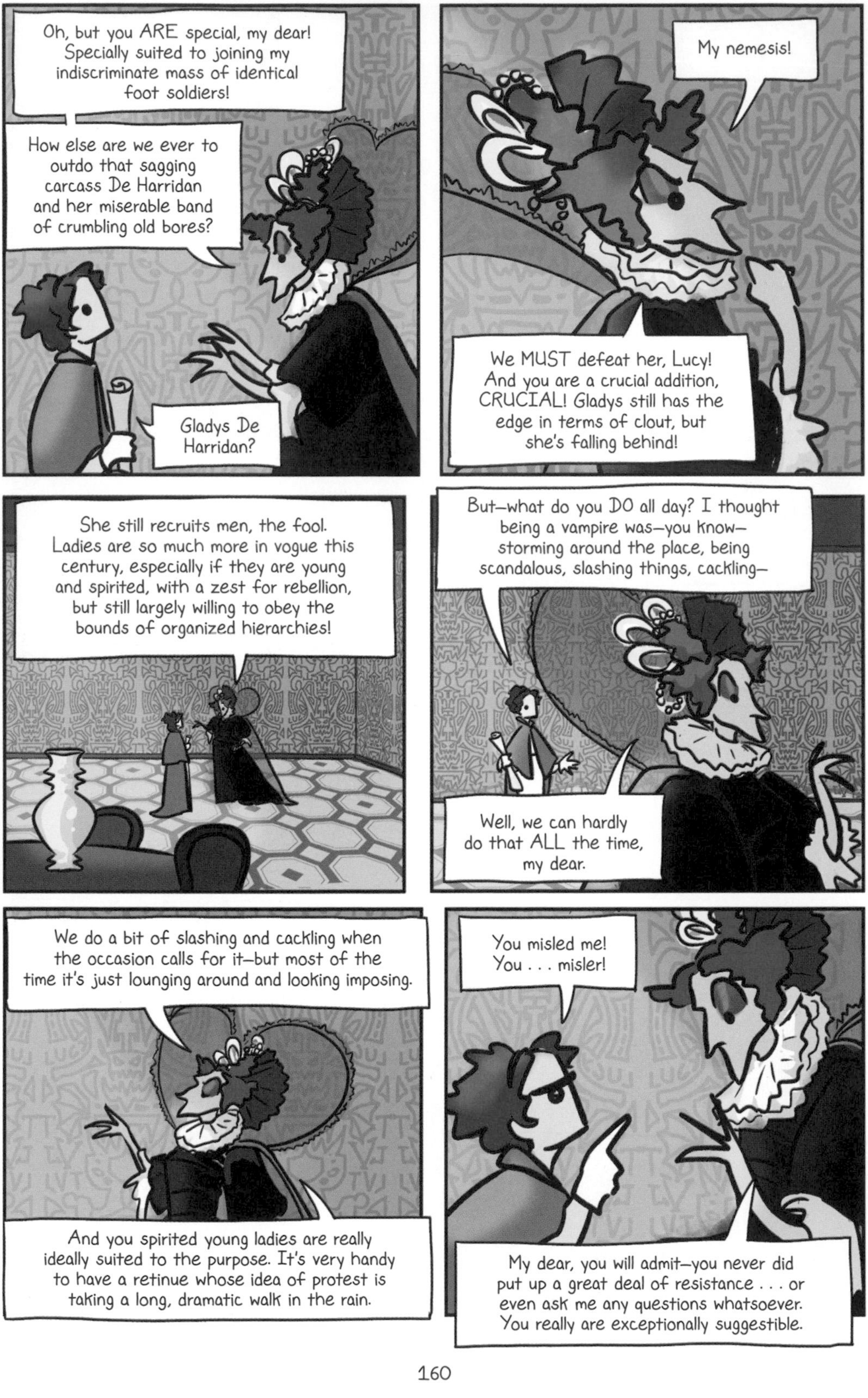
Oh, but you ARE special, my dear! Specially suited to joining my indiscriminate mass of identical foot soldiers!
How else are we ever to outdo that sagging carcass De Harridan and her miserable band of crumbling old bores?
Gladys De Harridan?
My nemesis!
We MUST defeat her, Lucy! And you are a crucial addition, CRUCIAL! Gladys still has the edge in terms of clout, but she's falling behind!
She still recruits men, the fool. Ladies are so much more in vogue this century, especially if they are young and spirited, with a zest for rebellion, but still largely willing to obey the bounds of organized hierarchies!
But—what do you DO all day? I thought being a vampire was—you know—storming around the place, being scandalous, slashing things, cackling—
Well, we can hardly do that ALL the time, my dear.
We do a bit of slashing and cackling when the occasion calls for it—but most of the time it's just lounging around and looking imposing.
And you spirited young ladies are really ideally suited to the purpose. It's very handy to have a retinue whose idea of protest is taking a long, dramatic walk in the rain.
You misled me! You . . . misler!
My dear, you will admit—you never did put up a great deal of resistance . . . or even ask me any questions whatsoever. You really are exceptionally suggestible.

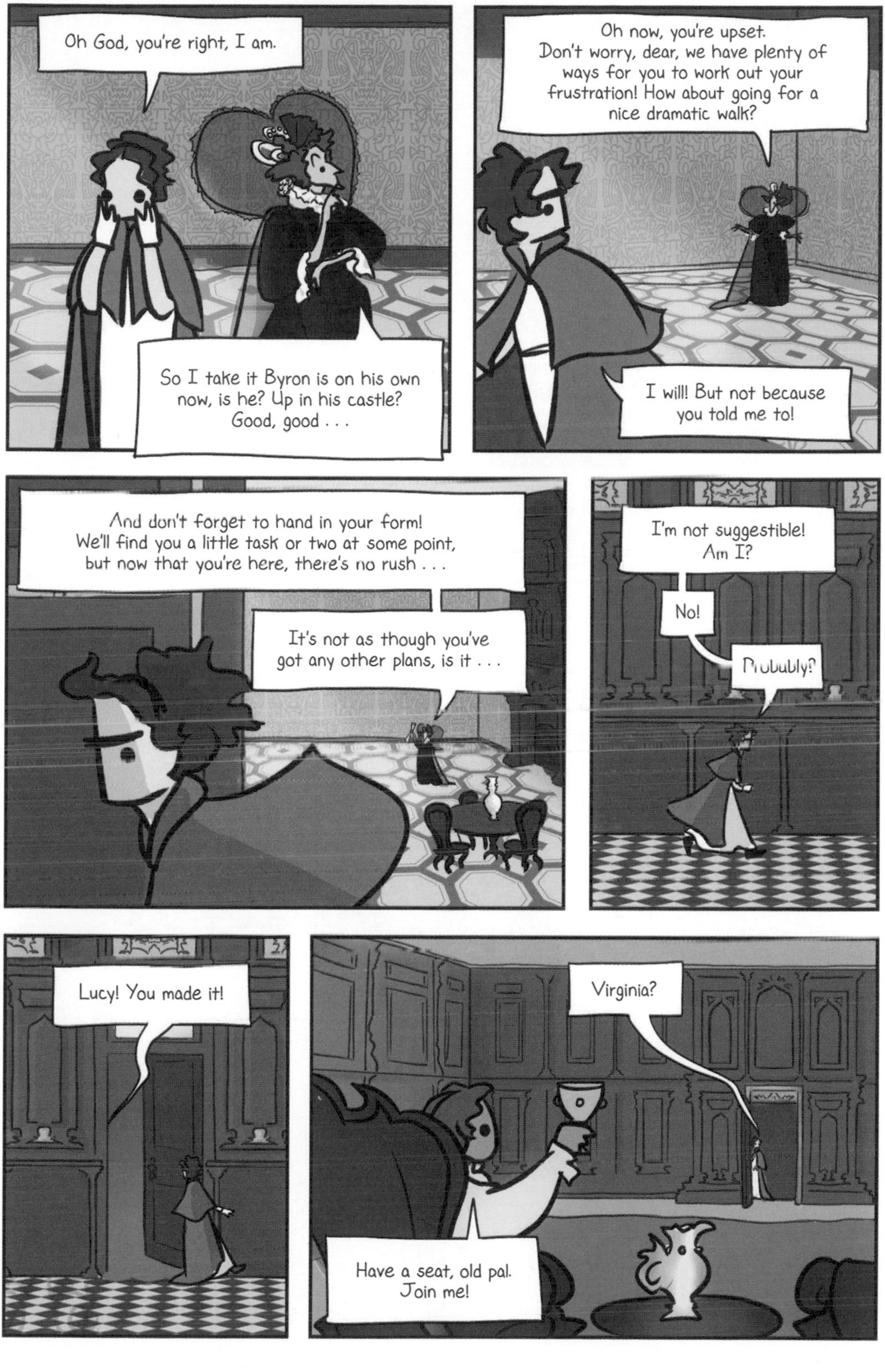
Oh God, you're right, I am.
So I take it Byron is on his own now, is he? Up in his castle? Good, good . . .
Oh now, you're upset. Don't worry, dear, we have plenty of ways for you to work out your frustration! How about going for a nice dramatic walk?
I will! But not because you told me to!
And don't forget to hand in your form! We'll find you a little task or two at some point, but now that you're here, there's no rush . . .
It's not as though you've got any other plans, is it . . .
I'm not suggestible! Am I?
No!
Probably?
Lucy! You made it!
Virginia?
Have a seat, old pal. Join me!

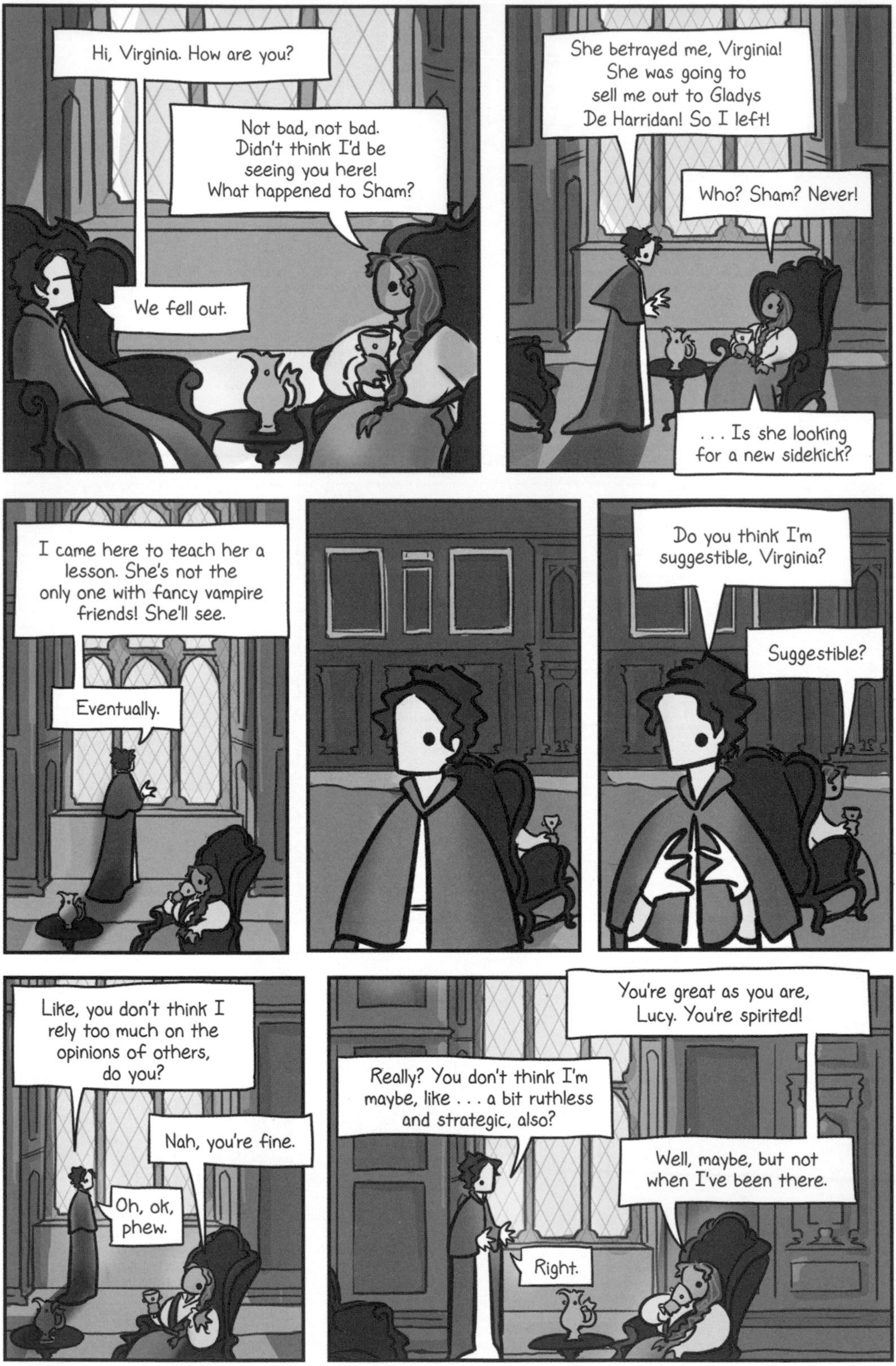
Hi, Virginia. How are you?
Not bad, not bad. Didn't think I'd be seeing you here! What happened to Sham?
We fell out.
She betrayed me, Virginia! She was going to sell me out to Gladys De Harridan! So I left!
Who? Sham? Never!
. . . Is she looking for a new sidekick?
I came here to teach her a lesson. She's not the only one with fancy vampire friends! She'll see.
Eventually.
Do you think I'm suggestible, Virginia?
Suggestible?
Like, you don't think I rely too much on the opinions of others, do you?
Nah, you're fine.
Oh, ok, phew.
You're great as you are, Lucy. You're spirited!
Really? You don't think I'm maybe, like . . . a bit ruthless and strategic, also?
Well, maybe, but not when I've been there.
Right.

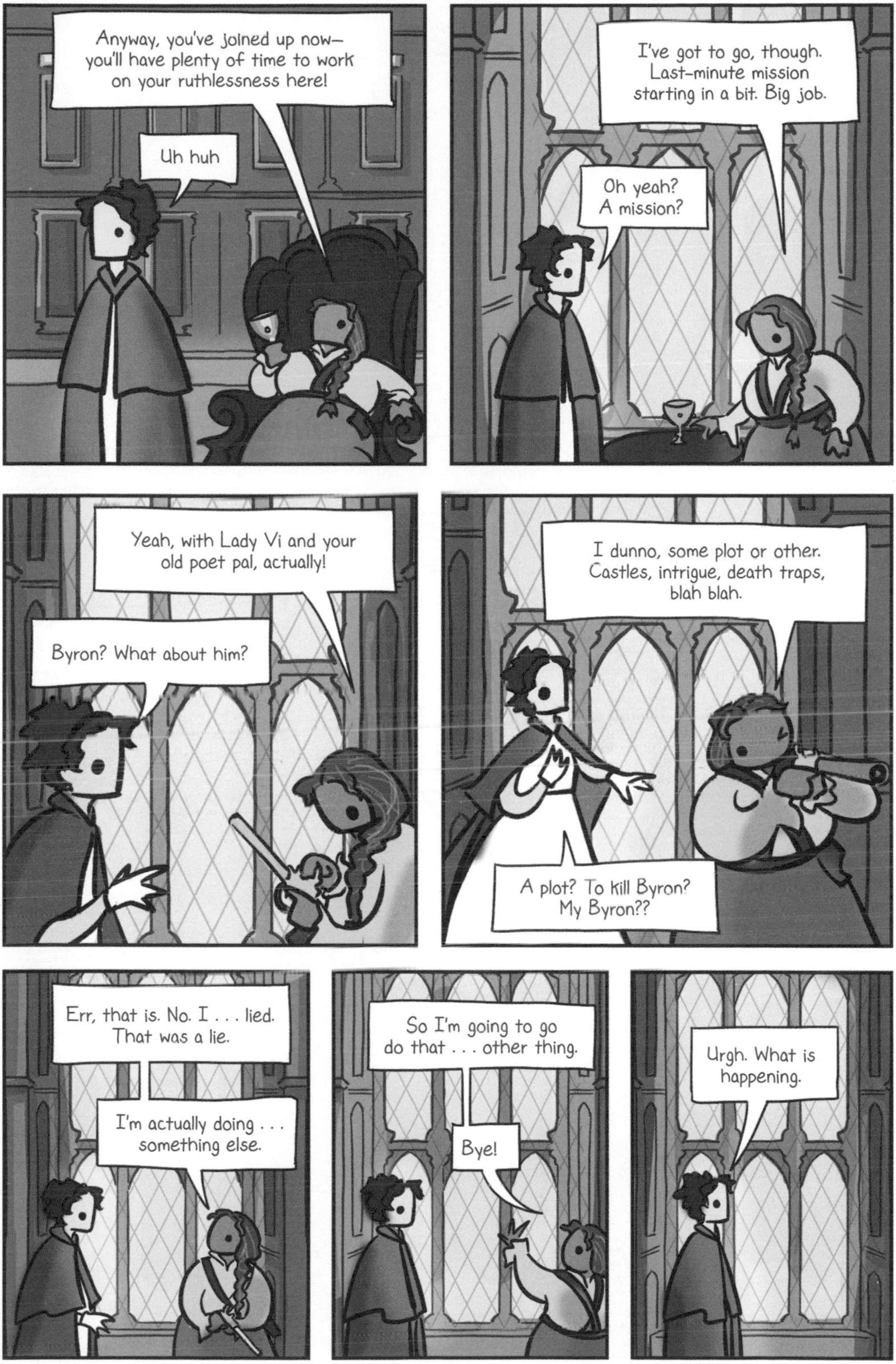
Anyway, you've joined up now—you'll have plenty of time to work on your ruthlessness here!
Uh huh
I've got to go, though. Last-minute mission starting in a bit. Big job.
Oh yeah? A mission?
Yeah, with Lady Vi and your old poet pal, actually!
Byron? What about him?
I dunno, some plot or other. Castles, intrigue, death traps, blah blah.
A plot? To kill Byron? My Byron??
Err, that is. No. I . . . lied. That was a lie.
I'm actually doing . . . something else.
So I'm going to go do that . . . other thing.
Bye!
Urgh. What is happening.

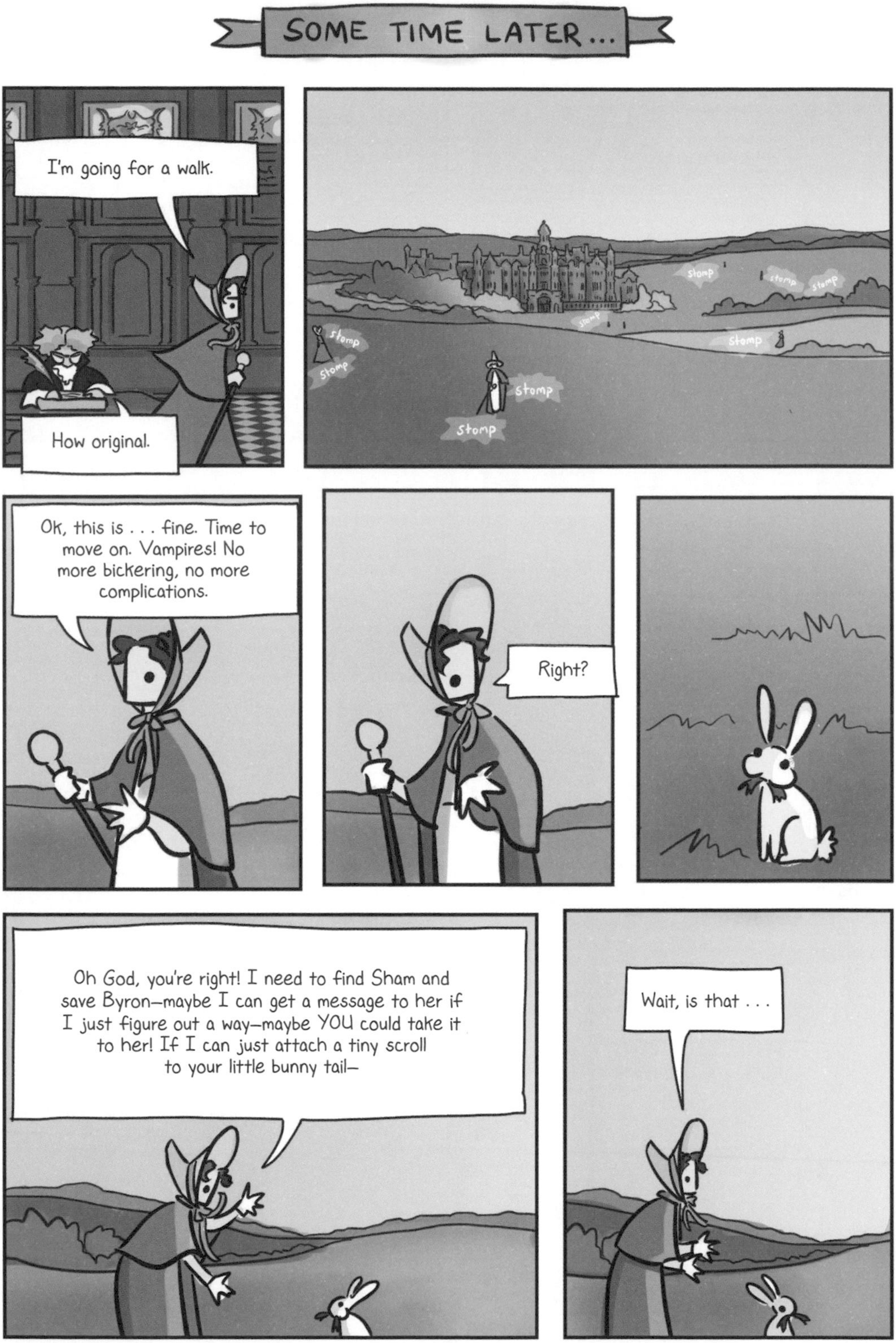
SOME TIME LATER...
I'm going for a walk.
How original.
Stomp
Stomp
Stomp
Stomp
Stomp
Stomp
Ok, this is . . . fine. Time to move on. Vampires! No more bickering, no more complications.
Right?
Oh God, you're right! I need to find Sham and save Byron—maybe I can get a message to her if I just figure out a way—maybe YOU could take it to her! If I can just attach a tiny scroll to your little bunny tail—
Wait, is that . . .

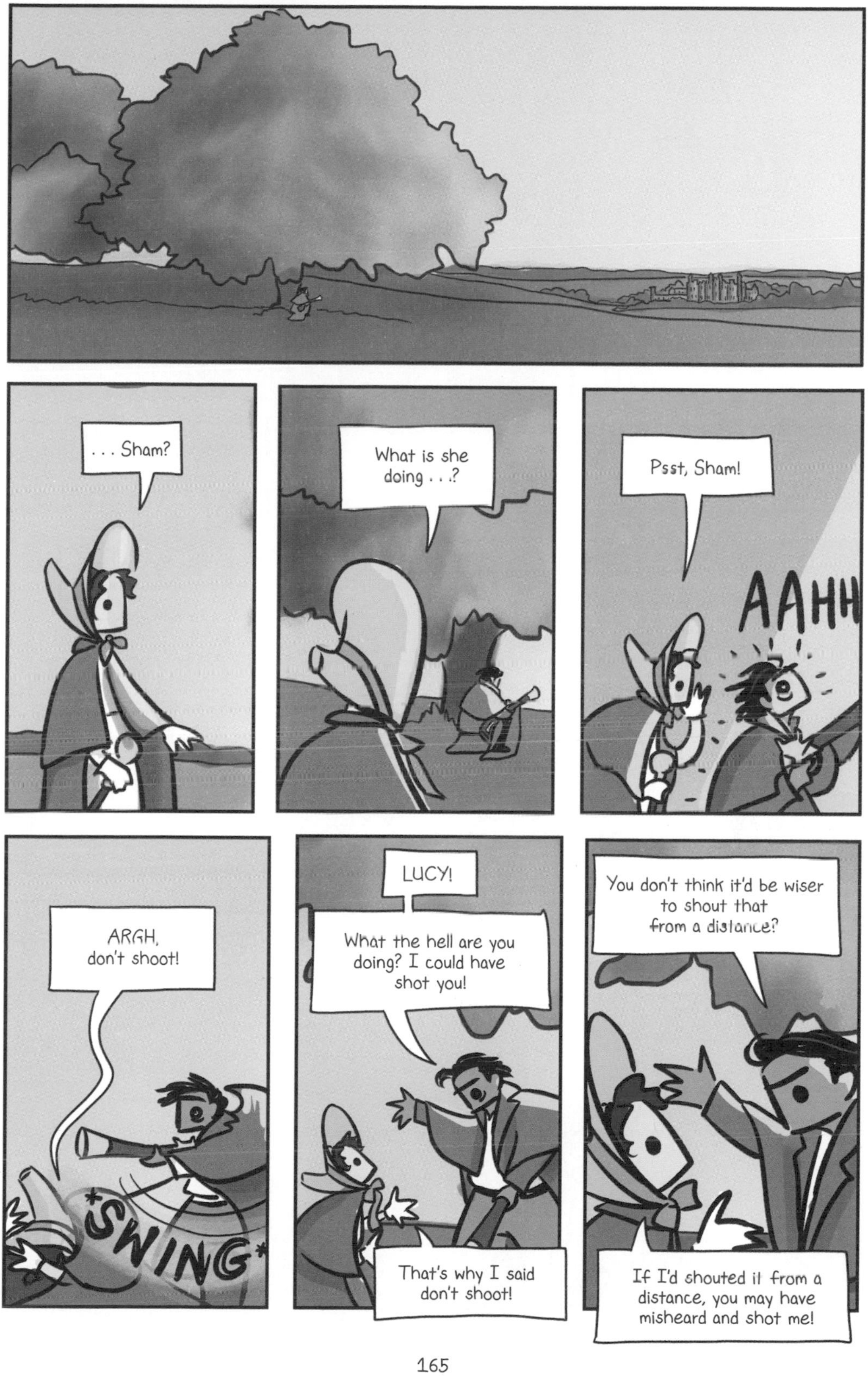

. . . Sham?
What is she doing . . .?
Psst, Sham!
AAHH
ARGH, don't shoot!
SWING
LUCY!
What the hell are you doing? I could have shot you!
That's why I said don't shoot!
You don't think it'd be wiser to shout that from a distance?
If I'd shouted it from a distance, you may have misheard and shot me!

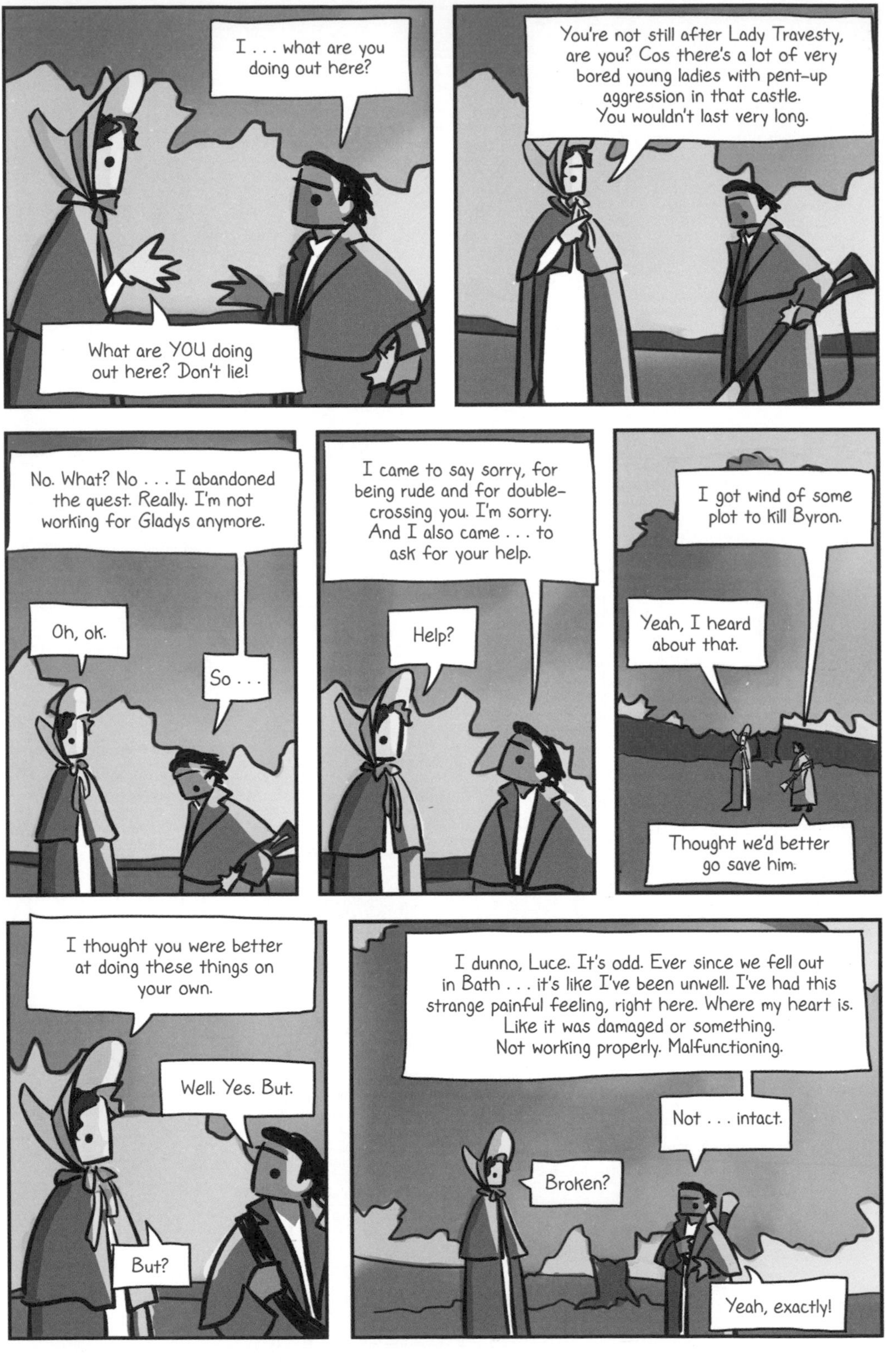
I . . . what are you doing out here?
What are YOU doing out here? Don't lie!
You're not still after Lady Travesty, are you? Cos there's a lot of very bored young ladies with pent-up aggression in that castle. You wouldn't last very long.
No. What? No . . . I abandoned the quest. Really. I'm not working for Gladys anymore.
Oh, ok.
So . . .
I came to say sorry, for being rude and for double-crossing you. I'm sorry. And I also came . . . to ask for your help.
Help?
I got wind of some plot to kill Byron.
Yeah, I heard about that.
Thought we'd better go save him.
I thought you were better at doing these things on your own.
Well. Yes. But.
But?
I dunno, Luce. It's odd. Ever since we fell out in Bath . . . it's like I've been unwell. I've had this strange painful feeling, right here. Where my heart is. Like it was damaged or something. Not working properly. Malfunctioning.
Not . . . intact.
Broken?
Yeah, exactly!

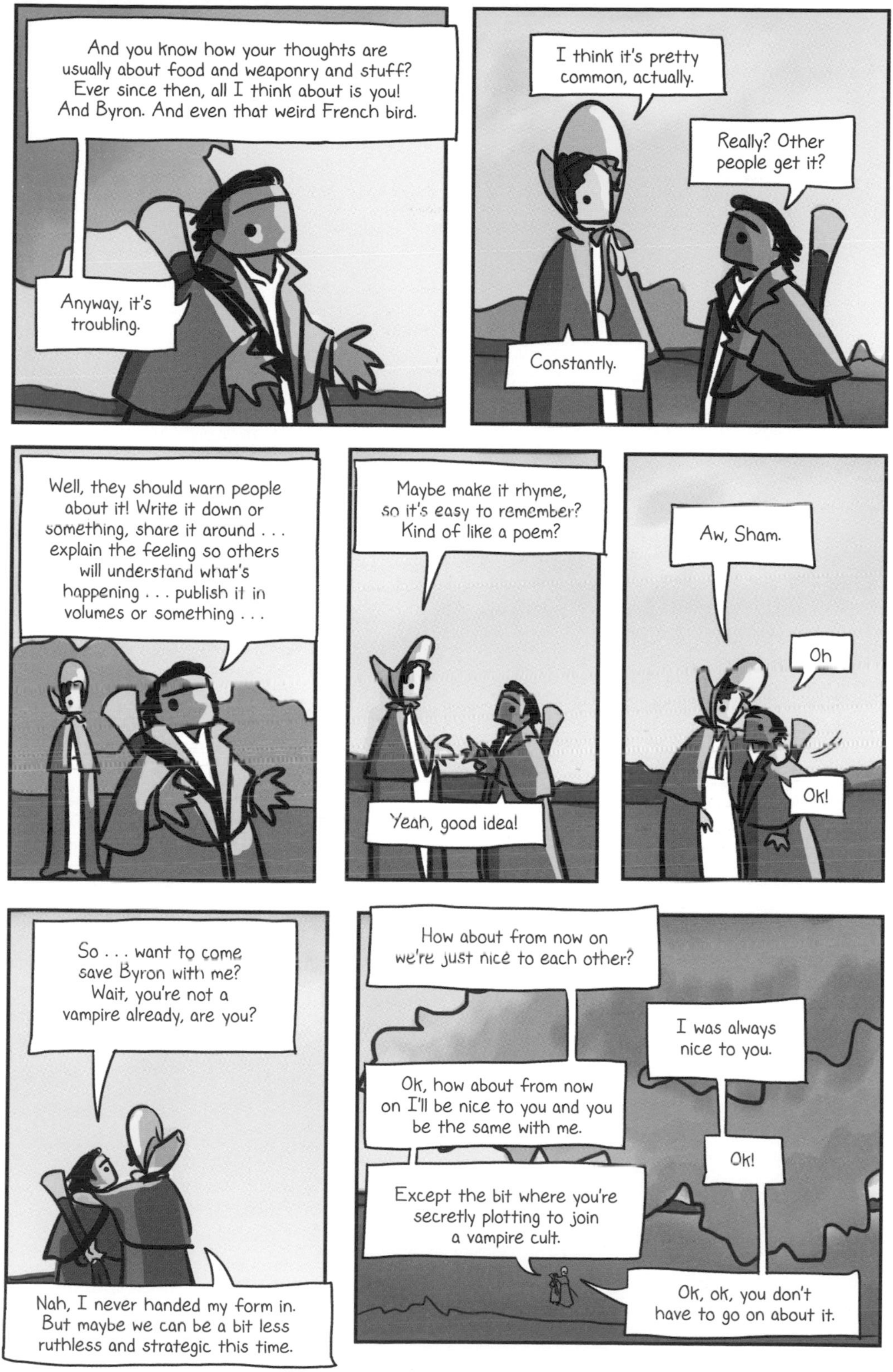

And you know how your thoughts are usually about food and weaponry and stuff? Ever since then, all I think about is you! And Byron. And even that weird French bird.
Anyway, it's troubling.
I think it's pretty common, actually.
Really? Other people get it?
Constantly.
Well, they should warn people about it! Write it down or something, share it around . . . explain the feeling so others will understand what's happening . . . publish it in volumes or something . . .
Maybe make it rhyme, so it's easy to remember? Kind of like a poem?
Yeah, good idea!
Aw, Sham.
Oh
Ok!
So . . . want to come save Byron with me? Wait, you're not a vampire already, are you?
Nah, I never handed my form in. But maybe we can be a bit less ruthless and strategic this time.
How about from now on we're just nice to each other?
I was always nice to you.
Ok, how about from now on I'll be nice to you and you be the same with me.
Ok!
Except the bit where you're secretly plotting to join a vampire cult.
Ok, ok, you don't have to go on about it.

CHAPTER XI – THE CLUB AGAIN

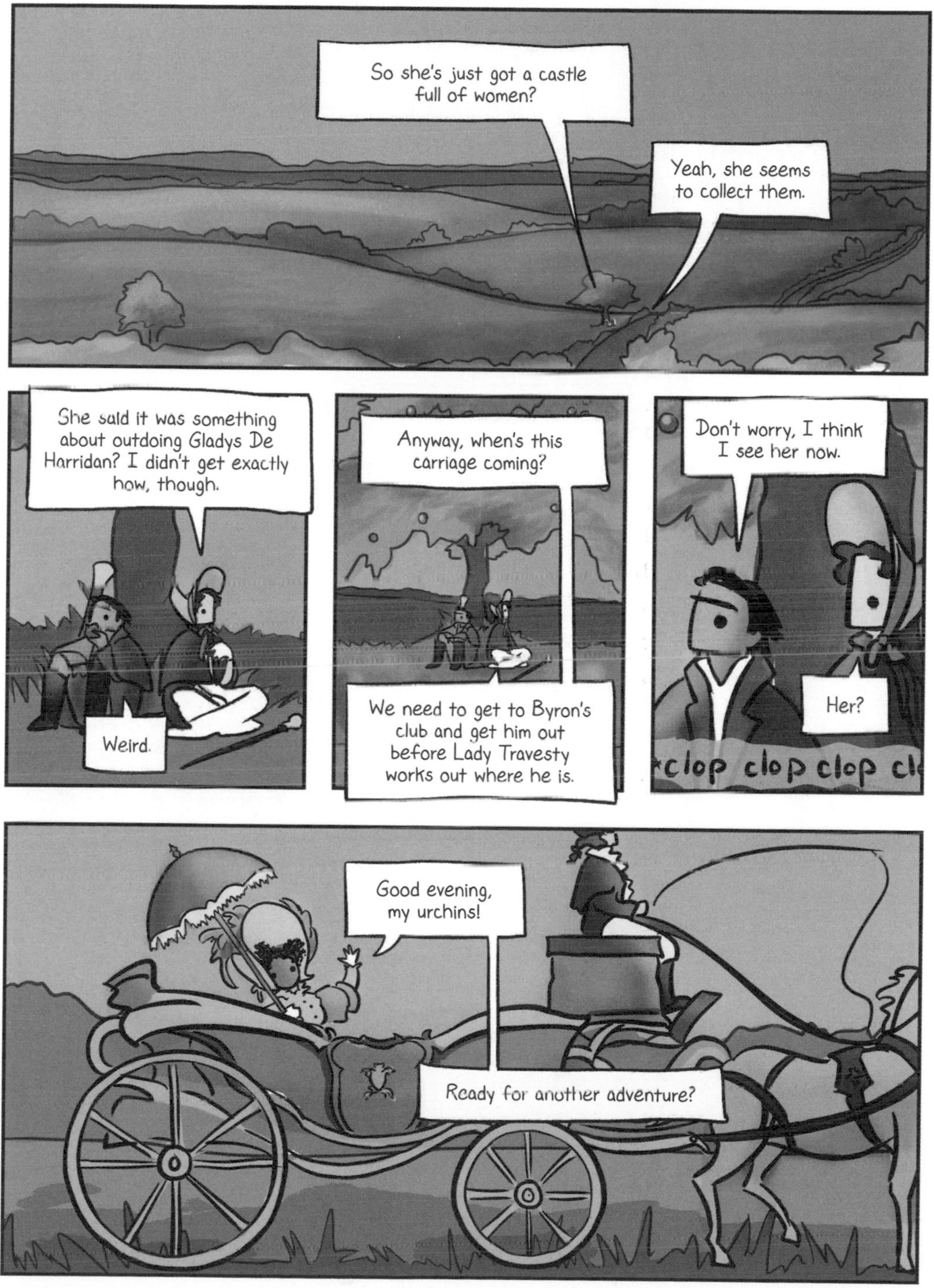
So she's just got a castle full of women?
Yeah, she seems to collect them.
She said it was something about outdoing Gladys De Harridan? I didn't get exactly how, though.
Weird.
Anyway, when's this carriage coming?
We need to get to Byron's club and get him out before Lady Travesty works out where he is.
Don't worry, I think I see her now.
Her?
*clop clop clop cl
Good evening, my urchins!
Ready for another adventure?

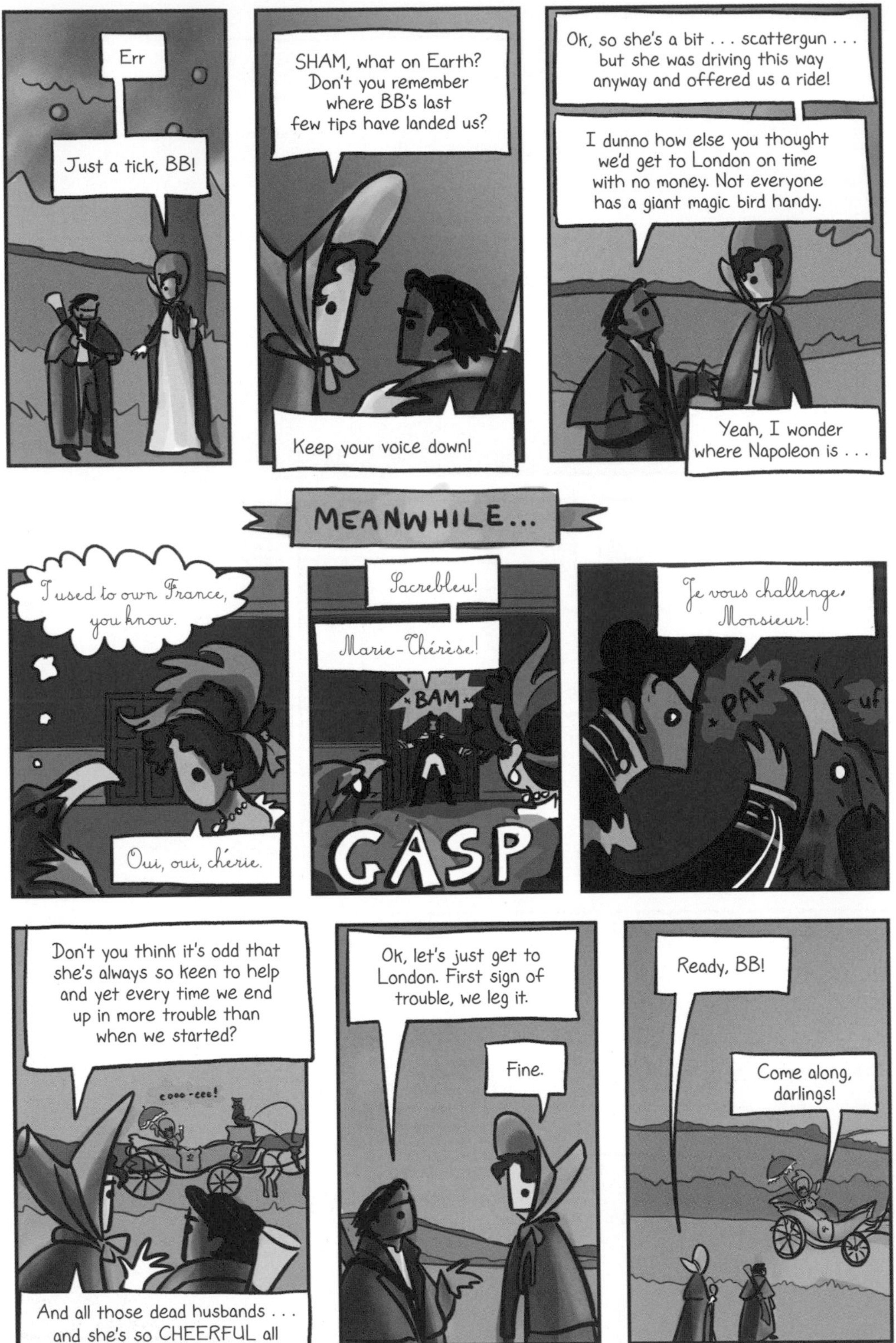
Err
Just a tick, BB!
SHAM, what on Earth? Don't you remember where BB's last few tips have landed us?
Keep your voice down!
Ok, so she's a bit . . . scattergun . . . but she was driving this way anyway and offered us a ride!
I dunno how else you thought we'd get to London on time with no money. Not everyone has a giant magic bird handy.
Yeah, I wonder where Napoleon is . . .
MEANWHILE...
I used to own France, you know.
Oui, oui, chérie.
Sacrebleu!
Marie-Thérèse!
BAM
GASP
Je vous challenge, Monsieur!
PAF
uf
Don't you think it's odd that she's always so keen to help and yet every time we end up in more trouble than when we started?
cooo-eee!
And all those dead husbands . . . and she's so CHEERFUL all the time! It's suspicious!
Ok, let's just get to London. First sign of trouble, we leg it.
Fine.
Ready, BB!
Come along, darlings!

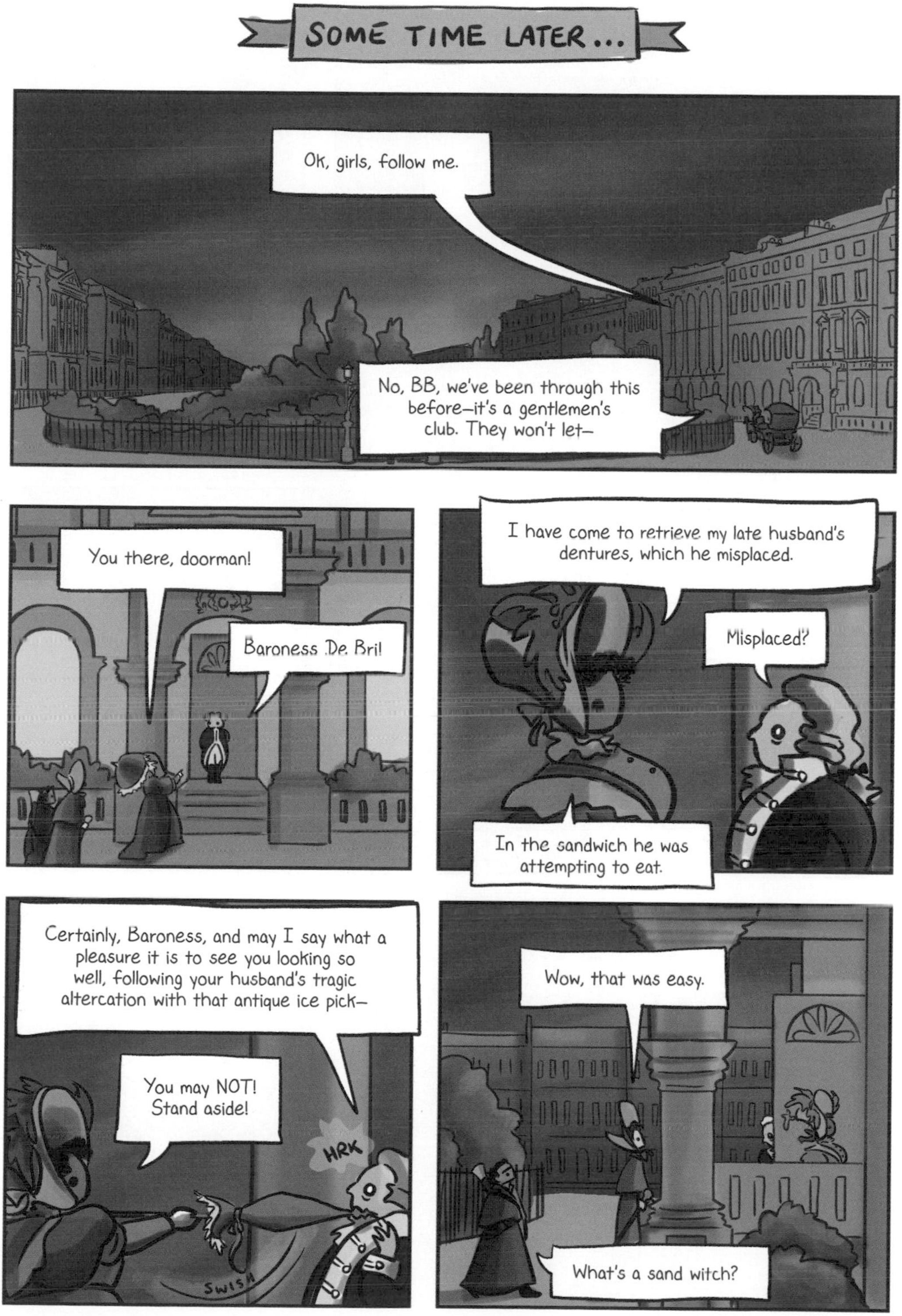
SOME TIME LATER...
Ok, girls, follow me.
No, BB, we've been through this before—it's a gentlemen's club. They won't let—
You there, doorman!
Baroness De Bril
I have come to retrieve my late husband's dentures, which he misplaced.
Misplaced?
In the sandwich he was attempting to eat.
Certainly, Baroness, and may I say what a pleasure it is to see you looking so well, following your husband's tragic altercation with that antique ice pick—
You may NOT! Stand aside!
HRK
SWISH
Wow, that was easy.
What's a sand witch?

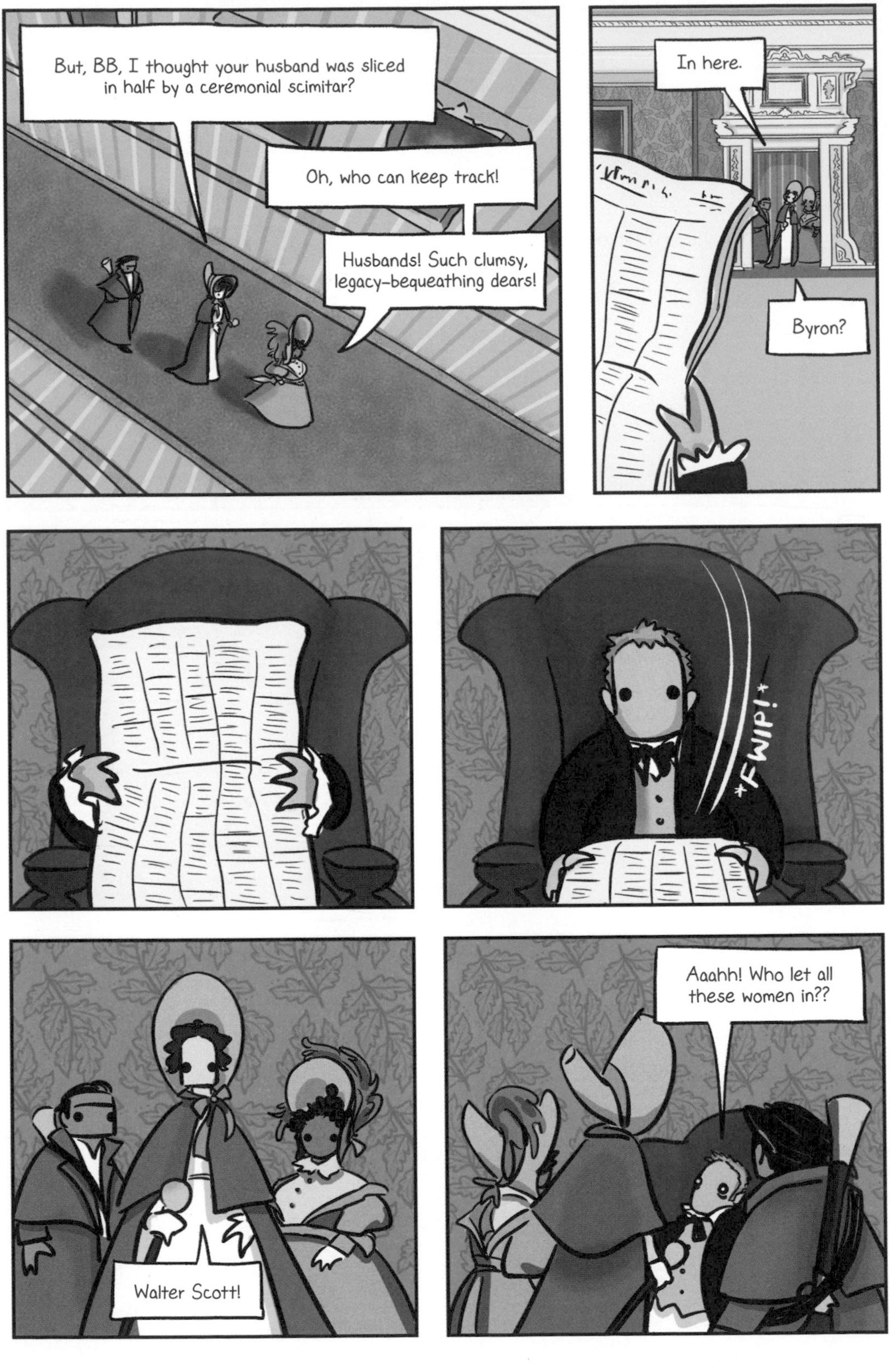
But, BB, I thought your husband was sliced in half by a ceremonial scimitar?
Oh, who can keep track!
Husbands! Such clumsy, legacy-bequeathing dears!
In here.
Byron?
FWIP!
Walter Scott!
Aaahh! Who let all these women in??

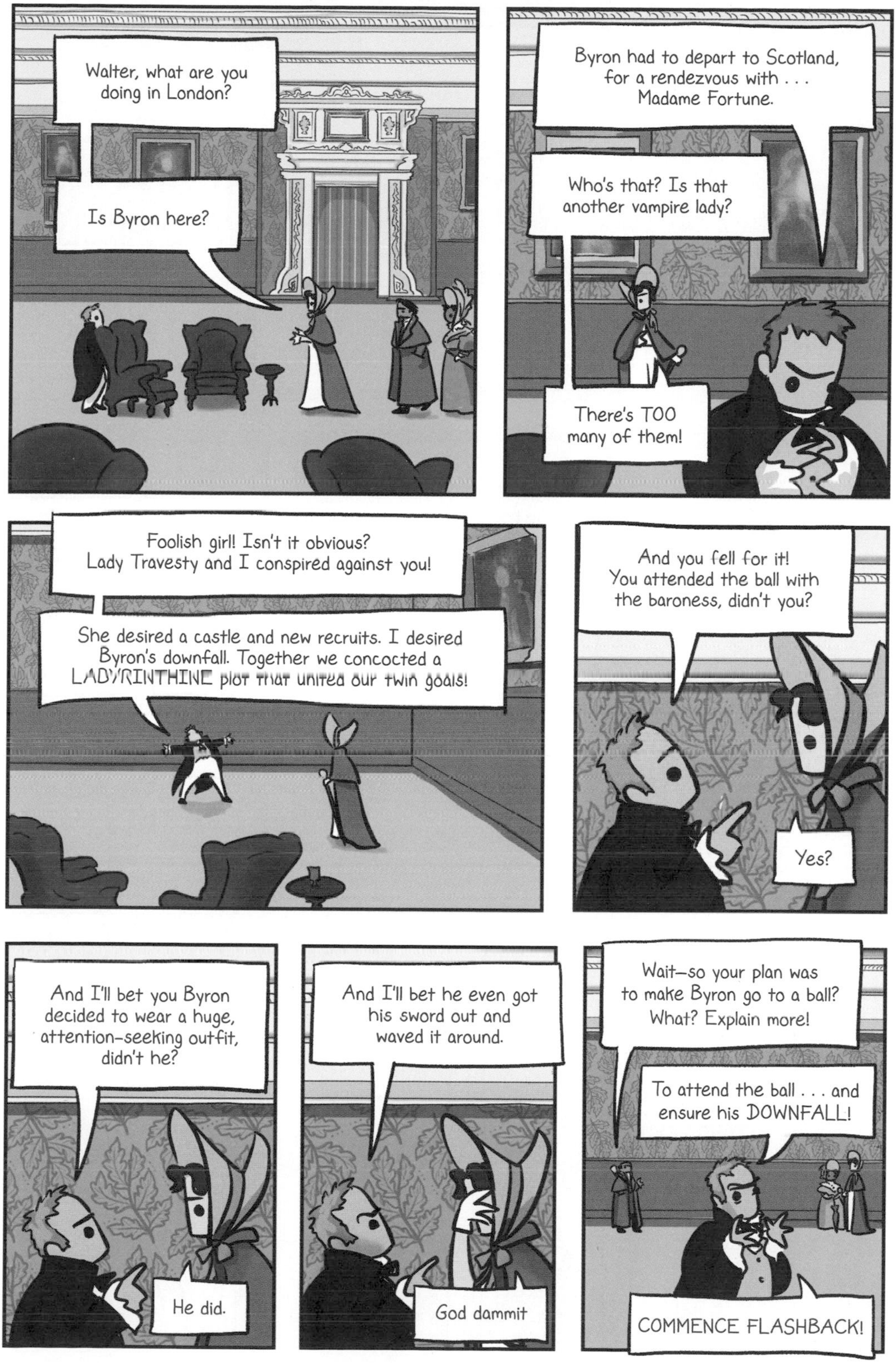
Walter, what are you doing in London?
Is Byron here?
Byron had to depart to Scotland, for a rendezvous with . . . Madame Fortune.
Who's that? Is that another vampire lady?
There's TOO many of them!
Foolish girl! Isn't it obvious? Lady Travesty and I conspired against you!
She desired a castle and new recruits. I desired Byron's downfall. Together we concocted a LABYRINTHINE plot that united our twin goals!
And you fell for it! You attended the ball with the baroness, didn't you?
Yes?
And I'll bet you Byron decided to wear a huge, attention-seeking outfit, didn't he?
He did.
And I'll bet he even got his sword out and waved it around.
God dammit
Wait—so your plan was to make Byron go to a ball? What? Explain more!
To attend the ball . . . and ensure his DOWNFALL!
COMMENCE FLASHBACK!

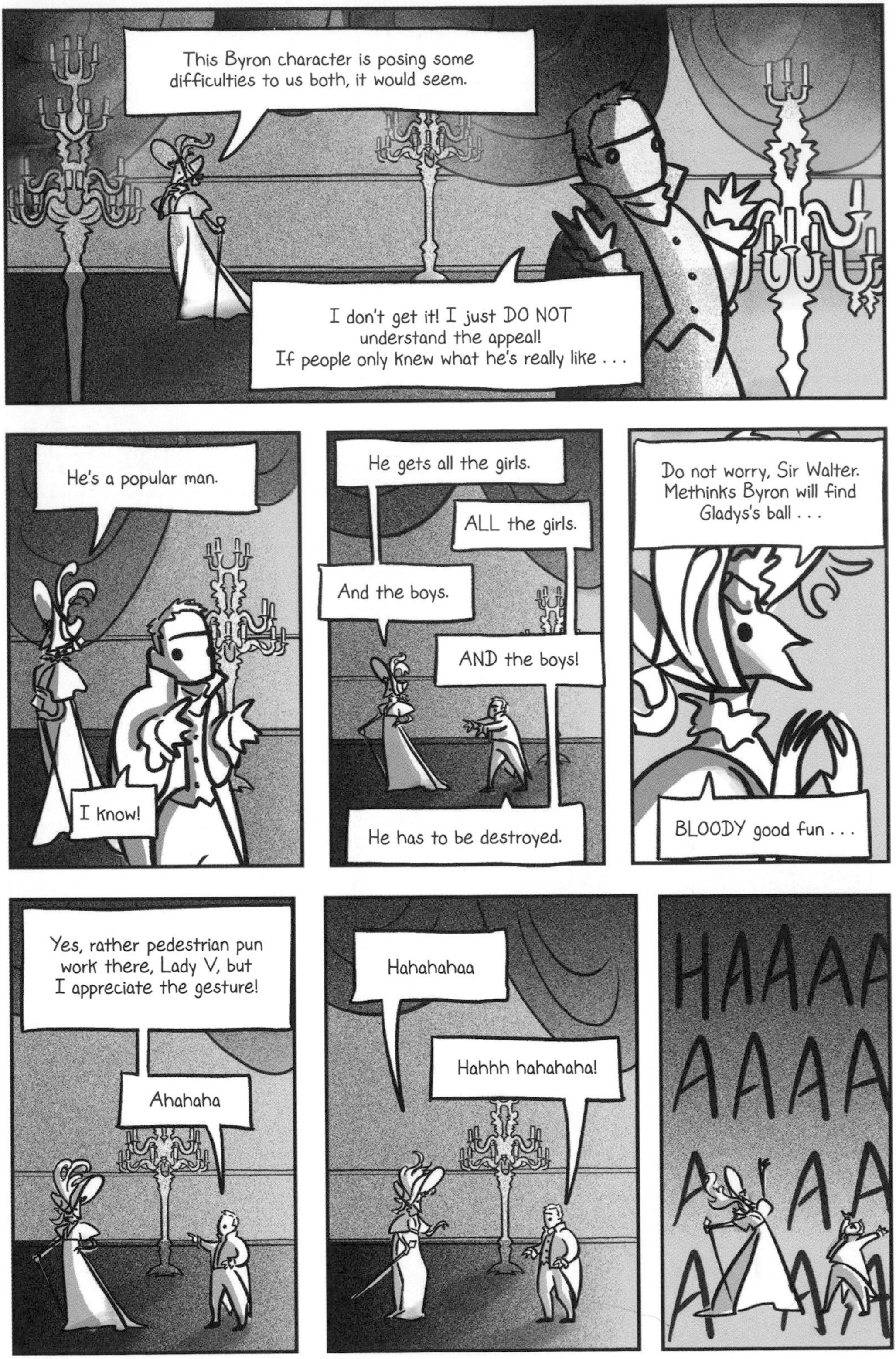
This Byron character is posing some difficulties to us both, it would seem.
I don't get it! I just DO NOT understand the appeal! If people only knew what he's really like . . .
He's a popular man.
I know!
He gets all the girls.
ALL the girls.
And the boys.
AND the boys!
He has to be destroyed.
Do not worry, Sir Walter. Methinks Byron will find Gladys's ball . . .
BLOODY good fun . . .
Yes, rather pedestrian pun work there, Lady V, but I appreciate the gesture!
Ahahaha
Hahahahaa
Hahhh hahahaha!
HAAAAAAAAAAAA

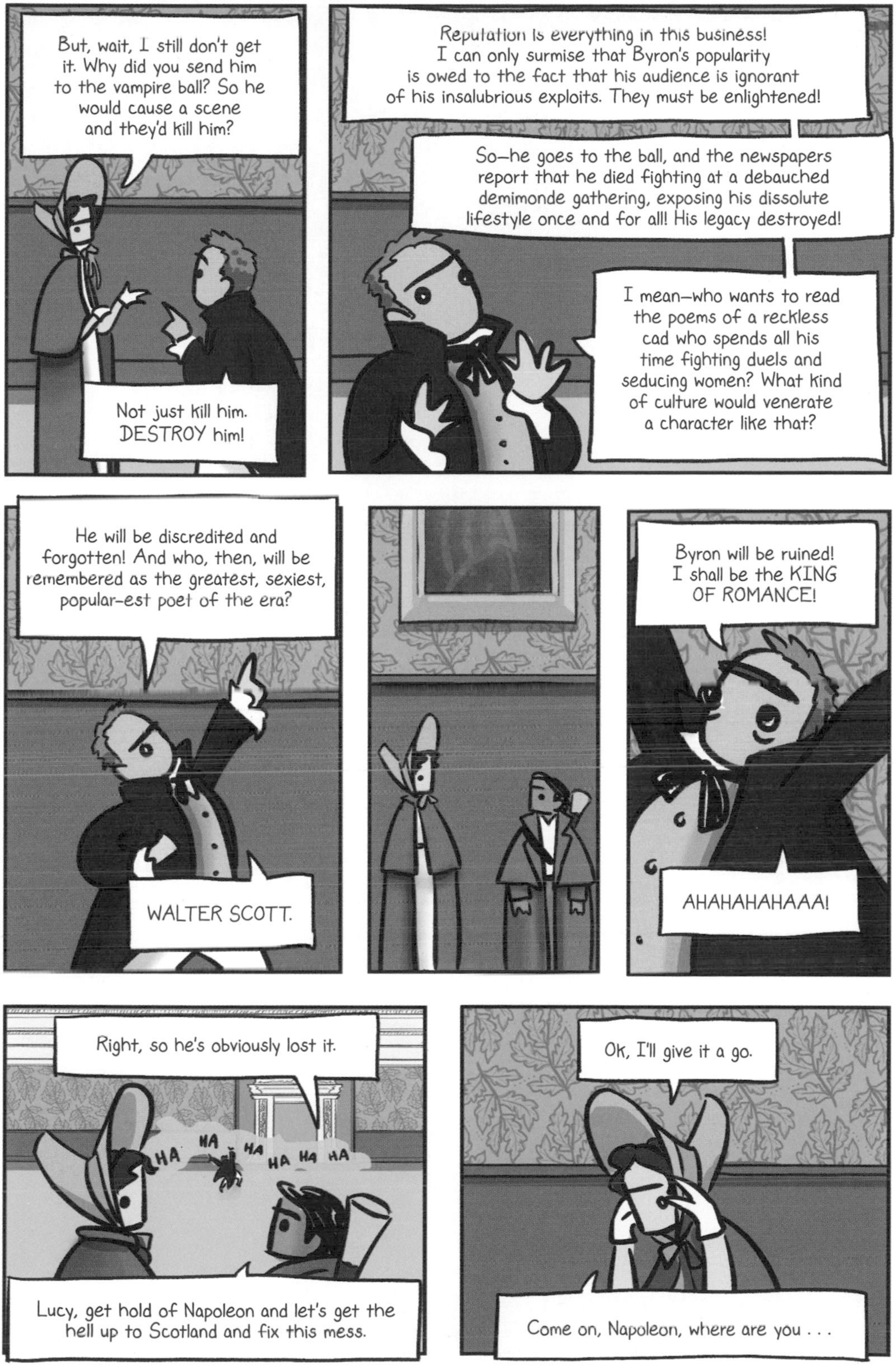
But, wait, I still don't get it. Why did you send him to the vampire ball? So he would cause a scene and they'd kill him?
Not just kill him. DESTROY him!
Reputation is everything in this business! I can only surmise that Byron's popularity is owed to the fact that his audience is ignorant of his insalubrious exploits. They must be enlightened!
So—he goes to the ball, and the newspapers report that he died fighting at a debauched demimonde gathering, exposing his dissolute lifestyle once and for all! His legacy destroyed!
I mean—who wants to read the poems of a reckless cad who spends all his time fighting duels and seducing women? What kind of culture would venerate a character like that?
He will be discredited and forgotten! And who, then, will be remembered as the greatest, sexiest, popular-est poet of the era?
WALTER SCOTT.
Byron will be ruined! I shall be the KING OF ROMANCE!
AHAHAHAHAAA!
Right, so he's obviously lost it.
HA HA HA HA HA HA
Lucy, get hold of Napoleon and let's get the hell up to Scotland and fix this mess.
Ok, I'll give it a go.
Come on, Napoleon, where are you . . .

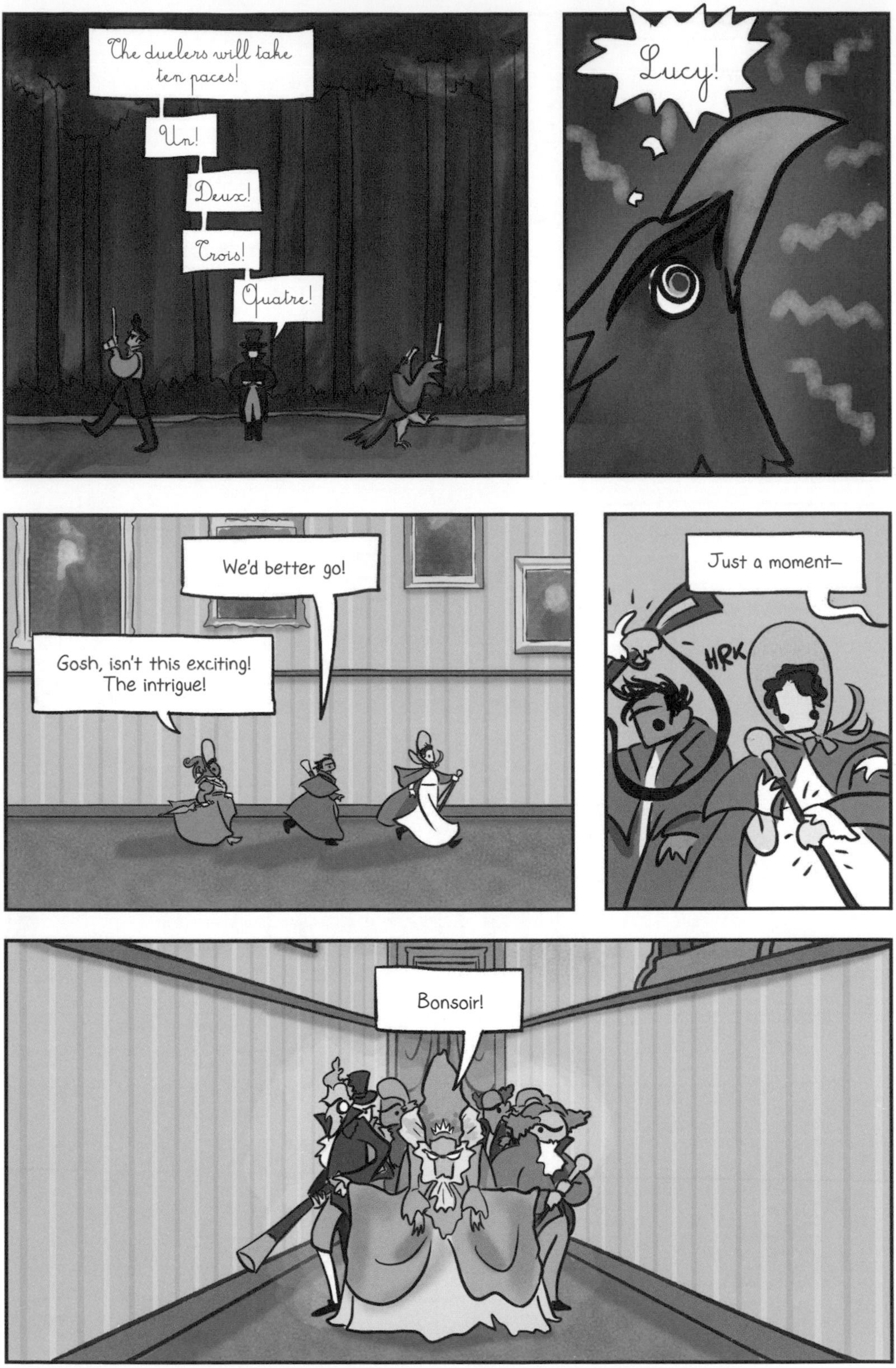
The duelers will take ten paces!
Un!
Deux!
Trois!
Quatre!
Lucy!
We'd better go!
Gosh, isn't this exciting! The intrigue!
Just a moment—
HRK
Bonsoir!

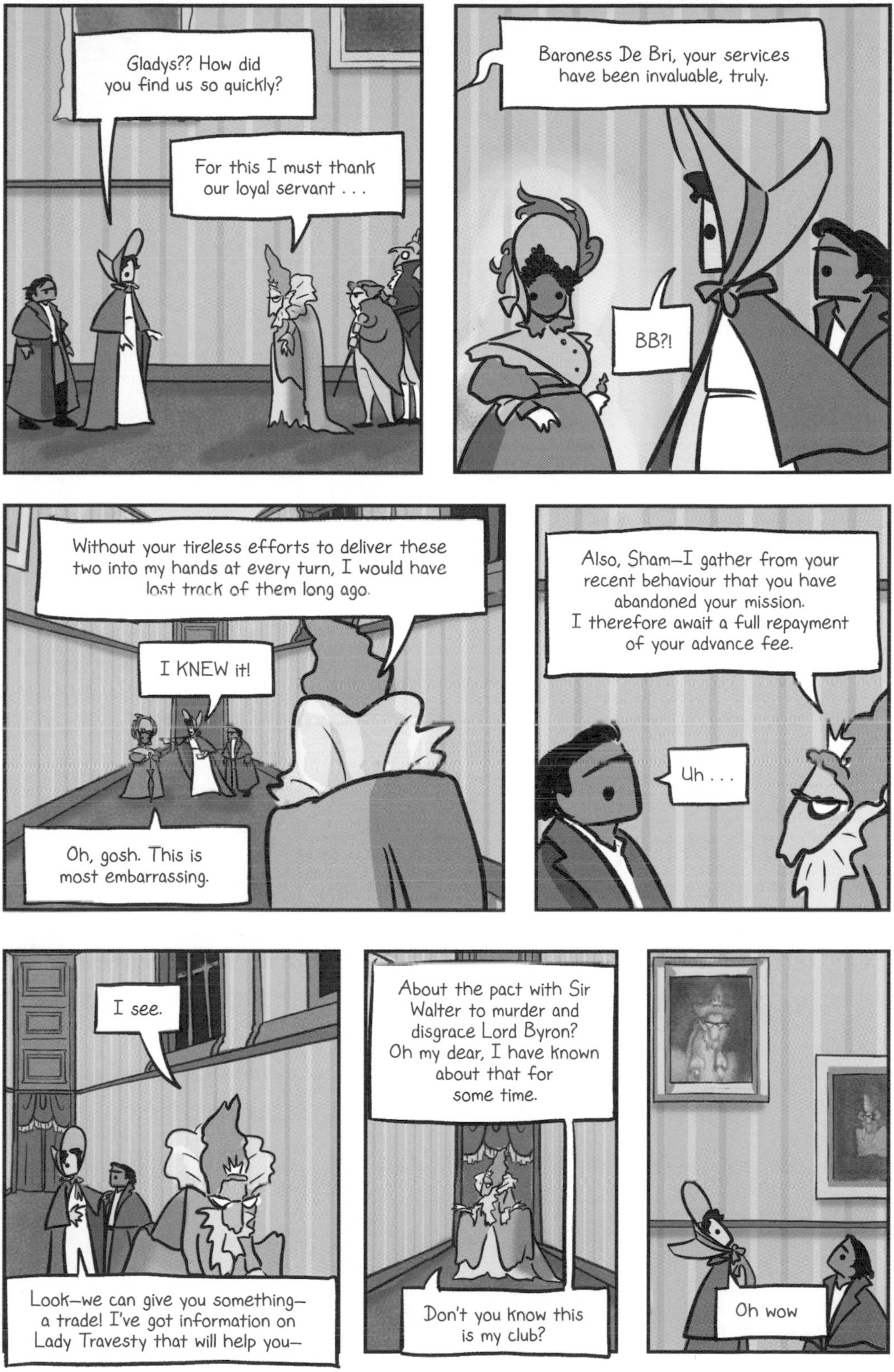
Gladys?? How did you find us so quickly?
For this I must thank our loyal servant . . .
Baroness De Bri, your services have been invaluable, truly.
BB?!
Without your tireless efforts to deliver these two into my hands at every turn, I would have lost track of them long ago.
I KNEW it!
Oh, gosh. This is most embarrassing.
Also, Sham—I gather from your recent behaviour that you have abandoned your mission. I therefore await a full repayment of your advance fee.
Uh . . .
I see.
Look—we can give you something—a trade! I've got information on Lady Travesty that will help you—
About the pact with Sir Walter to murder and disgrace Lord Byron? Oh my dear, I have known about that for some time.
Don't you know this is my club?
Oh wow

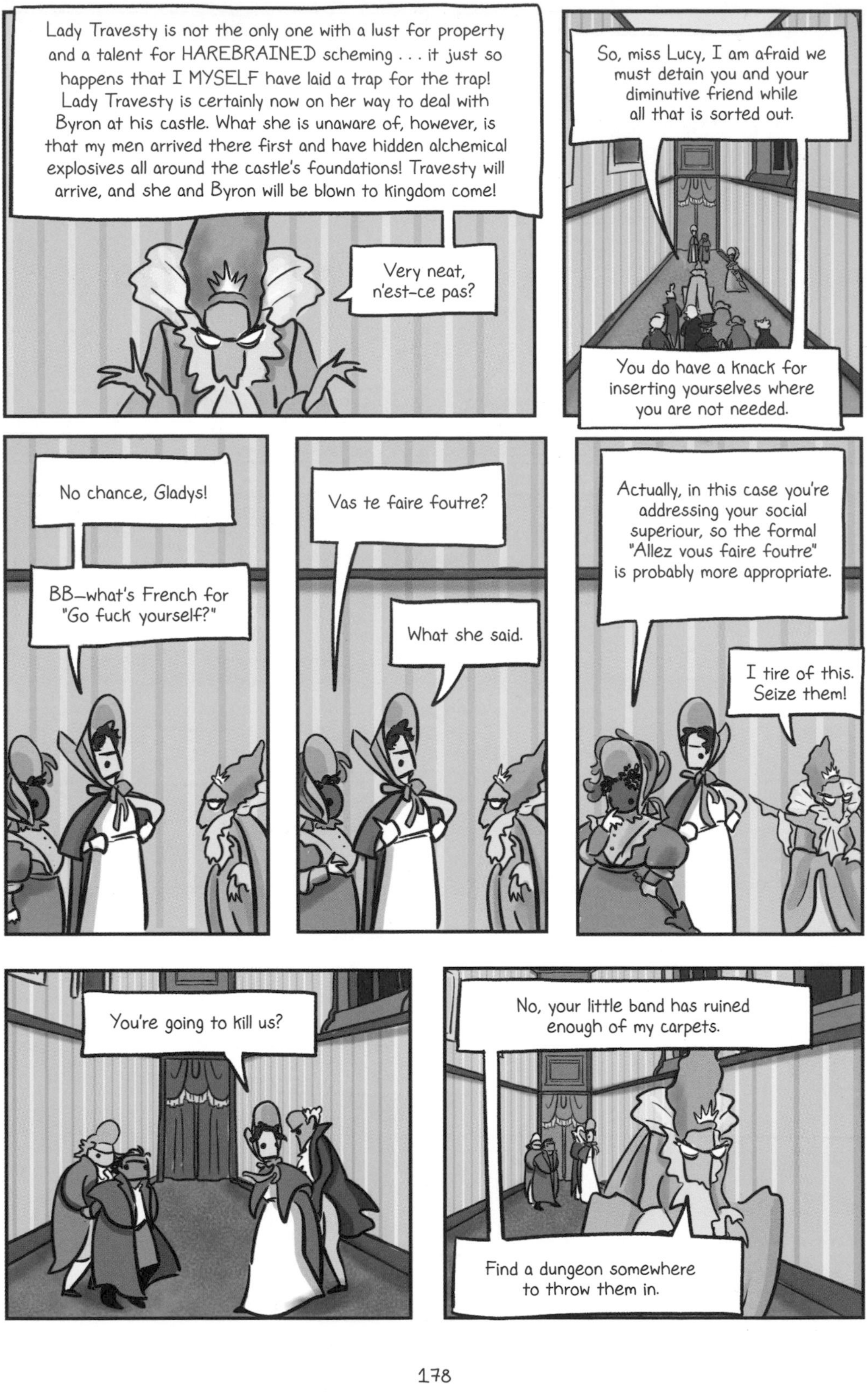
Lady Travesty is not the only one with a lust for property and a talent for HAREBRAINED scheming . . . it just so happens that I MYSELF have laid a trap for the trap! Lady Travesty is certainly now on her way to deal with Byron at his castle. What she is unaware of, however, is that my men arrived there first and have hidden alchemical explosives all around the castle's foundations! Travesty will arrive, and she and Byron will be blown to kingdom come!
Very neat, n'est-ce pas?
So, miss Lucy, I am afraid we must detain you and your diminutive friend while all that is sorted out.
You do have a knack for inserting yourselves where you are not needed.
No chance, Gladys!
BB—what's French for "Go fuck yourself?"
Vas te faire foutre?
What she said.
Actually, in this case you're addressing your social superiour, so the formal "Allez vous faire foutre" is probably more appropriate.
I tire of this. Seize them!
You're going to kill us?
No, your little band has ruined enough of my carpets.
Find a dungeon somewhere to throw them in.

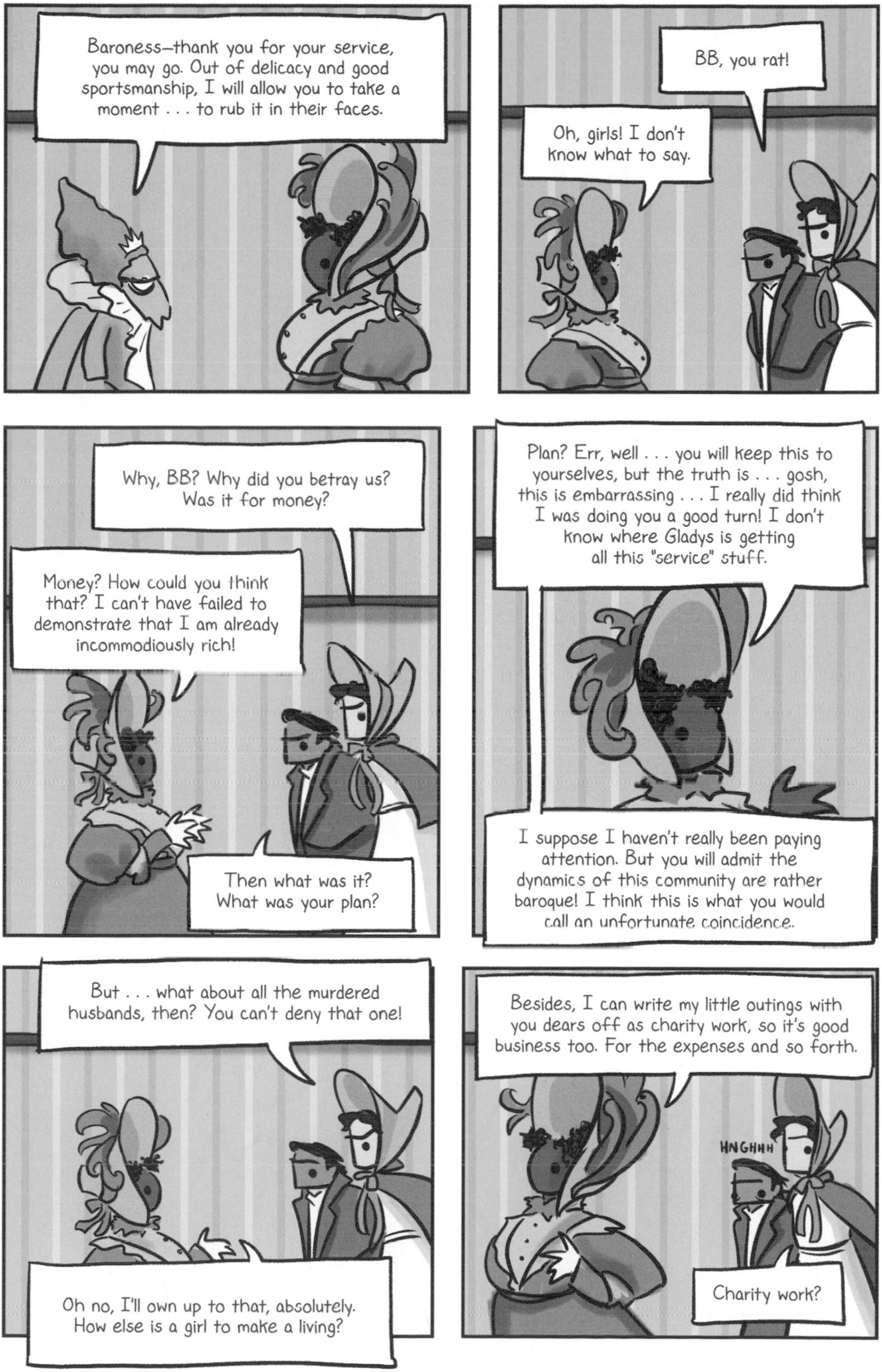
Baroness—thank you for your service, you may go. Out of delicacy and good sportsmanship, I will allow you to take a moment . . . to rub it in their faces.
BB, you rat!
Oh, girls! I don't know what to say.
Why, BB? Why did you betray us? Was it for money?
Money? How could you think that? I can't have failed to demonstrate that I am already incommodiously rich!
Then what was it? What was your plan?
Plan? Err, well . . . you will keep this to yourselves, but the truth is . . . gosh, this is embarrassing . . . I really did think I was doing you a good turn! I don't know where Gladys is getting all this "service" stuff.
I suppose I haven't really been paying attention. But you will admit the dynamics of this community are rather baroque! I think this is what you would call an unfortunate coincidence.
But . . . what about all the murdered husbands, then? You can't deny that one!
Oh no, I'll own up to that, absolutely. How else is a girl to make a living?
Besides, I can write my little outings with you dears off as charity work, so it's good business too. For the expenses and so forth.
HNGHHH
Charity work?

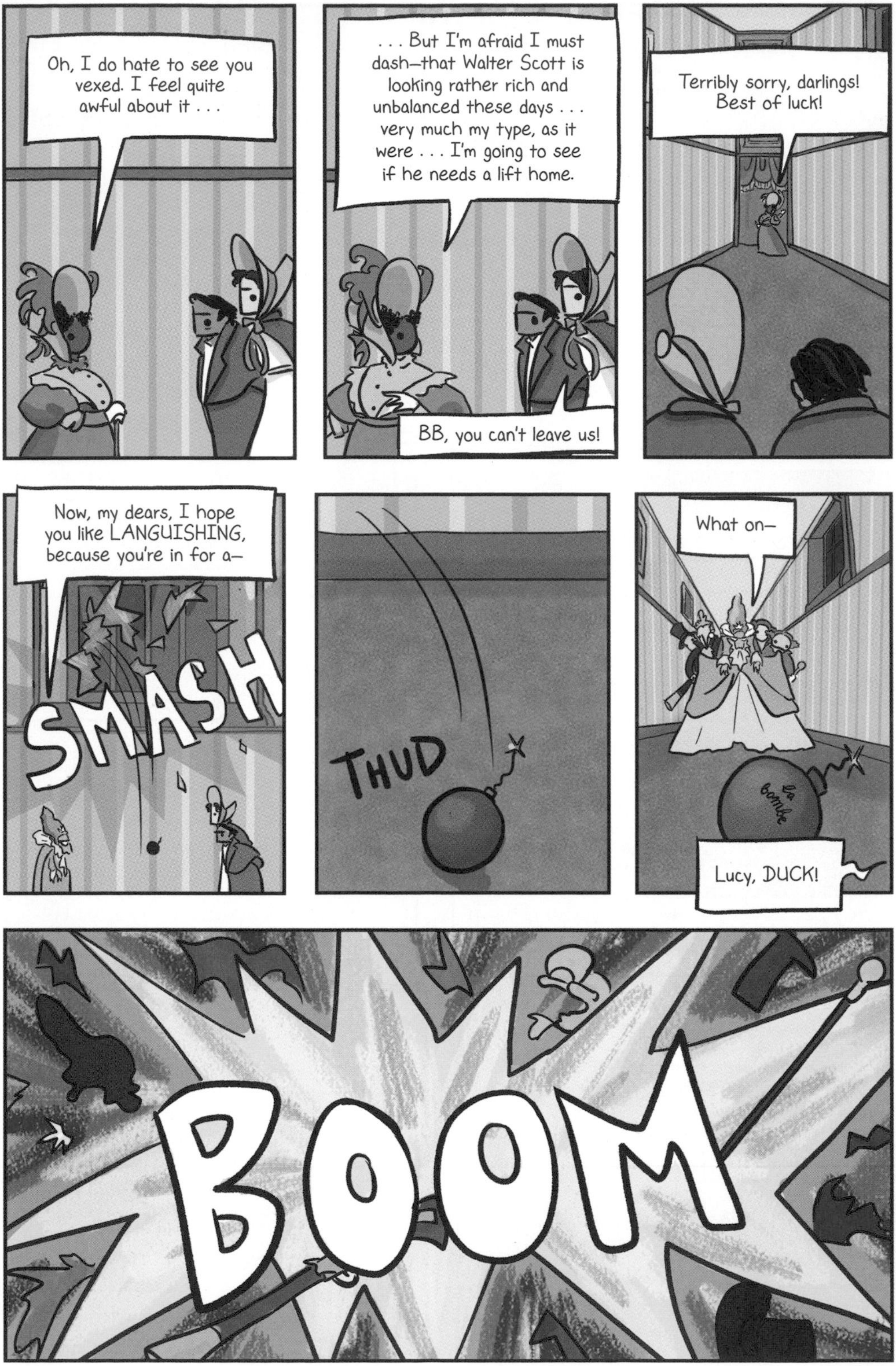
Oh, I do hate to see you vexed. I feel quite awful about it . . .
. . . But I'm afraid I must dash—that Walter Scott is looking rather rich and unbalanced these days . . . very much my type, as it were . . . I'm going to see if he needs a lift home.
BB, you can't leave us!
Terribly sorry, darlings! Best of luck!
Now, my dears, I hope you like LANGUISHING, because you're in for a—
SMASH
THUD
What on—
la bombe
Lucy, DUCK!
BOOM

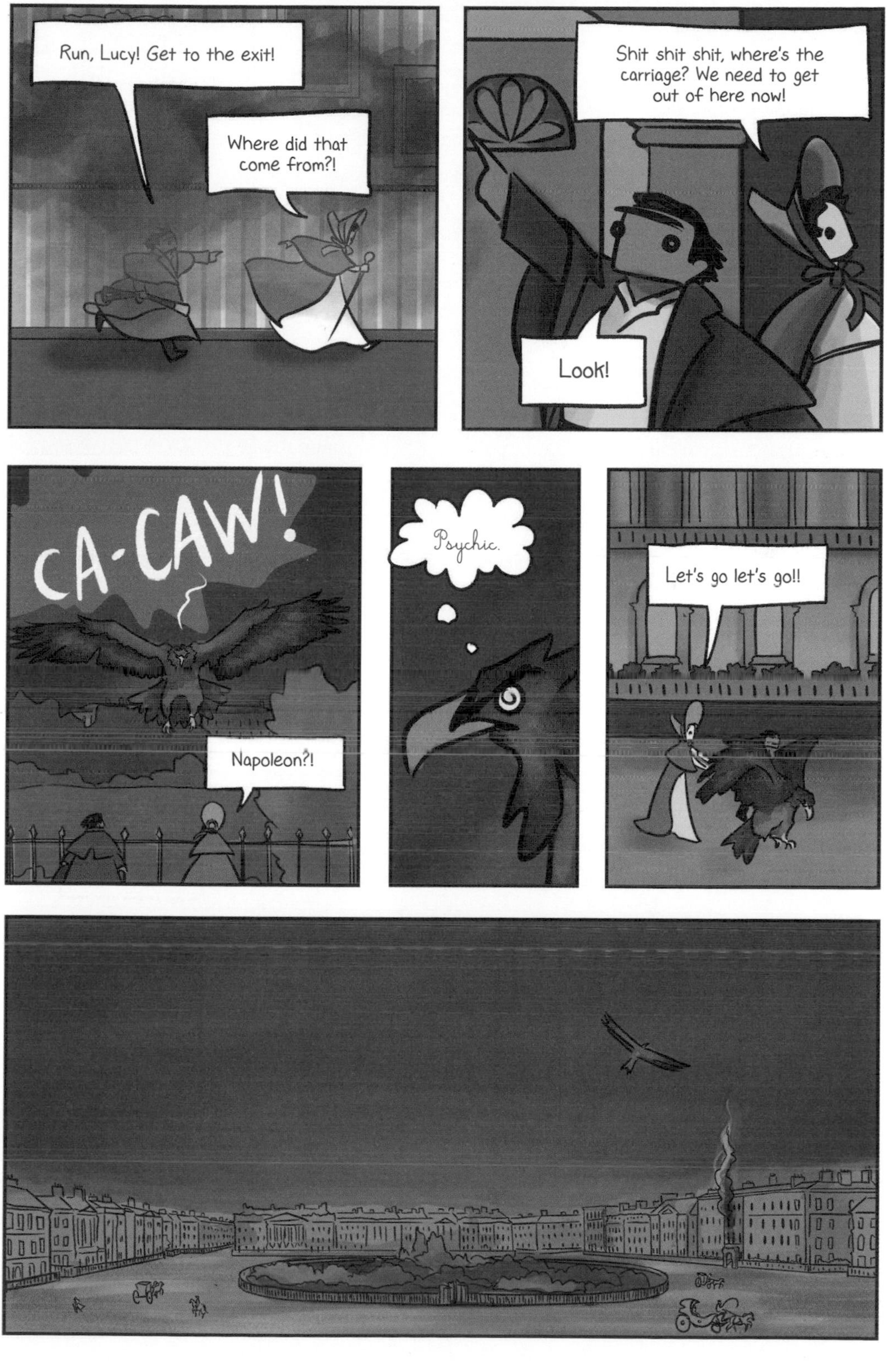
Run, Lucy! Get to the exit!
Where did that come from?!
Shit shit shit, where's the carriage? We need to get out of here now!
Look!
CA-CAW!
Napoleon?!
Psychic.
Let's go let's go!!

CHAPTER XII - THE END

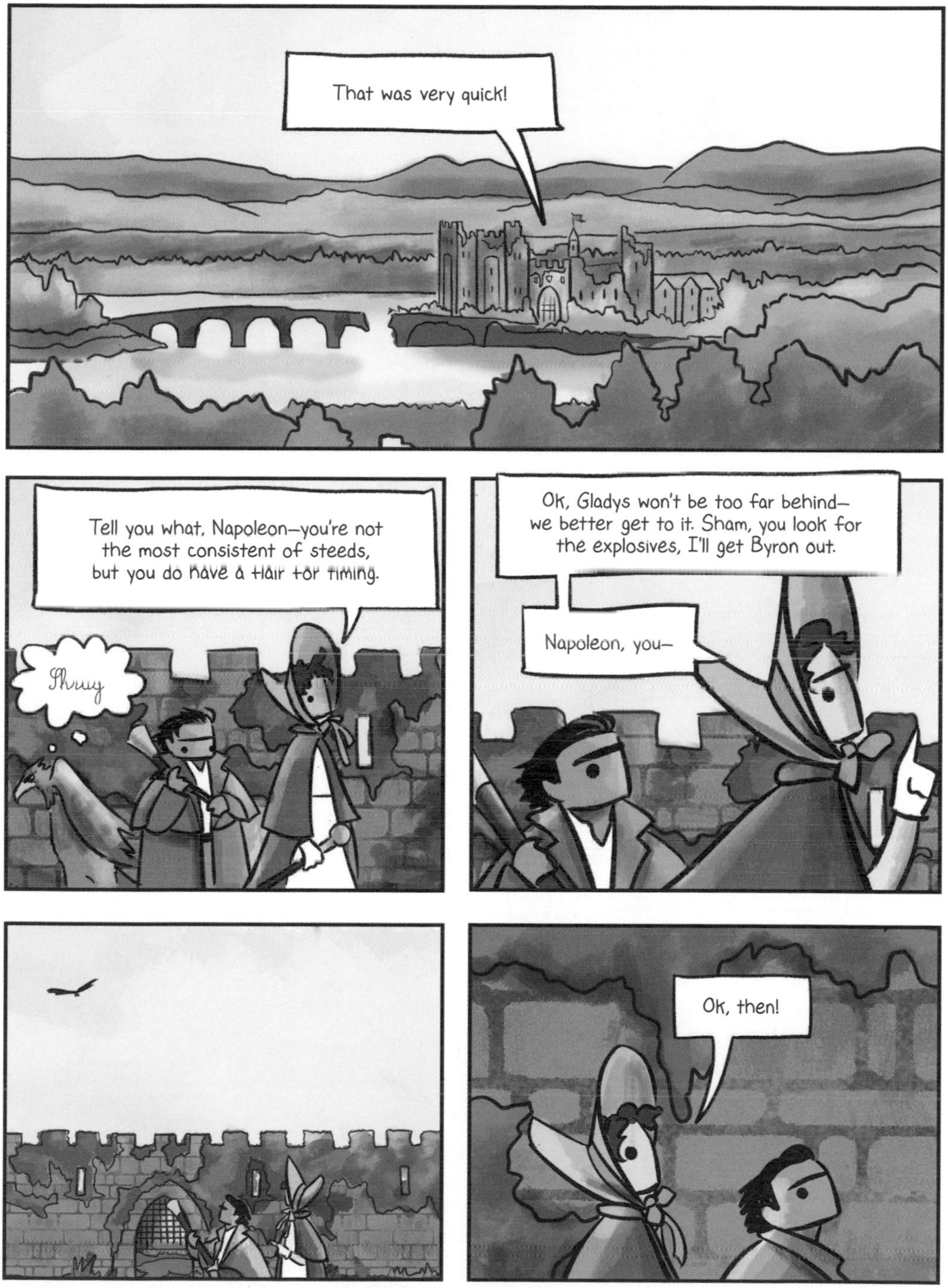
That was very quick!
Tell you what, Napoleon—you're not the most consistent of steeds, but you do have a flair for timing.
Shrug
Ok, Gladys won't be too far behind— we better get to it. Sham, you look for the explosives, I'll get Byron out.
Napoleon, you—
Ok, then!

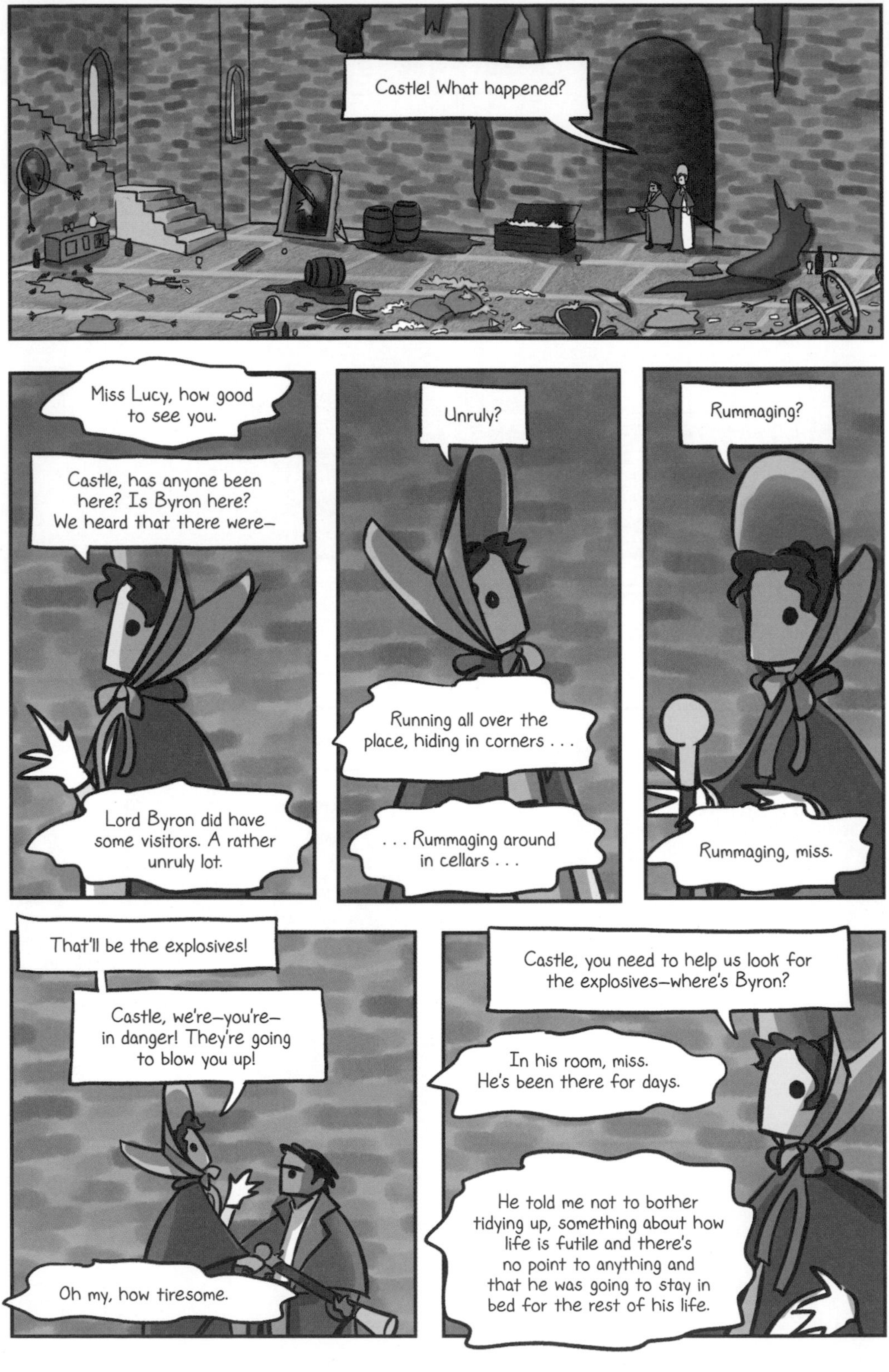
Castle! What happened?
Miss Lucy, how good to see you.
Castle, has anyone been here? Is Byron here? We heard that there were–
Lord Byron did have some visitors. A rather unruly lot.
Unruly?
Running all over the place, hiding in corners . . .
. . . Rummaging around in cellars . . .
Rummaging?
Rummaging, miss.
That'll be the explosives!
Castle, we're–you're–in danger! They're going to blow you up!
Oh my, how tiresome.
Castle, you need to help us look for the explosives–where's Byron?
In his room, miss. He's been there for days.
He told me not to bother tidying up, something about how life is futile and there's no point to anything and that he was going to stay in bed for the rest of his life.

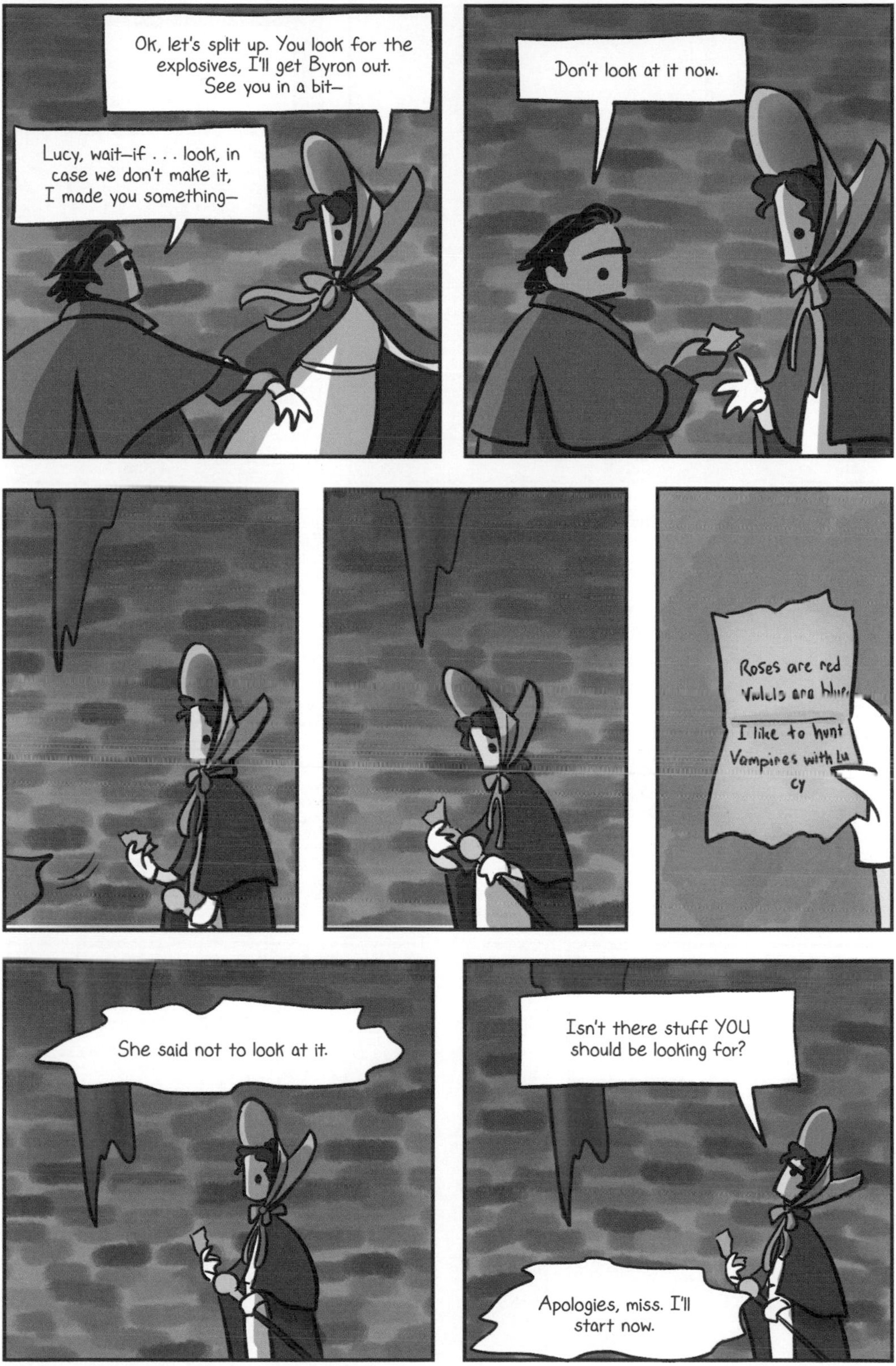
Ok, let's split up. You look for the explosives, I'll get Byron out. See you in a bit—
Lucy, wait—if . . . look, in case we don't make it, I made you something—
Don't look at it now.
Roses are red
Vwlels are blue
I like to hunt
Vampires with Lu
cy
She said not to look at it.
Isn't there stuff YOU should be looking for?
Apologies, miss. I'll start now.

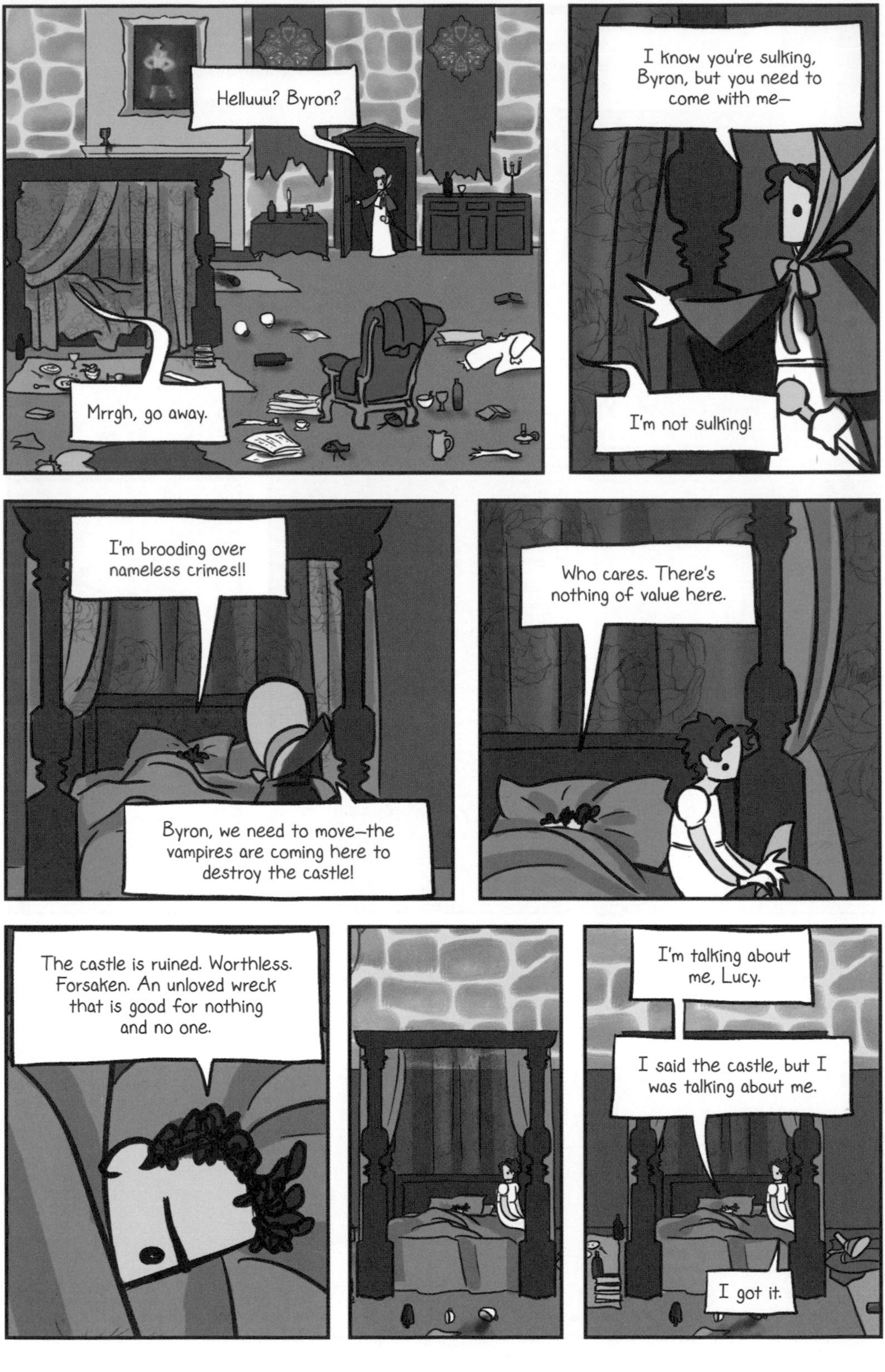
Helluuu? Byron?
Mrrgh, go away.
I know you're sulking, Byron, but you need to come with me–
I'm not sulking!
I'm brooding over nameless crimes!!
Byron, we need to move–the vampires are coming here to destroy the castle!
Who cares. There's nothing of value here.
The castle is ruined. Worthless. Forsaken. An unloved wreck that is good for nothing and no one.
I'm talking about me, Lucy.
I said the castle, but I was talking about me.
I got it.

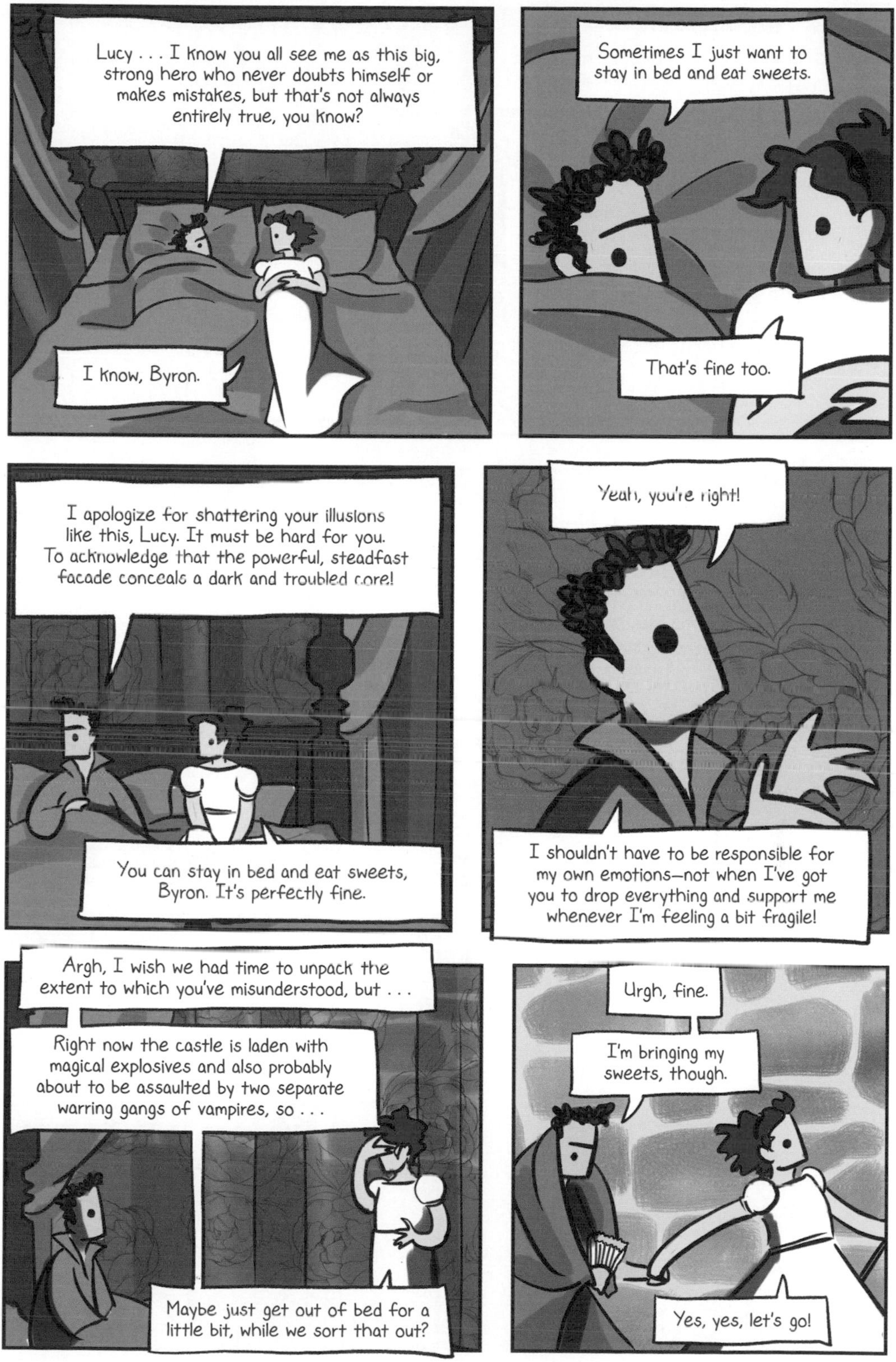
Lucy . . . I know you all see me as this big, strong hero who never doubts himself or makes mistakes, but that's not always entirely true, you know?
I know, Byron.
Sometimes I just want to stay in bed and eat sweets.
That's fine too.
I apologize for shattering your illusions like this, Lucy. It must be hard for you. To acknowledge that the powerful, steadfast facade conceals a dark and troubled core!
You can stay in bed and eat sweets, Byron. It's perfectly fine.
Yeah, you're right!
I shouldn't have to be responsible for my own emotions—not when I've got you to drop everything and support me whenever I'm feeling a bit fragile!
Argh, I wish we had time to unpack the extent to which you've misunderstood, but . . .
Right now the castle is laden with magical explosives and also probably about to be assaulted by two separate warring gangs of vampires, so . . .
Maybe just get out of bed for a little bit, while we sort that out?
Urgh, fine.
I'm bringing my sweets, though.
Yes, yes, let's go!

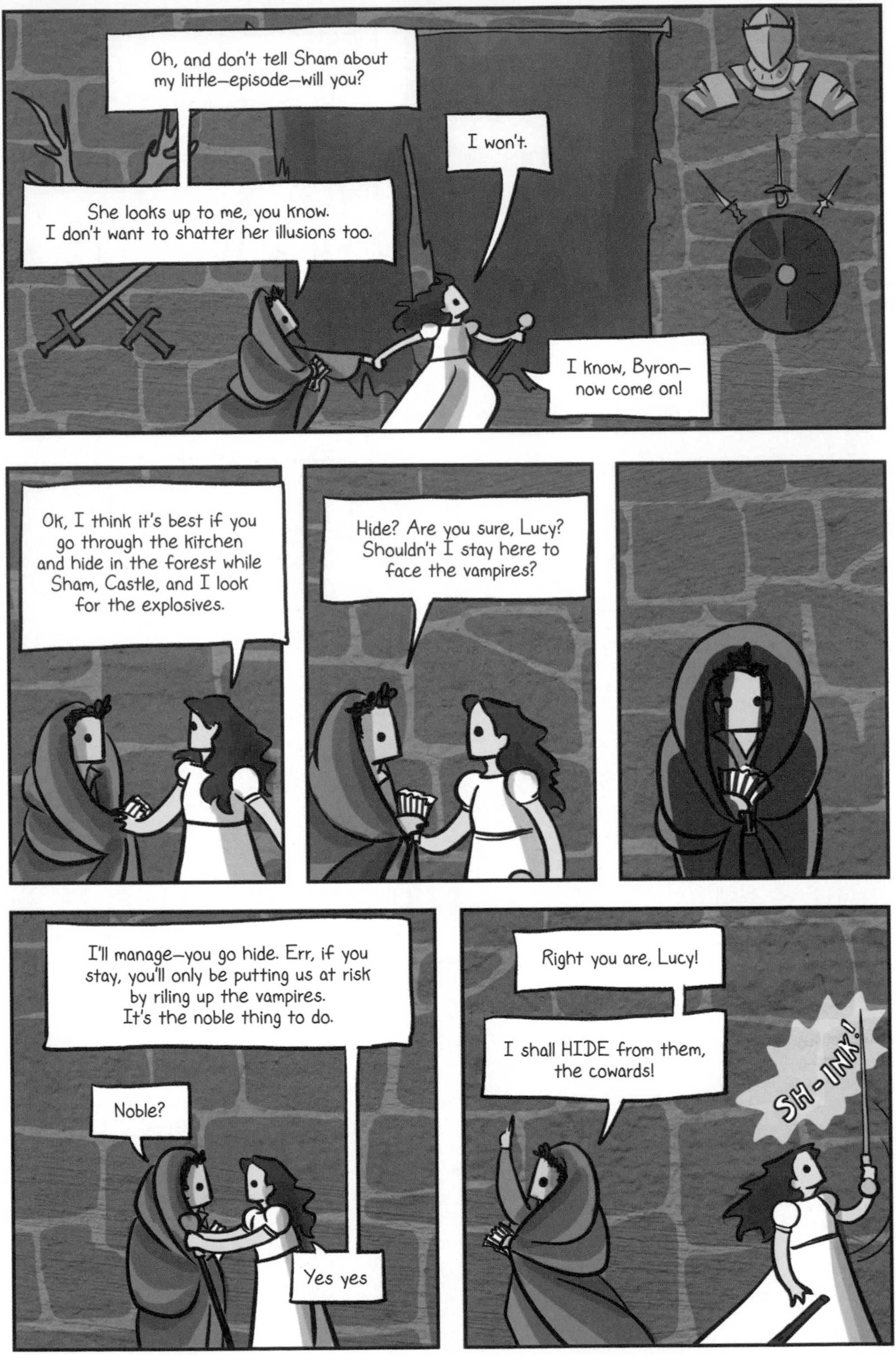
Oh, and don't tell Sham about my little—episode—will you?
She looks up to me, you know. I don't want to shatter her illusions too.
I won't.
I know, Byron— now come on!
Ok, I think it's best if you go through the kitchen and hide in the forest while Sham, Castle, and I look for the explosives.
Hide? Are you sure, Lucy? Shouldn't I stay here to face the vampires?
I'll manage—you go hide. Err, if you stay, you'll only be putting us at risk by riling up the vampires. It's the noble thing to do.
Noble?
Yes yes
Right you are, Lucy!
I shall HIDE from them, the cowards!
SH-INK!

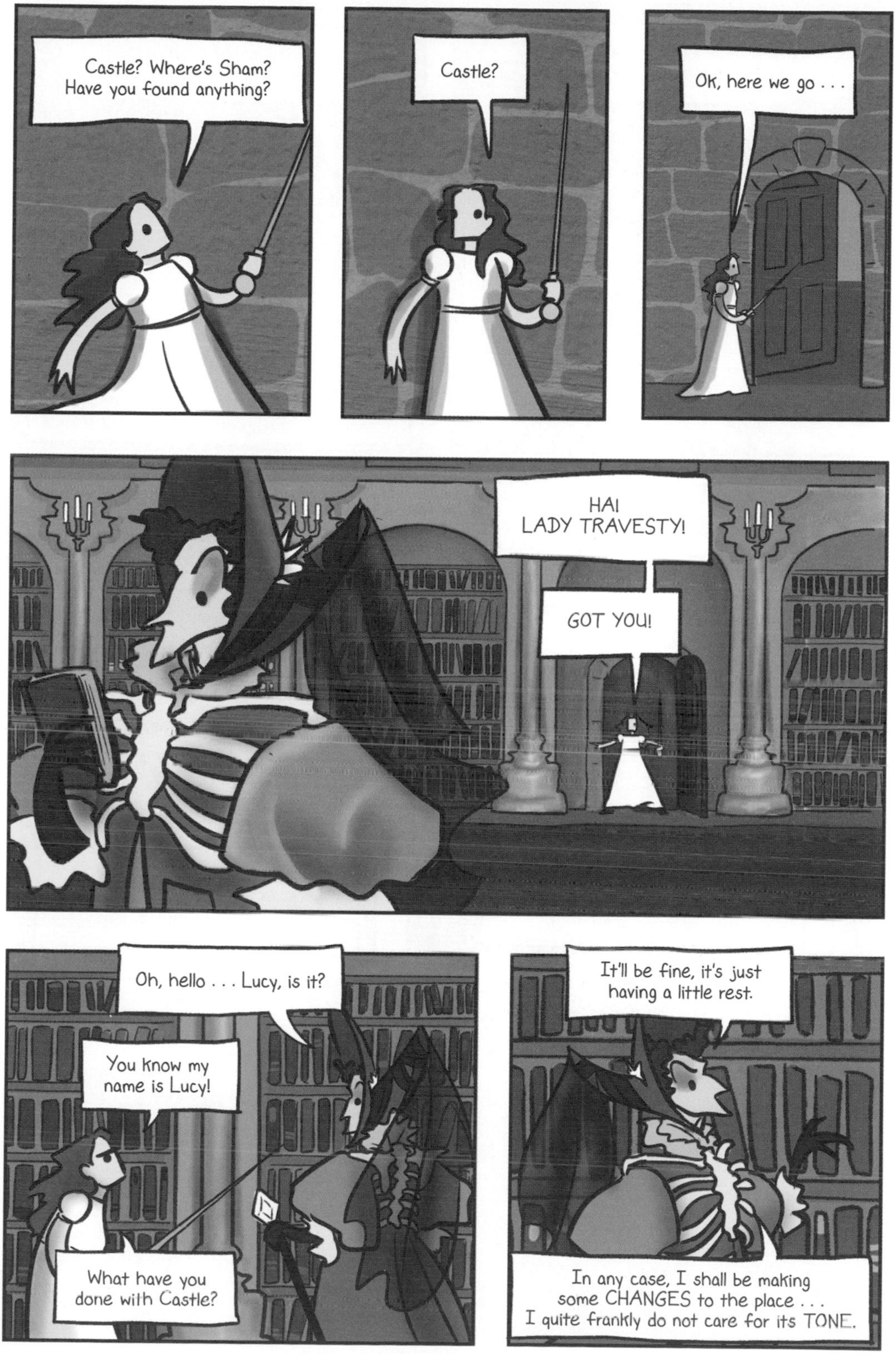
Castle? Where's Sham? Have you found anything?
Castle?
Ok, here we go . . .
HAI LADY TRAVESTY!
GOT YOU!
Oh, hello . . . Lucy, is it?
You know my name is Lucy!
What have you done with Castle?
It'll be fine, it's just having a little rest.
In any case, I shall be making some CHANGES to the place . . . I quite frankly do not care for its TONE.

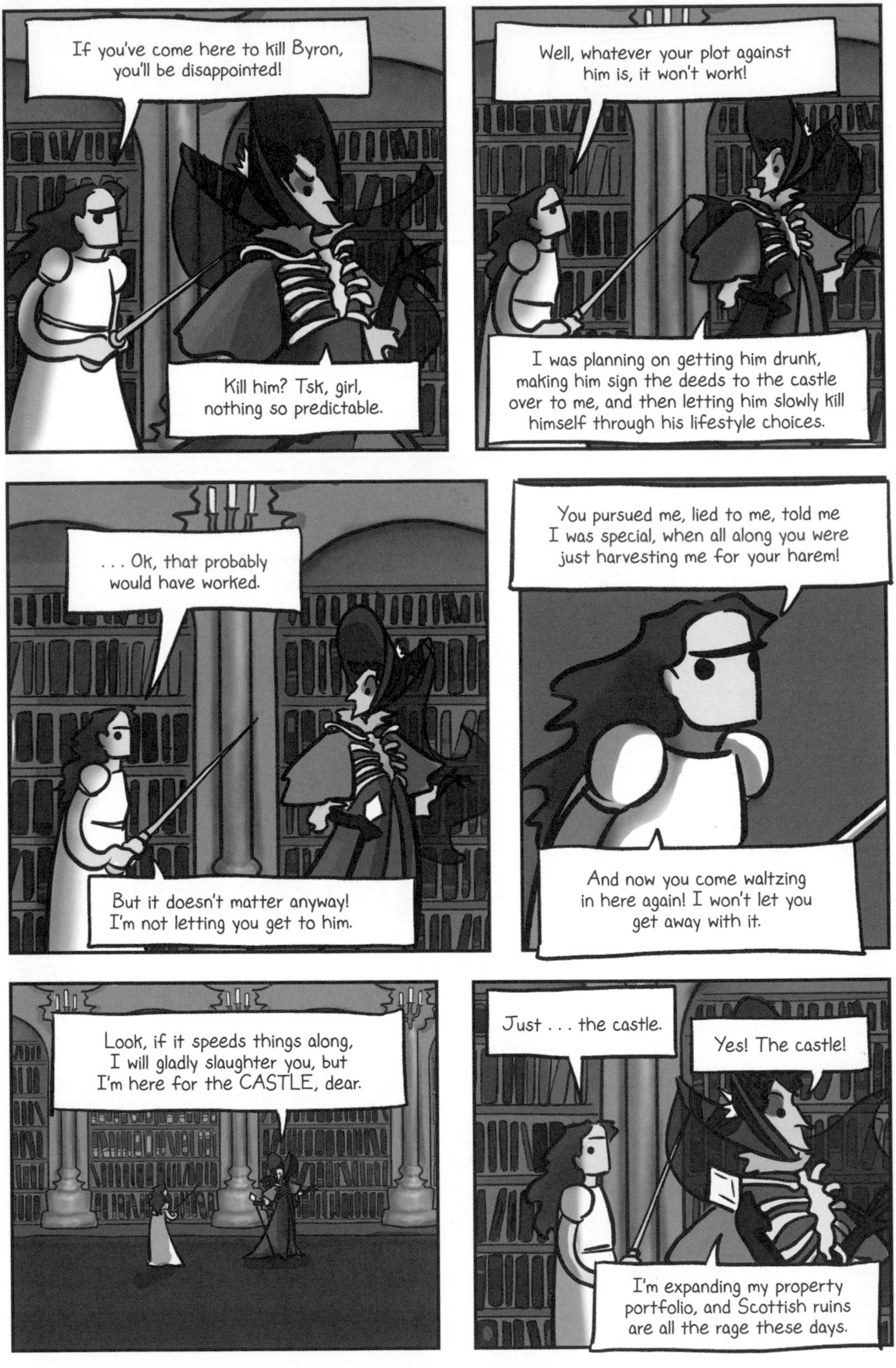
If you've come here to kill Byron, you'll be disappointed!
Kill him? Tsk, girl, nothing so predictable.
Well, whatever your plot against him is, it won't work!
I was planning on getting him drunk, making him sign the deeds to the castle over to me, and then letting him slowly kill himself through his lifestyle choices.
. . . Ok, that probably would have worked.
But it doesn't matter anyway! I'm not letting you get to him.
You pursued me, lied to me, told me I was special, when all along you were just harvesting me for your harem!
And now you come waltzing in here again! I won't let you get away with it.
Look, if it speeds things along, I will gladly slaughter you, but I'm here for the CASTLE, dear.
Just . . . the castle.
Yes! The castle!
I'm expanding my property portfolio, and Scottish ruins are all the rage these days.

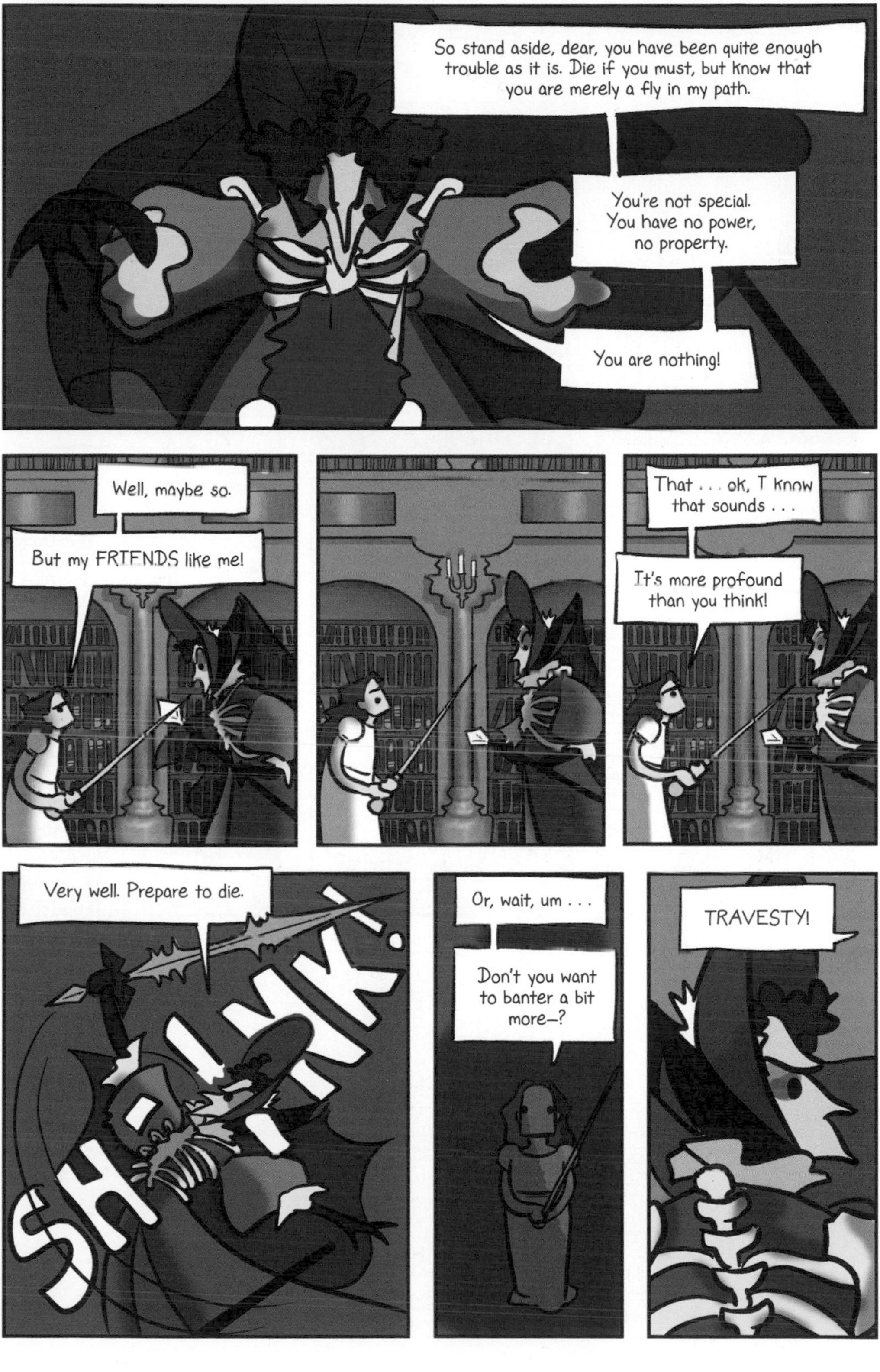
So stand aside, dear, you have been quite enough trouble as it is. Die if you must, but know that you are merely a fly in my path.
You're not special. You have no power, no property.
You are nothing!
Well, maybe so.
But my FRIENDS like me!
That . . . ok, I know that sounds . . .
It's more profound than you think!
Very well. Prepare to die.
SHIIINK!
Or, wait, um . . .
Don't you want to banter a bit more–?
TRAVESTY!

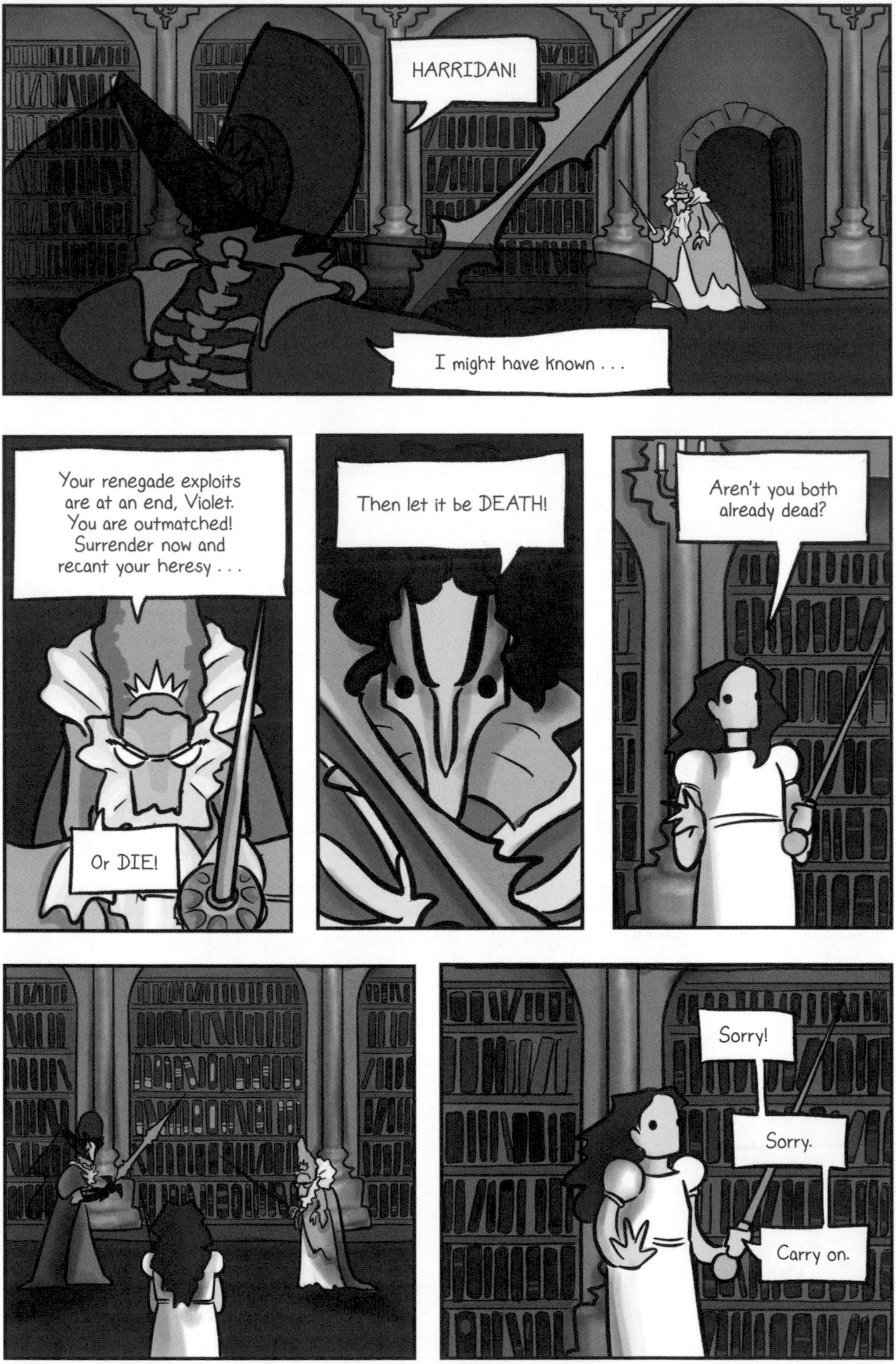
HARRIDAN!
I might have known . . .
Your renegade exploits are at an end, Violet. You are outmatched! Surrender now and recant your heresy . . .
Or DIE!
Then let it be DEATH!
Aren't you both already dead?
Sorry!
Sorry.
Carry on.

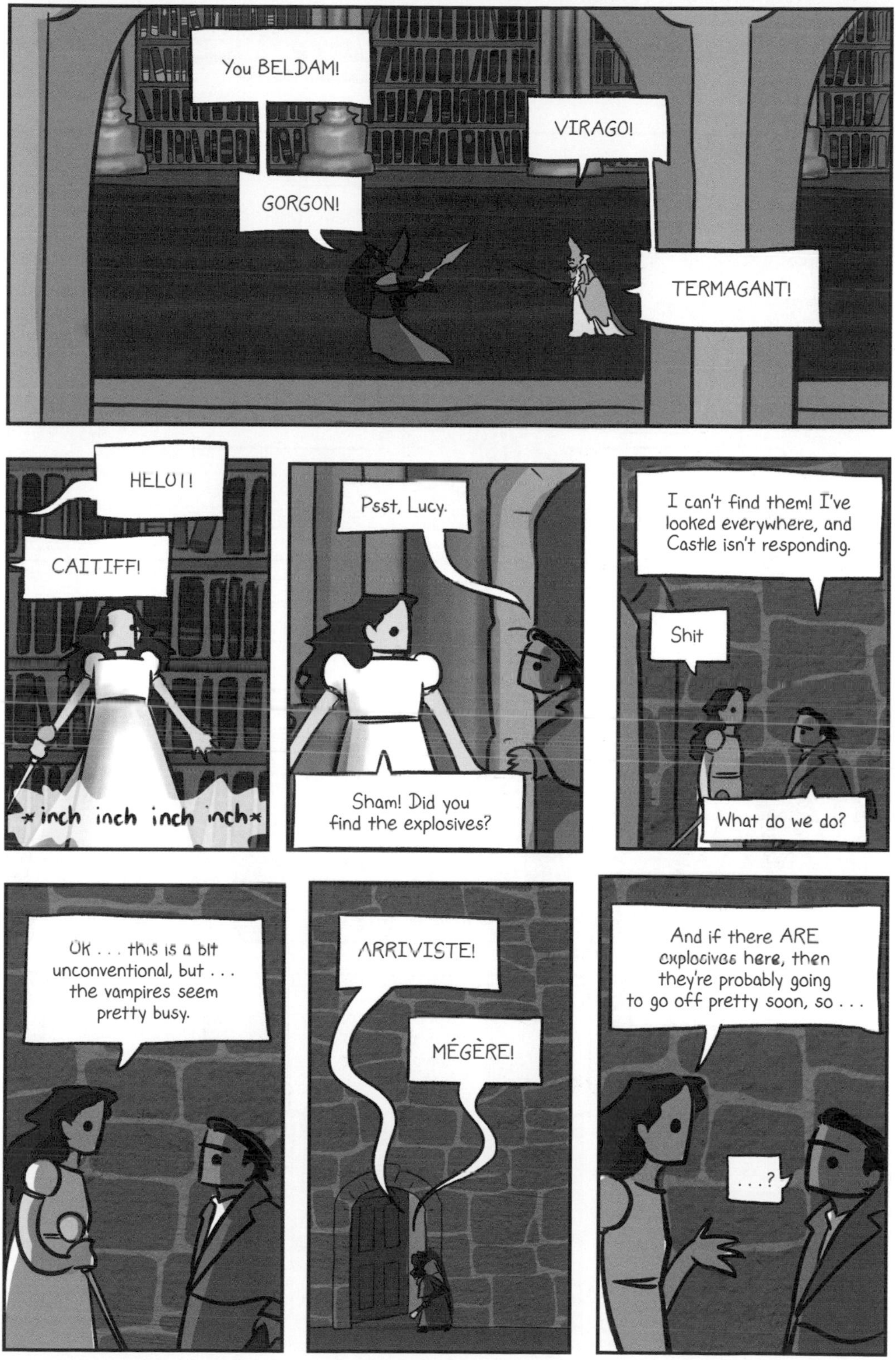
You BELDAM!
GORGON!
VIRAGO!
TERMAGANT!
HELOT!
CAITIFF!
inch inch inch inch
Psst, Lucy.
Sham! Did you find the explosives?
I can't find them! I've looked everywhere, and Castle isn't responding.
Shit
What do we do?
OK . . . this is a bit unconventional, but . . . the vampires seem pretty busy.
ARRIVISTE!
MÉGÈRE!
And if there ARE explosives here, then they're probably going to go off pretty soon, so . . .
. . . ?

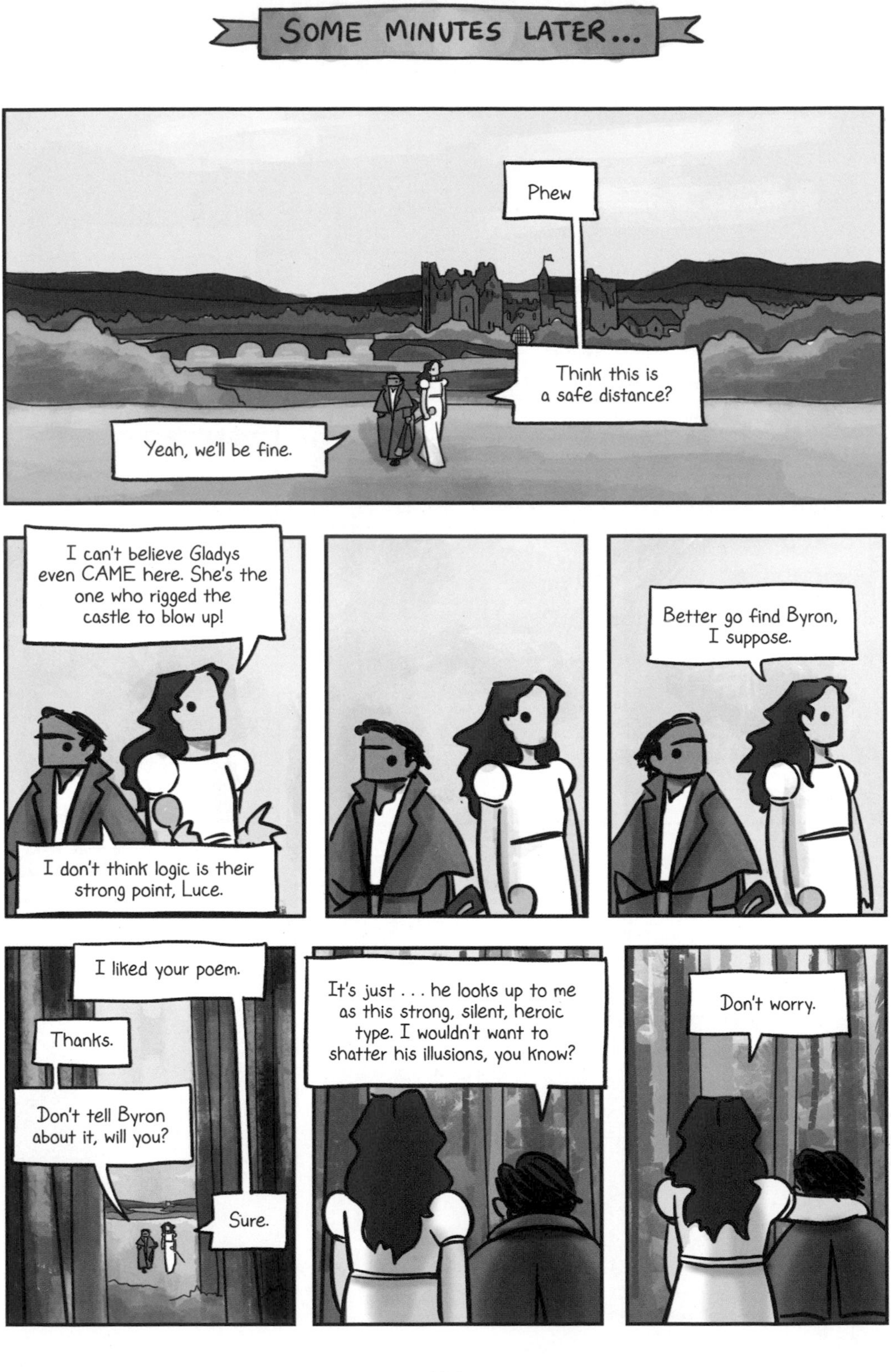
SOME MINUTES LATER...
Phew
Think this is a safe distance?
Yeah, we'll be fine.
I can't believe Gladys even CAME here. She's the one who rigged the castle to blow up!
I don't think logic is their strong point, Luce.
Better go find Byron, I suppose.
I liked your poem.
Thanks.
Don't tell Byron about it, will you?
Sure.
It's just . . . he looks up to me as this strong, silent, heroic type. I wouldn't want to shatter his illusions, you know?
Don't worry.

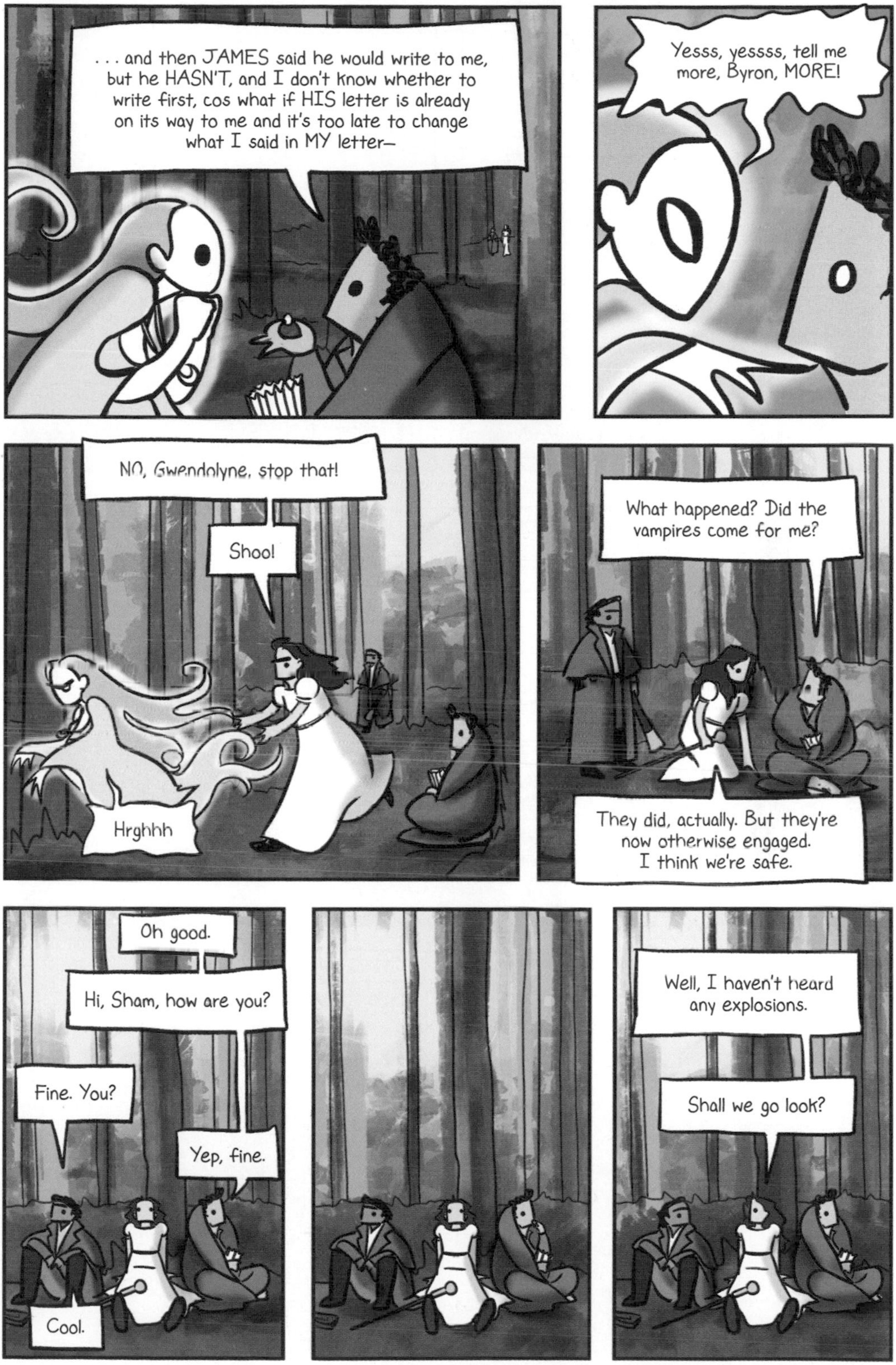
. . . and then JAMES said he would write to me, but he HASN'T, and I don't know whether to write first, cos what if HIS letter is already on its way to me and it's too late to change what I said in MY letter—
Yesss, yessss, tell me more, Byron, MORE!
NO, Gwendolyne, stop that!
Shoo!
Hrghhh
What happened? Did the vampires come for me?
They did, actually. But they're now otherwise engaged. I think we're safe.
Oh good.
Hi, Sham, how are you?
Fine. You?
Yep, fine.
Cool.
Well, I haven't heard any explosions.
Shall we go look?

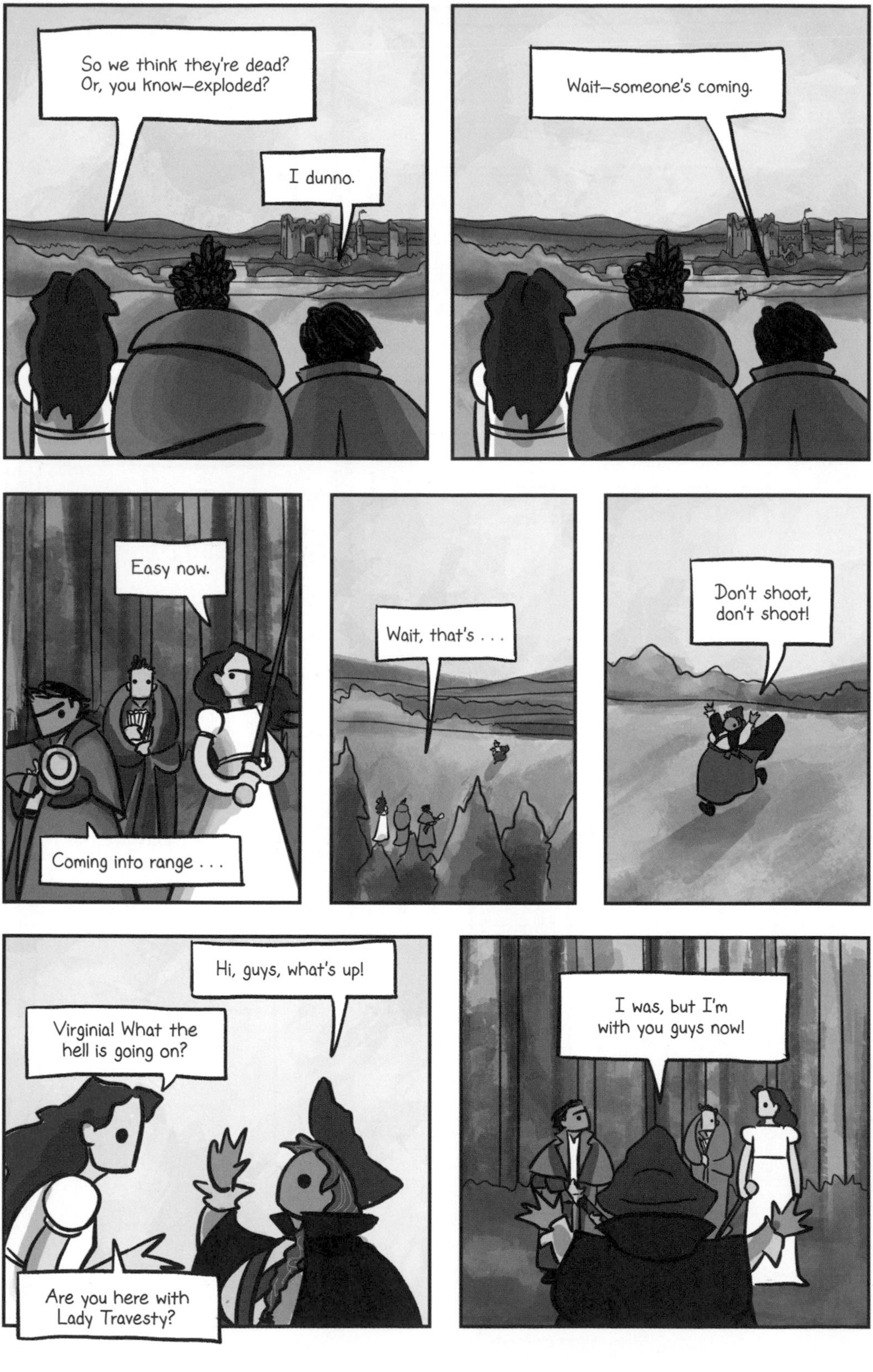
So we think they're dead? Or, you know—exploded?
I dunno.
Wait—someone's coming.
Easy now.
Coming into range . . .
Wait, that's . . .
Don't shoot, don't shoot!
Hi, guys, what's up!
Virginia! What the hell is going on?
Are you here with Lady Travesty?
I was, but I'm with you guys now!

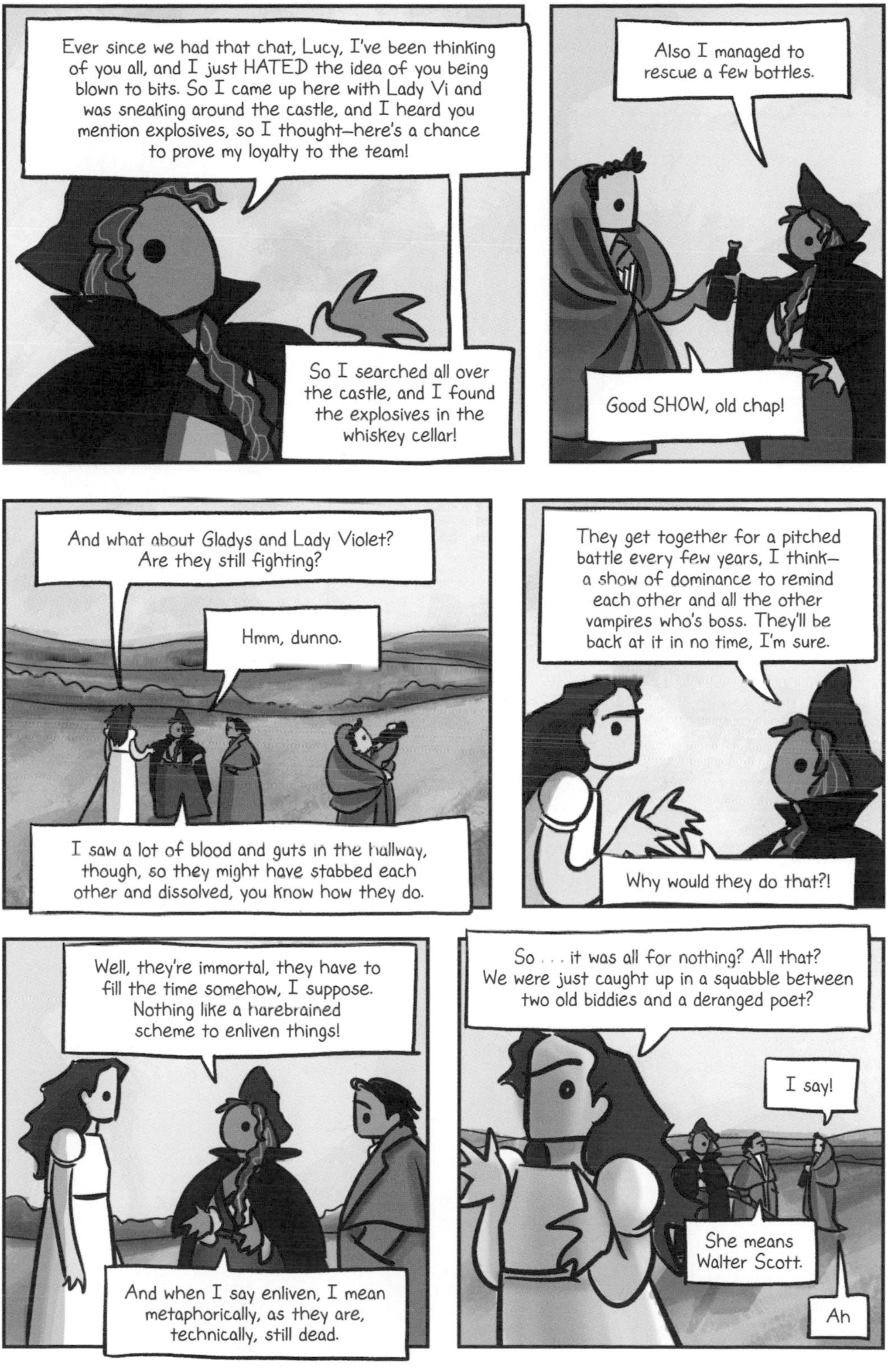
Ever since we had that chat, Lucy, I've been thinking of you all, and I just HATED the idea of you being blown to bits. So I came up here with Lady Vi and was sneaking around the castle, and I heard you mention explosives, so I thought—here's a chance to prove my loyalty to the team!
So I searched all over the castle, and I found the explosives in the whiskey cellar!
Also I managed to rescue a few bottles.
Good SHOW, old chap!
And what about Gladys and Lady Violet? Are they still fighting?
Hmm, dunno.
I saw a lot of blood and guts in the hallway, though, so they might have stabbed each other and dissolved, you know how they do.
They get together for a pitched battle every few years, I think—a show of dominance to remind each other and all the other vampires who's boss. They'll be back at it in no time, I'm sure.
Why would they do that?!
Well, they're immortal, they have to fill the time somehow, I suppose. Nothing like a harebrained scheme to enliven things!
And when I say enliven, I mean metaphorically, as they are, technically, still dead.
So . . . it was all for nothing? All that? We were just caught up in a squabble between two old biddies and a deranged poet?
I say!
She means Walter Scott.
Ah

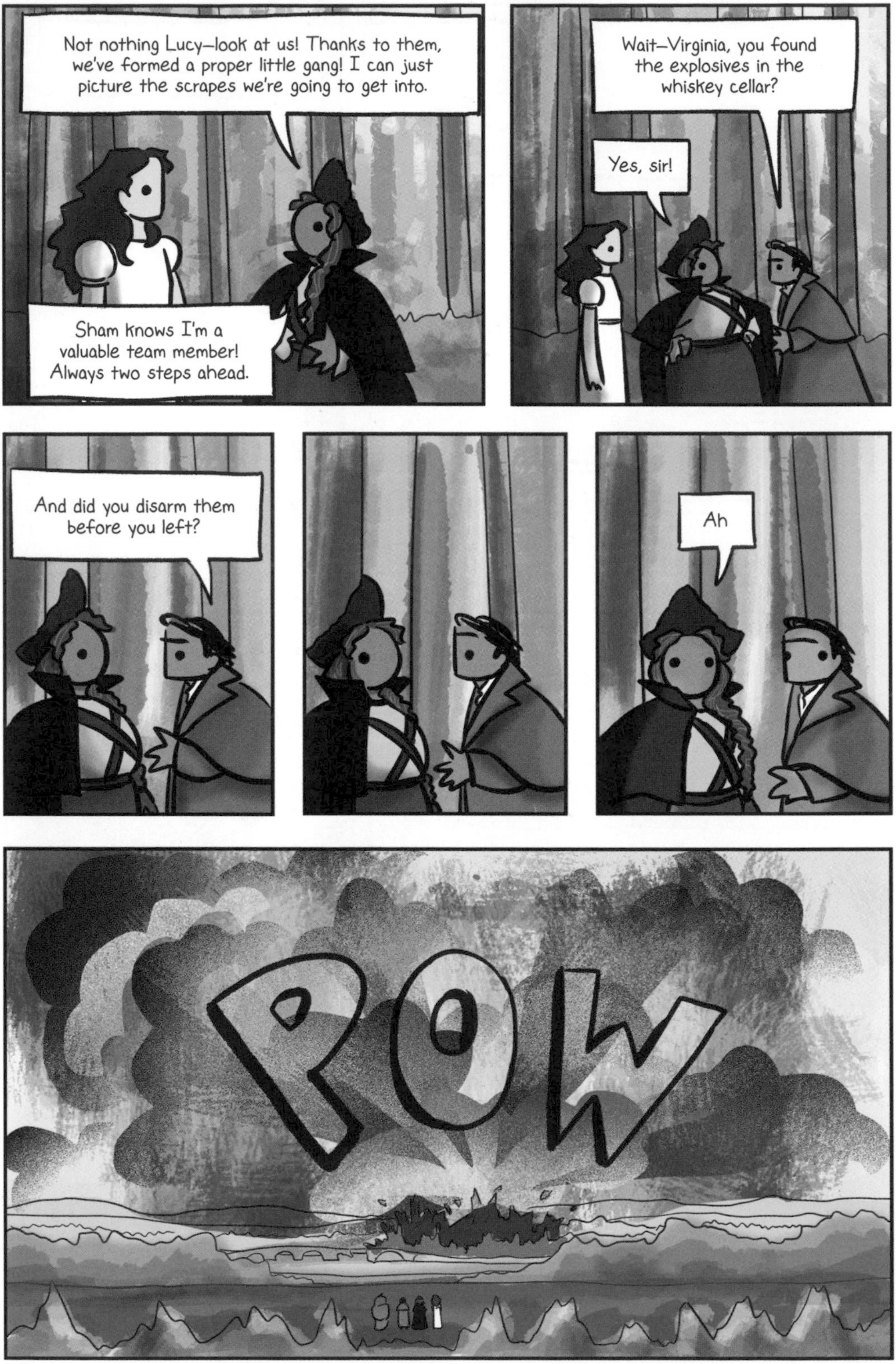
Not nothing Lucy—look at us! Thanks to them, we've formed a proper little gang! I can just picture the scrapes we're going to get into.
Sham knows I'm a valuable team member! Always two steps ahead.
Wait—Virginia, you found the explosives in the whiskey cellar?
Yes, sir!
And did you disarm them before you left?
Ah
POW

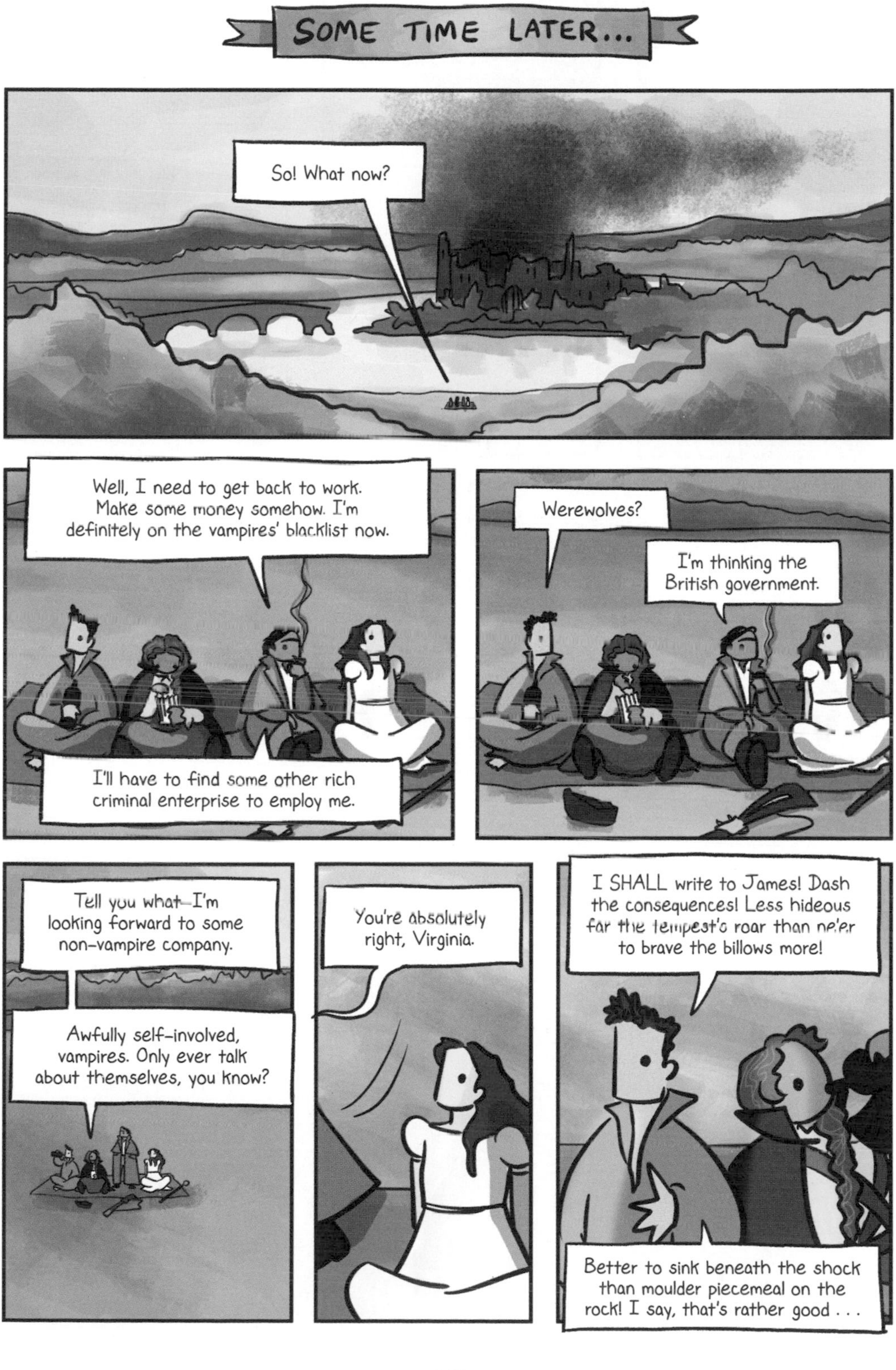
SOME TIME LATER...
So! What now?
Well, I need to get back to work. Make some money somehow. I'm definitely on the vampires' blacklist now.
I'll have to find some other rich criminal enterprise to employ me.
Werewolves?
I'm thinking the British government.
Tell you what—I'm looking forward to some non-vampire company.
Awfully self-involved, vampires. Only ever talk about themselves, you know?
You're absolutely right, Virginia.
I SHALL write to James! Dash the consequences! Less hideous far the tempest's roar than ne'er to brave the billows more!
Better to sink beneath the shock than moulder piecemeal on the rock! I say, that's rather good . . .

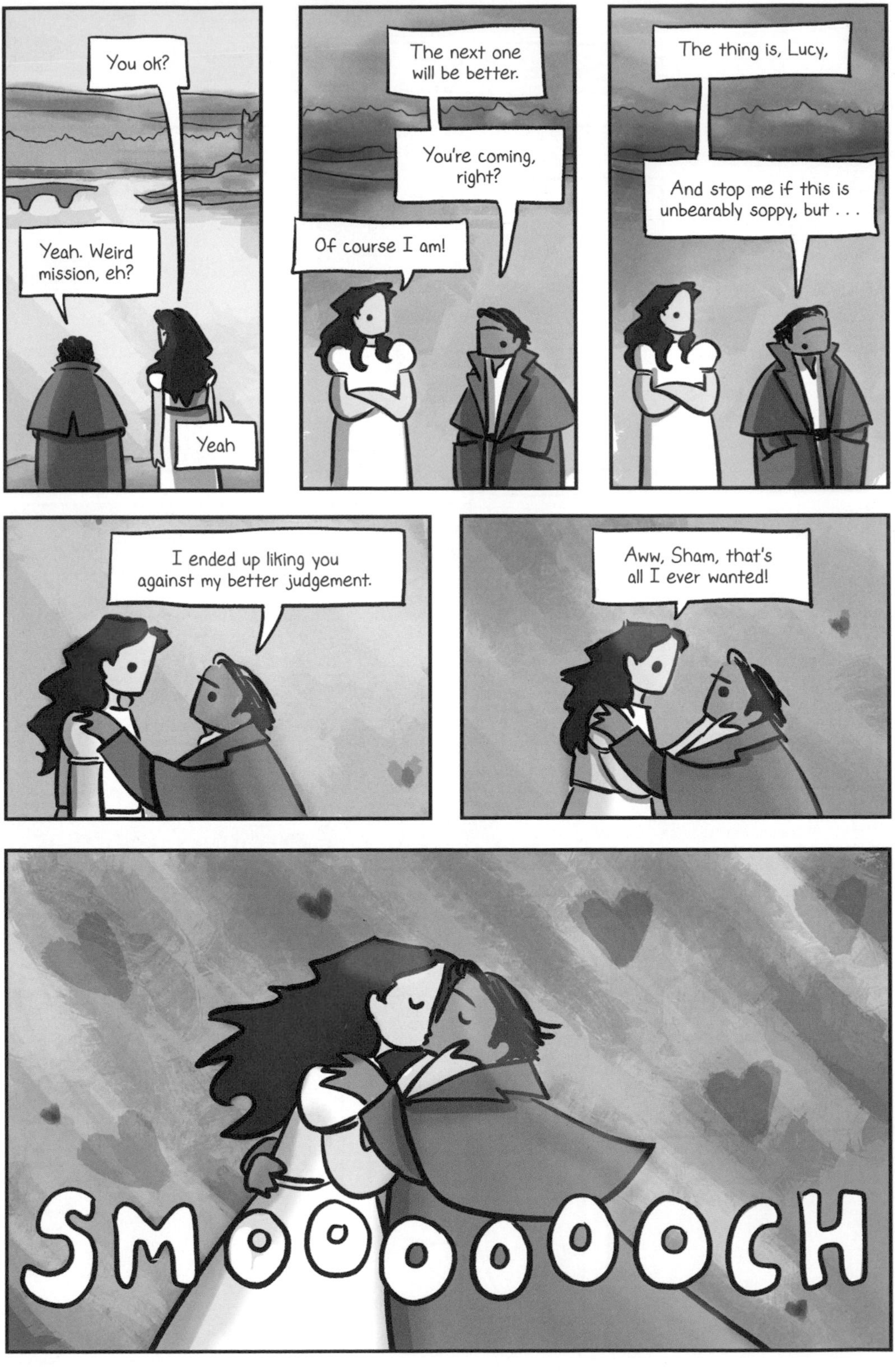
You ok?
Yeah. Weird mission, eh?
Yeah
The next one will be better.
You're coming, right?
Of course I am!
The thing is, Lucy,
And stop me if this is unbearably soppy, but . . .
I ended up liking you against my better judgement.
Aww, Sham, that's all I ever wanted!
SMOOOOOOCH

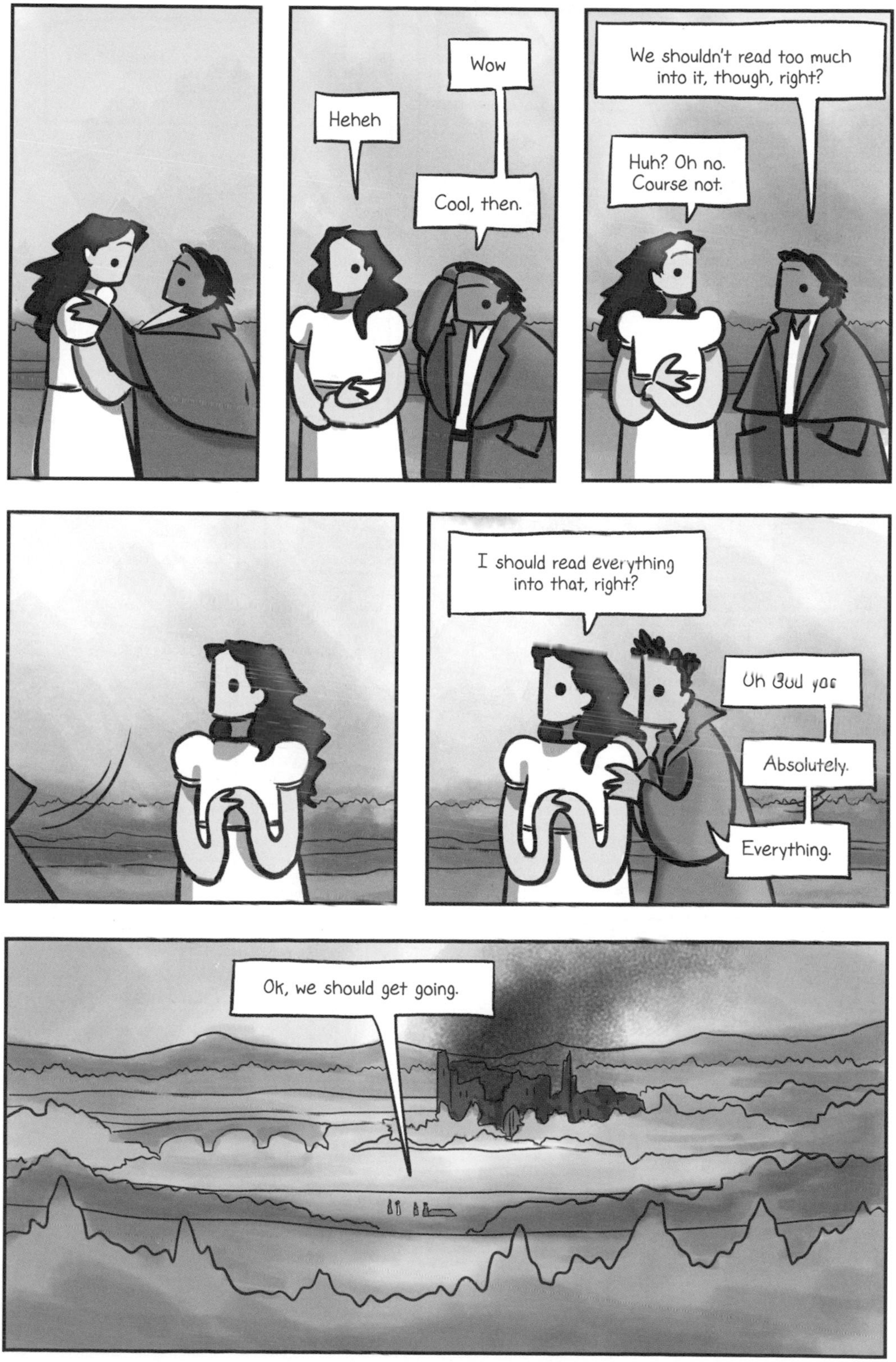
Heheh
Wow
Cool, then.
We shouldn't read too much into it, though, right?
Huh? Oh no. Course not.
I should read everything into that, right?
Absolutely.
Everything.
Ok, we should get going.

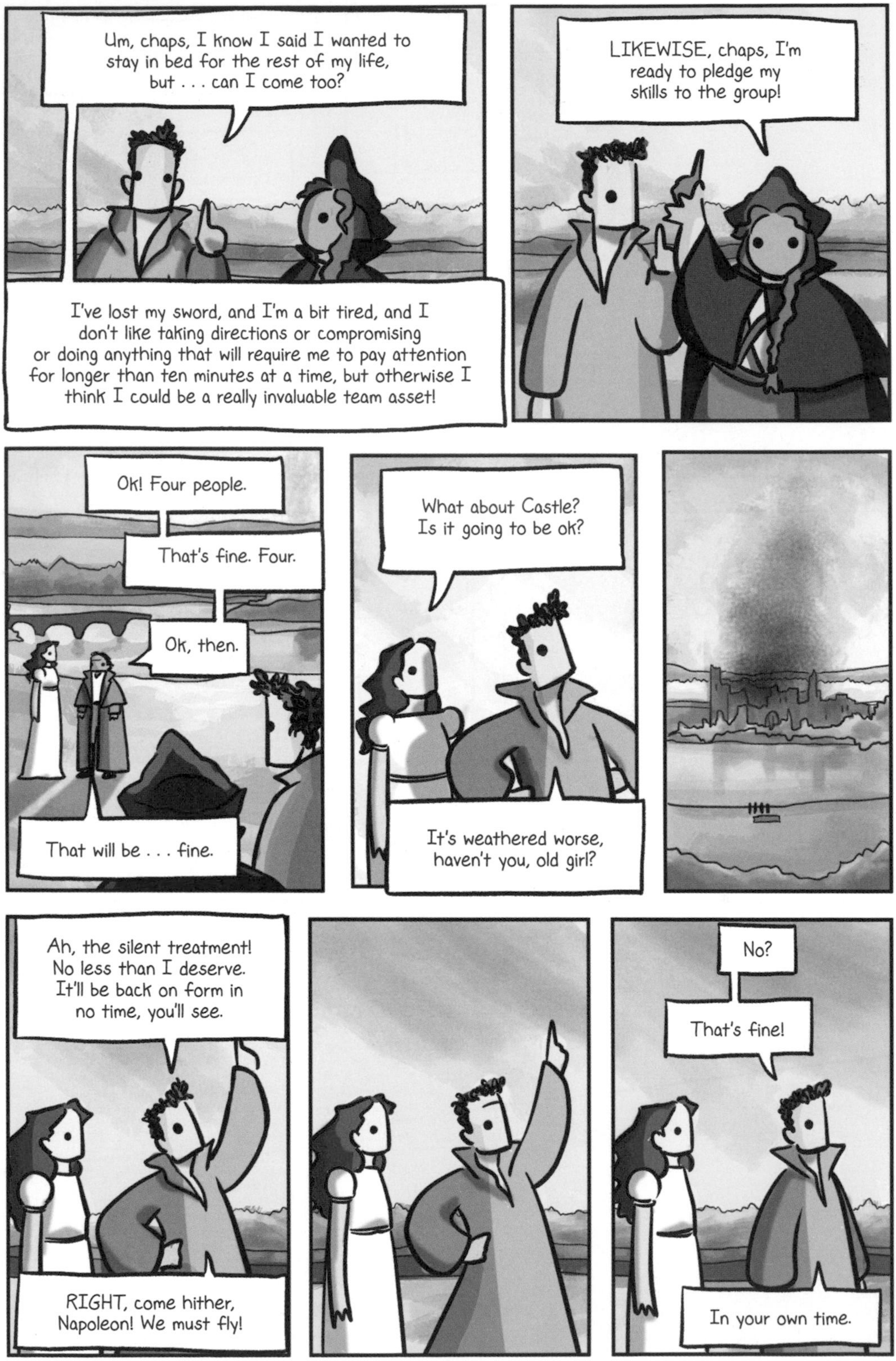
Um, chaps, I know I said I wanted to stay in bed for the rest of my life, but . . . can I come too?
I've lost my sword, and I'm a bit tired, and I don't like taking directions or compromising or doing anything that will require me to pay attention for longer than ten minutes at a time, but otherwise I think I could be a really invaluable team asset!
LIKEWISE, chaps, I'm ready to pledge my skills to the group!
Ok! Four people.
That's fine. Four.
Ok, then.
That will be . . . fine.
What about Castle? Is it going to be ok?
It's weathered worse, haven't you, old girl?
Ah, the silent treatment! No less than I deserve. It'll be back on form in no time, you'll see.
RIGHT, come hither, Napoleon! We must fly!
No?
That's fine!
In your own time.

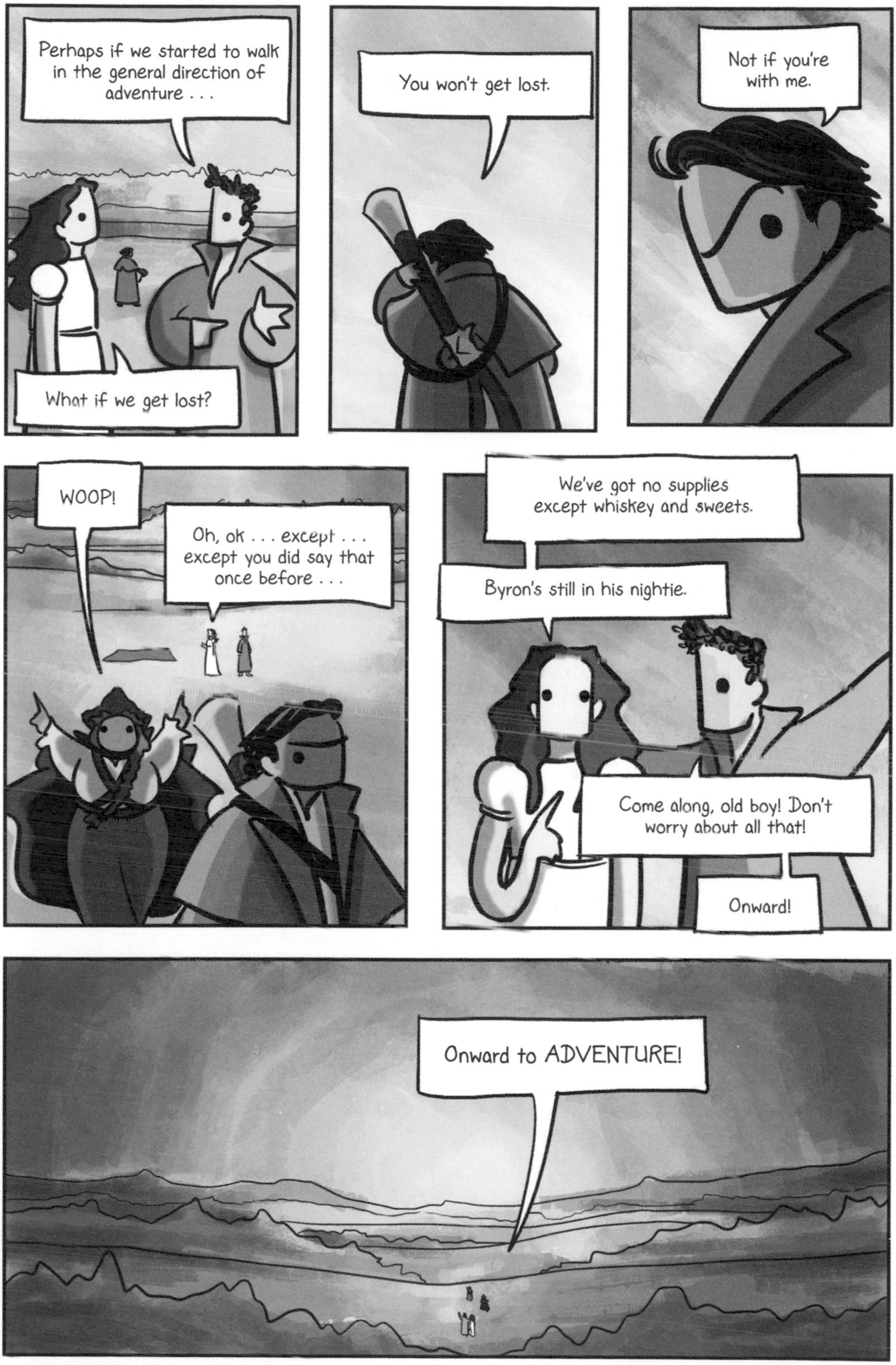
Perhaps if we started to walk in the general direction of adventure . . .
What if we get lost?
You won't get lost.
Not if you're with me.
WOOP!
Oh, ok . . . except . . . except you did say that once before . . .
We've got no supplies except whiskey and sweets.
Byron's still in his nightie.
Come along, old boy! Don't worry about all that!
Onward!
Onward to ADVENTURE!

Acknowledgments

Thanks to Rebekah Rarely, Heather Flaherty, Melissa Zahorsky, Siân Docksey, Zeba Clarke, and Michael McGovern for their support, hard work, and invaluable advice in the making of this book.

Thanks also to Leo, Aisling, Agnes, Jenny, Alice, Lucie, Shabnam, Léa, Jasper, Fliss, and Jessica for coming to my rescue at one time or another, and to Norma, Ed, Patrick, and Michael for absolutely everything.

About the Author

Emily McGovern grew up in Brussels and writes bios for herself in the third person cos it looks way more professional. She graduated from University College London in 2014 with a degree in Russian Studies. She now works as a full-time cartoonist and is the creator of the webcomic *My Life as a Background Slytherin*. This is her first graphic novel.